"Every phrase reflects to the highest degree integrity and stylistic mastery. To read *Revolutionary Road* is to have forced upon us a fresh sense of our critical modern shortcomings: failures of work, education, community, family, marriage . . . and plain nerve." —*The New Republic*

"Richard Yates is a writer of commanding gifts. His prose is urbane yet sensitive, with passion and irony held deftly in balance. And he provides unexpected pleasures in a flood of freshly minted phrases and in the thrust of sudden insight, precise notation of feeling, and mordant unsentimental perceptions." —*Saturday Review*

"A powerful treatment of a characteristically American theme, which might be labeled 'trapped.' . . . A highly impressive performance. It is written with perception, force and awareness of complexity and ambiguity, and it tells a moving and absorbing story." —*The Atlantic Monthly*

Richard Yates

REVOLUTIONARY ROAD

Richard Yates was born in 1926 in New York and lived in California. His prize-winning stories began to appear in 1953 and his first novel, *Revolutionary Road*, was nominated for the National Book Award in 1961. He is the author of eight other works, including the novels *A Good School*, *The Easter Parade*, and *Disturbing the Peace*, and two collections of short stories, *Eleven Kinds of Loneliness* and *Liars in Love*. He died in 1992.

ALSO BY RICHARD YATES

REVOLUTIONARY

ROAD

REVOLUTIONARY
ROAD

Richard Yates

VINTAGE CONTEMPORARIES

Vintage Books
A Division of Random House, Inc.
New York

FIRST VINTAGE CONTEMPORARIES
MASS MARKET EDITION, JANUARY 2009

Copyright © 1961, copyright renewed 1989 by Richard Yates

All rights reserved. Published in the United States by Vintage Books, a division of
Random House, Inc., New York, and in Canada by Random House of Canada Limited,
Toronto. Originally published in hardcover in the United States by
Little, Brown & Co., Boston, Massachusetts, in 1961.

Vintage and colophon are registered trademarks and Vintage
Contemporaries is a trademark of Random House, Inc.

This is a work of fiction. Names, characters, places, and incidents are either the
product of the author's imagination or are used fictitiously. Any resemblance to actual
persons, living or dead, events, or locales is entirely coincidental.

Library of Congress Cataloging-in-Publication Data
Yates, Richard, 1926–1992.
Revolutionary road / Richard Yates. —
Vintage Contemporaries ed.
p. cm.
1. Married people—Connecticut—Fiction.
2. Suburban life—Connecticut—Fiction. I. Title.
PS3575.A83 R4   2000
813'54—dc21 99-055503

Vintage Mass Market ISBN 978-0-307-45478-2

Book design by Christopher M. Zucker

www.vintagebooks.com

Printed in the United States of America
10   9   8   7   6   5   4   3   2   1

To Sheila

Alas! when passion is both meek and wild!

—JOHN KEATS

PART ONE

ONE

THE FINAL DYING SOUNDS of their dress rehearsal left the Laurel Players with nothing to do but stand there, silent and helpless, blinking out over the footlights of an empty auditorium. They hardly dared to breathe as the short, solemn figure of their director emerged from the naked seats to join them on stage, as he pulled a stepladder raspingly from the wings and climbed halfway up its rungs to turn and tell them, with several clearings of his throat, that they were a damned talented group of people and a wonderful group of people to work with.

"It hasn't been an easy job," he said, his glasses glinting soberly around the stage. "We've had a lot of problems here, and quite frankly I'd more or less resigned myself not to expect too much. Well, listen. Maybe this sounds corny, but something happened up here tonight. Sitting out there tonight I suddenly knew, deep down, that you were all putting your hearts into your work for the first time." He let the fingers of one hand splay out across the pocket of his shirt to show what a simple, physical thing the heart was; then he made the same hand into a fist, which he shook slowly and wordlessly in a long dramatic pause, closing one eye and allowing his moist lower lip to curl out in a grimace of triumph and pride. "Do that again tomorrow night," he said, "and we'll have one hell of a show."

They could have wept with relief. Instead, trembling, they cheered and laughed and shook hands and kissed one another, and somebody went out for a case of beer and they all sang songs around the auditorium piano until the time came to agree, unanimously, that they'd better knock it off and get a good night's sleep.

"See you tomorrow!" they called, as happy as children, and riding home under the moon they found they could roll down the windows of their cars and let the air in, with its health-giving smells of loam and young flowers. It was the first time many of the Laurel Players had allowed themselves to acknowledge the coming of spring.

The year was 1955 and the place was a part of western Connecticut where three swollen villages had lately been merged by a wide and clamorous highway called Route Twelve. The Laurel Players were an amateur company, but a costly and very serious one, carefully recruited from among the younger adults of all three towns, and this was to be their maiden production. All winter, gathering in one another's living rooms for excited talks about Ibsen and Shaw and O'Neill, and then for the show of hands in which a common-sense majority chose *The Petrified Forest*, and then for preliminary casting, they had felt their dedication growing stronger every week. They might privately consider their director a funny little man (and he was, in a way: he seemed incapable of any but a very earnest manner of speaking, and would often conclude his remarks with a little shake of the head that caused his cheeks to wobble) but they liked and respected him, and they fully believed in most of the things he said. "Any play deserves the best that any actor has to give," he'd told them once, and another time: "Remember this. We're not just putting on a play here. We're establishing a community theater, and that's a pretty important thing to be doing."

The trouble was that from the very beginning they had been afraid they would end by making fools of themselves, and they had compounded that fear by being afraid to admit it. At first their rehearsals had been held on Saturdays—always, it seemed, on the kind of windless February or March afternoon when the sky is white, the trees are black, and the brown fields and hummocks of the earth lie naked and tender between curds of shriveled snow. The Players, coming out of their various kitchen doors and hesitating for a minute to button their coats or pull on their gloves, would see a landscape in which only a few very old, weathered houses seemed to belong; it made their own homes look as weightless and impermanent, as foolishly misplaced as a great many bright new toys that had been left outdoors overnight and rained on. Their automobiles didn't look right either—unnecessarily wide and gleaming in the colors of candy and ice cream, seeming to wince at each splatter of mud, they crawled apologetically down the broken roads that led from all directions to the deep, level slab of Route Twelve. Once there the cars seemed able to relax in an environment all their own, a long bright valley of colored plastic and plate glass and stainless steel—KING KONE, MOBILGAS, SHOPORAMA, EAT—but eventually they had to turn off, one by one, and make their way up the winding country road that led to the central high school; they had to pull up and stop in the quiet parking lot outside the high-school auditorium.

"Hi!" the Players would shyly call to one another.

"Hi! . . ." "Hi! . . ." And they'd go reluctantly inside.

Clumping their heavy galoshes around the stage, blotting at their noses with Kleenex and frowning at the unsteady print of their scripts, they would disarm each other at last with peals of forgiving laughter, and they would agree, over and over, that there was plenty of time to smooth the thing out. But there wasn't plenty of time, and they all knew it, and a doubling and redoubling of their rehearsal schedule seemed only to make matters worse. Long after the time had come for what the director called "really getting this thing off the ground; really making it happen," it remained a static, shapeless, inhumanly heavy weight; time and again they read the promise of failure in each other's eyes, in the apologetic nods and smiles of their parting and the spastic haste with which they broke for their cars and drove home to whatever older, less explicit promises of failure might lie in wait for them there.

And now tonight, with twenty-four hours to go, they had somehow managed to bring it off. Giddy in the unfamiliar feel of make-up and costumes on this first warm evening of the year, they had forgotten to be afraid: they had let the movement of the play come and carry them and break like a wave; and maybe it sounded corny (and what if it did?) but they had all put their hearts into their work. Could anyone ever ask for more than that?

The audience, arriving in a long clean serpent of cars the following night, were very serious too. Like the

Players, they were mostly on the young side of middle age, and they were attractively dressed in what the New York clothing stores describe as Country Casuals. Anyone could see they were a better than average crowd, in terms of education and employment and good health, and it was clear too that they considered this a significant evening. They all knew, of course, and said so again and again as they filed inside and took their seats, that *The Petrified Forest* was hardly one of the world's great plays. But it was, after all, a fine theater piece with a basic point of view that was every bit as valid today as in the thirties ("Even more valid," one man kept telling his wife, who chewed her lips and nodded, seeing what he meant; "even more valid, when you think about it"). The main thing, though, was not the play itself but the company—the brave idea of it, the healthy, hopeful sound of it: the birth of a really good community theater right here, among themselves. This was what had drawn them, enough of them to fill more than half the auditorium, and it was what held them hushed and tense in readiness for pleasure as the house lights dimmed.

The curtain went up on a set whose rear wall was still shaking with the impact of a stagehand's last-minute escape, and the first few lines of dialogue were blurred by the scrape and bang of accidental offstage noises. These small disorders were signs of a mounting hysteria among the Laurel Players, but across the footlights they seemed only to add to a sense of impending excellence. They seemed to say, engagingly: Wait a minute; it hasn't really started yet. We're all a little nervous here, but please bear with us. And soon there was no further need for apologies, for the audience was watching the girl who played the heroine, Gabrielle.

Her name was April Wheeler, and she caused the whispered word "lovely" to roll out over the auditorium the first time she walked across the stage. A little later there were hopeful nudges and whispers of "She's *good*," and there were stately nods of pride among the several people who happened to know that she had attended one of the leading dramatic schools of New York less than ten years before. She was twenty-nine, a tall ash blonde with a patrician kind of beauty that no amount of amateur lighting could distort, and she seemed ideally cast in the role. It didn't even matter that bearing two children had left her a shade too heavy in the hips and thighs, for she moved with the shyly sensual grace of maidenhood; anyone happening to glance at Frank Wheeler, the round-faced, intelligent-looking young man who sat biting his fist in the last row of the audience, would have said he looked more like her suitor than her husband.

"Sometimes I can feel as if I were sparkling all over,"

she was saying, *"and I want to go out and do something that's absolutely crazy, and marvelous. . . ."*

Backstage, huddled and listening, the other actors suddenly loved her. Or at least they were prepared to love her, even those who had resented her occasional lack of humility at rehearsals, for she was suddenly the only hope they had.

The leading man had come down with a kind of intestinal flu that morning. He had arrived at the theater in a high fever, insisting that he felt well enough to go on, but five minutes before curtain time he had begun to vomit in his dressing room, and there had been nothing for the director to do but send him home and take over the role himself. The thing happened so quickly that nobody had time to think of going out front to announce the substitution; a few of the minor actors didn't even know about it until they heard the director's voice out there in the lights, speaking the familiar words they'd expected to hear from the other man. He was doing his fervent best and delivering each line with a high semi-professional finish, but there was no denying that he looked all wrong in the part of Alan Squiers—squat and partly bald and all but unable to see without his glasses, which he'd refused to wear on stage. From the moment of his entrance he had caused the supporting actors to interrupt each other and forget where to stand, and now in the middle of his important first-act speech about his own futility—"*Yes, brains without purpose; noise without sound; shape without substance*—" one of his gesturing hands upset a glass of water that flooded the table. He tried to cover it with a giggle and a series of improvised lines—"*You see? That's how useless I am. Here, let me help you wipe it up*—" but the rest of the speech was ruined. The virus of calamity, dormant and threatening all these weeks, had erupted now and spread from the helplessly vomiting man until it infected everyone in the cast but April Wheeler.

"*Wouldn't you like to be loved by me?*" she was saying.

"*Yes, Gabrielle,*" said the director, gleaming with sweat. "*I should like to be loved by you.*"

"*You think I'm attractive?*"

Under the table the director's leg began to jiggle up and down on the spring of its flexed foot. "*There are better words than that for what you are.*"

"*Then why don't we at least make a start at it?*"

She was working alone, and visibly weakening with every line. Before the end of the first act the audience could tell as well as the Players that she'd lost her grip, and soon they were all embarrassed for her. She had begun to alternate between false theatrical gestures and a white-knuckled immobility; she was carrying her shoulders high and square, and despite her heavy make-up you could see the warmth of humiliation rising in her face and neck.

Then came the bouncing entrance of Shep Campbell, the burly young red-haired engineer who played the gangster, Duke Mantee. The whole company had worried about Shep from the beginning, but he and his wife, Milly, who had helped with the props and the publicity, were such enthusiastic and friendly people that nobody'd had the heart to suggest replacing him. The result of this indulgence now, and of Campbell's own nervous guilt about it, was that he forgot one of his key lines, said others in a voice so quick and faint that it couldn't be heard beyond the sixth row, and handled himself less like an outlaw than an obliging grocery clerk, bobbing head, rolled-up sleeves and all.

At intermission the audience straggled out to smoke and wander in uncomfortable groups around the high-school corridor, examining the high-school bulletin board and wiping damp palms down their slim-cut trousers and their graceful cotton skirts. None of them wanted to go back and go through with the second and final act, but they all did.

And so did the Players, whose one thought now, as plain as the sweat on their faces, was to put the whole sorry business behind them as fast as possible. It seemed to go on for hours, a cruel and protracted endurance test in which April Wheeler's performance was as bad as the others, if not worse. At the climax, where the stage directions call for the poignance of the death scene to be *punctuated with shots from outside and bursts from* DUKE's *Tommy gun,* Shep Campbell timed his bursts so sloppily, and the answering offstage gunfire was so much too loud, that all the lovers' words were lost in a deafening smoky shambles. When the curtain fell at last it was an act of mercy.

The applause, not loud, was conscientiously long enough to permit two curtain calls, one that caught all the Players in motion as they walked to the wings, turned back and collided with one another, and another that revealed the three principals in a brief tableau of human desolation: the director blinking myopically, Shep Campbell looking appropriately fierce for the first time all evening, April Wheeler paralyzed in a formal smile.

Then the house lights came up, and nobody in the auditorium knew how to look or what to say. The uncertain voice of Mrs. Helen Givings, the real-estate broker, could be heard repeating *"Very* nice," over and over again, but most of the people were silent and stiff, fingering packs of cigarettes as they rose and turned to the aisles. An efficient high-school boy, hired for the evening to help with the lights, vaulted up onto the stage with a squeak of his sneakers and began calling instructions to an unseen partner high in the flies. He stood posing self-consciously in the footlights, managing to keep most of his bright pimples in shadow while proudly turning his body to show that the tools of the electrician's trade—knife, pliers, coils of wire—were slung in a professional-looking holster of oiled leather and worn low on one tense buttock of his dungarees. Then the bank of lights clicked off, the boy made a pale exit and the curtain became a dull wall of green velvet, faded and streaked with dust. There was nothing to watch now but the massed faces of the audience as they pressed up the aisles and out the main doors. Anxious, round-eyed, two by two, they looked and moved as if a calm and orderly escape from this place had become the one great necessity of their lives; as if, in fact, they wouldn't be able to begin to live at all until they were out beyond the rumbling pink billows of exhaust and the crunching gravel of this parking lot, out where the black sky went up and up forever and there were hundreds of thousands of stars.

TWO

FRANKLIN H. WHEELER WAS AMONG the few who bucked the current. He did so with apologetic slowness and with what he hoped was dignity, making his way in sidling steps down the aisle toward the stage door, saying "Excuse me. . . . Excuse me," nodding and smiling to several faces he knew, carrying one hand in his pocket to conceal and dry the knuckles he had sucked and bitten throughout the play.

He was neat and solid, a few days less than thirty years old, with closely cut black hair and the kind of unemphatic good looks that an advertising photographer might use to portray the discerning consumer of well-made but inexpensive merchandise (Why Pay More?). But for all its lack of structural distinction, his face did have an unusual mobility: it was able to suggest wholly different personalities with each flickering

change of expression. Smiling, he was a man who knew
perfectly well that the failure of an amateur play was
nothing much to worry about, a kindly, witty man who
would have exactly the right words of comfort for his
wife backstage; but in the intervals between his smiles,
when he shouldered ahead through the crowd and you
could see the faint chronic fever of bewilderment in his
eyes, it seemed more that he himself was in need of
comforting.

The trouble was that all afternoon in the city, stul-
tified at what he liked to call "the dullest job you can
possibly imagine," he had drawn strength from a mental projection of scenes to unfold tonight: himself
rushing home to swing his children laughing in the air,
to gulp a cocktail and chatter through an early dinner
with his wife; himself driving her to the high school,
with her thigh tense and warm under his reassuring
hand ("If only I weren't so *nervous*, Frank!"); himself
sitting spellbound in pride and then rising to join a
thunderous ovation as the curtain fell; himself glowing
and disheveled, pushing his way through jubilant backstage crowds to claim her first tearful kiss ("Was it
really good, darling? Was it really good?"); and then
the two of them, stopping for a drink in the admiring
company of Shep and Milly Campbell, holding hands
under the table while they talked it all out. Nowhere in
these plans had he foreseen the weight and shock of

reality; nothing had warned him that he might be overwhelmed by the swaying, shining vision of a girl he hadn't seen in years, a girl whose every glance and gesture could make his throat fill up with longing (*"Wouldn't you like to be loved by me?"*), and that then before his very eyes she would dissolve and change into the graceless, suffering creature whose existence he tried every day of his life to deny but whom he knew as well and as painfully as he knew himself, a gaunt constricted woman whose red eyes flashed reproach, whose false smile in the curtain call was as homely as his own sore feet, his own damp climbing underwear, and his own sour smell.

At the door he paused to withdraw and examine the pink-blotched hand from his pocket, half expecting to find it torn to a pulp of blood and gristle. Then, pulling his coat straight, he went through the door and up the steps into a high dusty chamber filled with the raw glare and deep shadows cast by naked light bulbs, where the Laurel Players, ablaze with cosmetics, stood talking to their sallow visitors in nervous, widely spaced groups of two and three around the floor. She wasn't there.

"No, I mean seriously," somebody was saying. "Could you hear me, or not?" And somebody else said, "Well, hell, it was a lot of fun anyway." The director, in a scanty cluster of his New York friends, was pulling

hungrily on a cigarette and shaking his head. Shep
Campbell, pebbled with sweat, still holding his Tommy
gun but clearly himself again, was standing near the
curtain rope with his free arm around his small, rumpled wife, and they were both demonstrating their
decision to laugh the whole thing off.

"Frank?" Milly Campbell had waved and risen on
tiptoe to shout his name through cupped hands, as if
pretending that the crowd were thicker and noisier
than it really was. "Frank! We'll see you and April
later, okay? For a drink?"

"Fine!" he called back. "Couple of minutes!" And
he winked and nodded as Shep raised his machine gun
in a comic salute.

Around the corner he found one of the lesser gang-
sters talking with a plump girl who had caused a thirty-
second rupture in the first act by missing her entrance
cue, who had evidently been crying but now was hilar-
iously pounding her temple and saying "God! I could've
killed myself!" while the gangster, tremulously wiping
grease paint from his mouth, said "No, but I mean it
was a lot of fun anyway, you know what I mean? That's
the main thing, in a thing like this."

"Excuse me," Frank Wheeler said, squeezing past
them to the door of the dressing room that his wife
shared with several other women. He knocked and

waited, and when he thought he heard her say "Come in," he opened it tentatively and peeked inside.

She was alone, sitting very straight at a mirror and removing her make-up. Her eyes were still red and blinking, but she gave him a small replica of her curtain-call smile before turning back to the mirror. "Hi," she said. "You ready to leave?"

He closed the door and started toward her with the corners of his mouth stretched tight in a look that he hoped would be full of love and humor and compassion; what he planned to do was bend down and kiss her and say "Listen: you were wonderful." But an almost imperceptible recoil of her shoulders told him that she didn't want to be touched, which left him uncertain what to do with his hands, and that was when it occurred to him that "You were wonderful" might be exactly the wrong thing to say—condescending, or at the very least naive and sentimental, and much too serious.

"Well," he said instead. "I guess it wasn't exactly a triumph or anything, was it?" And he stuck a cigarette jauntily in his lips and lit it with a flourish of his clicking Zippo.

"I guess not," she said. "I'll be ready in a minute."

"No, that's okay, take your time."

He pocketed both hands and curled the tired toes inside his shoes, looking down at them. Would "You were wonderful" have been a better thing to say, after all? Almost anything, it now seemed, would have been a better thing to say than what he'd said. But he would have to think of better things to say later; right now it was all he could do to stand here and think about the double bourbon he would have when they stopped on the way home with the Campbells. He looked at himself in the mirror, tightening his jaw and turning his head a little to one side to give it a leaner, more commanding look, the face he had given himself in mirrors since boyhood and which no photograph had ever quite achieved, until with a start he found that she was watching him. Her own eyes were there in the mirror, trained on his for an uncomfortable moment before she lowered them to stare at the middle button of his coat.

"Listen," she said. "Will you do me a favor? The thing is—" It seemed that all the slender strength of her back was needed to keep her voice from wavering. "The thing is, Milly and Shep wanted us to go out with them afterwards. Will you say we can't? Say it's because of the baby sitter, or something?"

He moved well away and stood stiff-legged and hump-shouldered, hands in his pockets, like a stage lawyer considering a fine point of ethics. "Well," he said, "the thing is, I already said we could. I mean I just saw them out there and I said we would."

"Oh. Then would you mind going out again and saying you were mistaken? That should be simple enough."

"Look," he said. "Don't start getting this way. The point is I thought it might be fun, is all. Besides, it's going to look kind of rude, isn't it? I mean isn't it?"

"You mean you won't." She closed her eyes. "All right, I will, then. Thanks a lot." Her face in the mirror, nude and shining with cold cream, looked forty years old and as haggard as if it were set to endure a physical pain.

"Wait a second," he told her. "Take it easy, will you please? I didn't say that. I just said they're going to think it's damn rude, that's all. And they are. I can't help that."

"All right. You go along with them, if you want to, and give me the car keys."

"Oh, Jesus, don't start this business about the car keys. Why do you always have to—"

"Look, Frank." Her eyes were still shut. "I'm not going out with those people. I don't happen to feel very well, and I—"

"Okay." He was backing away, holding out both stiff trembling hands like a man intently describing the length of a short fish. "Okay. Okay. I'm sorry. I'll tell them. I'll be right back. I'm sorry."

The floor rode under his feet like the deck of a

moving ship as he made his way back to the wings, where a man was taking pictures with a miniature flash camera ("Hold it now—that's fine. That's fine") and the actor who played Gabrielle's father was telling the plump girl, who looked ready to cry again, that the only thing to do was write the whole thing off to experience.

"You folks about ready?" Shep Campbell demanded.

"Well," Frank said, "actually, I'm afraid we'll have to cut out. April promised this baby sitter we'd be home early, you see, and we really—"

Both their faces sagged in hurt and disappointment. Milly drew a section of her lower lip between her teeth and slowly released it. "Gee," she said. "I guess April feels awful about this whole thing, doesn't she? Poor kid."

"No, no, she's okay," he told them. "Really, it's not that. She's okay. It's just this business of the baby sitter, you see." It was the first lie of its kind in the two years of their friendship, and it caused them all three to look at the floor as they labored through a halting ritual of smiles and goodnights; but it couldn't be helped.

She was waiting for him in the dressing room, ready with a pleasant social face for any of the Laurel Players they might happen to meet on the way out, but they managed to avoid them all. She led him through a

side door that opened onto fifty yards of empty, echoing high-school corridor and they walked without
touching each other and without speaking, moving in
and out of the oblongs of moonlight that lay on the
marble floor.

The smell of school in the darkness, pencils and
apples and library paste, brought a sweet nostalgic pain
to his eyes and he was fourteen again, and it was
the year he'd lived in Chester, Pennsylvania—no, in
Englewood, New Jersey—and spent all his free time in
a plan for riding the rails to the West Coast. He had
traced several alternate routes on a railroad map, he
had rehearsed many times the way he would handle
himself (politely, but with fist fights if necessary) in the
hobo jungles along the way, and he'd chosen all the
items of his wardrobe from the window of an Army
and Navy store: Levi jacket and pants, an army-type
khaki shirt with shoulder tabs, high-cut work shoes
with steel caps at heel and toe. An old felt hat of his
father's, which could be made to fit with a wad of
newspaper folded into its sweatband, would lend the
right note of honest poverty to the outfit, and he could
take whatever else he needed in his Boy Scout knap-
sack, artfully reinforced with adhesive tape to conceal
the Boy Scout emblem. The best thing about the plan
was its absolute secrecy, until the day in the school corridor when he impulsively asked a fat boy named

Krebs, who was the closest thing to a best friend he had that year, to go along with him. Krebs was dumbfounded—"On a *freight* train, you mean?"—and soon he was laughing aloud. "Jeez, you kill me, Wheeler. How far do you think *you'd* get on a freight train? Where do you get these weird ideas, anyway? The movies or someplace? You want to know something, Wheeler? You want to know why everybody thinks you're a jerk? Because you're a jerk, that's why."

Walking now through the same smells and looking at the pale shape of April's profile as she walked beside him, he allowed his rising sense of poignance to encompass her as well, and the sadness of her own childhood. He wasn't often able to do this, for most of her memories were crisply told and hard to sentimentalize ("I always knew nobody cared about me and I always let everybody know I knew it"), but the school smell made him think of one particular time she had told about, a morning in Rye Country Day when a menstrual flow of unusual suddenness and volume had taken her by surprise in the middle of a class. "At first I just sat there," she'd told him. "That was the stupid thing; and then it was too late." And he thought of how she must have lurched from her desk and run from the room with a red stain the size of a maple leaf on the seat of her white linen skirt while thirty boys and girls looked up in dumb surprise, how she must have fled down the corridor in a nightmarish silence past the doors of other murmuring classrooms, spilling books and picking them up and running again, leaving a tidy, well-spaced trail of blood drops on the floor, how she had run to the first-aid room and been afraid to go inside, how instead she had run all the way down another corridor to a fire-exit door, where she pulled off her cardigan and tied it around her waist and hips; how then, hearing or imagining the approach of footsteps in her wake, she had pushed through to the sunny lawn outside and set off for home, walking not too quickly and with her head high, so that anyone happening to glance from any of a hundred windows would think her on some perfectly normal errand from school, wearing her sweater in a perfectly normal way.

Her face must have looked almost exactly the way it did now, as they opened this other fire-exit door and walked out across these other school grounds not many miles from Rye, and her way of walking must have been similar too.

He had hoped she would sit close to him in the car—he wanted to hold her shoulders while he drove—but she made herself very small and pressed against the passenger's door, turning away to watch the passing lights and shadows of the road. This caused his eyes to grow round and his mouth solemn as he steered and shifted gears, until finally, licking his lips, he thought of something to say.

"You know something? You were the only person in that whole play. No kidding, April. I mean it."

"All right," she said. "Thank you."

"It's just that we never should've let you get mixed up in the damned thing, is all." With his free hand he opened his collar, both to cool his neck and to find reassurance in the grown-up, sophisticated feel of the silk tie and Oxford shirt. "I'd just like to get my hands on that what's his name, that's all. That director."

"It wasn't his fault."

"Well, the whole pack of them, then. God knows they all stank. The whole point is we should've known better in the first place. *I* should've known better, is what it amounts to. You never would've joined the damn group if the Campbells and I hadn't talked you into it. Remember when we first heard about it? And you said they'd probably turn out to be a bunch of idiots? Well, I should've listened to you, that's all."

"All right. Could we sort of stop talking about it now?"

"Sure we will." He tried to pat her thigh but it was out of reach across the wide seat. "Sure we will. I just don't want you feeling bad about it, that's all."

With a confident, fluid grace he steered the car out of the bouncing side road and onto the hard clean straightaway of Route Twelve, feeling that his attitude was on solid ground at last. A refreshing wind rushed in to ruffle his short hair and cool his brains, and he began to see the fiasco of the Laurel Players in its true perspective. It simply wasn't worth feeling bad about. Intelligent, thinking people could take things like this in their stride, just as they took the larger absurdities of deadly dull jobs in the city and deadly dull homes in the suburbs. Economic circumstance might force you to live in this environment, but the important thing was to keep from being contaminated. The important thing, always, was to remember who you were.

And now, as it often did in the effort to remember who he was, his mind went back to the first few years after the war and to a crumbling block of Bethune Street, in that part of New York where the gentle western edge of the Village flakes off into silent waterfront warehouses, where the salt breeze of evening and the deep river horns of night enrich the air with a promise of voyages. In his very early twenties, wearing the proud mantles of "veteran" and "intellectual" as bravely as he wore his carefully aged tweed jacket and washed-out khakis, he had owned one of three keys to a one-room apartment on that street. The other two keys, and rights to "the use of the place" every second and third week, had belonged to two of his Columbia College classmates, each of whom paid a third of its twenty-seven-dollar rent. These other two, an ex–fighter pilot and an ex-marine, were older and more relaxed in their worldliness than Frank—they seemed able to draw on endless reserves of willing girls with whom to use the place—but it wasn't long before Frank, to his own shy amazement, began to catch up with them; that was a time of wondrously rapid catching-up in many ways, of dizzily mounting self-confidence. The solitary tracer of railroad maps had never hopped his freight, but it had begun to seem unlikely that any Krebs would ever call him a jerk again. The army had taken him at eighteen, had thrust him into the final spring offensive of the war in Germany and given him a confused but exhilarating tour of Europe for another year before it set him free, and life since then had carried him from strength to strength. Loose strands of his character—the very traits that had kept him dreaming and lonely among schoolboys and later among soldiers—these seemed suddenly to have coalesced into a substantial and attractive whole. For the first time in his life he was admired, and the fact that girls could actually want to go to bed with him was only slightly more remarkable than his other concurrent discovery—that men, and intelligent men at that, could actually want to listen to him talk. His marks at school were seldom better than average, but there was nothing average about his performance in the beery, all-night talks that had begun to form around him—talks that would often end in a general murmur of agreement, accompanied by a significant tapping of temples, that old Wheeler really had it. All he would ever need, it was said, was the time and the freedom to find himself. Various ultimate careers were predicted for him, the consensus being that his work would lie somewhere "in the humanities" if not precisely in the arts—it would, at any rate, be something that called for a long and steadfast dedication— and that it would involve his early and permanent withdrawal to Europe, which he often described as the only part of the world worth living in. And Frank himself, walking the streets at daybreak after some of those talks, or lying and thinking on Bethune Street on nights when he had the use of the place but had no girl to use it with, hardly ever entertained a doubt of his own exceptional merit. Weren't the biographies of all great men filled with this same kind of youthful groping, this same kind of rebellion against their fathers and their fathers' ways? He could even be grateful in a sense that he had no particular area of interest: in avoiding specific goals he had avoided specific limitations. For the time being the world, life itself, could be his chosen field.

But as college wore on he began to be haunted by numberless small depressions, and these tended to increase in the weeks after college was over, when the other two men had taken to using their keys less and less frequently and he was staying alone in the Bethune Street place, taking odd jobs to buy his food while he thought things out. It nagged him, in particular, that none of the girls he'd known so far had given him a sense of unalloyed triumph. One had been very pretty except for unpardonably thick ankles, and one had been intelligent, though possessed of an annoying tendency to mother him, but he had to admit that none had been first-rate. Nor was he ever in doubt of what he meant by a first-rate girl, though he'd never yet come close enough to one to touch her hand. There had been two or three of them in the various high schools he'd attended, disdainfully unaware of him in their concern with college boys from out of town; what few he'd seen in the army had most often been seen in flickering miniature, on strains of dance music, through the distant golden windows of an officers' club, and though he'd seen plenty of them since then, in New York, they had always been climbing in or out of taxicabs, followed by the grimly hovering presences of men who looked as if they'd never been boys at all.

Why not let well enough alone? As an intense, nicotine-stained, Jean-Paul Sartre sort of man, wasn't it simple logic to expect that he'd be limited to intense, nicotine-stained, Jean-Paul Sartre sorts of women? But this was the counsel of defeat, and one night, bolstered by four straight gulps of whiskey at a party in Morningside Heights, he followed the counsel of victory. "I guess I didn't get your name," he said to the exceptionally first-rate girl whose shining hair and splendid legs had drawn him halfway across a roomful of strangers. "Are you Pamela?"

"No," she said. "That's Pamela over there. I'm April. April Johnson."

Within five minutes he found he could make April Johnson laugh, that he could not only hold the steady attention of her wide gray eyes but could make their pupils dart up and down and around in little arcs while he talked to her, as if the very shape and texture of his face were matters of absorbing interest.

"What do you do?"

"I'm a longshoreman."

"No, I mean really."

"I mean really too." And he would have showed her his palms to prove it if he hadn't been afraid she could tell the difference between calluses and blisters. For the past week, under the guidance of a roughhewn college friend, he had been self-consciously "shaping up" on the docks each morning and swaying under the weight of fruit crates. "Starting Monday, though, I've got a better job. Night cashier in a cafeteria."

"Well but I don't mean things like that. I mean what are you really interested in?"

"Honey—" (and he was still young enough so that the audacity of saying "Honey" on such short acquaintance made him blush) "—Honey, if I had the answer to that one I bet I'd bore us both to death in half an hour."

Five minutes later, dancing, he found that the small of April Johnson's back rode as neatly in his hand as if it had been made for that purpose; and a week after that, almost to the day, she was lying miraculously nude beside him in the first blue light of day on Bethune Street, drawing her delicate forefinger down his face from brow to chin and whispering: "It's true, Frank. I mean it. You're the most interesting person I've ever met."

"Because it's just not worth it," he was saying now, allowing the blue-lit needle of the speedometer to tremble up through sixty for the final mile of highway. They were almost home. They would have a few drinks and maybe she would cry a little—it would do her good—and then they would laugh about it and shut themselves in the bedroom and take off their clothes, and in the moonlight her plump little breasts would nod and sway and point at him, and there wasn't any reason why it couldn't be like the old days.

"I mean it's bad enough having to *live* among all

these damn little suburban types—and I'm including
the Campbells in that, let's be honest—it's bad enough
having to *live* among these people, without letting our-
selves get hurt by every little half-assed—what'd you
say?" He glanced briefly away from the road and was
startled to see, by the light of the dashboard, that she
was covering her face with both hands.

"I said *yes. All right*, Frank. Could you just please
stop talking now, before you drive me crazy?"

He slowed down quickly and brought the car to a
sandy halt on the shoulder of the road, cutting the
engine and the lights. Then he slid across the seat and
tried to take her in his arms.

"No, Frank, please don't do that. Just leave me
alone, okay?"

"Baby, it's only that I want to—"

"Leave me alone. Leave me *alone*!"

He drew himself back to the wheel and put the
lights on, but his hands refused to undertake the job of
starting the car. Instead he sat there for a minute, listening to the beating of blood in his eardrums.

"It strikes me," he said at last, "that there's a considerable amount of bullshit going on here. I mean you
seem to be doing a pretty good imitation of Madame
Bovary here, and there's one or two points I'd like to
clear up. Number one, it's not my fault the play was
lousy. Number two, it's sure as hell not my fault you

didn't turn out to be an actress, and the sooner you get over *that* little piece of soap opera the better off we're all going to be. Number three, I don't happen to fit the role of dumb, insensitive suburban husband; you've been trying to hang that one on me ever since we moved *out* here, and I'm damned if I'll wear it. Number four—"

She was out of the car and running away in the headlights, quick and graceful, a little too wide in the hips. For a second, as he clambered out and started after her, he thought she meant to kill herself—she was capable of damn near anything at times like this—but she stopped in the dark roadside weeds thirty yards ahead, beside a luminous sign that read NO PASSING. He came up behind her and stood uncertainly, breathing hard, keeping his distance. She wasn't crying; she was only standing there, with her back to him.

"What the hell," he said. "What the hell's this all about? Come on back to the car."

"No. I will in a minute. Just let me stand here a minute, all right?"

His arms flapped and fell; then, as the sound and the lights of an approaching car came up behind them, he put one hand in his pocket and assumed a conversational slouch for the sake of appearances. The car overtook them, lighting up the sign and the tense shape of her back; then its taillights sped away and the drone of its tires flattened out to a buzz in the distance, and finally to silence. On their right, in a black marsh, the spring peepers were in full and desperate song. Straight ahead, two or three hundred yards away, the earth rose high above the moonlit telephone wires to form the mound of Revolutionary Hill, along whose summit winked the friendly picture windows of the Revolutionary Hill Estates. The Campbells lived in one of those houses; the Campbells might well be in one of the cars whose lights were coming up behind them right now.

"April?"

She didn't answer.

"Look," he said. "Couldn't we sit in the car and talk about it? Instead of running all over Route Twelve?"

"Haven't I made it clear," she said, "that I don't particularly want to talk about it?"

"*Okay*," he said. "*Okay*. Jesus, April, I'm trying as hard as I can to be nice about this thing, but I—"

"How kind of you," she said. "How terribly, terribly kind of you."

"*Wait* a minute—" He pulled the hand from his pocket and stood straight, but then he put it back because other cars were coming. "Listen a minute." He tried to swallow but his throat was very dry. "I don't know what you're trying to prove here," he said, "and frankly I don't think you do either. But I do know one thing. I know damn well I don't deserve this."

"You're always so wonderfully definite, aren't you," she said, "on the subject of what you do and don't deserve." She swept past him and walked back to the car.

"Now, *wait* a minute!" He was stumbling after her in the weeds. Other cars were rushing past now, both ways, but he'd stopped caring. "*Wait* a minute, God damn it!"

She leaned the backs of her thighs against the fender and folded her arms in an elaborate display of resignation while he jabbed and shook a forefinger in her face.

"You listen to me. This is one time you're not going to get away with twisting everything I say. This just happens to be *one* damn time I *know* I'm not in the wrong. You know what you are when you're like this?"

"Oh God, if only you'd stayed home tonight."

"You know what you are when you're like this? You're sick. I really mean that."

"And do you know what you are?" Her eyes raked him up and down. "You're disgusting."

Then the fight went out of control. It quivered their arms and legs and wrenched their faces into shapes of hatred, it urged them harder and deeper into each other's weakest points, showing them cunning ways around each other's strongholds and quick chances to switch tactics, feint, and strike again. In the space of a gasp for breath it sent their memories racing back over the years for old weapons to rip the scabs off old wounds; it went on and on.

"Oh, you've never fooled me, Frank, never once. All your precious moral maxims and your 'love' and your mealy-mouthed little—do you think I've *forgotten* the time you hit me in the face because I said I wouldn't forgive you? Oh, I've always known I had to be your conscience and your guts—*and* your punching bag. Just because you've got me safely in a trap you think you—"

"*You* in a trap! *You* in a trap! *Jesus*, don't make me laugh!"

"Yes, me." She made a claw of her hand and clutched at her collarbone. "Me. Me. Me. Oh, you poor, self-deluded—*Look* at you! *Look* at you, and tell me how by any *stretch*"—she tossed her head, and the grin of her teeth glistened white in the moonlight—"by any *stretch* of the imagination you can call yourself a man!"

He swung out one trembling fist for a backhanded blow to her head and she cowered against the fender in an ugly crumple of fear; then instead of hitting her he danced away in a travesty of boxer's footwork and brought the fist down on the roof of the car with all his strength. He hit the car four times that way: *Bong! Bong! Bong! Bong!*—while she stood and watched. When he was finished, the shrill, liquid chant of the peepers was the only sound for miles.

"God damn you," he said quietly. "God damn you, April."

"All right. Could we please go home now?"

With parched, hard-breathing mouths, with wobbling heads and shaking limbs, they settled themselves in the car like very old and tired people. He started the engine and drove carefully away, down to the turn at the base of Revolutionary Hill and on up the winding blacktop grade of Revolutionary Road.

This was the way they had first come, two years ago, as cordially nodding passengers in the station wagon of Mrs. Helen Givings, the real-estate broker. She had been polite but guarded over the phone—so many city people were apt to come out and waste her time demanding impossible bargains—but from the moment they'd stepped off the train, as she would later tell her husband, she had recognized them as the kind of couple one did take a little trouble with, even in the low-price bracket. "They're *sweet*," she told her husband. "The girl is *ab*solutely ravishing, and I think the boy must do something very brilliant in town—he's very nice, rather reserved—and really, it *is* so refreshing to deal with people of that sort." Mrs. Givings had understood at once that they wanted something out of the ordinary—a small remodeled barn or carriage house, or an old guest cottage—something with a little charm—and she did hate having to tell them that those things simply weren't available any more. But she implored them not to lose heart; she did know of one little place they might like.

"Now of course it isn't a very desirable road down at this end," she explained, her glance switching bird-like between the road and their pleased, attentive faces as she made the turn off Route Twelve. "As you see, it's mostly these little cinder-blocky, pickup-trucky places—plumbers, carpenters, little local people of that sort. And then *eventually*"—she aimed the stiff pistol of her index finger straight through the windshield in fair warning, causing a number of metal bracelets to jingle and click against the steering wheel—"*eventually* it leads on up and around to a perfectly dreadful new development called Revolutionary Hill Estates—great hulking split levels, all in the most nauseous pastels and dreadfully expensive too, I can't think why. No, but the place I want to show you has absolutely no connection with that. One of our nice little local builders put it up right after the war, you see, before all the really awful building began. It's really rather a sweet little house and a sweet little setting. Simple, clean lines, good lawns, marvelous for children. It's right around this next curve, and you see the road *is* nicer along in here, isn't it? Now you'll see it—there. See the little white one? Sweet, isn't it? The perky way it sits there on its little slope?"

"Oh yes," April said as the house emerged through the spindly trunks of second-growth oak and slowly turned toward them, small and wooden, riding high on its naked concrete foundation, its outsized central window staring like a big black mirror. "Yes, I think it's sort of—nice, don't you, darling? Of course it does have the picture window; I guess there's no escaping that."

"I guess not," Frank said. "Still, I don't suppose one picture window is necessarily going to destroy our personalities."

"Oh, that's *marvelous*," Mrs. Givings cried, and her laughter enclosed them in a warm shelter of flattery as they rolled up the driveway and climbed out to have a look. She hovered near them, reassuring and protective, while they walked the naked floors of the house in whispering speculation. The place did have possibilities. Their sofa could go here and their big table there; their solid wall of books would take the curse off the picture window; a sparse, skillful arrangement of furniture would counteract the prim suburban look of this too-symmetrical living room. On the other hand, the very symmetry of the place was undeniably appealing— the fact that all its corners made right angles, that each of its floorboards lay straight and true, that its doors hung in perfect balance and closed without scraping in efficient clicks. Enjoying the light heft and feel of these doorknobs, they could fancy themselves at home here. Inspecting the flawless bathroom, they could sense the pleasure of steaming in its ample tub; they could see their children running barefoot down this hallway free of mildew and splinters and cockroaches and grit. It did have possibilities. The gathering disorder of their lives might still be sorted out and made to fit these rooms, among these trees; and what if it did take time? Who could be frightened in as wide and bright, as clean and quiet a house as this?

Now, as the house swam up close in the darkness with its cheerful blaze of kitchen and carport lights, they tensed their shoulders and set their jaws in attitudes of brute endurance. April went first, swaying blindly through the kitchen, pausing to steady herself against the great refrigerator, and Frank came blinking behind her. Then she touched a wall switch, and the living room exploded into clarity. In the first shock of light it seemed to be floating, all its contents adrift, and even after it held still it had a tentative look. The sofa was here and the big table there, but they might just as well have been reversed; there was the wall of books, obediently competing for dominance with the picture window, but it might as well have been a lending library. The other pieces of furniture had indeed removed the suggestion of primness, but they had failed to replace it with any other quality. Chairs, coffee table, floor lamp and desk, they stood like items arbitrarily grouped for auction. Only one corner of the room showed signs of pleasant human congress—carpet worn, cushions dented, ash trays full—and this was the alcove they had established with reluctance less than six months ago: the province of the television set ("Why not? Don't we really owe it to the kids? Besides, it's silly to go on being snobbish about television. . . .").

Mrs. Lundquist, the baby sitter, had fallen asleep on the sofa and lay hidden beneath its back. Now she rose abruptly into view as she sat up squinting and trying to smile, her false teeth clacking and her hands fumbling at the pins of her loosened white hair.

"Mommy?" came a high wide-awake voice from the children's room down the hall. It was Jennifer, the six-year-old. "Mommy? Was it a good play?"

Frank took two wrong turns in driving Mrs. Lundquist home (Mrs. Lundquist, lurching against door and dashboard, tried to cover her fear by smiling fixedly in the darkness; she thought he was drunk), and all the way back, alone, he rode with one hand pressed to his mouth. He was doing his best to reconstruct the quarrel in his mind, but it was hopeless. He couldn't even tell whether he was angry or contrite, whether it was forgiveness he wanted or the power to forgive. His throat was still raw from shouting and his hand still throbbed from hitting the car—he remembered that part well enough—but his only other memory was of the high-shouldered way she had stood in the curtain call, with that false, vulnerable smile, and this made him weak with remorse. Of all the nights to have a fight! He had to hold the wheel tight in both hands because the road lights were blurring and swimming in his eyes.

The house was dark, and the sight of it as he drove up, a long milky shape in the greater darkness of trees and sky, made him think of death. He padded quickly through the kitchen and living room and went down the hall on careful tiptoe, past the children's room and into the bedroom, where he softly shut the door behind him.

"April, listen," he whispered. Stripping off his coat, he went to the dim bed and sat slumped on its edge in a classic pose of contrition. "Please listen. I won't touch you. I just want to say I'm—there isn't anything to say except I'm sorry."

This was going to be a bad one; it was going to be the kind that went on for days. But at least they were here, alone and quiet in their own room, instead of shouting on the highway; at least the thing had passed into its second phase now, the long quiet aftermath that always before, however implausibly, had led to reconciliation. She wouldn't run away from him now, nor was there any chance of his boiling into a rage again;

they were both too tired. Early in his marriage these numb periods had seemed even worse than the humiliating noise that set them off: each time he would think, There can't be any dignified way out of it this time. But there always had been a way, dignified or not, discovered through the simple process of apologizing first and then waiting, trying not to think about it too much. By now the feel of this attitude was as familiar as an unbecoming, comfortable old coat. He could wear it with a certain voluptuous ease, for it allowed him a total suspension of will and pride.

"I don't know what happened back there," he said, "but whatever it was, believe me, I—April?" Then his reaching hand discovered that the bed was empty. The long shape he'd been talking to was a wad of thrown-back covers and a pillow; she had torn the bed apart.

"April?"

He ran frightened to the empty bathroom and down the hall.

"Please go away," her voice said. She was rolled up in a blanket on the living-room sofa, where Mrs. Lundquist had lain.

"Listen a minute. I won't touch you. I just want to say I'm sorry."

"That's wonderful. Now will you please leave me alone?"

THREE

A SHRILL METALLIC WHINE CUT through the silence of his sleep. He tried to hide from it, huddling deeper into a cool darkness where the mists of an absorbing dream still floated, but it came tearing back again and again until his eyes popped open in the sunshine.

It was after eleven o'clock, Saturday morning. Both his nostrils were plugged as if with rubber cement, his head ached, and the first fly of the season was crawling up the inside of a clouded whiskey glass that stood on the floor beside a nearly empty bottle. Only after making these discoveries did he begin to remember the events of the night—how he'd sat here drinking until four in the morning, methodically scratching his scalp with both hands, convinced that sleep was out of the question. And only after remembering this did his mind come into focus on an explanation of the noise: it was his own rusty lawnmower, which needed oiling. Somebody was cutting the grass in the back yard, a thing he had promised to do last weekend.

He rolled heavily upright and groped for his bathrobe, moistening the wrinkled roof of his mouth. Then he went and squinted through the brilliant window. It was April herself, stolidly pushing and hauling the old machine, wearing a man's shirt and a pair of loose, flapping slacks, while both children romped behind her with handfuls of cut grass.

In the bathroom he used enough cold water and toothpaste and Kleenex to revive the working parts of his head; he restored its ability to gather oxygen and regained a certain muscular control over its features. But nothing could be done about his hands. Bloated and pale, they felt as if all their bones had been painlessly removed. A command to clench them into fists would have sent him whimpering to his knees. Looking at them, and particularly at the bitten-down nails that never in his life had had a chance to grow, he wanted to beat and bruise them against the edge of the sink. He thought then of his father's hands, and this reminded him that his dream just now, just before the lawnmower and the headache and the sun, had been of a dim and deeply tranquil time long ago. Both his parents had been there, and he'd heard his mother say "Oh, don't wake him, Earl; let him sleep." He tried his best to remember more of it, and couldn't; but the tenderness of it brought him close to tears for a moment until it faded away.

They had both been dead for several years now, and it sometimes troubled him that he could remember neither of their faces very well. To his waking memory, without the aid of photographs, his father was a vague bald head with dense eyebrows and a mouth forever fixed in the shape either of disgruntlement or exasperation, his mother a pair of rimless spectacles, a hair net, and a timorous smear of lipstick. He remembered too, of both of them, that they'd always been tired. Middle-aged at the time of his birth and already tired then from having raised two other sons, they had grown steadily more and more tired as long as he'd known them, until finally, tired out, they had died with equal ease, in their sleep, within six months of each other. But there had never been anything tired about his father's hands, and no amount of time and forgetfulness had ever dimmed their image in his mind's eye.

"Open it!" That was one of his earliest memories: the challenge to loosen one big fist, and his frantic two-handed efforts, never succeeding, to uncoil a single finger from its massively quivering grip, while his father's laughter rang from the kitchen walls. But it wasn't only their strength he envied, it was their sureness and sensitivity—when they held a thing, you could see how it felt—and the aura of mastery they imparted to everything Earl Wheeler used: the creaking pigskin handle of his salesman's briefcase, the hafts of all his woodworking tools, the thrillingly dangerous stock and trigger of his shotgun. The briefcase had been of particular fascination to Frank at the age of five or six; it always stood in the shadows of the front hallway in the evenings, and sometimes after supper he would saunter manfully up to it and pretend it was his own. How fine and smooth, yet how impossibly thick its handle felt! It was heavy (Whew!) yet how lightly it would swing at his father's side in the morning! Later, at ten or twelve, he had become familiar with the carpentry tools as well, but none of his memories of them were pleasant. "No, boy, no!" his father would shout over the scream of the power saw. "You're ruining it! Can't you see you're ruining it? That's no way to handle a tool." The tool, whatever obstinate thing it was, chisel or gouge or brace-and-bit, would be snatched away from the failure of its dismally sweat-stained woodwork and held aloft to be minutely inspected for damage. Then there would be a lecture on the proper care and handling of tools, to be followed by a gracefully expert demonstration (during which the grains of wood clung like gold in the hair of his father's forearm) or more likely by a sigh of manly endurance pressed to the breaking point and the quiet words: "All right. You'd better go on upstairs." Things had always ended that way in the woodworking shop, and even today he could never breathe the yellow smell of sawdust without a sense of humiliation. The shotgun, luckily, had never come to a test. By the time he was old enough to go along on one of his father's increasingly rare hunting trips the chronic discord between them had long precluded any chance of it. It would never have occurred to the old man to suggest such a thing, and what's more—for this was the period of his freight-train dreams—it would never have occurred to Frank to desire the suggestion. Who wanted to sit in a puddle and kill a lot of ducks? Who, for that matter, wanted to be good with hobbyist's tools? And who wanted to be a dopey salesman in the first place, acting like a big deal with a briefcase full of boring catalogues, talking about machines all day to a bunch of dumb executives with cigars?

Yet even in those days and afterwards, even in the extremities of rebellion on Bethune Street, when his father had become a dreary, querulous old fool nodding to sleep over the *Reader's Digest*, then as now he continued to believe that something unique and splendid had lived in his father's hands. On Earl Wheeler's very deathbed, when he was shrunken and blind and cackling ("Who's that? Frank? Is that Frank?") the dry clasp of his hands had been as positive as ever, and when they lay loose and still on the hospital sheet at last they still looked stronger and better than his son's.

"Boy, I guess the headshrinkers could really have a ball with me," he liked to say, wryly, among friends. "I mean the whole deal of my relationship with my father alone'd be enough to fill a textbook, not to mention my mother. Jesus, what a little nest of neuroses we must've been." All the same, in moments of troubled solitude like this, he was glad he could muster some vestige of honest affection for his parents. He was grateful that however uneasy the rest of his life had turned out to be, it had once contained enough peace to give him pleasant dreams; and he often suspected, with more than a little righteousness, that this might be what kept him essentially more stable than his wife. Because if the headshrinkers could have a ball with him, God only knew what kind of a time they would have with April.

In all the scanty stories she told about them, her parents were as alien to his sympathetic understanding as anything in the novels of Evelyn Waugh. Had people like that ever really existed? He could picture them only as flickering caricatures of the twenties, the Playboy and the Flapper, mysteriously rich and careless and cruel, married by a ship's captain in mid-Atlantic and divorced within a year of the birth of their only child.

"I think my mother must've taken me straight from

the hospital to Aunt Mary's," she'd told him. "At any rate I don't think I ever lived with anyone but Aunt Mary until I was five, and then there were a couple of other aunts, or friends of hers or something, before I went to Aunt Claire, in Rye." The rest of the story was that her father had shot himself in a Boston hotel room in 1938, and that her mother had died some years later after long incarceration in a West Coast alcoholic retreat.

"Jesus," Frank said on first hearing these facts, one irritably hot summer night in the Bethune Street place (though he wasn't quite sure at the time, as he hung and shook his head, whether what he felt was sorrow for the unhappiness of the story or envy because it was so much more dramatic a story than his own). "Well," he said. "I guess your aunt always really seemed like your mother, though, didn't she?"

But April shrugged, drawing her mouth a little to one side in a way that he'd lately decided he didn't like—her "tough" look. "Which aunt do you mean? I hardly remember Mary, or the others in between, and I always hated Claire."

"Oh, come on. How can you say you 'always hated' her? I mean maybe it seems that way now, looking back, but over the years she must've given you a certain feeling of—*you* know, love, and security and everything."

"She didn't, though. The only real fun I ever had was when one of my parents came for a visit. They were the ones I loved."

"But they hardly ever *came* for visits. I mean you couldn't have had much sense of their *being* your parents, in a deal like that; you didn't even know them. How could you love them?"

"I did, that's all." And she began picking up and putting away again, in her jewelry box, the souvenirs she had spread before him on the bed: snapshots of herself at various ages, on various lawns, standing with one or the other parent; a miniature painting of her mother's pretty head; a yellowed, leather-framed photograph showing both parents, tall and elegantly dressed beside a palm tree, with the inscription *Cannes, 1925;* her mother's wedding ring; an ancient brooch containing a lock of her maternal grandmother's hair; a tiny white plastic horse, the size of a watch charm, which had a net value of two or three cents and had been saved for years because "my father gave it to me."

"Oh, all right, sure," he conceded. "Maybe they did seem romantic and everything; they probably seemed very dazzling and glamorous and all that. The point is, I don't mean that. I mean love."

"So do I. I did love them." Her grave silence following this statement, as she fastened the clasp of the jewelry box, was so prolonged that he thought she had finished with the subject. He decided he was finished with it anyway, at least for the time being. It was too hot a night to have an argument. But it turned out that she was only thinking it over, preparing her next words with great care to make sure they would say exactly what she meant. When she began to speak at last she looked so much like the little girl in the photographs that he was ashamed of himself. "I loved their clothes," she said. "I loved the way they talked. I loved to hear them tell about their lives."

And there was nothing for him to do but take her in his arms, full of pity for the meagerness of her treasure and full of a reverent, silent promise, soon to be broken, that he would never again disparage it.

A small stain of drying milk and cereal on the table was all that remained of the children's breakfast; the rest of the kitchen gleamed to an industrial perfection of cleanliness. He planned, as soon as he'd had some coffee, to get dressed and go out and take the lawn-mower away from her, by force if necessary, in order to restore as much balance to the morning as possible. But he was still in his bathrobe, unshaven and fumbling at the knobs of the electric stove, when Mrs. Givings's station wagon came crackling up the driveway. For a second he thought of hiding, but it was too late. She had already seen him through the screen door, and April, trudging along the far border of the back yard, had already escaped her with a wave across the wide expanse of grass and gone on mowing. He was caught. He had to open the door and stand there in an attitude of welcome. Why did this woman keep bothering them all the time?

"I can't stay a minute!" she cried, staggering toward him under the weight of a damp cardboard box full of earth and wobbling vegetation. "I just wanted to bring over this sedum for the rocky place at the foot of your drive. My, don't you look comfy."

He bent into an ungainly pose, trying to hold the door open with one trailing foot while he took the box from her arms. "Well," he said, smiling very close to her tense, powdery face. Mrs. Givings's cosmetics seemed always to have been applied in a frenzy of haste, of impatience to get the whole silly business over and done with, and she was constantly in motion, a trim, leather-skinned woman in her fifties whose eyes expressed a religious belief in the importance of keeping busy. Even when she stood still there was kinetic energy in the set of her shoulders and the hang of her loose, angrily buttoned-up clothes; when sitting was inevitable she always chose straight chairs and used them sparingly, and it was hard to imagine her ever lying down. Nor was it easy to picture her face asleep, free from the tension of its false smiles, its little bursts of social laughter and its talk.

"I really think this is just what's called for down there, don't you?" she was saying. "Have you worked with this type of sedum before? You'll find it's the most marvelous ground cover, even in this acid soil."

"Well," he said again. "That's fine. Thanks a lot, Mrs. Givings." Nearly two years ago she had asked them to call her Helen, a name his tongue seemed all but unable to pronounce. Usually he solved the problem by calling her nothing, covering the lack with friendly nods and smiles, and she had taken to calling him nothing either. Now, as her small eyes seemed to take in for the first time the fact that his wife was cutting the grass while he lounged around the kitchen in a bathrobe, they stood smiling at each other with uncommon brilliance. He let the screen clap shut behind him and adjusted his grip on the box, which wobbled in his arms and sent a fine stream of sand down his naked ankle.

"What should we—you know, do with it?" he asked her. "I mean, *you* know, to make it grow and everything."

"Well, nothing really. All it wants is just a tiny dollop of water the first few days, and then you'll find it absolutely thrives. It's rather like the European houseleek, you see, except of course that has the lovely pink flower and this has the yellow."

"Oh, yeah," he said. "House leak." She told him a

good many other things about the plants, while he nodded and watched her and wished she would go away, listening to the whir and whine of the lawn-mower. "Well," he said when her voice stopped. "That's swell, thanks a lot. Can I—offer you a cup of coffee?"

"Oh, no, thanks ever so much—" She skittered four or five feet away, retreating, as if he had offered her a soiled handkerchief to blow her nose in. Then, from the safety of her new position, she displayed all her long teeth in an elaborate smile. "Do tell April we loved the play last night—or wait, I'll tell her myself." She craned and squinted into the sun, judging the distance her voice would have to travel, and then she let it loose:

"*April! April!* I just wanted to *tell* you we *loved* the *play!*" Her strained, shouting face could have been the picture of a woman in agony.

After a second the sound of the lawnmower stopped and April's distant voice said "What's that?"

"I say, we LOVED, the PLAY!"

And at last, on hearing April's faint "Oh—thanks, Helen," she was able to slacken her features. She turned back to Frank, who was still clumsily holding the box. "You really do have a very gifted wife. I can't tell you how much Howard and I enjoyed it."

"Good," he said. "Actually, I think the general consensus is that it wasn't too great. I mean I think most people seemed to feel that way."

"Oh, no, it was charming. I did think your nice friend up on the Hill was rather unfortunately cast—Mr. Crandall?—but otherwise—"

"Campbell, yes. Actually, I don't think he was any worse than some of the others; and of course he did have a difficult part." He always felt it necessary to defend the Campbells to Mrs. Givings, whose view seemed to be that anyone who lived in the Revolutionary Hill Estates deserved at best a tactful condescension.

"I suppose that's true. I was surprised not to see *Mrs.* Crandall in the group—or Campbell, is it? Still, I don't expect she'd have the time, with all those children."

"She worked backstage." He was trying to shift the box so that the sand would stop trickling, or trickle somewhere else. "She was quite active in the whole thing, as a matter of fact."

"Oh, good. I'm sure she would be; such a friendly, willing little soul. All right, then—" She began sidling toward her car. "I won't keep you." This was the moment for her saying "Oh, one other thing, while I think of it." She nearly always did that, and the other thing would turn out to be the thing she had really come for in the first place. Now she hesitated, visibly wondering whether to say it or not; then her face showed her decision not to, under the circumstances. Whatever it was would have to wait. "Fine, then. I simply love the stone path you've started down the front lawn."

"Oh," he said. "Thanks. I haven't hardly started it yet."

"Oh, I know," she assured him. "It *is* hard work." Then she trilled a gracious little two-note song of goodbye and twitched into her station wagon, which rolled slowly away.

"Mommy, look what Daddy's got," Jennifer was calling. "Mrs. Givings brought it."

And Michael, the four-year-old, said, "It's flowers. Is it flowers, or what?"

They were hurrying toward him over the cropped grass, while April slowly and heavily brought up the rear, pulling the lawnmower behind her, blowing damp strands of hair away from her eyes with a stuck-out lower lip. Everything about her seemed determined to prove, with a new, flat-footed emphasis, that a sensible middle-class housewife was all she had ever wanted to be and that all she had ever wanted of love was a husband who would get out and cut the grass once in a while, instead of sleeping all day.

"It's leaking, Daddy," Jennifer said.

"I know it's leaking. Quiet a minute. Listen," he said to his wife, without quite looking at her. "Would you mind telling me what I'm supposed to do with this stuff?"

"How should I know? What is it?"

"I don't know what the hell it is. It's European house leak or something."

"European what?"

"Oh no, wait a second. It's *like* house leak, only it's pink instead of yellow. Yellow instead of pink. I thought you'd probably know all about it."

"Whatever made you think that?" She came up close to squint at the plants, fingering one of their fleshy stems. "What's it for? Didn't she say?"

His mind was a blank. "Wait a second. It's called beecham. Or wait—seecham. I'm pretty sure it's seecham." He licked his lips and changed his grip on the box. "It's marvelous in acid soil. Does that ring a bell?"

The children were switching their hopeful eyes from one parent to the other, and Jennifer was beginning to look worried.

April ran her fingers into her hip pockets. "Marvelous for what? You mean you didn't even ask her?"

The plants were quivering in his arms. "Look, could you kind of take it easy? I haven't had any coffee yet, and I—"

"Oh, this is swell. What am I supposed to do with this stuff? What am I supposed to *tell* the woman the next time I see her?"

"Tell her any God damn thing you like," he said. "Maybe you could tell her to mind her own God damn business for a change."

"Don't *shout*, Daddy." Jennifer was bouncing up and down in her grass-stained sneakers, flapping her hands and starting to cry.

"I'm *not* shouting," he told her, with all the indignation of the falsely accused. She held still then and put her thumb in her mouth, which seemed to make her eyes go out of focus, while Michael clutched at the fly of his pants and took two backward steps, solemn with embarrassment.

April sighed and raked back a lock of hair. "All right," she said. "Take it down to the cellar, then. The least we can do is get it out of sight. Then you'd better get dressed. It's time for lunch."

He carried the box down the cellar stairs, dropped it on the floor with a rustling thud and kicked it into a corner, sending a sharp pain through the tendon of his big toe.

He spent the afternoon in an old pair of army pants and a torn shirt, working on his stone path. The idea was to lay a long, curving walk from the front door to the road, to divert visitors from coming in through the kitchen. It had seemed simple enough last weekend, when he'd started it, but now as the ground sloped off more sharply he found that flat stones wouldn't work.

He had to make steps, of stones nearly as thick as they were wide, stones that had to be dislodged from the steep woods behind the house and carried on tottering legs around to the front lawn. And he had to dig a pit for each step, in ground so rocky that it took ten minutes to get a foot below the surface. It was turning into mindless, unrewarding work, the kind of work that makes you clumsy with fatigue and petulant with lack of progress, and it looked as if it would take all summer.

Even so, once the first puffing and dizziness was over, he began to like the muscular pull and the sweat of it, and the smell of the earth. At least it was a man's work. At least, squatting to rest on the wooded slope, he could look down and see his house the way a house ought to look on a fine spring day, safe on its carpet of green, the frail white sanctuary of a man's love, a man's wife and children. Lowering his eyes with the solemnity of this thought, he could take pleasure in the sight of his own flexed thigh, lean and straining under the old O.D., and of the heavily veined forearm that lay across it and the dirty hand that hung there—not to be compared with his father's hand, maybe, but a serviceable, good-enough hand all the same—so that his temples ached in zeal and triumph as he heaved a rock up from the suck of its white-wormed socket and let it roll end over end down the shuddering leafmold, because he was a man. Following it down to the edge of the lawn, he squatted over it again, grunted, wrestled it up to his thighs and from there to his waist, cradling it in the tender flesh of his forearms; then he moved out, glassy-eyed and staggering on the soft grass, out around the white blur of the house and into the sun of the front lawn and all the way over to the path, where he dropped it and nearly fell in a heap on top of it.

"We're helping you, aren't we, Daddy?" Jennifer said. Both children had come to sit near him on the grass. The sun made perfect circles of yellow on their two blond heads and gave their T-shirts a dazzling whiteness.

"You sure are," he said.

"Yes, because you like to have us keep you company, don't you?"

"I sure do, baby. Don't get too close now, you'll kick dirt in the hole." And he fell to work with the long-handled shovel to deepen the hollow he had dug, enjoying the rhythmic rasp and grip of the blade against a loosening edge of buried rock.

"Daddy?" Michael inquired. "Why does the shovel make sparks?"

"Because it's hitting rock. When you hit rock with steel, you get a spark."

"Why don't you take the rock out?"

"That's what I'm trying to do. Don't get so close now, you might get hurt."

The piece of rock came free at last; he lifted it out and knelt to claw at the sliding tan pebbles of the pit until the depth and the shape of it looked right. Then he heaved and rolled the boulder into place and packed it tight, and another step was completed. A light swarm of gnats had come to hover around his head, tickling and barely visible as they hung and flicked past his eyes.

"Daddy?" Jennifer said. "How come Mommy slept on the sofa?"

"I don't know. Just happened to feel like it, I guess. You wait here, now, while I go and get another stone."

And the more he thought about it, as he plodded back up through the trees behind the house, the more he realized that this was the best answer he could have given, from the standpoint of simple honesty as well as tact. She just happened to feel like it. Wasn't that, after all, the only reason there was? Had she ever had a less selfish, more complicated reason for doing anything in her life?

"I love you when you're nice," she'd told him once, before they were married, and it had made him furious.

"Don't *say* that. Christ's sake, you don't 'love' people when they're 'nice.' Don't you see that's the same as saying 'What's in it for me?' Look." (They were standing on Sixth Avenue in the middle of the night, and he was holding her at arm's length, his hands placed firmly on either side of the warm rib cage inside her polo coat.) "Look. You either love me or you don't, and you're going to have to make up your mind."

Oh, she'd made up her mind, all right. It had been easy to decide in favor of love on Bethune Street, in favor of walking proud and naked on the grass rug of an apartment that caught the morning sun among its makeshift chairs, its French travel posters, and its bookcase made of packing-crate slats—an apartment where half the fun of having an affair was that it was just like being married, and where later, after a trip to City Hall and back, after a ceremonial collecting of the other two keys from the other two men, half the fun of being married was that it was just like having an affair. She'd decided in favor of that, all right. And why not? Wasn't it the first love of any kind she'd ever known? Even on the level of practical advantage it must have held an undeniable appeal: it freed her from the gritty round of disappointment she would otherwise have faced as an only mildly talented, mildly enthusiastic graduate of dramatic school; it let her languish attractively through a part-time office job ("just until my husband finds the kind of work he really wants to do") while saving her best energies for animated discussions of books and pictures and the shortcomings of other people's personalities, for trying new ways of fixing her hair and new kinds of inexpensive clothes ("Do you really like the sandals, or are they too Villagey?") and for hours of unhurried dalliance deep in their double bed. But even in those days she'd held herself poised for immediate flight; she had always been ready to take off the minute she happened to feel like it ("Don't *talk* to me that way, Frank, or I'm *leaving*. I *mean* it") or the minute anything went wrong.

And one big thing went wrong right away. According to their plan, which called for an eventual family of four, her first pregnancy came seven years too soon. That was the trouble, and if he'd known her better then he might have guessed how she would take it and what she would happen to feel like doing about it. At the time, though, coming home from the doctor's office in a steaming crosstown bus, he was wholly in the dark. She refused to look at him as they rode; she carried her head high in a state of shock or disbelief or anger or blame—it could have been any or all or none of these things, for all he knew. Pressed close and sweating beside her with his jaw set numbly in a brave smile, trying to think of things to say, he knew only that everything was out of kilter. Whatever you felt on hearing the news of conception, even if it was chagrin instead of joy, wasn't it supposed to be something the two of you shared? Your wife wasn't supposed to turn away from you, was she? You weren't supposed to have to work and wheedle to win her back, with little jokes and hand-holdings, as if you were afraid she might evaporate at the very moment of this first authentic involvement of your lives—that couldn't be right. Then what the hell was the matter?

It wasn't until a week later that he came home to find her stalking the apartment with folded arms, her eyes remote and her face fixed in the special look that meant she had made up her mind about something and would stand for no nonsense.

"Frank, listen. Try not to start talking until I finish, and just listen." And in an oddly stifled voice, as if she'd rehearsed her speech several times without allowing for the fact that she'd have to breathe while delivering it, she told him of a girl in dramatic school who knew, from first-hand experience, an absolutely infallible way to induce a miscarriage. It was simplicity itself: you waited until just the right time, the end of the third month; then you took a sterilized rubber syringe and a little bit of sterilized water, and you very carefully. . . .

Even as he filled his lungs for shouting he knew it wasn't the idea itself that repelled him—the idea itself, God knew, was more than a little attractive—it was that she had done all this on her own, in secret, had sought out the girl and obtained the facts and bought the rubber syringe and rehearsed the speech; that if she'd thought about him at all it was only as a possible hitch in the scheme, a source of tiresome objections that would have to be cleared up and disposed of if the thing were to be carried out with maximum efficiency. That was the intolerable part of it; that was what enriched his voice with a tremor of outrage:

"Christ's *sake*, don't be an idiot. You want to kill yourself? I don't even want to hear about it."

She sighed patiently. "All right, Frank. In that case there's certainly no need for you to hear about it. I only told you because I thought you might be willing to help me in this thing. Obviously, I should have known better."

"Listen. *Listen* to me. You do this—you do this and I swear to God I'll—"

"Oh, you'll what? You'll leave me? What's that supposed to be—a threat or a promise?"

And the fight went on all night. It caused them to hiss and grapple and knock over a chair, it spilled outside and downstairs and into the street ("Get *away* from me! Get *away* from me!"); it washed them trembling up against the high wire fence of a waterfront junkyard, until a waterfront drunk came to stare at them and make them waver home, and he could feel the panic and the shame of it even now, leaning here against this tree with these gnats tickling his neck. All that saved him, all that enabled him now to crouch and lift a new stone from its socket and follow its rumbling fall with the steady and dignified tread of self-respect, was that the next day he had won. The next day, weeping in his arms, she had allowed herself to be dissuaded.

"Oh, I know, I know," she had whispered against his shirt, "I know you're right. I'm sorry. I love you. We'll name it Frank and we'll send it to college and everything. I promise, promise."

And it seemed to him now that no single moment of his life had ever contained a better proof of manhood than that, if any proof were needed: holding that tamed, submissive girl and saying "Oh, my lovely; oh, my lovely," while she promised she would bear his child. Lurching and swaying under the weight of the stone in the sun, dropping it at last and wiping his sore hands, he picked up the shovel and went to work again, while the children's voices fluted and chirped around him, as insidiously torturing as the gnats.

And I didn't even *want* a baby, he thought to the rhythm of his digging. Isn't that the damnedest thing? I didn't want a baby any more than *she* did. Wasn't it true, then, that everything in his life from that point on had been a succession of things he hadn't really wanted to do? Taking a hopelessly dull job to prove he could be as responsible as any other family man, moving to an overpriced, genteel apartment to prove his mature belief in the fundamentals of orderliness and good health, having another child to prove that the first one hadn't been a mistake, buying a house in the country because that was the next logical step and he had to prove himself capable of taking it. Proving, proving; and for no other reason than that he was married to a woman who had somehow managed to put him forever on the defensive, who loved him when he was nice, who lived according to what she happened to feel like doing and who might at any time—this was the hell of it—who might at any time of day or night just happen to feel like leaving him. It was as ludicrous and as simple as that.

"Are you hitting rock again, Daddy?"

"Not this time," he said. "This is a root. I think it's too deep to matter, though. If you'll just get out of the way now, I'll try and fit the stone in."

Kneeling, he rolled the boulder into place, but it wouldn't settle. It wobbled, and it sat three inches too high.

"That's too high, Daddy."

"I know it, baby." He laboriously pried the stone out again and began hacking at the root, trying to cut it, using the shovel like a clumsy ax. It was as tough as cartilage.

"Sweetie, I said don't come so *close*. You're kicking *dirt* in the hole."

"I'm *helping*, Daddy."

Jennifer looked hurt and surprised, and he thought she might be going to cry again. He tried to make his voice very low and gentle. "Look, everybody. Why don't you find something else to do? You've got the whole yard to play in. Come on, now. That's the idea. I'll call you if I need any help."

But in a minute they were back, sitting too close and talking quietly together. Dizzy with effort and blind with sweat, he was straddling the pit and holding the shovel vertically, like a pile driver, lifting it high and bringing it down with all his strength on the root. He had torn a ragged wound in it, laying open its moist white meat, but it wouldn't break, it wouldn't give, and it made the children laugh each time the shovel bounced and rang in his hands. The delicate noise of their laughter, the look of their tulip-soft skin and of their two sunny skulls, as fragile as eggshell, made a terrible contrast to the feel of biting steel and shuddering pulp, and it was his sense of this that made his eyes commit a distortion of truth. For a split second, in the act of bringing the shovel blade down, he thought he saw Michael's white sneaker slip into its path. Even as he swerved and threw the shovel away with a clang he knew it hadn't really happened—but it *could* have happened, that was the point—and his anger was so quick that the next thing he knew he had grabbed him by the belt and spun him around and hit him hard on the buttocks with the flat of his hand, twice, surprised at the stunning vigor of the blows and at the roar of his own voice: "Get *outa* here now! Get *outa* here!"

Leaping and twisting, clutching the seat of his pants with both hands, Michael found his need to cry so sudden and so deep that for several seconds after the first shocked squeal no sound could break from him. His eyes wrinkled shut, his mouth opened and was locked in that position while his lungs fought for breath; then out it came, a long high wail of pain and humiliation. Jennifer watched him, round-eyed, and in the next breath her own face began to twitch and crumple and she was crying too.

"I kept telling you and telling you," he explained to them, waving his arms. "I *told* you there'd be trouble if you got too close. Didn't I? Didn't I? All right now, take off. Both of you."

They didn't need to be told. They were moving steadily away from him across the grass, crying, looking back at him with infinite reproachfulness. In another second he might have been running after them with apologies, he might have been crying too, if he hadn't forced himself to pick up the shovel and bang it at the root again; and as he worked he prepared an anxious, silent brief in his own defense. Well, damn it, I *did* keep telling them and telling them, he assured himself, and by now his mind had mercifully amended the facts. The kid put his foot right the hell in my *way*, for God's sake. If I hadn't swerved just in time he wouldn't *have* a foot, for God's sake. . . .

When he looked up again he saw that April had come out of the kitchen door and around the side of the house, and he saw that the children had run to her and hidden their faces in her trousers.

FOUR

THEN IT WAS SUNDAY, with the living room deep in the rustling torpor of Sunday newspapers, and no words had passed between Frank Wheeler and his wife for what seemed a year. She had gone alone to the second and final performance of *The Petrified Forest*, and afterwards had slept on the sofa again.

He was trying now to take his ease in an armchair, looking through the magazine section of the *Times*, while the children played quietly in the corner and April washed the dishes in the kitchen. He had thumbed through the magazine more than once, put it down and picked it up again, and he kept returning to a full-page, dramatically lighted fashion photograph whose caption began "A frankly flattering, definitely feminine dress to go happily wherever you go . . ." and whose subject was a tall, proud girl with deeper breasts

and hips than he'd thought fashion models were supposed to have. At first he thought she looked not
unlike a girl in his office named Maureen Grube; then
he decided this one was much better looking and probably more intelligent. Still, there was a distinct resemblance; and as he studied this frankly flattering,
definitely feminine girl his mind slid away in a fuddled
erotic reverie. At the last office Christmas party, not
nearly as drunk as he was pretending to be, he had
backed Maureen Grube up against a filing cabinet and
kissed her long and hard on the mouth.

Displeased with himself, he dropped the paper
on the rug and lit a cigarette without noticing that
another one, quite long, was smoldering in the ash tray
beside him. Then, if only because the afternoon was
bright and the children were quiet and the fight with
April was now another day in the past, he went into the
kitchen and took hold of both her elbows as she bent
over a sinkful of suds.

"Listen," he whispered. "I don't care who's right or
who's wrong or what this whole damn thing is all
about. Couldn't we just cut it out and start acting like
human beings for a change?"

"Until the next time, you mean? Make everything
all nice and comfy-cozy until the next time? I'm afraid
not, thanks. I'm tired of playing that game."

"Don't you see how unfair you're being? What do you want from me?"

"Two things, at the moment. I want you to take your hands off me and I want you to keep your voice down."

"Will you tell me one thing? Will you tell me just what the hell you're trying to do?"

"Certainly. I'm trying to wash the dishes."

"Daddy?" Jennifer said when he went back to the living room.

"What?"

"Would you please read us the funnies?"

The shyness of this request, and the sight of their trusting eyes, made him want to weep. "You bet I will," he said. "Let's sit down over here, all three of us, and we'll read the funnies."

He found it hard to keep his voice from thickening into a sentimental husk as he began to read aloud, with their two heads pressed close to his ribs on either side and their thin legs lying straight out on the sofa cushions, warm against his own. *They* knew what forgiveness was; *they* were willing to take him for better or worse; they loved him. Why couldn't April realize how simple and necessary it was to love? Why did she have to complicate everything?

The only trouble was that the funnies seemed to go

on forever; the turning of each dense, muddled page of them brought the job no nearer to completion. Before long his voice had become a strained, hurrying monotone and his right knee had begun to jiggle in a little dance of irritation.

"Daddy, we skipped a funny."

"No we didn't, sweetie. That's just an advertisement. You don't want to read that."

"Yes I do."

"I do too."

"But it isn't a *funny*. It's just made to look like one. It's an advertisement for some kind of toothpaste."

"Read us it anyway."

He set his bite. All the nerves at the roots of his teeth seemed to have entwined with the nerves at the roots of his scalp in a tingling knot. "All right," he said. "See, in the first picture this lady wants to dance with this man but he won't ask her to, and here in the next picture she's crying and her friend says maybe the reason he won't dance with her is because her breath doesn't smell too nice, and then in the next picture she's talking to this dentist, and he says . . ."

He felt as if he were sinking helplessly into the cushions and the papers and the bodies of his children like a man in quicksand. When the funnies were finished at last he struggled to his feet, quietly gasping,

and stood for several minutes in the middle of the carpet, making tight fists in his pockets to restrain himself
from doing what suddenly seemed the only thing in
the world he really and truly wanted to do: picking up
a chair and throwing it through the picture window.

What the hell kind of a life was this? What in God's
name was the point or the meaning or the purpose of a
life like this?

When evening came, heavy with beer, he began to
look forward to the fact that the Campbells were coming over. Ordinarily it might have depressed him
("Why don't we ever see anyone else? Do you realize
they're practically the only friends we have?"), but
tonight it held a certain promise. At least she would
have to laugh and talk in their company; at least she
would have to smile at him from time to time and call
him "darling." Besides, it couldn't be denied that the
Campbells did seem to bring out the best in both of
them.

"Hi!" They called to one another.

"Hi! . . ." "Hi! . . ."

This one glad syllable, borne up through the gathering twilight and redoubling back from the Wheelers'
kitchen door, was the traditional herald of an evening's

entertainment. Then came the handshakings, the stately puckered kissings, the sighs of amiable exhaustion—"Ah-h-h"; "Who-o-o"—suggesting that miles of hot sand had been traveled for the finding of this oasis or that living breath itself had been held, painfully, against the promise of this release. In the living room, having sipped and grimaced at the first frosty brimming of their drinks, they pulled themselves together for a moment of mutual admiration; then they sank into various postures of controlled collapse.

Milly Campbell dropped her shoes and squirmed deep into the sofa cushions, her ankles snug beneath her buttocks and her uplifted face crinkling into a good sport's smile—not the prettiest girl in the world, maybe, but cute and quick and fun to have around.

Beside her, Frank slid down on the nape of his spine until his cocked leg was as high as his head. His eyes were already alert for conversational openings and his thin mouth already moving in the curly shape of wit, as if he were rolling a small, bitter lozenge on his tongue.

Shep, massive and dependable, a steadying influence on the group, set his meaty knees wide apart and worked his tie loose with muscular fingers to free his throat for gusts of laughter.

And finally, the last to settle, April arranged herself with careless elegance in the sling chair, her head thrown back on the canvas to blow sad, aristocratic spires of cigarette smoke at the ceiling. They were ready to begin.

At first it seemed, to everyone's surprise and relief, that the delicate topic of the Laurel Players could be rapidly disposed of. A brief exchange of words and a few deprecating, head-shaking chuckles seemed to take care of it. Milly insisted that the second performance had really been much better than the first—"I mean at least the audience did seem more—well, more appreciative, I thought. Didn't you, sweetie?" Shep said that he personally was glad to have the damn thing over with; and April, to whom all their anxious glances now turned, put them at ease with a smile.

"To coin a phrase," she said, "it was a lot of fun anyway. Wasn't it awful how many people were saying that last night? I must've heard those same words fifty times."

Within a minute the talk had turned to children and disease (the Campbells' eldest boy was underweight and Milly wondered if he might be suffering from an obscure blood ailment, until Shep said that whatever he was suffering from it sure hadn't weakened his throwing arm), and from there to an agreement that the elementary school was really doing a fine job, considering the reactionary board it was saddled with, and from there to the fact that prices had been unaccountably high in the supermarket. It was only then, during a dissertation by Milly on lamb chops, that an almost palpable discomfort settled over the room. They shifted in their seats, they filled awkward pauses with elaborate courtesies about the freshening of drinks, they avoided one another's eyes and did their best to avoid the alarming, indisputable knowledge that they had nothing to talk about. It was a new experience.

Two years or even a year ago it could never have happened, for then if nothing else there had always been a topic in the outrageous state of the nation. "How do you *like* this Oppenheimer business?" one of them would demand, and the others would fight for the floor with revolutionary zeal. The cancerous growth of Senator McCarthy had poisoned the United States, and with the pouring of second or third drinks they could begin to see themselves as members of an embattled, dwindling intellectual underground. Clippings from the *Observer* or the *Manchester Guardian* would be produced and read aloud, to slow and respectful nods; Frank might talk wistfully of Europe—"God, I wish we'd taken off and gone there when we had the chance"—and this might lead to a quick general lust for expatriation: "Let's *all* go!" (Once it went as far as a practical discussion of how much they'd need for boat fare and rent and schools, until Shep, after a sobering round of coffee, explained what he'd read about the difficulty of getting jobs in foreign countries.)

And even after politics had palled there had still been the elusive but endlessly absorbing subject of Conformity, or The Suburbs, or Madison Avenue, or American Society Today. "Oh Jesus," Shep might begin, "you know this character next door to us? Donaldson? The one that's always out fooling with his power mower and talking about the rat race and the soft sell? Well, listen: did I tell you what he said about his barbecue pit?" And there would follow an anecdote of extreme suburban smugness that left them weak with laughter.

"Oh, I don't believe it," April would insist. "Do they really talk that way?"

And Frank would develop the theme. "The point is it wouldn't be so bad if it weren't so typical. It isn't only the Donaldsons—it's the Cramers too, and the whaddyacallits, the Wingates, and a million others. It's all the idiots I ride with on the train every day. It's a disease. Nobody thinks or feels or cares any more; nobody gets excited or believes in anything except their own comfortable little God damn mediocrity."

Milly Campbell would writhe in pleasure. "Oh, that's so true. Isn't that true, darling?"

They would all agree, and the happy implication

was that they alone, the four of them, were painfully alive in a drugged and dying culture. It was in the face of this defiance, and in tentative reply to this loneliness, that the idea of the Laurel Players had made its first appeal. Milly had brought the news: some people she'd met from the other side of the Hill were trying to organize a theater group. They planned to hire a New York director and to produce serious plays, if only they could arouse enough community interest. Oh, it probably wouldn't amount to much—Milly knew that—but she wondered, shyly, if it might not be fun. April had been disdainful at first: "Oh, God, I know these damn little artsy-craftsy things. There'll be a woman with blue hair and wooden beads who met Max Reinhardt once, and there'll be two or three slightly homosexual young men and seven girls with bad complexions." But then a tasteful advertisement began to appear in the local paper ("We are looking for actors. . . ."); then the Wheelers met the people too, at an otherwise boring party, and had to admit that they were what April called "genuine." At Christmastime they met the director himself and agreed with Shep that he did seem like a man who knew what he was doing, and within a month they were all committed. Even Frank, while refusing to try out for a part ("I'd be lousy"), helped write some of the promotional material and got it multigraphed at his office, and it was Frank who talked most hopefully about the larger social and philosophical possibilities of the thing. If a really good, really serious community theater could be established here, wouldn't it be a step in the right direction? God knew they would probably never inspire the Donaldsons—and who cared?—but at least they might give the Donaldsons pause; they might show the Donaldsons a way of life beyond the commuting train and the Republican Party and the barbecue pit. Besides, what did they have to lose?

Whatever it was, they had lost it now. Blame for the failure of the Laurel Players could hardly be fobbed off on Conformity or The Suburbs or American Society Today. How could new jokes be told about their neighbors when these very neighbors had sat and sweated in their audience? Donaldsons, Cramers, Wingates and all, they had come to *The Petrified Forest* with a surprisingly generous openness of mind, and had been let down.

Milly was talking about gardening now, about the difficulty of raising a healthy lawn on Revolutionary Hill, and her eyes were taking on a glaze of panic. Her voice had been the only sound in the room for ten minutes or more, and it had been continuous. She seemed keenly aware of this, but aware too that if she allowed herself to stop the house would fill with a silence as thick as water, an impossibly deep, wide pool in which she would flounder and drown.

It was Frank who came to her rescue. "Oh, hey listen, Milly. I meant to ask you. Do you know what seecham is? Or beecham? A kind of plant?"

"Seecham," she repeated, pretending to think, while a blush of gratitude suffused her softening face. "Offhand I'm afraid I don't know, Frank. I can certainly look it *up* for you, though. We have this book at home."

"Doesn't really matter, I guess," he said. "It's just that Mrs. Givings came barrel-assing over here yesterday with a big box of this crazy—"

"Mrs. Givings!" Milly cried in a sudden ecstasy of remembrance and relief. "Oh my goodness, I haven't even *told* you people about that! I guess I haven't even told Shep yet, have I, sweetie? About their son? It's fantastic."

She was off again, but this was a wholly different kind of monologue: everyone was listening. The urgency of her voice and the eager way she leaned forward to tug her skirt down over her wrinkled knees had galvanized them all with the promise of a new theme, and Milly savored the capture of her audience, wanting to let the revelation come out as slowly as possible. First of all, did the Wheelers know the Givingses had a son?

Certainly they did; and Milly sat nodding wisely, allowing herself to be interrupted, while they reminded each other of the thin sailor whose photograph had grinned from the Givingses' mantelpiece the one time they had gone there for dinner; they remembered Mrs. Givings explaining that this was John, who had loathed the navy, had done marvelously well at M.I.T. and now was doing marvelously well as an instructor of mathematics at some Western university.

"Well," Milly said. "He isn't teaching any mathematics now, and he isn't out West either. You know where he is? You know where he's been for the past two months? He's over here in Greenacres. *You* know," she added, when they all looked blank. "The State hospital. The insane asylum."

They all began chattering at once, drawing close and tense together in the fog of cigarette smoke; it was almost like old times. Wasn't this the damnedest, weirdest, saddest thing? Was Milly absolutely certain of her facts?

Oh yes, oh yes, she was certain. "And what's more," she went on, "he didn't just *go* to Greenacres. He was taken in and put there, by the State Police."

A Mrs. Macready, who worked for the Givingses as a part-time cleaning woman, had told Milly the whole story only yesterday, at the shopping center, unable to believe she hadn't heard it long before. "She said she thought everybody'd heard it by now. Anyway, it seems he's been—you know, mentally disturbed for a long time. She said they practically went broke trying to pay for this private sanatorium out in California; he'd go in there for months at a time and then come out—that's when he'd teach, I guess—and then go back again. Then he seemed all right for a long time, until he suddenly quit his job out there and disappeared. Then he turned up here, without any warning, and came storming into the house and sort of held them captive there for about three days." She giggled uneasily at this, aware that a phrase like "held them captive" might sound too melodramatic to be true. "That's what Mrs. Macready called it anyway. I mean he probably didn't have a gun or a knife or anything, but he must've scared them half to death. Especially with Mr. Givings being so old and all, and his heart trouble. What he did was, he locked them in and cut the telephone wires and said he wasn't going to leave until they gave him what he'd come for, only he wouldn't say what it *was* he'd come for. One time he said it was his birth certificate, and they looked through all their old papers and stuff until they found it and gave it to him, and he tore it up. The rest of the time he just walked around talking and talking—raving, I guess—and breaking things. Furniture, pictures off the wall, dishes—everything. And in the middle of it all Mrs. Macready came over to go to work and he locked her in too—that's how she found out, you see—and I guess she was there for about ten hours before she got out through the garage. Then she called the State Troopers, and they came and took him to Greenacres."

"God," April said. "The State Troopers. How awful." And they all shook their heads in solemn agreement.

Shep was inclined to doubt the cleaning woman's veracity—"After all, the whole thing's just hearsay"—but the others talked him down. Hearsay or not, it had the unmistakable ring of truth to it.

April pointed out how significant it now seemed that Mrs. Givings had been dropping in so often lately for seemingly aimless little visits: "It's the funniest thing, I've always had the feeling she wanted something here, or wanted to tell us something and couldn't quite get the words out—haven't you felt that?" (Here she turned to her husband, but without quite meeting his eyes and without adding the "darling" or even the "Frank" that would have filled his heart with hope. He muttered that he guessed he had.) "God, isn't that sad," April said. "She's probably been dying to talk about it, or to find out how much we know, or something."

Milly, happily relaxing, wanted to explore the thing from the woman's angle. What *would* a mother feel on learning that her only child was mentally deranged? Shep hitched his chair up close to Frank, excluding the girls, bent on a plain, hard-headed discussion of the practical aspects. What was the deal? Could a man be forcibly committed to the nuthouse just like that? Didn't it sound fishy somehow, from a legal standpoint?

Frank began to see that if he allowed things to go on this way the excitement of the topic would soon be dispelled; without it, the evening might then degenerate into the dreariest kind of suburban time filler, the very kind of evening he had always imagined the Donaldsons and the Wingates and the Cramers having, in which women consulted with women about recipes and clothes, while men settled down with men to talk of jobs and cars. In a minute Shep might even say, "How's the job going, Frank?" in dead earnest, just as if Frank hadn't made it clear, time and again, that his job was the very least important part of his life, never to be mentioned except in irony. It was time to act.

He took a deep drink, leaned forward, and raised his voice enough to leave no doubt of his intention to address the group. Wasn't this, he asked, a beautifully typical story of these times and this place? A man could rant and smash and grapple with the State Police, and still the sprinklers whirled at dusk on every lawn and the television droned in every living room. A woman's only son came home insane, confronting her with God only knew what agonies of grief and guilt, and still she busied herself with the doings of the zoning board, with little chirrups of neighborly good cheer and card-board boxes full of garden plants.

"I mean talk about decadence," he declared, "how decadent can a society get? Look at it this way. This country's probably the psychiatric, psychoanalytical capital of the world. Old Freud himself could never've dreamed up a more devoted bunch of disciples than the population of the United States—isn't that right? Our whole damn culture is geared to it; it's the new religion; it's everybody's intellectual and spiritual sugar-tit. And for all that, look what happens when a man really does blow his top. Call the Troopers, get him out of sight quick, hustle him off and lock him up before he wakes the neighbors. Christ's sake, when it comes to any kind of a showdown we're still in the Middle Ages. It's as if everybody'd made this tacit agreement to live in a state of total self-deception. The hell with reality! Let's have a whole bunch of cute little winding roads and cute little houses painted white and pink and baby blue; let's all be good consumers and have a lot of Togetherness and bring our children up in a bath of sentimentality—Daddy's a great man because he makes a living, Mummy's a great woman because she's stuck by Daddy all these years—and if old reality ever does pop out and say Boo we'll all get busy and pretend it never happened."

It was the kind of outburst that normally won their

clamorous approval, or at the very least caused Milly to cry "Oh that's so true!" But it seemed to have no effect. The three of them sat watching politely while he talked, and when he stopped they looked mildly relieved, like pupils at the end of a lecture.

There was nothing for him to do but get up and collect the glasses and retreat to the kitchen, where he petulantly wrenched and banged at the ice tray. The black kitchen window gave him a vivid reflection of his face, round and full of weakness, and he stared at it with loathing. That was when he remembered something—and the thought seemed to follow rather than precede the stricken look it caused on his mirrored face—something that shocked him and then filled him with a sense of ironic justice. The face in the glass, again seeming to anticipate rather than reflect his mood, had changed now from a look of dismay to a wise and bitter smile, and it nodded at him several times. Then he busied himself with the drinks, anxious to get back to the company. The thing he had remembered, whatever else it might mean, would be something to talk about.

"I just thought of something," he announced, and they all looked up. "Tomorrow's my birthday."

"Well!" the Campbells said in tired, congratulatory unison.

"I'll be thirty years old. Can you beat that?"

"Hell yes, I can beat it," said Shep, who was thirty-two, and Milly, who was thirty-four, began brushing cigarette ashes off her lap.

"No, but I mean it's funny to think you're not in your twenties any more," he said, re-establishing himself on the sofa. "It's kind of—*you* know, the end of an era or something. I don't know." He was getting drunk; he was drunk already. In another minute he'd be saying even sillier things than this, and repeating himself—he knew that, and the desperation of knowing it made him talk all the more.

"Birthdays," he was saying. "It's funny how they all run together when you look back. I do remember one of them damn well, though, and that was my twentieth." And he began to tell them how he had spent it, or part of it, pinned down by mortar and machine-gun fire in the last week of the war. One small, cold-sober part of his mind knew why he was doing this: it was because humorous talk of the army and the war had more than once turned out to be the final salvation of evenings with the Campbells. There was nothing Shep seemed to relish more, and though the girls might laugh in the wrong places and jokingly insist they would never fathom the interests and the loyalties of men, there was no denying that their listening faces would shine with a glow of romance. One of the most memorable nights of the whole friendship, in fact, had been built on a series of well-turned army stories and had found its climax in a roar of masculine song. Shep Campbell and Frank Wheeler, exultantly laughing and sweating and bathed in the sleepy admiration of their wives, had thumped their fists in marching cadence on the coffee table and bellowed out, at three in the morning:

> *"Oh-h-h-h—*
> *Hidey, tidey, Christ Almighty*
> *Who the hell are we?*
> *Flim, flam, God damn*
> *We're the infantry . . ."*

And so he told his anecdote, as carefully and well as he could, using all the tricks of wry self-disparagement that had come to form his style of military reminiscence over the years. It wasn't until he got to the part that went "—so I poked the guy next to me and said 'Hey, what day is this?'" that he began to feel uneasy, and by then it was too late. There was nothing to do but finish it: "And it turned out to be my birthday." He knew now that he'd told this same story to the Campbells before, using almost the same words; it must have been a year ago that he'd told it, in connection with his turning twenty-nine.

Both the Campbells made conscientious little

clucks of amusement, and Shep discreetly inspected his watch. But the worst part—the worst part of the whole weekend, if not of his life to date—was the way April was looking at him. He had never seen such a stare of pitying boredom in her eyes.

It haunted him all night, while he slept alone; it was still there in the morning, when he swallowed his coffee and backed down the driveway in the crumpled old Ford he used for a station car. And riding to work, one of the youngest and healthiest passengers on the train, he sat with the look of a man condemned to a very slow, painless death. He felt middle-aged.

FIVE

THE ARCHITECTS OF THE KNOX BUILDING had wasted no time in trying to make it look taller than its twenty stories, with the result that it looked shorter. They hadn't bothered trying to make it handsome, either, and so it was ugly: slab-sided and flat-topped, with a narrow pea-green cornice that jutted like the lip of a driven stake. It stood in an appropriately hum-drum section of lower midtown, and from the very day of its grand opening, early in the century, it must clearly have been destined to settle deep into that smoke-hung clutter of numberless rectilinear shapes out of which, in aerial photographs, the mightier tow-ers of New York emerge and rise.

But for all its plainness, the Knox Building did con-vey a quality of massive common sense. If it lacked grandeur, at least it had bulk; if there was nothing heroic about it, there was certainly nothing frivolous; it was a building that meant business.

"There it is, Frank," Earl Wheeler said to his son on a summer morning in 1935. "Straight ahead. That's the Home Office. Better take my hand here, this is a bad crossing . . ."

It was the only time Frank had ever been brought to New York by his father, and it had come as the climax to an exhilarating several weeks that always seemed, in retrospect, the only time his father could ever have been described as jovial. During that time the cryptic phrase "Oat Fields" had flown in happy profusion through his father's dinner-table talk, along with "New York" and "The Home Office," and had repeatedly caused his mother to say "Oh, that's wonderful, Earl," and "Oh, I'm so glad." Frank had eventually figured out that Oat Fields had nothing whatever to do with Quaker Oats but was in fact the odd name of a man—Mr. Oat Fields—a man remarkable not only in his size ("One of the biggest men in the Home Office") but in his intellectual astuteness. And he'd scarcely put this information straight in his mind before being presented, by his mother, with some startling news. Mr. Oat Fields, upon learning that Mr. Earl Wheeler had a son of ten, had invited that son to accompany his father on a visit to the Home Office. Father and son would then be the guests of Mr. Fields at luncheon (it was the first time he'd ever heard her use that word instead of lunch), following which Mr. Fields would take them to a ball game at Yankee Stadium. In the next few days the suspense had grown all but intolerable until it threatened to spoil everything on the morning of the trip: he very nearly threw up his breakfast from tension and trainsickness on the way to town, and might have done it in the taxi too if they hadn't gotten out to walk the last several blocks in the fresh air; but with the clearing of his head as they walked it began to seem that everything was going to be fine.

"There," his father said when they'd crossed the street. "Now, here's the barbershop, that's where we're going for our haircuts in a minute, and here's the sub-way—see how they've built the subway entrance right into the building? —and look over here, this is the display room. These windows run the entire length of the building, from here on. Lot bigger than our dinky old showroom out home, isn't it? And look—these are just a few of the products we make. Here's your typewriters, of course, and your adders and calculators and some of your different kinds of filing systems, and that's one of the new bookkeeping machines back there in the corner; and then look over here, in the next window. These are your punched-card machines. That big one is your tabulator, and the little one beside it is your sorter. When you watch a demonstration of that baby, it's really a sight to see. Fella takes a deck of punched cards, stacks 'em, puts 'em in there and presses a button, and those old cards go flying through there lickety-split."

But Frank's eyes kept wandering from the machines to his own reflection in the plate glass. He thought he looked surprisingly dignified in his new suit, with its coat and tie almost exactly like his father's, and it pleased him to see this bright image of the two of them, man and boy, with the endless swarm of people moving past on the sidewalk behind them. After a minute he backed several steps away and looked straight up, until his collar cramped the back of his neck, and Wow! He would admit he'd hoped for a skyscraper, but the last of his disappointment was vanishing now in this one long look. Up and up and up the tiers of windows rose, each smaller and more foreshortened than the one beneath, until their ever-narrowing sills and lintels seemed to merge. Imagine falling from the very top floor! Then he saw that the high, high cornice was moving slowly and steadily forward against the sky—the building was falling over on them!—but there was no time for panic before he saw his mistake: it was the sky that moved, white clouds floating back over the ledge of the roof, and at the instant his mind came into focus on this fact he felt a shiver of wonder down his spine at the enormous granite strength and stillness of the building. Wow!

"All set?" his father was saying. "Let's go to the barber's, then, and get fixed up, and then we'll go on inside. We're going to ride the elevator all the way up to the top."

But as things turned out, that preliminary moment on the sidewalk was the high point of the day. The barbershop proved to be nice enough, and so did the echoing marble-flagged lobby, which smelled of cigars and umbrellas and ladies' perfume, but from there on the pleasures of the day began to dwindle steadily. The elevator gave no sense of flight, for one thing, but only of confinement and nausea. Of the office itself, the top floor, he remembered only an acre of white lights and a very thin lady whose openwork blouse revealed an incredible number of straps that were apparently connected with her underwear, who called him Sonny and showed him how the water cooler worked ("Look, Sonny; watch the big bubble come up when I press the button—Blurp!—isn't that funny? Here, you try it"); and he would never forget the instantaneous revulsion he felt in the presence of Mr. Oat Fields, who if not the biggest was certainly the fattest man he had ever seen. Oat Fields's glasses mirrored staring images of the office lights, so that you couldn't see what his eyes were doing when he talked to you, and he talked in a very loud voice without seeming to hear your replies.

"Well, aren't *you* a big fella! What's your name? Huh? You like school? Well, that's fine. You like baseball? Huh?"

The worst part of him was his mouth, which was so wet that a dozen shining strands of spittle clung and trembled between his moving lips; and it was this as much as anything that hampered Frank's enjoyment of the lunch, or luncheon, which took place in the restaurant of a great hotel. Oat Fields's mouth did not close while chewing and it left white streaks of food on the rim of his water glass. Once he softened the hard crust of a roll by holding it submerged in the gravy boat for some time before he lifted it to his reaching lips, allowing part of it to fall and leave a bright tan stain on his vest.

"You're absolutely right, Oat," Earl Wheeler kept saying throughout the meal, and "I certainly do agree with you on that," and the few times he glanced at Frank it was with startled eyes, as if surprised to find him sitting there. The ball game was a letdown too: nobody hit a home run, and in Frank's limited knowledge of the game a home run was all that mattered. For the last hour of it the sun slanted straight in his eyes, giving him a headache, and he had to go to the bathroom but didn't know how to broach the subject. Then came the grimy ordeal of subway connections to Penn Station, during which his father took him angrily to task for having failed to say "Thank you I had a very nice time" to Oat Fields. In the bleak light of the train-shed, as they stood waiting for the gates to open, he stared unnoticed at the physical exhaustion and moral defeat in his father's face, which looked loose and porous and very old. Then, lowering his eyes, he discovered that his father's trouser leg was slightly and rhythmically twitching with the anxious movement of his pocketed fingers on his genitals.

And that, ultimately, would become his most vivid single remembrance of the day; at the time, though, later that same night as he staggered and crouched barefoot in the tilting, oddly shrunken bathroom of his home, it was his memory's vision of Oat Fields's eating mouth that made the spasms of vomiting come again and again.

Not until years later was he able to piece the simple facts of the case together. Earl Wheeler, having clung to an assistant branch managership in Newark through any number of Depression layoffs and cutbacks, had somehow come to Home Office attention as a candidate for the job of right-hand man to Oat Fields (and not until later still did he guess the explanation of that name—the fact that in a world of mandatory diminutives, a corporation of jolly Bills and Jacks and Herbs and Teds in which an unabbreviable given name like Earl must always have been a minor handicap, "Oat" was the best that could be done for a man with the given name of Otis). But the promotion had fallen through; higher authority had decreed that Oat Fields could get along without a right-hand man, and Earl Wheeler must either have learned or guessed this outcome at some point during the luncheon or the ball game.

And whether or not he ever came to accept the disappointment, Frank knew that to the end of his life he never understood it. It must, for that matter, have been the first of many events that passed Earl Wheeler's understanding, for it came at the beginning of his decline. In the years after that he was transferred from one field assignment to another until his retirement soon after the war (and not long after Oat Fields's own retirement and death), by which time he had slipped from the assistant-manager level to that of an ordinary salesman in Harrisburg, Pennsylvania. And in those years too, with increasing bewilderment, he had failed to understand the weakening of his health, the rapid difficult aging of his wife, the indifference of his two older sons—and finally the shrill rebellion, the desertion, and the moral collapse of his youngest.

A longshoreman! A cafeteria cashier! An ungrateful, spiteful, foul-mouthed weakling, boozing his way through Greenwich Village with God only knew what kind of companions; a punk kid with no more sense of decency than to drive his mother nearly out of her mind not writing for six, eight months and then mailing a letter with no return address and the postscript: "Got married last week—might bring her out sometime."

It was a lucky thing for Earl Wheeler, then, that he wasn't present in a cheap bar near the Columbia campus one noontime in 1948, when his son sat in conference with another slouching youth named Sam, a graduate student in philosophy who held a part-time job in the student placement office.

"So what's the problem, Frank? I thought you'd be back in Europe by now."

"Big joke. April's knocked up."

"Oh Jesus."

"No, but listen; there're all different kinds of ways of looking at a thing like this, Sam. Look at it this way. I need a job; okay. Is that any reason why the job I get has to louse me up? Look. All I want is to get enough dough coming in to keep us solvent for the next year or so, till I can figure things out; meanwhile I want to retain my own identity. Therefore the thing I'm most anxious to avoid is any kind of work that can be considered 'interesting' in its own right. I want something that can't possibly touch me. I want some big, swollen old corporation that's been bumbling along making money in its sleep for a hundred years, where they have to hire eight guys for every one job because none of them can be expected to care about whatever boring thing it is they're supposed to be doing. I want to go into that kind of place and say, Look. You can have my body and my nice college-boy smile for so many hours a day, in exchange for so many dollars, and beyond that we'll leave each other strictly alone. Get the picture?"

"I think so," said the philosophy student. "Come on back to the office." And there, adjusting his glasses and thumbing through a card index, Sam began to write out a list of companies that seemed to fit the picture: a great copper-and-brass manufacturer, a great public utility, a gigantic firm that made all kinds of paper bags . . .

But when Frank saw the awesome name of Knox Business Machines being added to the list he thought there must be some mistake. "Hey, no, wait a minute; I know that can't be right—" and he gave a brief oral summary of his father's career, which caused the philosophy student to enjoy a pleasant chuckle.

"I think you'll find things've changed a little since your old man's time, Frank," he said. "That was the Depression, don't forget. Besides, he was out in the field; you'd be in the home office. As a matter of fact this place is just what you're looking for. I happen to know they've got guys sitting around that building that never lift a finger except to pick up their checks. I'd certainly mention your father, though, when you go for the interview. Probably help things along."

But Frank, as he walked into the shadow of the Knox Building with the ghosts of that other visit crowding his head ("Better take my hand here, this is a bad crossing . . ."), decided it would be more fun not to mention his father in the interview at all. And he didn't, and he got a job that very day on the fifteenth floor, in something called the Sales Promotion Department.

"The sales what?" April inquired. "'Promotion'? I don't get it. What does that mean you're supposed to do?"

"Who the hell knows? They explained it to me for half an hour and I still don't know, and I don't think they do either. No, but it's pretty funny, isn't it? Old Knox Business Machines. Wait'll I tell the old man. Wait'll he hears I didn't even use his name."

And so it started as a kind of joke. Others might fail to see the humor of it, but it filled Frank Wheeler with a secret, astringent delight as he discharged his lazy duties, walking around the office in a way that had lately become almost habitual with him, if not quite truly characteristic, since having been described by his wife as "terrifically sexy"—a slow, catlike stride, proudly muscular but expressing a sleepy disdain of tension or hurry. And the best part of the joke was what happened every afternoon at five. Buttoned-up and smiling among the Knox men, nodding goodnight as the elevator set him free, he would take a crosstown bus and a downtown bus to Bethune Street, where he'd mount two flights of slope-treaded, creaking stairs, open a white door so overlayed with many generations of soiled and blistered paint that its surface felt like the flesh of a toadstool, and let himself into a wide clean room that smelled faintly of cigarettes and candlewax and tangerine peel and eau de cologne; and there a beautiful, disheveled girl would be waiting, a girl as totally unlike the wife of a Knox man as the apartment was unlike a Knox man's home. Instead of after-work cocktails they would make after-work love, sometimes on the bed and sometimes on the floor; sometimes it was ten o'clock before they roused themselves and strolled into the gentle evening streets for dinner, and by then the Knox Building could have been a thousand miles away.

By the end of the first year the joke had worn thin, and the inability of others to see the humor of it had become depressing. "Oh, you mean your *father* worked there," they would say when he tried to explain it, and their eyes, as often as not, would then begin to film over with the look that people reserve for earnest, obedient, unadventurous young men. Before long (and particularly after the second year, with both his parents dead) he had stopped trying to explain that part of it, and begun to dwell instead on other comic aspects of the job: the absurd discrepancy between his own ideals and those of Knox Business Machines; the gulf between the amount of energy he was supposed to give the company and the amount he actually gave. "I mean the great advantage of a place like Knox is that you can sort of turn off your mind every morning at nine and leave it off all day, and nobody knows the difference."

More recently still, and particularly since moving to the country, he had taken to avoiding the whole topic whenever possible by replying, to the question of what he did for a living, that he didn't do anything, really; that he had the dullest job you could possibly imagine.

On the Monday morning after the end of the Laurel Players, he walked into the Knox Building like an automaton. The show windows were featuring a new display, bright cardboard images of thin, fashionable young women who grinned and pointed their pencils at emblazoned lists of product benefits—SPEED, ACCURACY, CONTROL—and beyond them, across the deep-carpeted expanse of the display floor, a generous sampling of the products themselves stood poised for demonstration. Some of them, the simpler ones, were much like the machines that had kindled his father's enthusiasm twenty years before, though the angular black designs of those days had all been modified to fit the globular "sculptured forms" of their new casings, which were the color of oyster meat; but there were others equipped to deal with the facts of business at speeds more lickety-split than anything Earl Wheeler could have dreamed of. These, ready to purr and blink with electronic mystery, grew more and more imposing across the floor until they culminated in the big inscrutable components of the Knox "500" Electronic Computer, a machine which, according to the museum card displayed at its base, could "perform the lifetime work of a man with a desk calculator in thirty minutes."

But Frank moved past the display room without a glance, and his actions on entering the lobby were absent-mindedly expert: he obeyed the pointed finger of the elevator starter without quite being aware of it, nor did he notice which of the six elevator operators it was who sleepily made him welcome (he almost never did, unless it happened to be one of the two whose presence could be faintly oppressive: the very old man whose knees were so sprung that painful-looking bulges pressed against the backs of his trousers, or the enormous boy whom some glandular disorder had afflicted with the high hips of a woman and the downy head and beardless face of an infant). Pressed well back in the polite bondage of the car, he heard the sliding door clamp shut and the safety gate go rattling after it, and as the car began to rise he was surrounded by the dissonant conversations of his colleagues. He heard a deep, measured voice of the Great Plains, rich with distance and travel and the best accommodations (". . . course, we did hit a little bumpy weather comin' inta Chicawgo . . ."), sound out in counterpoint to the abrupt and sibilant accents of the city (". . . so I siz 'Whaddya—kiddin'?' He siz 'No, listen, *I'm* not kiddin' . . .") while a softer medley of eight or ten voices, male and female, repeated their hushed morning courtesies under the buzz of the overhead fan; then it was time to begin the nodding, side-stepping ritual of making way for the people who edged toward the front with murmurs of "Out, please . . . Out, please" and to wait while the door slid open and shut, open and shut again. The eighth, the eleventh, the twelfth, the fourteenth . . .

At first glance, all the upper floors of the Knox Building looked alike. Each was a big open room, ablaze with fluorescent ceiling lights, that had been divided into a maze of aisles and cubicles by shoulder-high partitions. The upper panels of these dividers, waist to shoulder, were made of thick unframed plate glass that was slightly corrugated to achieve a blue-white semi-transparency; and the overall effect of this, to a man getting off the elevator and looking out across the room, was that of the wide indoor lake in which swimmers far and near were moving, some making steady headway, some treading water, others seen in the act of breaking to the surface or going under, and many submerged, their faces loosened into wavering pink blurs as they drowned at their desks. But the illusion was quickly dispelled on walking farther into the office, for here the air was of an overwhelming dryness—it was, as Frank Wheeler often complained, "enough to dry your God damned eyeballs out."

For all his complaints, though, he was sometimes guiltily aware of taking a dim pleasure in the very discomfort of the office. When he said, as he'd been saying for years, that in a funny way he guessed he would miss old Knox when he quit, he meant of course that it was the people he would miss ("I mean hell, they're a pretty decent crowd; some of them, anyway") and yet in all honesty he could not have denied a homely affection for the place itself, the Fifteenth Floor. Over the years he had discovered slight sensory distinctions between it and all the others of the building; it was no more or less pleasant, but different for being "his" floor. It was his bright, dry, daily ordeal, his personal measure of tedium. It had taught him new ways of spacing out the hours of the day—almost time to go down for coffee; almost time to go out for lunch; almost time to go home—and he had come to rely on the desolate wastes of time that lay between these pleasures as an invalid comes to rely on the certainty of recurring pain. It was a part of him.

"Morning, Frank," said Vince Lathrop.

"Morning, Frank," said Ed Small.

"Morning, Mr. Wheeler," said Grace Mancuso, who worked for Herb Underwood in Market Research.

His feet knew where to turn at the aisle marked SALES PROMOTION, and they knew how many steps would bring him past the first three cubicles and where he would have to turn again to enter the fourth; he could have done it in his sleep.

"Hello," said Maureen Grube, who served as floor receptionist and worked in Mrs. Jorgensen's typing pool. She said it in a frankly flattering, definitely feminine way, and as she swayed aside to let him pass he wanted to put his arm around her and lead her away somewhere (the mail room? the freight elevator?) where he could sit down and take her on his lap and remove her royal blue sweater and fill his mouth with one and then the other of her breasts.

It wasn't the first time this idea had occurred to him; the difference was that this time it had no sooner occurred to him than he thought, Why not?

His feet had led him to the entrance of the cubicle whose plastic nameplate read:

J. R. ORDWAY

F. H. WHEELER

and he paused there, one hand hooked over the rim of the plate glass, to turn and look back at her. She was all the way down to the end of the aisle, now, her buttocks moving nicely in her flannel skirt, and he watched her until she disappeared beneath the waterline of partition tops to take her place at the reception desk.

Take it easy, he counseled himself. A thing like this would need a little planning. The first thing to do, he knew, was to go on inside and say good morning to Jack Ordway and take off his coat and sit down. He did that, instantly shutting out his view of everything beyond the cubicle walls, and as he settled himself sideways at his desk with his right foot automatically toeing open a lower drawer and using its edge as a foot rest (the pressure of his shoe over the years had worn a little saddle in the edge of that particular drawer), he allowed a slow wave of delight to break over him. Why not? Hadn't she given him every possible encouragement for months? Undulating past him in the aisle like that, bending close over his desk to hand him a folder, smiling in a special, oblique way that he'd never seen her use on anyone else? And that time at the Christmas party (he could still remember the taste of her mouth) hadn't she trembled in his arms, and hadn't she whispered "You're sweet"?

Why not? Oh, not in the mail room or the freight elevator, but didn't she probably have an apartment somewhere, with a roommate, and wouldn't the roommate probably be out all day?

Jack Ordway was talking to him, requiring him against his will to look up and say "What's that?" An intrusion by almost anyone else wouldn't have mattered—he could have nodded and made the right replies while keeping most of his mind free for Maureen Grube—but Ordway was different.

"I said I'm going to need your help this morning, Franklin," he was saying. "This is an emergency. I'm dead serious, old scout." He was apparently studying a sheaf of typewritten papers on his desk, the picture of concentration; only someone who knew what to look for could have told that the hand which seemed to be shading his eyes was really holding his head up, and that his eyes were shut. In his early forties, slight and trim, with the graying hair and wittily handsome face of a romantic actor, he was the kind of borderline alcoholic whose salvation seems to lie in endless renewals of his ability to laugh the whole thing off, and he was the sentimental hero of the office. Everybody loved

Jack Ordway. Today he was wearing his English suit—
the suit he had ordered from a touring London tailor
some years before, at the cost of half a month's salary,
the suit whose cuff buttons really buttoned and whose
high-backed trousers could only be worn with sus-
penders, or "braces," the suit that was never seen without a fresh linen handkerchief spilling from its breast
pocket—but his long narrow feet, which lay splayed
with childish awkwardness under the desk, betrayed a
pitifully all-American look. They were encased in
cheap orange-brown loafers, badly scuffed; and the
reason for this clashing note was that the one thing
Jack Ordway could not do in the grip of a really bad
hangover was to tie a pair of shoelaces.

"For the next—" he was saying in a hoarse,
unsteady voice, "for the next two or possibly three
hours you're to warn me of Bandy's every approach;
you're to protect me from Mrs. Jorgensen, and you
may have to screen me from public view in case I begin
to throw up. It's that bad."

The capsuled story of Jack Ordway's life had
become a minor legend of the Fifteenth Floor: everyone
knew of how he'd married a rich girl and lived on her
inheritance until it vanished just before the war, how
since then his business career had been spent entirely in
the Knox Building, in one glass cubicle after another,
and how it had been distinguished by an almost flawless

lack of work. Even here in Sales Promotion, where nobody worked very hard except old Bandy, the manager, he had managed to retain his unique reputation. Except when a really bad hangover laid him low he was up and around and talking all day, setting off little choruses of laughter wherever he went, sometimes even winning a tolerant chuckle from Bandy himself, driving Mrs. Jorgensen into fits of helpless giggles that made her weep.

"First of all," he was saying now, "on Saturday these crazy friends of Sally's flew in from the Coast all eager for the treat. Could we show them the town? Oh, indeed we could. Old, old buddies of hers and all that, and besides, they always bring pocketfuls of loot. So. Started off with lunch at André's, and dear God you've never seen such whopping great martinis in your life. Oh, and none of this sissy business of one or two apiece, either, buddy. I lost count. And then let's see. Oh, yes. Then there was nothing to do but sit around and drink until cocktail time. Then came cocktail time." He had abandoned his working posture now, pushed the false papers aside and leaned delicately back in the chair to hold his head with both hands; he was moving it from side to side in the rhythm of his narrative, laughing and talking through his laughter, while Frank watched him with a mixture of pity and distaste. Most of his hangover stories seemed to begin with a flying-in of Sally's crazy friends from the Coast, or from the Bahamas, or from Europe, with pocketfuls of loot, and Sally herself was always featured at the center of the fun—the former debutante, the chic, childless wife and irrepressible playmate. That, at least, was the way his listeners on the Fifteenth Floor were expected to picture her; Frank had been able to do so, and to picture their apartment as a kind of Noël Coward stage setting, until the time he went home with Ordway for a drink and found that Sally was massively soft and wrinkled, a sodden, aging woman with lips forever painted in the petulant cupid's bow of her youth. Her every whining intonation of Jack's name that night, as she swayed bewildered through rooms of rotting leather and dusty silver and glass, showed how deeply she blamed him for allowing the world to collapse; once she had turned up her eyes to the paint-flaked ceiling as if calling on God to punish him—this weak, foolish little man for whom she'd sacrificed her very life, who poisoned all her friendships with his endless counting of pennies, who insisted on grubbing at his dreary, dreary white-collar job and bringing dreary office people home with him. And Jack, apologetically hovering and making little jokes, had called her "Mother."

". . . and as for how we got *back* from Idlewild," he was saying, "it's a thing I'll never know. My last completely clear recollection is of standing in the Idlewild lounge at three o'clock this morning and wondering if someone would please tell me how we'd gotten there in the first place. Or no, wait. After that there was something about a hamburger joint—or no, I think that was earlier. . . ." When the story was over at last he removed his hands from his head, experimentally, and frowned and blinked several times. Then he announced that he was beginning to feel a little better.

"Good." Frank dropped his foot from the drawer and got settled at his desk. He had to think, and the best way to think was to go through the motions of working. This morning's batch of papers was waiting in his IN basket, on top of last Friday's, and so his first action was to turn the whole stack upside down on his desk and start from the bottom. As he did each day (or rather on the days when he bothered with the IN basket, for there were many days when he left it alone) he tried first to see how many papers he could get rid of without actually reading their contents. Some could be thrown away, others could be almost as rapidly disposed of by scrawling "What about this?" in their margins, with his initials, and sending them to Bandy, or by writing "Know anything on this?" and sending them to someone like Ed Small, next door; but the danger here was that the same papers might come back in a few days marked "Do" from Bandy and "No" from

Small. A safer course was to mark a thing "File" for Mrs. Jorgensen and the girls, after the briefest possible glance had established that it wasn't of urgent importance; if it was, he might mark it "File & Follow 1 wk.," or he might put it aside and go on to the next one. The gradual accumulation of papers put aside in this way was what he turned to as soon as he was finished with, or tired of, the IN basket. Arranging them in an approximate order of importance, he would interleave them, in the same order, with those of the six- or eight-inch stack that always lay near the center of the desk, held down by a glazed ceramic paperweight that Jennifer had made for him in kindergarten. This was his current work pile. Many of the papers in it bore the insignia of Bandy's "Do" or Ed Small's "No," and some had been through the "File & Follow" cycle as many as three or four times; some, bearing notes like "Frank—might look into this," were the gifts of men who used him as he used Small. Occasionally he would remove a piece of current work and place it in the equally high secondary pile that lay on the far right-hand corner of the desk, under a leaden scale model of the Knox "500" Electronic Computer. This was the pile of things he couldn't bring himself to face just now, and the worst of them, sometimes whole bulging folders filled with scrawled-over typewritten sheets and loose, sliding paper clips, would eventually go into the stuffed bottom right-hand drawer of the desk. The papers in there were of the kind that Ordway called Real Goodies, and that drawer, opposite to the one that served as a foot rest, had come to occupy a small nagging place in Frank's conscience: he was as shy of opening it as if it held live snakes.

Why not? Wouldn't it be perfectly easy to walk up and ask her out to lunch? No, it wouldn't; that was the trouble. An unspoken rule of the Fifteenth Floor divided the men from the girls on all but business matters, except at Christmas parties. The girls made separate arrangements for lunch in the same inviolable way that they used a separate lavatory, and only a fool would openly defy the system. This would need a little planning.

He was still in the middle of the IN basket when a thin smiling face and a round solemn one appeared above the glass wall, looking in from the next cubicle. They were the faces of Vince Lathrop and Ed Small, and this meant it was time to go down for coffee.

"Gentlemen," said Vince Lathrop. "Shall we dance?"

Half an hour later they were back in the office, having heard at some length about Ed Small's difficulties with grass seed and lawn care in Roslyn, Long Island. The coffee had helped to strengthen Ordway, though it was clear now that what he really needed was a drink, and to prove how much better he felt he was pacing up and down the cubicle and going through his impersonation of Bandy, wobbling his head and repeatedly sucking at a side tooth with little kissing sounds.

"Well, but I wonder if we're really being effective, that's the thing (kiss). Because if we really want to be effective, then we're going to have to get in there and be more, be more (kiss), be more *effective* . . ."

Frank was trying for the second or third time to read the top paper on his current work pile, which seemed to be a letter from the branch manager in Toledo; but its paragraphs were as opaque as if it had been typed in a foreign language. He closed his eyes and rubbed them and tried again, and this time he made it.

The branch manager in Toledo, who in the Knox tradition referred to himself as "we," wished to know what action had been taken on his previous correspondence with regard to the many serious errors and misleading statements in SP-1109, a copy of which was attached. This proved to be a thick, coated-stock, four-color brochure entitled *Pinpoint Your Production Control with the Knox "500,"* and the sight of it brought back uneasy memories. It had been produced many months before by a nameless copywriter in an agency that had since lost its Knox account, and had been released to the field in tens of thousands of copies marked

"Address all inquiries F. H. Wheeler, Home Office." Frank had known at the time that it was a mess—its densely printed pages defied simple logic, as well as readership, and its illustrations were only sporadically related to its text—but he'd let it go anyway, chiefly because Bandy had confronted him in the aisle one day with a kiss of the side tooth and said "Haven't we released that brochure yet?"

Since then the inquiries addressed to F. H. Wheeler had come in slow, embarrassing streams from all parts of the United States, and he was dimly aware of something particularly urgent about those that had been coming from Toledo. The next paragraph reminded him.

As you will recall, it was our intention to order 5,000 additional copies of the brochure for distribution at the annual NAPE Convention (Nat'l. Assn. of Production Executives) here June 10–13. However, as stated in previous correspondence, the brochure is in our opinion so inferior that it does not fulfill its purpose in any way, shape, or manner.

Therefore please advise immediately re our inquiry in previous correspondence, namely: what arrangements are being made to have a revised version of the brochure in our office not later than June 8 in the required number of copies?

He looked quickly at the upper left-hand corner and was relieved to find that the letter had not carried a carbon to Bandy. That was a piece of luck; but even so, this had all the earmarks of a Real Goody. Even if there were still time to arrange for a new brochure to be produced (and there probably wasn't), he would have to clear the job through Bandy, and Bandy would want to know why he hadn't been told about it two months earlier.

He was in the act of laying the thing on his secondary pile when the beginnings of a bright idea came through his confusion; and suddenly he was out of the cubicle and walking toward the front of the office with his heart in his mouth.

She was at her desk in the reception area with nothing to do, and when she looked up her eyes were so full of pleased expectancy—of complicity, it almost seemed—that he nearly forgot what it was he had to pretend he'd come for.

"Maureen," he said, moving up close and taking hold of the back of her chair, "if you're not too busy here I wonder if you'd help me find some stuff in the central file. You see this?" He laid the brochure on her desk as if it were an intimate revelation, and she leaned forward from the hips to examine it, so that her breasts swung close to his pointing hand.

"Mm?"

"The thing is, it's got to be revised. That means I've got to dig up all the material that went into it, right from scratch. Now, if you'll look in the inactive file under SP-1109 you'll find copies of all the stuff we sent to the agency; then if you check each of those papers you'll find another code number referring you to other files; that way we can trace the thing back to original sources. Come on, I'll help you get started."

"All right."

As he moved up the aisle behind her hips he felt the promise of triumph in his expanding chest, and soon they were alone together in the labyrinth of the central file, enveloped in her perfume as they fingered nervously through a drawer of folders.

"Eleven-oh-what, did you say?"

"Eleven-oh-nine. Should be right there somewhere."

For the first time he allowed himself to scrutinize her face. It was round and wide-nosed and not really very pretty—he could afford to admit that now—and its too-heavy make-up was probably there to hide a bad complexion, just as the little black tails she had drawn at the corners of her eyes were there to make the eyes look larger and farther apart. Her carefully arranged hair was probably her greatest problem—it must have been a shapeless frizzled bush when she was a child, and must still give her trouble in the rain—but her mouth was wonderful: perfect teeth and plump, subtly shaped lips that had the texture of marzipan. He found that if he focused his eyes on her mouth so that the rest of her face was slightly blurred, and then drew back to include the whole length and shape of her in that hazy image, it was possible to believe he was look-ing at the most desirable woman in the world.

"Here," she said. "Now, you want all the folders relating to all these other code numbers. Is that it?"

"That's it. It may take a little time; I hope you weren't planning on an early lunch."

"No. I didn't have any special plans."

"Good. I'll stop back in a while and see how you're doing. Thanks a lot, Maureen."

"You're very welcome."

And he went back to his cubicle and sat down. It was a perfect arrangement. He could wait here until the rest of the floor had emptied out for lunch; then he would go back and get her. His only problem now was to think up an excuse for not going out to lunch in the usual way, with the usual crowd—an excuse, if possi-ble, that would cover him for the rest of the afternoon.

"Eat?" a deep masculine voice inquired, and this time three heads hung above the partition. They were the heads of Lathrop, Small, and the man who had spoken, a gray mountain of a man with heavy eyebrows and a clenched pipe, whose bulk rose high enough above the glass to reveal that he wore a defiantly unbusinesslike checked shirt, hairy wool tie, and pepper-and-salt jacket. This was Sid Roscoe, the literary and political sage of the Fifteenth Floor, a self-described "old newspaper guy" who contemptuously edited the employee house organ, *Knox Knews*. "Come on, you characters," he said heartily. "On your feet."

Jack Ordway obeyed him, pausing only to murmur "Ready, Franklin?" But Frank held back, inspecting his watch with the look of a man pressed for time.

"Guess I won't be able to make it today," he said. "Got some people to see uptown this afternoon; I'll probably stop for a bite up there."

"Oh, for God's sake, Wheeler," Ordway said, turning on him. There was a disproportionate amount of shock and disappointment in his face, a look of But you've *got* to come with us; and it took Frank a second to realize what the trouble was. Ordway needed him. With Frank along for moral support, it would be possible to steer the group to what Ordway called the Nice place, the dark German restaurant where a round of weak but adequate martinis came floating to your table almost as a matter of course; without him, under

Roscoe's leadership, they would almost certainly go to the Awful place—a bright, mercilessly clean luncheon-ette called Waffle Heaven where you couldn't even get a glass of beer and where the cloying smells of melting butter and maple syrup were enough to make you retch into your tiny paper napkin. There would then be nothing for Jack Ordway to do but sit and hold himself together until they brought him back to the office and set him free to slip out again for the couple of quick ones he would need to survive the afternoon. *Please*, his comically round eyes implored as they led him away, *please* don't let this happen to me.

But Frank sat firm, thumbing the edges of his cur-rent work file. He waited until they were safely in the elevator, and then he continued to wait. Ten minutes went by, and twenty, and still the office seemed much too crowded; then at last he half rose from his chair and peeked out over the surface of the partition-tops in all directions.

Maureen's head moved alone above the waterline of the central file. There were a few other heads bunched near the elevators and a few others scattered in far corners, but there was no point in waiting any longer. The office would never be emptier than this. He buttoned his coat and stalked out of the cubicle.

"That's fine, Maureen," he said, bearing down on

her and taking the batch of folders and papers from her hand. "I don't think we'll need any more than that."

"Well, but it's only about half the stuff, though. I mean didn't you want all of it?"

"Tell you what: let's not worry about it. How about some lunch?"

"All right. I'd love to."

He was all action as he hurried back to his desk to drop the papers and dodged into the men's room to wash up, but when he went to stand by the elevators, waiting for her to come out of the ladies' room, he was all worry. The small crowd around the elevators was beginning to include people coming *back* from lunch; if she didn't hurry up they might run into Ordway and the others. What the hell was she doing in there? Standing with her arms around three other girls in a paralysis of laughter at the very idea of going out with Mr. Wheeler?

Then suddenly she was walking toward him in a light coat, and the elevator door was sliding open and the operator's voice was saying "Down!"

He stood a little behind her and held himself in a rigid parade rest as they dropped through space. All the restaurants for blocks around would be loaded with Knox people; he would have to get her out of the neighborhood, and as they moved through the lobby he touched her elbow as hesitantly as if it were her breast. "Listen," he mumbled. "There aren't any decent places to eat around here. You mind taking a short trip?"

They were out on the sidewalk now, jostled by the crowd, and he stood smiling like an idiot for what seemed a full minute of indecision before the word "taxi" popped into his head; then all at once it made him feel so fine to see one slowing down under the command of his wagging arm, and so splendid to see her smile and bend and climb gracefully into its deep seat, that he didn't give a damn about what he saw from the corner of his eye at that moment: the unmistakable bulk of Sid Roscoe in the crowd, flanked by the familiar shapes of Lathrop and Small and Ordway, coming from the direction of the Awful place. It was impossible to tell whether they'd seen him or not, and he instantly decided that it didn't matter. He slammed the door and allowed himself one more glance through the window of the cab as it pulled away from the curb, and he wanted to laugh aloud at the sight of Jack Ordway's orange loafers flapping along through the forest of legs and feet.

SIX

"EVERYTHING'S SORT OF GOING OUT of focus," she said. "I mean I feel fine and everything, but I guess we'd better eat something."

They were in an expensive brick-walled restaurant on West Tenth Street, and Maureen had talked for half an hour in a breathless autobiographical rush, pausing only once to let him telephone Mrs. Jorgensen and arrange for one of the other girls to take the reception desk for the afternoon. ("The thing is," he had explained, "I had to borrow Maureen to help me locate some stuff here in Visual Aids, and it looks like we're going to be tied up here for the rest of the day." There was no department or subdepartment anywhere in the Knox Building called Visual Aids, but he was reasonably sure that Mrs. Jorgensen didn't know it, and that anyone she'd be likely to ask would not be certain either. He had handled the call so adroitly that he didn't realize how close he was to being drunk until he came within an inch of upsetting a tray of French pastries on his way back from the phone booth.) The rest of his time had been devoted to steady drinking and listening, with mixed emotions.

These were some of the things he'd learned: that she was twenty-two and came from a town far upstate, where her father owned a hardware store; that she hated her name ("I mean 'Maureen's' all right but 'Grube' sounds so awful with it; I guess that was one reason I was so crazy to get married"); that she'd been married at eighteen and had it annulled six months later—"It was completely ridiculous"—and had spent the following year or two "just moping around home and working at the gas company and feeling depressed" until it struck her that what she'd always really and truly wanted to do was to come to New York "and live."

All this was pleasing, and so was the way she had shyly slipped into calling him "Frank," and so was the news that she did indeed have an apartment with another girl—a "perfectly adorable" apartment right here in the Village—but after a while he found he had to keep reminding himself to be pleased. The trouble, he guessed, was mainly that she talked too much. It was also that so much of her talk rang false, that so many of its possibilities for charm were blocked and buried under the stylized ceremony of its cuteness. Soon he was able to guess that most if not all of her inanity could be blamed on her roommate, whose name was Norma and for whom she seemed to feel an unqualified admiration. The more she told him about this other girl, or "gal"—that she was older and twice divorced, that she worked for a big magazine and knew "all sorts of fabulous people"—the more annoyingly clear it became that she and Norma enjoyed classic roles of mentor and novice in an all-girl orthodoxy of fun. There were signs of this tutelage in Maureen's too-heavy make-up and too-careful hairdo, as well as in her every studied mannerism and prattling phrase— her overuse of words like "mad" and "fabulous" and "appalling," her wide-eyed recitals of facts concerning apartment maintenance, and her endless supply of anecdotes involving sweet little Italian grocers and sweet little Chinese laundrymen and gruff but lovable cops on the beat, all of whom, in the telling, became the stock supporting actors in a confectionery Hollywood romance of bachelor-girls in Manhattan.

Under the oppressive weight of this outpouring he had called for round after round of drinks, and now her meek announcement that everything was sort of out of focus filled him with guilt. All Norma's brittle animation had fled from Maureen's face; she looked as honest and as helpless as a child about to be sick on her party dress. He called the waiter and helped her to choose the most wholesome items on the menu with all the care of a conscientious father; and when she had settled down to eat, looking up now and then to assure him that she felt much better, it was his turn to talk.

He made the most of it. Sentences poured from him, paragraphs composed themselves and took wing, appropriate anecdotes sprang to his service and fell back to make way for the stately passage of epigrams.

Beginning with a quick, audacious dismantling of the Knox Business Machines Corporation, which made her laugh, he moved out confidently onto broader fields of damnation until he had laid the punctured myth of Free Enterprise at her feet; then, just at the point where any further talk of economics might have threatened to bore her, he swept her away into cloudy realms of philosophy and brought her lightly back to earth with a wise-crack.

And how did she feel about the death of Dylan Thomas? And didn't she agree that this generation was the least vital and most terrified in modern times? He was at the top of his form. He was making use of material that had caused Milly Campbell to say "Oh that's so true, Frank!" and of older, richer stuff that had once helped to make him the most interesting person April Johnson had ever met. He even touched on his having been a longshoreman. Through it all, though, ran a bright and skillfully woven thread that was just for Maureen: a portrait of himself as decent but disillusioned young family man, sadly and bravely at war with his environment.

By the time the coffee came he could see that it was all taking effect. Her face had become an automatic register of quick responses to everything he said: he could make it leap into delighted laughter or frown and nod in solemn agreement or soften into romantic contemplation; if he'd wanted to he could very easily have made it weep. When she looked briefly away from him, down at her cup or off misty-eyed into the room, it was only for a kind of emotional catching of breath; once he could have sworn he saw her planning how she would tell Norma about him tonight ("*Oh, the most fascinating man . . .*"), and the way she seemed to melt when he helped her on with her coat, the way she swayed against him as they walked out of the place for a stroll in the sunshine, made it clear that the last shred of doubt could be safely abandoned. He had it made.

The only problem now was where to go. They were heading vaguely toward the trees of Washington Square; and the trouble with taking a walk in the park, aside from its waste of valuable time, was that this was the hour when the park would be full of women who had once been April's friends and neighbors. Anne

Snyder and Susan Cross and God only knew how many others would be there, lifting their softening cheeks to the sun or wiping ice cream from the mouths of their children as they talked of nursery schools and outrageous rents and perfectly marvelous Japanese movies, waiting until it was time to gather up their toys and graham crackers and stroll home to fix their husbands' cocktails, and they'd spot him in a minute ("Well, of *course* it's Frank Wheeler, but who's that *with* him? Isn't that funny?"). But he had scarcely allowed this uneasiness to develop before Maureen came to a stop on the sidewalk.

"This is my place. Would you like to come up for a drink or something?"

Then he was following her hips up a dim carpeted stairway, and then a door had clicked shut behind him and he was standing in a room that smelled of vacuum cleaning and breakfast bacon and perfume, a high, silent room where everything lay richly bathed in yellow light from windows whose blinds of split bamboo had turned the sun into fine horizontal stripes of tan and gold. He stood feeling tall and strong as she ducked and curtsied around him in her stockinged feet, straightening ash trays and magazines—"I'm afraid the place is an awful mess; won't you sit down?"—and when she sank one knee into a studio couch to reach across it for the cord that opened one of the blinds, he moved up close behind her and put his hand on her waist. That was all it took. With a moist little whimpering groan she turned and pressed herself into his arms, offering up her mouth. Then they were on the couch and the only problem in the world was the bondage of their clothing. Twisting and gasping together, they worked urgently at knots and buttons and buckles and hooks until the last impediment slipped away; and then in the warmth and rhythm of her flesh he found an overwhelming sense of *this* is what I needed; *this* is what I needed; his self-absorption was so complete that he was only dimly aware of her whispering, "Oh, yes; yes; yes . . ."

When it was over, though, when they had fallen apart and rejoined each other in a lightly sweating tangle of arms and legs, he knew he had never been more grateful to anyone in his life. The only trouble was that he couldn't think of anything to say.

He tried to get a look at her face, to give himself a clue, but she had clasped her head against his chest so that all he could see was the black disorder of her hair; she was waiting for him to speak first. He rolled his head a little and found he was looking through a crooked opening of the window blind, which she had managed to raise a few inches before falling into his arms. He studied the weathered brick cornice of a house across the street, whose chimney pots and television aerials made intricate silhouettes against the vibrant blue of the sky. From somewhere high and far away came the faint crawling drone of a plane. He looked the other way, into the room where everything—Picasso prints, Book-of-the-Month Club selections, sling chair, mantelpiece bristling with snapshots—everything swam in the vivid yellow light; and his first consecutive thought was that his flung coat and shirt were lying over there, near the chair, and his shoes and pants and underwear were here, closer at hand. He could be up and dressed and out of this place in thirty seconds.

"Well," he said at last, "I guess this wasn't exactly what you had in mind when you went to work this morning, was it?"

The silence continued, so complete that he was aware for the first time of the ticking of an alarm clock in the next room. Then:

"No," she said. "It certainly wasn't." And she quickly sat up. She groped for the royal blue sweater and snatched it up to cover herself. Then, hesitating, she seemed to decide that modesty could hardly be said to matter any more, and let it drop; but in a flurry of embarrassment she picked it up again, evidently wondering if this wasn't exactly the kind of a time when modesty mattered most, and covered her breasts with it again and crossed her arms over it. Her hair was as unattractively wild now as it must have been in childhood; it seemed to have exploded upward from her skull into hundreds of little kinks. She touched it delicately with her fingertips in several places, not in any effort to smooth it but rather in the furtive, half-conscious way that he himself had sometimes touched his pimples at sixteen, just to make sure the horrible things were still there. Her face and neck were pale but a deep red blush had begun to mottle both her cheeks, as if she'd been slapped, and she looked so vulnerable that for a second or two he was certain he could read her thoughts. What would Norma say? Would Norma be appalled at her for having been so easy to get? No; surely Norma's feeling would be that in a really adult, really sophisticated affair it was hopelessly banal to think in such terms as being "easy" or "hard" to "get." Yes, but still, if it was as adult and sophisticated as all that, why couldn't she decide what to do with her sweater? Why was she having such an awful time thinking of what in the world she could possibly *say* to the man?

Finally she composed herself. She lifted her chin as if to toss back a smooth, heavy lock of hair and willed her face into a drawing-room comedy smile, looking him straight in the eyes for the first time.

"Do you have a cigarette, Frank?"

"Sure. Here." And at last, mercifully, the dialogue began to flow.

"What was the name of that department you invented?"

"Mm?"

"You know. The place you told her we'd be. Mrs. Jorgensen."

"Oh. Visual Aids. I didn't really invent it. There used to be something called that, down on I think the eighth floor. Don't worry, though, she'll never figure it out."

"It does sound wonderfully real. Visual Aids. Excuse me a sec, Frank." And she skittered across the apartment, crouching awkwardly as if that would make her less naked, into the room where the alarm clock ticked.

When she came out, wearing a floor-length dressing gown and with her hair almost completely restored to its former shape, she found him fully dressed and politely inspecting the snapshots on the mantelpiece, like a visitor who hasn't yet been asked to sit down. She showed him where the bathroom was, and when he came back she had straightened up the couch and was moving indecisively around the kitchenette.

"Can I get you a drink or anything?"

"No thanks, Maureen. Actually, I guess I'd better be cutting out. It's getting kind of late."

"Gee, that's right, it is. Have you missed your train?"

"That's all right. I'll get the next one."

"It's a shame you have to rush off." She seemed determined to be calm and dignified, and she carried it off with elegance until the moment of her opening the door for him, when her eyes strayed to the corner near the couch and discovered that something flimsy and white, a brassiere or a garter belt, had been overlooked in her straightening-up and still lay twisted on the carpet. She started, visibly fighting an impulse to run over and grab it and stuff it behind the cushions—or possibly tear it to shreds—and when she turned back to him her eyes were pitiably wide and bright.

It couldn't be avoided; he would have to put something into words. But the only honest thing he could say was that he'd never felt more grateful to anyone—to thank her—and he wondered if this mightn't have exactly the wrong effect, almost as if he were offering her money. Another idea occurred to him: he could be sad and tender; he could take her by the shoulders and say "Look, Maureen. There can't be any future in a thing like this." But then she might say "Oh, I know," and hide her face in his coat, and that would leave him nothing to say but "I don't want to think I've taken any kind of unfair advantage here; if I have, well, I'm—" and that was the trouble. He would have to say "I'm sorry," and the last thing he wanted to do—the very last thing in God's world he wanted to do was apologize. Did the swan apologize to Leda? Did an eagle apologize? Did a lion apologize? Hell, no.

What he did instead was to smile at her—a subtle, worldly, attractive smile—and hold his face in that position until she falteringly smiled back. Then he bent and kissed her lightly on the lips and said, "Listen: you were swell. Take care, now."

He was down the stairs and out on the street and walking; before he'd gone half a block he had broken into an exultant run, and he ran all the way to Fifth Avenue. Once he had to swerve to keep from stepping into a baby carriage, and a woman shouted "Can't you watch where you're going?" but he refused, no less than an eagle or a lion would have refused, to look back. He felt like a man.

Could a man ride home in the rear smoker, primly adjusting his pants at the knees to protect their crease and rattling his evening paper into a narrow panel to give his neighbor elbow room? Could a man sit meekly massaging his headache and allowing himself to be surrounded by the chatter of beaten, amiable husks of men who sat and swayed and played bridge in a stagnant smell of newsprint and tobacco and bad breath and overheated radiators?

Hell, no. The way for a man to ride was erect and out in the open, out in the loud iron passageway where the wind whipped his necktie, standing with his feet set wide apart on the shuddering, clangoring floor-plates, taking deep pulls from a pinched cigarette until its burning end was a needle of fire and quivering paper ash and then snapping it straight as a bullet into the roaring speed of the roadbed, while the suburban towns wheeled slowly along the pink and gray dust of seven o'clock. And when he came to his own station, the way for a man to alight was to swing down the iron steps and leap before the train had stopped, to land running and slow down to an easy, athletic stride as he made for his parked automobile.

The curtains were drawn in the picture window. He saw that from the road before he'd reached the driveway; then, when he'd made the turn, he saw April come running from the kitchen door and stand waiting for him in the carport. She was wearing her black cocktail dress, ballet slippers, and a very small apron of crisp white gauze that he'd never seen before. And he'd barely had time to switch off the ignition before she wrenched open the car and took hold of his forearm with both hands, talking. Her hands were thinner and more nervous than Maureen Grube's; she was taller and older and used a completely different kind of perfume, and she spoke more rapidly in a higher-pitched voice.

"Frank, listen. Before you come in I've got to talk to you. It's terribly important."

"What?"

"Oh, so many things. First of all I missed you all day and I'm terribly sorry for everything and I love you. The rest can wait. Now come on inside."

If he'd had a year to devote to it and nothing else to do, he couldn't for the life of him have sorted out and weighed the emotions that filled him in the two or three seconds of his lumbering to the kitchen steps with April fastened to his arm. It was like walking through a sandstorm; it was like walking on the ocean floor; it was like walking on air. And this was the funny part: for all the depth of his bafflement he couldn't help noticing that April's voice, different as it was, possessed a quality that made it oddly similar to Maureen Grube's voice telling of the fabulous people Norma knew, or saying "Visual Aids"—a quality of play-acting, of slightly false intensity, a way of seeming to speak less to him than to some romantic abstraction.

"Wait here, my darling," she was saying. "Just for a minute, till I call you," and she left him alone in the kitchen, where the hot brown smell of roasting beef brought tears to his eyes. She handed him an Old-Fashioned glass full of ice and whiskey and disappeared into the darkened living room from which, now, he could hear an ill-suppressed giggle of children and the scrape of a match.

"All right," she called. "Now."

They were at the table, and he looked into all three of their faces before he saw what it was that bathed them in a flickering yellow light. It was a cake with candles. Then came their slow, shrill singing:

"Hap-py birth-day to you . . ."

Jennifer's voice was the loudest and April's was the only one in tune when they took the high note— "Hap-py *birth*-day, dear Dad-dy . . ." but Michael was doing the best he could, and his was the widest smile.

SEVEN

"FORGIVE YOU FOR *WHAT*, APRIL?" They were standing alone on the living room carpet, and she took a
tentative step toward him.

"Oh, for everything," she said. "For everything.
The way I was all weekend. The way I've been ever
since I got mixed up in that awful play. Oh, I've got so
much to tell you, and I've got the most wonderful *plan*,
Frank. Listen."

But it wasn't easy to listen to anything over the out-
raged silence in his head. He felt like a monster. He had
wolfed his dinner like a starving man and topped it off
with seven cloying forkfuls of chocolate cake; he had
repeatedly exclaimed, over the unwrapping of his birthday gifts, the very word he'd used to describe what Maureen Grube had been to him—"Swell . . . Swell . . ."—he
had heard his children's bedtime prayers and tiptoed

from their room; now he was allowing his wife to ask forgiveness, and at the same time, with a cold eye, he was discovering that she wasn't really very much to look at: she was too old and too tall and too intense.

He wanted to rush outdoors and make some dramatic atonement—smash his fist against a tree or run for miles, leaping stone walls, until he fell exhausted in a morass of mud and brambles. Instead he shut his eyes and reached out and drew her close against him, crushing her cocktail apron in a desperate embrace, letting all his torment dissolve in pressing and stroking the inward curve of her back while he urged his groaning, muttering mouth into her throat. "Oh, my lovely," he said. "Oh, my lovely girl."

"No, wait, listen. Do you know what I did all day? I missed you. And Frank, I've thought of the most wonderful—no, wait. I mean I love you and everything, but listen a minute. I—"

The only way to stop her talking and get her out of sight was to kiss her mouth; then the floor began to tilt at dangerous angles and they might have fallen into the coffee table if they hadn't taken three tottering steps and gone over instead into the voluptuous safety of the sofa.

"Darling?" she whispered, fighting for breath. "I do love you terribly, but don't you think we ought to—oh, no, don't stop. Don't stop."

"Ought to what?"

"Ought to sort of try and get into the bedroom first. But not if it makes you cross. We'll stay here if you like. I love you."

"No, you're right. We will." He forced himself up, dragging her with him. "I better take a shower first, too."

"Oh, no, don't. Please don't take a shower. I won't let you."

"I've got to, April."

"Why?"

"Just because. I've got to." It took all his will to move one heavy, swaying step at a time.

"I think you're terribly mean," she was saying, clinging to his arm. "Terribly, terribly mean. Frank, did you like the presents? Was the tie all right? I went to about fourteen different places and none of them had any decent ties."

"It's a swell tie. It's the nicest tie I've ever had."

Under the stiff pelting of hot water, in which Maureen Grube had become an adhesive second skin that only the most desperate scrubbing would shed, he decided he would have to tell her. He would soberly take hold of both her hands and say "Listen, April. This afternoon I—"

He turned off all the hot water and turned up the cold, a thing he hadn't done in years. The shock of it sent him dancing and gasping but he made himself stay under it until he'd counted to thirty, the way he used to do in the army, and he came out feeling like a million dollars. Tell her? Why, of course he wasn't going to tell her. What the hell would be the point of that?

"Oh, you look so clean," she said, whirling from the closet in her best white nightgown. "You look so clean and peaceful. Come sit beside me and let's talk a minute first, all right? Look what I've got."

She had set a bottle of brandy and two glasses on the night table, but it was a long time before he allowed her to pour it, or to say anything else. When she did pull away from him, once, it was only to remove the constriction of lace from her shoulders and let it fall away from her breasts, whose nipples were hardening and rising even before he covered them with his hands.

For the second time that day he discovered that the act of love could leave him speechless, and he hoped she would be willing to let the talking wait for tomorrow. He knew that whatever she had to say would be said with that odd, theatrical emphasis, and he didn't feel equipped to deal with it just now. All he wanted was to lie here smiling in the dark, confused and guilty and happy, and submit to the gathering weight of sleep.

"Darling?" Her voice sounded very far away. "Darling? You're not going to sleep, are you? Because I do have so much to say and we're letting the brandy go to waste and I haven't even had a chance to tell you about my plan."

After a minute he found it easy to stay awake, if only for the pleasure of sitting with her under the double cloak of a blanket, sipping brandy in the moonlight and hearing the rise and fall of her voice. Play-acting or not, her voice in moods of love had always been a pretty sound. At last, with some reluctance, he began to pay attention to what she was saying.

Her plan, the idea born of her sorrow and her missing him all day and her loving him, was an elaborate new program for going to Europe "for good" in the fall. Did he realize how much money they had? With their savings, with the proceeds from the sale of house and car and with what they could save between now and September, they'd have enough to live comfortably for six months. "And it won't take anything like six months before we're established and self-supporting again for as long as we like—that's the best part."

He cleared his throat. "Look, baby. In the first place, what kind of a job could I possibly—"

"No kind of a job. Oh, I know you could get a job anywhere in the world if you had to, but that's not the point. The point is you won't be getting any kind of a job, because I will. Don't laugh—listen a minute. Have you any idea how much they pay for secretarial work in all these government agencies overseas? NATO and the ECA and those places? And do you realize how low the cost of living is, compared to here?" She had it all figured out; she had read an article in a magazine. Her skills at typing and shorthand would bring them enough to live on and more—enough for a part-time servant to take care of the children while she worked. It was, she insisted, such a marvelously simple plan that she was amazed at having never thought of it before. But she had to keep interrupting herself, with mounting impatience, to tell him not to laugh.

This laughter of his was not quite genuine, nor was the way he kept squeezing her shoulder as if to dismiss the whole thing as an endearing whimsy. He was trying to conceal from her, if not from himself, that the plan had instantly frightened him.

"I'm serious about this, Frank," she said. "Do you think I'm kidding or something?"

"No, I know. I just have a couple of questions, is all. For one thing, what exactly am I supposed to be doing while you're out earning all this dough?"

She drew back and tried to examine his face in the dim light, as if she couldn't believe he had failed to understand. "Don't you see? Don't you see that's the whole idea? You'll be doing what you should've been

allowed to do seven years ago. You'll be finding yourself. You'll be reading and studying and taking long
walks and thinking. You'll have *time*. For the first time
in your life you'll have time to find out what it is you
want to do, and when you find it you'll have the time
and the freedom to start doing it."

And that, he knew as he chuckled and shook his
head, was what he'd been afraid she would say. He had
a quick disquieting vision of her coming home from a
day at the office—wearing a Parisian tailored suit,
briskly pulling off her gloves—coming home and finding him hunched in an egg-stained bathrobe, on an
unmade bed, picking his nose.

"Look," he began. He let his hand slide off her
shoulder and work its way up under her arm to fondle
the shape and light weight of her breast. "In the first
place, all this is very sweet and very—"

"It's not 'sweet'!" She pronounced the word as if it
were the quintessence of everything she despised, and
she caught at his hand and threw it down as if it were
despicable too. "For God's sake, Frank, I'm not being
'sweet.' I'm not making any big altruistic sacrifice—
can't you see that?"

"Okay; okay; it's not sweet. Don't get sore. Whatever it is, though, I think you'll have to agree it isn't
very realistic; that's all I meant."

"In order to agree with that," she said, "I'd have to

have a very strange and very low opinion of reality. Because you see I happen to think *this* is unrealistic. I think it's unrealistic for a man with a fine mind to go on working like a dog year after year at a job he can't stand, coming home to a house he can't stand in a place he can't stand either, to a wife who's equally unable to stand the same things, living among a bunch of frightened little—my God, Frank, I don't have to tell you what's wrong with this environment—I'm practically *quoting* you. Just last night when the Campbells were here, remember what you said about the whole idea of suburbia being to keep reality at bay? You said everybody wanted to bring up their children in a bath of sentimentality. You said—"

"I know what I said. I didn't think you were listening, though. You looked sort of bored."

"I *was* bored. That's part of what I'm trying to say. I don't think I've ever been more bored and depressed and fed up in my life than I was last night. All that business about Helen Givings's son on top of everything else, and the way we all grabbed at it like dogs after meat; I remember looking at you and thinking 'God, if only he'd stop talking.' Because everything you said was based on this great premise of ours that we're somehow very special and superior to the whole thing, and I wanted to say 'But we're not! Look at us! We're just like the people you're talking about! We *are* the people you're talking about!' I sort of had—I don't know, contempt for you, because you couldn't see the terrific fallacy of the thing. And then this morning when you left, when you were backing the car around down at the turn, I saw you look back up at the house as if it was going to bite you. You looked so miserable I started to cry, and then I started feeling lonely as hell and I thought, Well, how *did* everything get so awful then? If it's not his fault, whose fault is it? How did we ever get *into* this strange little dream world of the Donaldsons and the Cramers and the Wingates—oh yes, and the Campbells, too, because another thing I figured out today is that both those Campbells are a big, big, big, colossal waste of time. And it suddenly began to dawn on me—honestly, Frank, it was like a revelation or something—I was standing there in the kitchen and it suddenly began to dawn on me that it's my fault. It's always been my fault, and I can tell you when it began. I can tell you the exact moment in time when it began. Don't interrupt me."

But he knew better than to interrupt her now. She must have spent the morning in an agony of thought, pacing up and down the rooms of a dead-silent, dead-clean house and twisting her fingers at her waist until they ached; she must have spent the afternoon in a frenzy of action at the shopping center, lurching her car imperiously through mazes of NO LEFT TURN signs and angry traffic cops, racing in and out of stores to buy the birthday gifts and the roast of beef and the cake and the cocktail apron. Her whole day had been a heroic build-up for this moment of self-abasement; now it was here, and she was damned if she'd stand for any interference.

"It was way back on Bethune Street," she said. "It was when I first got pregnant with Jennifer and told you I was going to—you know abort it, abort her. I mean up until that moment you didn't want a baby any more than I did—why *should* you have?—but when I went out and bought that rubber syringe I put the whole burden of the thing on you. It was like saying, All right, then, if you want this baby it's going to be All Your Responsibility. You're going to have to turn yourself inside out to provide for us. You'll have to give up any idea of being anything in the world but a father. Oh, Frank, if only you'd given me what I deserved—if only you'd called me a bitch and turned your back on me, you could've called my bluff in a minute. I'd probably never have gone through with the thing—I probably wouldn't have had the courage, for one thing—but you didn't. You were too good and young and scared; you played right along with it, and that's how the whole thing started. That's how we both got committed to this enormous delusion—because that's what it is, an enormous, obscene delusion—this idea that people have to resign from real life and 'settle down' when they have families. It's the great sentimental lie of the suburbs, and I've been making you subscribe to it all this time. I've been making you *live* by it! My God, I've even gone as far as to work up this completely corny, soap-opera picture of myself—and I guess this is what really brought it home to me—this picture of myself as the girl who could have been The Actress if she hadn't gotten married too young. And I mean you know perfectly well I was never any kind of an actress and never really wanted to be; you know I only went to the Academy to get away from home, and I know it too. I've always known it. And here for three months I've been walking around with this noble, bittersweet expression on my face—I mean how self-deluded can you get? Do you see how neurotic all this is? I wanted to have it both ways. It wasn't enough that I'd spoiled your life; I wanted to bring the whole monstrous thing full-circle and make it seem that you'd spoiled mine, so I could end up being the victim. Isn't that awful? But it's true! It's true!"

And at each "true!" she thumped a tight little fist on her naked knee. "Now do you see what you have to forgive me for? And why we have to get out of here and over to Europe as fast as we possibly can? It isn't a case of my being 'sweet' or generous or anything else. *I'm* not doing you any favors. All I'm giving you is what you've always been entitled to, and I'm only sorry it has to come so late."

"All right. Can I talk now?"

"Yes. You do understand, though, don't you? And could I have a little more of the brandy? Just a splash—that's fine. Thanks." When she'd sipped at it she threw back her hair, allowing the blanket to slide from her shoulders, and drew a little away from him in order to sit back against the wall, tucking her legs up beneath her. She looked wholly relaxed and confident, ready to listen, happy in the knowledge that she'd stated her case. The blue-white luminescence of her body was a powerful force; he knew he wouldn't be able to think straight if he looked at her, so he willed himself to look at the moonlit floor between his feet, and he took longer than necessary over the lighting of a cigarette, stalling for time. He would have to get his bearings. When she came home to the Paris apartment her spike-heeled pumps would click decisively on the tile floor and her hair would be pulled back into a neat bun; her face would be drawn with fatigue so that the little vertical line between her eyes would show, even when she smiled. On the other hand . . .

"In the first place," he said at last, "I think you're being much too hard on yourself. Nothing's ever that black and white. You didn't force me to take the job at Knox. Besides, look at it this way. You say you've always known you weren't really an actress, and therefore it's not too legitimate for you to go around feeling cheated. Well, let's face it: isn't it just possible the same thing applies to me? I mean who ever said I was supposed to be a big deal?"

"I don't know what you mean," she said calmly. "I think it might be rather tiresome if you *were* a big deal. But if you mean who ever said you were exceptional, if you mean who ever said you had a first-rate, original mind—well my God, Frank, the answer is everybody. When I first met you, you were—"

"Oh, hell, I was a little wise guy with a big mouth. I was showing off a lot of erudition I didn't have. I was—"

"You were not! How can you talk that way? Frank, has it gotten so bad that you've lost all your belief in yourself?"

Well, no; he had to admit it hadn't gotten quite that bad. Besides, he was afraid he could detect a note of honest doubt in her voice—a faint suggestion that it might be possible to persuade her he *had* been a little wise guy, after all—and this was distressing.

"Okay," he conceded. "Okay, let's say I was a promising kid. The point is there were plenty of promising kids at Columbia; that doesn't necessarily mean—"

"There weren't plenty like you," she said, sounding reassured. "I'll never forget what's-his-name, you know? The one you always admired so much? The one who'd been the fighter pilot and had all the girls? Bill Croft. I'll never forget the way he used to talk about you. He said to me once: 'If I had half that guy's brains I'd quit worrying.' And he meant it! Everybody knew there was nothing in the world you couldn't do or be if you only had a chance to find yourself. Anway, all that's beside the point. You wouldn't have to be the least bit exceptional, and this would still be a thing that has to be done. Don't you see that?"

"Will you let me finish? In the first place . . ." But instead of allowing his voice to run on he felt a need to be quiet for a minute. He took a deep drink of brandy, letting it burn the roof of his mouth and send out waves of warmth across his shoulders and down his spine as he solemnly stared at the floor.

Had Bill Croft really said that?

"Everything you say might make a certain amount of sense," he began again, and one of the ways he could tell he was losing the argument was that his voice had taken on a resonance that made it every bit as theatrical as hers. It was the voice of a hero, a voice befitting the kind of person Bill Croft could admire. "Might make a certain amount of sense if I had some definite, measurable talent. If I were an artist, say, or a writer, or a—"

"Oh, Frank. Can you really think artists and writers are the only people entitled to lives of their own?

Listen: I don't care if it takes you five years of doing nothing at all; I don't care if you decide after five years that what you really want is to be a bricklayer or a mechanic or a merchant seaman. Don't you see what I'm saying? It's got nothing to do with definite, measurable talents—it's your very *essence* that's being stifled here. It's what you *are* that's being denied and denied and denied in this kind of life."

"And what's that?" For the first time he allowed himself to look at her—not only to look but to put down his glass and take hold of her leg, and she covered and pressed his hand with both of her own.

"Oh, don't you know?" She brought his hand gently up her hip and around to the flat of her abdomen, where she pressed it close again. "Don't you know? You're the most valuable and wonderful thing in the world. You're a man."

And of all the capitulations in his life, this was the one that seemed most like a victory. Never before had elation welled more powerfully inside him; never had beauty grown more purely out of truth; never in taking his wife had he triumphed more completely over time and space. The past could dissolve at his will and so could the future; so could the walls of this house and the whole imprisoning wasteland beyond it, towns and trees. He had taken command of the universe because he was a man, and because the marvelous creature who opened and moved for him, tender and strong, was a woman.

At the first bright, hesitant calls of awakening birds, when the massed trees were turning from gray to olive green in a rising mist, she gently touched his lips with her fingertips.

"Darling? We really are going to do it, aren't we? I mean it hasn't just been a lot of talk or anything, has it?"

He was on his back, taking pleasure in the slow rise and fall of his own chest, which felt broad and deep and muscled enough to fill the modeling of a medieval breastplate. Was there anything he couldn't do? Was there any voyage he couldn't undertake and any prize in life he couldn't promise her?

"No," he said.

"Because I mean I'd like to get started on it right away. Tomorrow. Writing letters and whatnot, and seeing about the passports. And I think we ought to tell Niffer and Mike about it right away too, don't you? They'll need a little time to get used to it, and besides, I want them to know before anybody else. Don't you?"

"Yes."

"But I mean I don't want to tell them unless you're absolutely sure."

"I'm absolutely sure."

"That's wonderful. Oh darling, look at the time. And it's practically light outside. You'll be dead tired."

"No I won't. I can sleep on the train. I can sleep at the office. It's all right."

"All right. I love you."

And they fell asleep like children.

PART TWO

ONE

THERE NOW BEGAN A TIME of such joyous derange-
ment, of such exultant carelessness, that Frank
Wheeler could never afterwards remember how long
it lasted. It could have been a week or two weeks or
more before his life began to come back into focus,
with its customary concern for the passage of time and
its anxious need to measure and apportion it; and by
then, looking back, he was unable to tell how long it
had been otherwise. The only day that would always
stand clear and sharp in his memory was the first one,
the day after his birthday.

He did sleep on the train, riding with his head
fallen back on the dusty plush and his *Times* sliding
from his lap; and he stood for a long time over scalding
cups of coffee in the echoing tan vault of Grand Central, allowing himself to be late for work. How small

and neat and comically serious the other men looked, with their gray-flecked crew cuts and their button-down collars and their brisk little hurrying feet! There were endless desperate swarms of them, hurrying through the station and the streets, and an hour from now they would all be still. The waiting midtown office buildings would swallow them up and contain them, so that to stand in one tower looking out across the canyon to another would be to inspect a great silent insectarium displaying hundreds of tiny pink men in white shirts, forever shifting papers and frowning into telephones, acting out their passionate little dumb show under the supreme indifference of the rolling spring clouds.

In the meantime, Frank Wheeler's coffee was delicious, his paper napkin was excellently white and dry, and the grandmotherly woman who served him was so courteous and so clearly pleased with the rhythm of her own efficiency ("Yes, sir, thank *you* sir; will that be all, sir?") that he wanted to lean over and press a kiss into her wrinkled cheek. By the time he reached the office he had passed into that euphoria of half-refreshed exhaustion in which all sounds are muffled, all sights are blurred, and every task is easy.

First things first: and the first thing he had to do, when the elevator door slid open at the Fifteenth Floor, was to walk up and deal like a man with Maureen Grube. She was alone at her reception desk, in a dark suit that she'd probably worn because it was the most severe, least provocative thing in her wardrobe, and when she saw him coming she looked badly flustered. But his smile was so expert—not the least bit furtive or the least bit vain, a perfectly open, friendly smile—that he could see the assurance come back into her face before he got to the desk. Had she been afraid he would think her a tramp? That he'd spend the day whispering and chuckling about her with the other men? If so, the smile told her she could relax. Had she been afraid, on the other hand, that he would try to make a big romantic thing out of it? That he'd embarrass the life out of her with messy little importunings in corners ("I've got to see you. . . .")? The smile told her she could stop worrying about that, too; and these two possibilities, for the moment, were the only ones that seemed likely enough to bother with.

"Hi," he said kindly. "You have any trouble about yesterday? With Mrs. Jorgensen, I mean?"

"No. She didn't say anything." She seemed to be having some difficulty in meeting his eyes; she was looking mostly at the knot of his tie. Standing there and smiling down at her, with the constant hum and bustle of people milling just out of earshot in the dry lake beyond them, he could easily have been stopping to pass the time of day or to ask her about a typing job;

there was nothing in his face or his stance to arouse the curiosity of onlookers. Yet at close range, from where she sat, he knew there could be no doubt of his intimate sincerity.

"Look, Maureen," he began. "If I thought there was anything to be gained by it, for either of us, I'd say let's go somewhere this afternoon and have a talk. And if you want to, if there's anything at all you want to tell me or ask me, that's what we'll do. Is there?"

"No. Except that I—well, no. There isn't really. You're right."

"It isn't a question of being 'right.' I don't want you to think I'm—well, never mind. But listen: the important thing in a thing like this is not to have any regrets. I don't; I hope you don't, and if you do I hope you'll tell me."

"No," she said. "I don't."

"I'm glad. And listen: You're swell, Maureen. If there's ever anything I can—you know, do for you or anything, I hope you'll let me know. I guess that sounds sort of crummy. All I mean is that I'd like us to be friends."

"All right," she said. "So would I."

And he walked away up the aisle of cubicles, moving slowly and confidently in a new, more mature version of the old "terrifically sexy walk" of Bethune Street. As simple as that! If he'd spent days planning and rehearsing it, filling page after page of scratch paper with revised and crossed-out sentences, he could never have come up with a more dignified, more satisfactory speech. And all on the spur of the moment! Was there anything in the world he couldn't do?

"Morning, Dad," he said to Jack Ordway.

"Franklin, my son. How good to see your shining morning face."

But first things first; and the next thing now was his IN basket. No; it was the batch of papers he'd dropped on the middle of his desk yesterday, the things Maureen had pulled from the central file, which brought up the whole disorderly problem of the branch manager in Toledo and the production control brochure. Was he going to let a thing like that harass him? Certainly not.

"Intra-company letter to Toledo," he said into the mouthpiece of his Dictaphone, leaning back in his swivel chair and working his foot into its wooden saddle on the drawer edge. "Attention B. F. Chalmers, branch manager. Subject: NAPE conference. Paragraph. With regard to recent and previous correspondence, this is to advise that the matter has been very satisfactorily taken in hand, period, paragraph."

He went that far without any idea of how the matter was going to be taken in hand, if at all; but as he sat fingering the mouthpiece he began to get ideas, and soon he was intoning one smooth sentence after another, pausing only to smile in satisfaction. The branch manager in Toledo was turning out to be as easy to handle as Maureen Grube.

F. H. Wheeler, or "we," wholly agreed that the existing brochure was unsuitable. Fortunately, the problem had now been solved in a way which "we" were confident would meet with the branch manager's approval. As the branch manager doubtless knew, the NAPE delegates would be given dozens of competitive promotion brochures, most of which were certain to end up in the wastebaskets of the convention floor. The problem, then, was to develop something different for Knox—something that would catch the delegate's eye, that he would want to put in his pocket and take back to his hotel room. Just such a piece was now in production, designed specifically for the NAPE conference: a brief, straightforward sales message entitled "Speaking of Production Control." As the branch manager would see, this document relied on no slick format, no fancy artwork or advertising jargon to tell its story. Crisply printed in large, easy-to-read type, in black and white, it had all the immediacy of plain talk. It would "give the NAPE delegate nothing more or less than what he wants, colon: the facts."

After putting a new belt in the Dictaphone machine, he leaned back again and said, "Copy for Veritype.

Heading: Speaking of Production Control, dot, dot, dot. Paragraph. Production control is, comma, after all, comma, nothing more or less than the job of putting the right materials in the right place at the right time, comma, according to a varying schedule. Period, paragraph. This is simple arithmetic, period. Given all the variables, comma, a man can do it with a pencil and paper, period. But the Knox '500' Electronic Computer can do it—dash—literally—dash—thousands of times faster, period. That's why . . ."

"Coming down for coffee, Franklin?"

"I guess not, Jack. I better finish this thing."

And he did finish it, though it took him all morning. Fingering through the papers from the central file with his free hand, lifting a sentence here and a paragraph there, he continued to recite into the Dictaphone until he'd explained all the advantages of using a computer to coordinate the details of factory production. It sounded very authoritative when he played it back ("Once the bill of materials has been exploded," he heard his own voice saying, "the computer's next step is to scan the updated parts inventory"). No one could have told that he didn't quite know what he was talking about. When the typescript came back he would polish it up—maybe he'd have it checked over by one of the technical men, just to be safe—and then he'd have it Verityped and sent to Toledo in the required number of copies. For self-protection he would send one copy to Bandy, with a note saying "Hope this is okay—Toledo wanted something short & sweet for the NAPE thing," and with luck he'd be off the hook. In the meantime he could safely remove all the troublesome Toledo correspondence from the stack of things he couldn't bring himself to face just now, and put it in his OUT basket marked "File," along with all the brochure material.

This made such a surprising reduction in the clutter of his desk that he was encouraged, after lunch, to tackle two or three other matters in the stack of things he couldn't face. One of them involved a ticklish letter explaining why "we" had allowed an obsolete model of adding-machine demonstrator to be shipped to the Chicago Business Fair, and he made it an airtight masterpiece of evasion; another, a thick sheaf of letters that he'd been avoiding for weeks, turned out to be much simpler than he'd thought in that it all boiled down to a decision left squarely up to him. Should solid-gold tie clasps ($14.49) or solid-gold lapel buttons ($8.98) be offered as the prizes in a quota-breaking contest among the tabulating-equipment salesmen of Minneapolis–St. Paul? Tie clasps! And into the OUT basket it went.

He was a demon of energy; and it wasn't until four o'clock, walking blearily to the water cooler ("Watch the big bubble come up—Blurp!—Isn't that funny?")

that he realized why. It was because April had left a small pocket of guilt in his mind last night by saying that he'd "worked like a dog year after year." He had meant to point out that whatever it was he'd been doing here year after year, it could hardly be called working like a dog—but she hadn't given him a chance. And now, by trying to clear all the papers off his desk in one day, he guessed he was trying to make up for having misled her. But what kind of nonsense was that? How could it possibly matter what he'd been doing here year after year, or what she thought he'd been doing, or what he thought she thought he'd been doing? None of it mattered any more; couldn't he get that through his head? And as he stumbled back from the water cooler, wiping his cold mouth with a warm hand, he began to understand for the first time that in another few months he would leave this place forever. All of it—lights, glass partitions, chattering typewriters—the whole slow, dry agony of this place would be cut away from his life like a tumor from his brain; and good riddance.

His final act of that day in the office involved no work at all and very little energy, though it did take a certain amount of courage. He opened the big bottom drawer of his desk, carefully lifted out the whole stack of Real Goodies—it weighed as much as a couple of telephone books—and tipped it into the wastebasket.

For an indeterminate number of days after that, the
office all but vanished from his consciousness. He
went through the motions, shuffling his papers, having
conferences with Bandy, having lunch with Ordway
and the others, smiling with dignity whenever he
passed Maureen Grube in the corridors and even stopping to chat with her now and then, to show that they
were friends—but the fact was that the daytime had
ceased to have any meaning except as a period of rest
and preparation for the evening.

He never seemed to come fully awake until the
moment he swung down from the train at sunset and
climbed into his station car. Then came the stimula-
tion of drinks with April, while the children lay
silenced by television, and then the pleasure of dinner,
which in conversational intensity was very like the din-
ners they'd had before they were married. But the day
didn't really begin until later still, when the children
were in bed with their door firmly shut for the night.
Then they would take their places in the living room—
April curled attractively on the sofa, usually, and Frank
standing with his back to the bookcase, each with a cup
of black Italian coffee and a cigarette—and give way to
their love affair.

He would begin to pace slowly around and around

the room as he talked, and she would follow him with her eyes, often with the tilt of her whole head and shoulders. From time to time when he felt he'd made a trenchant point he would wheel and stare at her in triumph; then it would be her turn to talk, while he walked and nodded, and when her turn was over their looks would meet exultantly again. Sometimes there was a glint of humor in these embraces of the eye: I know I'm showing off, they seemed to say, but so are you, and I love you.

And what did it matter? The very substance of their talk, after all, the message and the rhyme of it, whatever else they might be saying, was that they were going to be new and better people from now on. April, tucked up on the sofa with her skirt arranged in a graceful whirl from waist to ankle, her tall neck very white in the soft light and her face held in perfect composure, bore hardly any resemblance to the stiff, humiliated actress who had stood in the curtain call— and still less to the angrily sweating wife who had hauled the lawnmower, or to the jaded matron who had endured the evening of false friendship with the Campbells, or to the embarrassed, embarrassingly ardent woman who had welcomed him to his birthday party. Her voice was subtle and low, as low as in the first act of *The Petrified Forest*, and when she tipped back her head to laugh or leaned forward to reach out and tap the ash from her cigarette, she made it a maneuver of classic beauty. Anyone could picture her conquering Europe.

And Frank was modestly aware that something of the same kind of change was taking place in himself. He knew for one thing that he had developed a new way of talking, slower and more deliberate than usual, deeper in tone and more fluent: he almost never had to recourse to the stammering, apologetic little bridges ("No, but I mean—I don't know—*you* know—") that normally laced his speech, nor did his head duck and weave in the familiar nervous effort to make himself clear. Catching sight of his walking reflection in the black picture window, he had to admit that his appearance was not yet as accomplished as hers—his face was too plump and his mouth too bland, his pants too well pressed and his shirt too fussily Madison Avenue—but sometimes late at night when his throat had gone sore and his eyes hot from talking, when he hunched his shoulders and set his jaw and pulled his necktie loose and let it hang like a rope, he could glare at the window and see the brave beginnings of a personage.

It was a strange time for the children, too. What exactly did going to France in the fall mean? And why did their mother keep insisting it was going to be fun, as if daring them to doubt it? For that matter, why was she so funny about a lot of things? In the afternoons she would hug them and ask them questions in a rush of ebullience that suggested Christmas Eve, and then her eyes would go out of focus during their replies, and a minute later she'd be saying "Yes, darling, but don't talk *quite* so much, okay? Give Mommy a break."

Nor did their father's homecoming do much to help: he might throw them high in the air and give them airplane rides around the house until they were dizzy, but only after having failed to see them altogether during the disturbingly long time it took him to greet their mother at the kitchen door. And the talking at dinner! It was hopeless for either child to try and get a word in edgewise. Michael found he could jiggle in his chair, repeat baby words over and over in a shrill idiot's monotone or stuff his mouth with mashed potato and hang his jaws open, all without any adult reproof; Jennifer would sit very straight at the table and refuse to look at him, feigning great interest in whatever her parents were saying, though afterwards, waiting for bedtime, she would sometimes go off quietly by herself and suck her thumb.

There was one consolation: they could go to sleep without any fear of being waked in an hour by the abrupt, thumping, hard-breathing, door-slamming sounds of a fight; all that, apparently, was a thing of the past. They could lie drowsing now under the sound of kindly voices in the living room, a sound whose intricately rhythmic rise and fall would slowly turn into the shape of their dreams. And if they came awake later to turn over and reach with their toes for new cool places in the sheets, they knew the sound would still be there—one voice very deep and the other soft and pretty, talking and talking, as substantial and soothing as a blue range of mountains seen from far away.

"This whole country's *rotten* with sentimentality," Frank said one night, turning ponderously from the window to walk the carpet. "It's been spreading like a disease for years, for generations, until now everything you touch is flabby with it."

"Exactly," she said, enraptured with him.

"I mean isn't that really what's the matter, when you get right down to it? I mean even more than the profit motive or the loss of spiritual values or the fear of the bomb or any of those things? Or maybe it's the result of those things; maybe it's what happens when all those things start working at once without any real cultural tradition to absorb them. Anyway, whatever it's the result of, *it's* what's killing the United States. I mean isn't it? This steady, insistent vulgarizing of every idea and every emotion into some kind of pre-digested intellectual baby food; this optimistic, smiling-through, easy-way-out sentimentality in everybody's view of life?"

"Yes," she said. "Yes."

"And I mean is it any wonder all the men end up emasculated? Because that *is* what happens; that *is* what's reflected in all this bleating about 'adjustment' and 'security' and 'togetherness'—and I mean Christ, you see it everywhere: all this television crap where every joke is built on the premise that daddy's an idiot and mother's always on to him; and these loathsome little signs people put up in their front yards—you ever notice those signs up on the Hill?"

"The 'The' signs, you mean; with the people's name in the plural? Like 'The Donaldsons'?"

"Right!" He turned and smiled down at her in triumphant congratulation for having seen exactly what he meant. "Never 'Donaldson' or 'John J. Donaldson' or whatever the hell his name is. Always 'The Donaldsons.' You picture the whole cozy little bunch of them sitting around all snug as bunnies in their pajamas, for God's sake, toasting marshmallows. I guess the Campbells haven't put up a sign like that yet, but give 'em time. The rate they're going now, they will." He paused here for a deep-throated laugh. "And my God, when you think how close *we* came to settling into that kind of an existence."

"But we didn't," she told him. "That's the important thing."

Another time, quite late, he walked up close to the

sofa and sat down on the edge of the coffee table, facing her. "You know what this is like, April? Talking like this? The whole idea of taking off to Europe this way?" He felt tense and keyed up; the very act of sitting on a coffee table seemed an original and wonderful thing to do. "It's like coming out of a Cellophane bag. It's like having been encased in some kind of Cellophane for years without knowing it, and suddenly breaking out. It's a little like the way I felt going up to the line the first time, in the war. I remember acting very grim and scared because that was the fashionable way to act, but I couldn't really put my heart in it. I mean I was scared, of course, but that's not the point. What I really felt didn't have anything to do with being scared or not scared. I just felt this terrific sense of life. I felt full of blood. Everything looked realer than real; the snow on the fields, the road, the trees, the terrific blue sky all marked up with vapor trails—everything. And all the helmets and overcoats and rifles, and the way the guys were walking; I sort of loved them, even the guys I didn't like. And I remember being very conscious of the way my own body worked, and the sound of the breathing in my nose. I remember we went through this shelled-out town, all broken walls and rubble, and I thought it was beautiful. Hell, I was probably just as dumb and scared as anybody else, but inside I'd never felt better. I kept thinking: this is really true. This is the truth."

"I felt that way once too," she said, and in the shyness of her lips he saw that something overpoweringly tender was coming next.

"When?" He was as bashful as a schoolboy, unable to look her full in the face.

"The first time you made love to me."

The coffee table tipped absurdly and banged straight again, rattling its cups, as he moved from its edge to the edge of the sofa and took her in his arms; and the evening was over.

It wasn't until a good many such evenings had passed—until the time, in fact, when he had again begun to think in terms of time passing—that the first faint discordances crept into their talk.

Once he interrupted her to say, "Listen, why do we keep talking about Paris? Don't they have government agencies pretty much all over Europe? Why not Rome? Or Venice, or some place like Greece, even? I mean let's keep an open mind; Paris isn't the only place."

"Of course it isn't." She was impatiently brushing a fleck of ash off her lap. "But it does seem the most logical place to start, doesn't it? With the advantage of your knowing the language and everything?"

If he'd looked at the window at that moment he would have seen the picture of a frightened liar. The language! Had he ever really led her to believe he could speak French?

"Well," he said, chuckling and walking away from her, "I wouldn't be too sure about that. I've probably forgotten most of what little I knew, and I mean I never did know the language in the sense of—you know, being able to speak it fluently or anything; just barely enough to get by."

"That's all we'll need. You'll pick it up again in no time. We both will. And besides, at least you've been there. You know how the city's laid out and what the various neighborhoods are like; that's important."

And he silently assured himself that this, after all, was substantially true. He knew where most of the picture-postcard landmarks were, on the strength of his several three-day passes in the city long ago; he also knew how to go from any of those places to where the American PX and Red Cross Club had once been established, and how to go from those points to the Place Pigalle, and how to choose the better kind of prostitute there and what her room would probably smell like. He knew those things, and he knew too that the best part of Paris, the part where the people really knew how to live, began around St. Germain des Prés and extended southeast (or was it southwest?) as far as the Café Dome. But this latter knowledge was based more on his reading of *The Sun Also Rises* in high school than in his real-life venturings into the district, which had mostly been lonely and footsore. He had admired the ancient delicacy of the buildings and the way the street lamps made soft explosions of light green in the trees at night, and the way each long, bright café awning would prove to reveal a sea of intelligently talking faces as he passed; but the white wine gave him a headache and the talking faces all seemed, on closer inspection, to belong either to intimidating men with beards or to women whose eyes could sum him up and dismiss him in less than a second. The place had filled him with a sense of wisdom hovering just out of reach, of unspeakable grace prepared and waiting just around the corner, but he'd walked himself weak down its endless blue streets and all the people who knew how to live had kept their tantalizing secret to themselves, and time after time he had ended up drunk and puking over the tailgate of the truck that bore him jolting back into the army.

Je suis, he practiced to himself while April went on talking; *tu es; nous sommes; vous êtes; ils sont.*

". . . better once we get settled," she was saying, "don't you think? You're not listening."

"Sure I am. No, I'm sorry, I guess I wasn't." And he sat down on the coffee table, smiling with what he hoped was a disarming candor. "I was just thinking that none of this is going to be easy—taking off to a foreign country with the kids and all. I mean, we'll be running into a lot of problems we can't even begin to anticipate from this end."

"Well, certainly we will," she said. "And certainly it's not going to be easy. Do you know anything worth doing that is?"

"Of course not. You're right. I'm just kind of tired tonight, I guess. Would you like a drink?"

"No thanks."

He went to the kitchen and got one for himself, which brightened him; and there were no further difficulties until the next night, or the next, when she made a startling disclosure about how she'd spent her day.

He had assumed that she too would be lazy and absent-minded in the daytime; he had pictured her taking long baths and devoting whole hours to the bedroom mirror, trying on different dresses and new ways of fixing her hair—perhaps leaving the mirror only to waltz lightly away on the strains of imaginary violins, whirling in a dream through the sunlit house and returning to smile over her shoulder at her own flushed image, and then having to hurry to get the beds made and the rooms in order in time for his homecoming. But it turned out that on this particular day she had driven to New York right after breakfast, had undergone an interview and filled out a lengthy job application with an overseas employment office, had gone from there to make the necessary arrangements for their passports, had obtained three travel brochures and the schedules of half a dozen steamship companies and airlines, had bought two new traveling bags, a French dictionary, a street guide to Paris, a copy of *Babar the Elephant* for the children and a book called *Brighter French* ("For Bright People Who Already Know Some"), and had sped home and relieved the baby sitter just in time to get the dinner started and mix a pitcherful of martinis.

"Aren't you tired?"

"Not really. It was sort of invigorating. Do you realize how long it's been since I spent a day in town? I was going to pop into the office at lunchtime and surprise you, but there wasn't time. What's the matter?"

"Nothing. It just sort of throws me, that's all; the amount of stuff you can get done in one day. Pretty impressive."

"You're annoyed," she said, "aren't you. Oh, and I don't blame you." She puckered her face into what looked distressingly like the understanding simper of the wife in a television comedy. "It must seem as if I'm sort of taking over, doesn't it—taking charge of everything."

"No," he protested, "no, listen, don't be silly; I'm not annoyed. It doesn't matter."

"It does matter, though. It's like when I mow the lawn, or something. I *knew* I should've left the passports and the travel agent for you to handle, but I was right there in the neighborhood and it seemed silly not to stop in. Oh, but I *am* sorry."

"Look, will you cut it out? I'm going to start *getting* annoyed in a minute, if you keep on at this. Will you please forget it?"

"All right."

"This probably won't be much use to us," he said, fingering through the pages of *Brighter French*. "I mean, I think it's a little advanced."

"Oh, that. Yes, I guess it's sort of a supercilious little book; I just grabbed it in a hurry. That's another thing I should've left for you to do. You're always much better at things like that than I am."

It was the night after that when she told him, looking remorseful, that she had some bad news. "I mean not really bad, but annoying. First of all Mrs. Givings called up today and issued this very formal invitation to dinner tomorrow night, and naturally I said no; I said we couldn't get a baby sitter. Then she started trying to pin me down for a night next week and I kept begging off, until I realized we *are* going to have to see her soon anyway, about putting the house on the market, so I said why didn't they come *here* for dinner."

"Oh Jesus."

"No, don't worry, they're not coming—you know how she is. She kept babbling about not wanting to put us to any trouble—Lord, what a pain that woman can be—and I kept insisting we did want to see her anyway, on business, and this went on for half an hour until I finally worked her around to saying she'd come over alone tomorrow night. So it'll be after dinner, strictly business, and with any kind of luck we'll never have to see her again except to sell the house."

"Fine."

"Yes, but here's the trouble. I'd completely forgotten we were supposed to be going to the Campbells' tomorrow night. So I called Milly and tried using the same lie about the baby sitter, and she seemed—I don't know, really upset. You know how Milly is sometimes? It's like dealing with a child. And the first thing I knew she had me saying yes, we'd come tonight instead. So there goes the weekend—Campbells tonight, Givings tomorrow. I'm awfully sorry, Frank."

"Hell, that's all right. Is that all you meant by bad news?"

"You're sure you don't mind?"

He didn't mind at all. In fact, he realized as he

washed up and changed his shirt, he was looking forward with eagerness to telling the Campbells of the plan. A thing like this never really seemed real until you'd told somebody about it.

"Listen, though, April," he said, stuffing in his shirttail. "When we're breaking it to Mrs. Givings, there isn't any reason why we have to tell her what we're going to *do* in Europe, is there? I mean I think she thinks I'm enough of a creep as it is."

"Of course not." She looked surprised at the very idea of telling Mrs. Givings anything at all beyond the simple fact of their wish to sell the house. "What possible business is it of hers? There's no need to tell the Campbells either, for that matter."

"Oh no," he said quickly, "we have to tell them—" and he almost said "They're our *friends*" before he caught himself. "I mean, *you* know; of course we don't have to. But why not?"

TWO

SHEPPARD SEARS CAMPBELL LOVED to shine his shoes. It was a love he had learned in the army (he was a veteran of three campaigns with a famous airborne division) and even now, though civilian cordovans were far less rewarding than the heavy jump boots of the old days, the acrid smell and crouching vigor of the job held rich associations of *esprit de corps*. He sang a kind of old-time, big-band swing while he did it, alternating the husky lyrics with a squint-eyed, loose-lipped sound—"Buddappa banh! Banh! Banh!"—to simulate the brass section, and now and then he would pause to take a swig from the can of beer that stood on the floor beside him. Then he would stretch his back, scratch the yellowed armpits of his T-shirt and permit himself a long and satisfying belch.

"What time the Wheelers coming, doll?" he asked

his wife, who was studying herself, sensibly, in the mirror of her flounced dressing table.

"Eight-thirty, sweetie."

"Jesus," he said. "If I want to get a shower, I better haul ass." Squinting, he flexed the toes in his right shoe to test its gleam before he crouched again, snapped his rag, and went to work on the left one.

The stolid peasant's look that glazed his face as he worked was only an occasional expression with Shep Campbell nowadays—he saved it for his shoe-shining mood or his tire-changing mood—but it held the vestige of a force that had once laid claim to the whole of his heart. For years, boy and man, he had yearned above all to be insensitive and ill-bred, to hold his own among the sullen boys and men whose real or imagined jeers had haunted his childhood, to deny by an effort of will what for a long time had been the most shameful facts of his life: that he'd been raised in a succession of brownstone and penthouse apartments in the vicinity of Sutton Place, schooled by private tutors and allowed to play with other children only under the smiling eye of his English nanny or his French ma'm'selle, and that his wealthily divorced mother had insisted, until he was eleven years old, on dressing him every Sunday in "adorable" tartan kilts that came from Bergdorf Goodman.

"She woulda made a God damn *lollypop* outa me!"

he sometimes ranted even now, to the few friends with whom he could bring himself to talk about his mother, but in calmer, wiser moments he had long since found the compassion to forgive her. Nobody's parents were perfect; and besides, whatever her intentions might have been, he knew she'd never really had a chance. From earliest adolescence, from the time his child's physique began to coarsen into the slope-shouldered build of a wrestler, if not before, he had been lost forever to her fluttering grasp. Anything in the world that could even faintly be connected with what his mother called "cultivated" or "nice" was anathema to Shep Campbell in those formative years, and everything she called "vulgar" was his heart's desire. At his small and expensive prep school he found it easy to become the ill-dressed, hell-raising lout of the student body, feared and admired and vaguely pitied on the assumption that he was one of the charity boys; after being expelled in his senior year he moved straight, to his mother's horror, into the swarm of a Manhattan high school, and into minor scrapes with the police, until the arrival of his eighteenth birthday sent him whooping and hollering into the paratroops, resolved to acquit himself not only with conspicuous bravery but with that other attribute so highly prized by soldiers, the quality of being a tough son of a bitch.

He made the grade on both counts, and the war

seemed only to deepen the urgency of his quest. Afterwards it seemed entirely logical for him to shrug off
all his mother's tearful arguments for Princeton or
Williams and go slouching away instead to a third-rate
institute of technology in the Middle West ("On the
G.I. Bill," he had always explained, as if any possibility
of private means would have made him effete). There,
dozing through his classes in a leather jacket or lurching at night in the spit-and-sawdust company of other
campus toughs, growling his beer-bloated disdain for
the very idea of liberal arts, he learned the unquestionably masculine, unquestionably middle-class trade of
mechanical engineering. It was there too that he found
his wife, a small, soft, worshipful clerk in the bursar's
office, and fathered the first of his sons; and it wasn't
until several years later that the great reaction set in.

What happened then—he was later to call it "the
time I sort of went crazy"—was that he woke up to find
himself employed in a hydraulic machinery plant a
hundred miles from Phoenix, Arizona, and living in
one of four hundred close-set, identical houses in the
desert, a sun-baked box of a house with four framed
mountain scenes from the dimestore on its walls and
five brown engineering manuals in the whole naked
width of its bookshelves, a box that rang every night to
the boom of television or the shrill noise of neighbors
dropping in for Canasta.

Sheppard Sears Campbell had to admit he felt for-lorn among these young men with blunt, prematurely settled faces, and these girls who shrieked in paralyz-ing laughter over bathroom jokes ("Harry, Harry, tell the one about the man got caught in the ladies' john!") or folded their lips in respectful silence while their husbands argued automobiles ("Now, you take the Chevy; far as I'm concerned you can have any Chevy ever built, bar none") and he rapidly began to see him-self as an impostor and a fool. All at once it seemed that the high adventure of pretending to be something he was not had led him into a way of life he didn't want and couldn't stand, that in defying his mother he had turned his back on his birthright.

Bright visions came to haunt him of a world that could and should have been his, a world of intellect and sensibility that now lay forever mixed in his mind with "the East." In the East, he then believed, a man went to college not for vocational training but in disci-plined search for wisdom and beauty, and nobody over the age of twelve believed that those words were for sissies. In the East, wearing rumpled tweeds and flan-nels, he could have strolled for hours among ancient elms and clock towers, talking with his friends, and his friends would have been the cream of their genera-tion. The girls of the East were marvelously slim and graceful; they moved with the authority of places like

Bennington and Holyoke; they spoke intelligently in low, subtle voices, and they never giggled. On sharp winter evenings you could meet them for cocktails at the Biltmore and take them to the theater, and afterwards, warmed with brandy, they would come with you for a drive to a snowbound New England inn, where they'd slip happily into bed with you under an eiderdown quilt. In the East, when college was over, you could put off going seriously to work until you'd spent a few years in a book-lined bachelor flat, with intervals of European travel, and when you found your true vocation at last it was through a process of informed and unhurried selection; just as when you married at last it was to solemnize the last and best of your many long, sophisticated affairs.

Brooding on these fantasies, it wasn't long before Shep Campbell gained a reputation as a snob at the hydraulics plant. He antagonized Milly, too, and frightened her, for he had become a moody listener to classical music and a sulking reader of literary quarterlies. He seldom talked to her, and when he did it was never in his old unique blend of New York street boy and Indiana farmer, a mixture she had always found "real cute," but in a new rhythm of brisk impatience that sounded alarmingly like an English accent. And then one Sunday night, after he'd been drinking all day and snapping at the children, she found herself cowering in tears with the baby at her breast while her husband called her an ignorant cunt and broke three bones of his fist against the wall.

A week later, still pale and shaken, she had helped him load clothes and blankets and kitchenware into the car and they'd set off on their dusty Eastward pilgrimage; and the six months in New York that followed, while he tried to decide whether to go on being an engineer—that period had been, Shep knew, the hardest time of Milly's life. The first rude surprise was that his mother's money was gone (there had never really been very much of it in the first place, and now there was barely enough to keep her decently in a residence hotel, a querulous, genteel old lady with a cat), and there were hundreds of other rude surprises in the overwhelming fact of New York itself, which turned out to be big and dirty and loud and cruel. Dribbling their savings away on cheap food and furnished rooms, never knowing where Shep was or what kind of a mood he'd be in when he came home, never knowing what to say when he talked disjointedly of graduate courses in music and philosophy, or when he wanted to lounge for hours in the dry fountain of Washington Square with a four-day growth of beard, she had more than once gone as far as to look up "psychiatrists" in the Classified New York Telephone Directory. But at last he had settled for the job with Allied Precision in

Stamford, they had moved out to a rented house and then to the Revolutionary Hill Estates, and Milly's life had taken on a normal texture once again.

For Shep, too, the past few years had been a time of comparative peace. Or so it seemed, at any rate, in the glowing dusk of this fine spring evening. He was pleasantly full of roast lamb and beer, he was looking forward to a session of good talk with the Wheelers, and things could have been an awful lot worse. True enough, the job in Stamford and the Revolutionary Hill Estates and the Laurel Players were not exactly what he'd pictured in his Arizona visions of the East, but what the hell. If nothing else, the mellowing of these past few years had enabled him to look back without regret.

Because who could deny that his tough-guy phase, neurotic or not, had done him a lot of good? Hadn't it helped him on the way to a Silver Star and a field commission at twenty-one? Those things were real, they were a damned sight more than most men his age could claim (Field commission! The very forming of the words in his mind could still make warm tendrils of pride spread out in his throat and chest) and no psychiatrist would ever be able to take them away. Nor was he plagued any longer by the sense of having culturally missed out and fallen behind his generation. He could certainly feel himself to be the equal of a man like

Frank Wheeler, for example, and Frank was a product of all the things that once had made him writhe in envy—the Eastern university, the liberal arts, the years of casual knocking around in Greenwich Village. What was so terrible, then, in having gone to State Tech?

Besides, if he hadn't gone to State Tech he would never have met Milly, and he didn't need any damn psychiatrist to tell him he would really be sick, really be in trouble, if he ever caught himself regretting that again. Maybe their backgrounds were different; maybe he'd married her for reasons that were hard to remember and maybe it wasn't the most romantic marriage in the world, but Milly was the girl for him. Two things about her had become a constant source of his sentimental amazement: that she had stuck right by him through all the panic in Arizona and New York—he vowed he would never forget it—and that she had taken so well to his new way of life.

The things she had learned! For a girl whose father was a semiliterate housepainter and whose brothers and sisters all said things like "It don't matter none," it couldn't have been easy. The more he thought about it, the more remarkable it was that she could dress very nearly as well as April Wheeler and talk very nearly as well on any subject you wanted to name; that she could live in an ugly, efficient suburban house like this and

know why and how it had to be apologized for in terms
of the job and the kids ("Otherwise of course we'd live
in the city, or else further out, in the real country . . .").
And she had managed to give every room of it the
spare, stripped-down, intellectual look that April
Wheeler called "interesting." Well, almost every
room. Feeling fond and tolerant as he rolled his shoe
rag into a waxy cylinder, Shep Campbell had to admit
that this particular room, this bedroom, was not a very
sophisticated place. Its narrow walls, papered in a big
floral design of pink and lavender, held careful bracket
shelves that in turn held rows of little winking frail
things made of glass; its windows served less as windows than as settings for puffed effusions of dimity
curtains, and the matching dimity skirts of its bed and
dressing table fell in overabundant pleats and billows
to the carpet. It was a room that might have been
dreamed by a little girl alone with her dolls and
obsessed with the notion of making things nice for
them among broken orange crates and scraps of cloth
in a secret shady corner of the back yard, a little girl
who would sweep the bald earth until it was as smooth
as breadcrust and sweep it again if it started to crum-
ble, a scurrying, whispering, damp-fingered little girl
whose cheeks would quiver with each primping of
gauze and tugging of soiled ribbon into place
("There . . . There . . .") and whose quick, frightened

eyes, as she worked, would look very much like the eyes that now searched this mirror for signs of encroaching middle age.

"Sweetie?" she said.

"Mm?"

She turned around slowly on the quilted bench, tense with a troubling thought. "Well—I don't know, you'll just laugh, but listen. Do you think the Wheelers are getting sort of—stuck up, or something?"

"Oh, now, don't be silly," he told her, allowing his voice to grow heavy and rich with common sense. "What makes you want to think a thing like that?"

"I don't know. I can just tell. I mean I know she was upset about the play and everything, but it wasn't *our* fault, was it? And then when we were over there the last time, everything seemed so sort of—I don't know. Remember when I tried to describe the way your mother looked at me that time? Well, April was looking at me that exact same way that night. And now this whole business of forgetting our invitation—I don't know. It's funny, that's all."

He snapped the lid on his can of shoe polish and put it away with the rolled-up rag and the brushes. "Honey," he said, "you're just imagining all that. You're going to spoil the whole evening for yourself."

"I knew you'd say that." She got to her feet, looking aimless and pathetic in her pink slip.

"I'm only saying what's true. Come on, now; let's just take it easy and have a good time." He walked over and gave her a little hug; but his smile froze into an anxious grimace against her ear, because in bending close to her shoulder he had caught a faint whiff of something rancid.

"Oh, I guess you're right," she was saying. "I'm sorry. You go and have your shower, now, and I'll finish up in the kitchen."

"No big rush," he said. "They're always a little late. Why don't you have a shower too, if you want to?"

"No, I'm all ready, soon as I put on my dress."

In the shower, pensively soaping and scrubbing, Shep Campbell wondered what the hell it was that made her smell that way sometimes. It wasn't that she didn't take enough baths—he knew damn well she'd had one last night—and it didn't have anything to do with the time of the month; he had checked that out long ago. It seemed to be a thing brought on by nerves, like a skin rash or a bad stomach; he guessed it was just that she tended to perspire more in times of tension.

But he had to acknowledge, as he toweled himself in the steam, that it was more than just the smell of sweat. That alone, God knew, could be an exciting thing on a woman. And suddenly he was full of the time last summer when he'd held April Wheeler half drunk on the stifling, jam-packed dance floor of Vito's

Log Cabin, when her soaked dress was stuck to her
back and her temple slid greasily under his cheek as
they swayed to the buzz and clip of a snare drum and
the moan of a saxophone. Oh, she was sweating, all
right, and the smell of her was as strong and clean as
lemons; it was the smell of her as much as the tall
rhythmic feel of her that had made his—that had made
him want to—oh, Jesus. It had happened nearly a year
ago, and the memory of it could still make his fingers
tremble in the buttoning of his shirt.

The house seemed unnaturally still. Carrying his
empty beer can, he went downstairs to see what Milly
was doing, and he was halfway across the living room
before he realized that he had four sons.

He almost tripped over them. They were lying on
their bellies in a row, their eight-, seven-, five-, and
four-year-old bodies identically dressed in blue knit
pajamas, all propped on their elbows to stare at the flickering blue of the television screen. Their four snub-
nosed blond faces, in profile, looked remarkably alike
and remarkably like Milly's, and their jaws were all
working in cadence on cuds of bubble gum, the pink
wrappers of which lay strewn on the carpet.

"Hi, gang," he said, but none of them looked up.
He walked carefully around them and out to the
kitchen, frowning. Did other men ever feel distaste at
the sight of their own children? Because it wasn't just

that they'd taken him by surprise; there was nothing unusual in that. Quite often, in fact, he would happen on them suddenly and think, Who are these four guys? And it would take him a second or two to bring his mind into focus on the fact that they were his own. But damn it, if anyone ever asked him what he *felt* at those moments, he could have described it in all honesty as a deep twinge of pleasure—the same feeling he got when he checked them in their beds at night or when they galloped under his high-thrown softball on the lawn. This was different. This time he had to admit that he'd felt a distinct, mild revulsion.

Milly was there in the kitchen, spreading some kind of meat paste on crackers, licking her fingers as she worked.

"'Scuse me, honey," he said, sidling around her. "I'll get right out of your way."

He got a cold, fresh can of beer from the refrigerator and took it out to the back lawn, where he sipped it soberly. From here, looking down over the shadowy tops of trees, he could just make out the edge of the Wheelers' roof; farther down, beyond it and to the right, under the telephone wires, the endless humming parade of cars on Route Twelve had just turned on its lights. He looked away into the shimmering distance of the highway for a long time, trying to figure it out.

If it wasn't revulsion he'd felt, what exactly was it?

An over-fastidious, snobbish disapproval, maybe, because their sprawled staring and chewing had made them look sort of knuckle-headed and—well, middle-class? But what kind of nonsense was that? Would he rather see them sitting at a God damn miniature tea table, for Christ's sake? Wearing tartan kilts? No, it had to be more than that. Probably it was just that the sight of them had broken in on his thoughts of April Wheeler—and he did have thoughts about her! All kinds of thoughts! Wasn't it healthier to own up to a thing like that than to hide from it?—had broken in on his thoughts of April Wheeler and shocked him a little; that was all. And now that he'd faced up to it, he gave himself permission to quit looking up Route Twelve and to concentrate instead on the Wheelers' roof. In winter, when the trees were bare, you could see most of the house and part of its lawn from here, and at night you could see the light in the bedroom window. He began to wonder what April was doing right now. Combing her hair? Putting on her stockings? He hoped she would wear her dark blue dress.

"I love you, April," he whispered, just to see what it felt like. "I love you. I love you."

"Sweetie?" Milly was calling. "What're you *doing* out there?" She was standing in the bright kitchen doorway, squinting out into the gloaming, and behind her smiled the Wheelers.

"Oh!" he said, starting back across the lawn. "Hi! Didn't see you folks drive up." Then, feeling foolish, he paused to drink the last of his beer and found he had drunk the last of it some minutes before; the can was already warm in his hand.

It was an awkward evening from the start—so awkward, in fact, that for the whole first hour of it Shep had to avoid meeting Milly's eyes for fear his own expression would confirm her worry. He couldn't deny it: there *was* something damned peculiar going on here. The Wheelers weren't participating; they didn't relax and move around. Neither of them wandered talking out to the kitchen to help with the drinks; all they did was sit politely glued to the sofa, side by side. It would have taken a pistol shot to separate them.

April had indeed decided to wear her dark blue dress, and she'd never been lovelier, but there was an odd, distant look in her eyes—the look of a cordial spectator more than a guest, let alone a friend—and it was all you could do to get anything more than a "Yes" or an "Oh, really" out of her.

And Frank was the same, only ten times worse. It wasn't just that he wasn't talking (though that alone, for Frank, was about as far out of character as you could get) or that he made no effort to conceal the fact that he wasn't listening to anything Milly said; it was that he was acting like a God damned snob. His eyes kept straying around the room, examining each piece of furniture and each picture as if he'd never found himself in quite such an amusingly typical suburban living room as this before—as if, for Christ's sake, he hadn't spent the last two years spilling his ashes and slopping his booze all over every available surface *in* this room; as if he hadn't burned a hole in the upholstery of this very sofa last summer and passed out drunk and snoring on this very rug. Once, while Milly was talking, he leaned slightly forward and squinted past her like a man peering in between the bars of a darkened rat cage, and it took Shep a minute to figure out what he was doing: he was reading the book titles on the shelves across the room. And the worst part of it was, that Shep, for all his annoyance, had to fight an impulse to spring jovially to his feet and start apologizing ("Well, of course it's not much of a library, I mean I'd hate to have you judge our reading tastes on the basis of—actually, they're mostly just the kind of junk that accumulates over the years, most of our really good books have a way of . . ."). Instead, with his jaws shut tight, he collected all the glasses and went out to the kitchen. Jesus!

He gave both the Wheelers double shots in their next drinks, to help things along, and he held Milly's down to half a shot because if she went on putting it away like this, in the shape she was in, she'd be out cold in another hour.

And at last the Wheelers began to loosen up—though by the time their loosening-up was over, Shep wasn't at all sure but that he'd liked them better the other way.

It began with Frank clearing his throat and saying, "Actually, we've got some pretty important news. We're going—" and there he stopped and blushed and looked at April. "You tell it."

April smiled at her husband—not like a spectator or a guest or a friend, but in a way that made Shep's envious heart turn over—and then she turned back to address her audience. "We're going to Europe," she said. "To Paris. For good."

What? When? How? Why? The Campbells, husband and wife, exploded in a ferocious battery of questions as the Wheelers subsided into laughing, kindly answerers. Everybody was talking at once.

". . . Oh, about a week or two now," April was saying in reply to Milly's insistence on knowing how long all this had been going on. "It's hard to remember. We just suddenly decided to go, that's all."

"Well, but I mean what's the deal?" Shep was demanding of Frank for the second or third time. "I mean, you get a job over there, or what?"

"Well—no, not exactly." And all the talking stopped dead while he and April looked at each other again in their private, infuriating way. All right, Shep wanted to say; tell us or don't tell us. Who the hell cares?

Then the talking began again. Leaning forward, interrupting each other and squeezing each other's hands like a pair of kids, the Wheelers came out with the whole story. Shep did what he always tried to do when a great many pieces of upsetting news hit him one after another: he rolled with the punch. He took each fact as it came and let it slip painlessly into the back of his mind, thinking, Okay, okay, I'll think about that one later; and that one; and that one; so that the alert, front part of his mind could remain free enough to keep him in command of the situation. That way, he was able to have the right expression constantly on his face and to say the right things; he could even take pleasure in realizing that at least the party had livened up, at least there was plenty of action now. And he was surprised and proud to see how well Milly was handling the thing.

"Gee, it sounds wonderful, kids," she said when they were finished. "I mean it; it really sounds wonderful. We'll certainly miss you, though—won't we, sweetie? Golly." Her eyes were glistening. "Golly. We're really going to miss you people a lot."

Shep agreed that this was true, and the Wheelers both withdrew into a graceful, polite sentimentality of their own. They would, they said, certainly miss the Campbells too. Very much.

Later, when it was all over and the Wheelers were gone and the house was quiet, Shep carefully allowed a little of the pain to rise up in him—just enough to remind him that his first duty, right now, was to his wife. He could hold the rest of it down for the time being.

"You know what I think, doll?" he began, coming to stand beside her as she rinsed out the glasses and the ash trays at the kitchen sink. "I think this whole thing of theirs sounds like a pretty immature deal." And he could see her shoulders slacken with gratitude.

"Oh, so do I. I mean I didn't want to say anything, but I thought that exact same thing. Immature is exactly the right word. I mean have either of them even stopped for a minute to think of their children?"

"Right," he said. "And that's only one thing. Another thing: what kind of half-assed idea is this about her supporting him? I mean what kind of a man is going to be able to take a thing like that?"

"Oh, that's so true," she said. "I was thinking that exact same thing. I mean I hate to say this because I really do like them both so much and they're—*you* know, they're really our best friends and everything, but it's true. I kept thinking that exact same—that really is exactly what I thought."

But later still, flat on his back in the darkness upstairs, he was of no use to her at all. He could feel the wide-awake tension of her lying there beside him; he could hear the light rasp of her breathing, with its little telltale quiver near the crest of each inhalation, and he knew that if he so much as touched her—if he so much as turned to her and let her know he was awake—she would be in his arms and sobbing, getting the whole thing out of her system into his neck, while he stroked her back and whispered, "What's the matter, baby? Huh? What's the matter? Tell Daddy."

And he couldn't do it. He couldn't make the effort. He didn't want her tears soaking into his pajama top; he didn't want her warm, shuddering spine in the palm of his hand. Not tonight, anyway; not now. He was in no shape to comfort anybody.

Paris! The very sound of the name of the place had gone straight to the tender root of everything, had taken him back to a time when the weight of the world rode as light and clean as the proud invisible bird whose talons seemed always to grip the place where the lieutenant's bar lay pinned on the shoulder of his Eisenhower jacket. Oh, he remembered the avenues of Paris, and the trees, and the miraculous ease of conquest in the evenings ("You want the big one, Campbell? Okay, you take the big one and I'll take the little one. Hey, Ma'm'selle . . . 'Scuse me, Ma'm'selle . . .")

and the mornings, the lost blue-and-yellow mornings with their hot little cups of coffee, their fresh rolls, and their promise of everlasting life.

And all right, all right; maybe that was kid stuff, soldier stuff, field commission stuff; all right.

But oh God, to be there with April Wheeler. To swing down those streets with April Wheeler's cool fingers locked in his own, to climb the stone stairway of some broken old gray house with her; to sway with her into some high blue room with a red-tiled floor; to have the light husky ripple of her laugh and her voice up there (*"Wouldn't you like to be loved by me?"*); to have the lemon-skin smell of her and the long, clean feel of her when he—when she—oh Jesus.

Oh, Jesus God, to be there with April Wheeler.

THREE

SINCE 1936, WHEN THEY MOVED OUT of the city forever, Mr. and Mrs. Howard Givings had changed their
place of residence every two or three years; and they
had always explained that this was because Helen had a
way with houses. She could buy one in a rundown con-
dition, move in, vigorously improve its value and sell it
at a profit, to be invested in the next house. Beginning
in Westchester, moving gradually north into Putnam
County and then over into Connecticut, she had done
that with six houses. But their present house, the seventh, was a different story. They had lived in it for five,
almost six years now, and they doubted if they'd ever
move away. As Mrs. Givings often said, she had fallen
in love with the place.

It was one of the few authentic pre-Revolutionary
dwellings left in the district, flanked by two of the few

remaining wine-glass elms, and she liked to think of it as a final bastion against vulgarity. The demands of the working day might take her deep into the ever-encroaching swarm of the enemy camp; she might have to stand smiling in the kitchens of horrid little ranch houses and split levels, dealing with impossibly rude people whose children ran tricycles against her shins and spilled Kool-Aid on her dress; she might have to breathe the exhaust fumes and absorb the desolation of Route Twelve, with its supermarkets and pizza joints and frozen custard stands, but these things only heightened the joy of her returning. She loved the last few hundred yards of shady road that meant she was almost there, and the brittle hiss of well-raked gravel under her tires, and the switching-off of the ignition in her neat garage, and the brave, tired walk past fragrant flowerbeds to her fine old Colonial door. And the first clean scent of cedar and floorwax inside, the first glimpse of the Currier and Ives print that hung above the charming old umbrella stand, never failed to fill her with the sentimental tenderness of the word "home."

This had been an especially harrowing day. Saturday was always the busiest day of the real estate week, and this afternoon, on top of everything else, she'd had to drive all the way out to Greenacres—not to visit her son, of course, for she never did that unless her husband was along—but for a conference with his doctor, a thing which always left her feeling soiled. Weren't psychiatrists supposed to be wise, deep-voiced, fatherly sorts of people? Then how could you feel anything but soiled in the presence of a red-eyed, nail-biting little man who used adhesive tape to hold his glasses together and a piece of Woolworth jewelry to keep his tie clamped flat against his white-on-white shirt—who had to thumb moistly through a dozen manila folders before he could remember which of his patients you had come to see him about, and who then said, "Yes; oh yes; and, what was your question?"

But now, by the grace of whichever saint it was that protected weary travelers, she was home. "Hello, dear!" she sang from the vestibule, for her husband was certain to be reading the paper in the living room, and without stopping to chat with him she went directly into the kitchen, where the cleaning woman had left the tea things set out. What a cheerful, comforting sight the steaming kettle made! And how clean and ample this kitchen was, with its tall windows. It gave her the kind of peace she could remember knowing only as a child, gossiping with the maids in the kitchen of her father's wonderful house in Philadelphia. And the funny thing, she often reflected, was that none of her other houses, some of which had been every bit as nice as this, or nicer, had ever made her feel this way.

Well, of course, people do change, she sometimes told herself; I suppose it's simply that I'm getting old and tired. But in her heart, shyly, she cherished quite a different explanation. Her ability to love this house, she truly believed, was only one of many changes in her nature these past few years—deep, positive changes that had brought her to a new perspective on the past.

"Because I love it," she could hear her own voice saying years and years ago, in reply to Howard's exasperated wish to know why she refused to quit her job in the city.

"It certainly can't be very interesting," he would say, "and it certainly isn't as if we needed the money. Why, then?" And her answer had always been that she loved it.

"You love the Horst Ball Bearing Company? You love being a stenographer? How can anybody love things like that?"

"It happens that I do. Besides, you know perfectly well we do need the money, if we're going to keep a full-time servant. And you know I'm not a stenographer." She was an administrative assistant. "Really, Howard, there's no point in discussing this."

And she'd never been able to explain or even to understand that what she loved was not the job—it could have been any job—or even the independence it gave her (though of course that was important for a

woman constantly veering toward the brink of divorce).
Deep down, what she'd loved and needed was work
itself. "Hard work," her father had always said, "is the
best medicine yet devised for all the ills of man—*and* of
woman," and she'd always believed it. The press and
bustle and glare of the office, the quick lunch sent up
on a tray, the crisp handling of papers and telephones,
the exhaustion of staying overtime and the final sweet
relief of slipping off her shoes at night, which always
left her feeling drained and pure and fit for nothing but
two aspirins and a hot bath and a light supper and
bed—that was the substance of her love; it was all that
fortified her against the pressures of marriage and par-
enthood. Without it, as she often said, she would have
gone out of her mind.

When she did quit the job and move to the country
to break into real estate, it had been a difficult transition. There simply wasn't enough work in the real
estate business. Not many people were buying property
in those days, and there was a limit to the amount of
time she could spend on the study of mortgage law and
building codes; there were whole days together with
nothing to do but rearrange the papers on her rose-
wood desk and wait for the phone to ring, with her
nerves so taut she was ready to scream, until she discovered that her passion could find release in the improve-
ment of the things around her. With her own hands she

scraped layers of wallpaper and plaster away to disclose
original oak paneling; she installed a new banister on
the staircase, took out the ordinary window sashes and
put in small-paned, Colonial-looking ones instead; she
drew the blueprints and closely supervised the building
of a new terrace and a new garage; she cleared and filled
and rolled and planted a hundred square feet of new
lawn. Within three years she had added five thousand
dollars to the market value of the place, had persuaded
Howard to sell it and buy another, and had made a
good start on improving the second one. Then came
the third one and the fourth, and so on, with her real
estate business growing all the time, so that during one
peak year she had been able to work eighteen hours a
day—ten on business and eight on the house. "Because
I *love* it," she had insisted, crouching far into the night
over the endless tasks of chipping and hammering and
varnishing and repair, "I *love* doing this kind of work—
don't you?"

And hadn't she been silly? In the sense of calm and
well-being that suffused her now, as she arranged the
tea things on their tray, Mrs. Givings breathed a tolerant sigh at the thought of how silly, how wrong and
foolish she had been in those years. Oh, she had
changed, there was no doubt of it. People did change,
and a change could be a bloom as well as a withering,
couldn't it? Because that was what it seemed to be: a

final bloom, a long-delayed emergence into womanliness.

Oh, the growth of her feeling for this house and the dwindling of her fixation on work were only the smallest, the most superficial symptoms of it; there were deeper things as well—disturbing, oddly pleasurable things; physical things. Sometimes a soaring phrase of Beethoven on the kitchen radio could make her want to weep with the pain of gladness. Sometimes, chatting with Howard, she would feel stirrings of—well, of desire: she would want to take him in her arms and press his dear old head to her breast.

"I thought we'd just have the plain tea today," she said, carrying the tray into the living room. "I hope you don't mind. The point is, if we fill up now we won't be hungry for dinner, and we'll be having a very early dinner you see because I'm expected over at the Wheelers' at eight. Rather awkward timing all around, I'm afraid." She set the tray gently on an antique coffee table whose surface was faintly scarred with glue, showing the places where it had split when John threw it across the room on the awful night the State Police came.

"Oh, isn't it lovely to sit *down*," Mrs. Givings said. "Is there anything nicer than sitting down after a hard day?"

It wasn't until she fixed his tea the way he liked it,

with three sugars, and held it out for him to take, that she looked up to make sure her husband was there. And it wasn't until that instant, suddenly smelling the tea and seeing her, that Howard Givings realized she was home. His hearing aid had been turned off all afternoon. The shock of it made his face flinch like a startled baby's, but she didn't notice. She went on talking while he put down his *Herald Tribune*, fumbled at the dial of the hearing aid with one unsteady hand and reached out the other to take the cup and saucer, which chattered in his grip.

Howard Givings looked older than sixty-seven. His whole adult life had been spent as a minor official of the seventh largest life insurance company in the world, and now in retirement it seemed that the years of office tedium had marked him as vividly as old seafaring men are marked by wind and sun. He was very white and soft. His face, instead of wrinkling or sinking with age, had puffed out into the delicate smoothness of infancy, and his hair was like a baby's too, as fine as milkweed silk. He had never been a sturdy man, and now his frailty was emphasized by the spread of a fat belly, which obliged him to sit with his meager knees wide apart. He wore a rather natty red-checked shirt, gray flannel trousers, gray socks, and an old pair of black, high-cut orthopedic shoes that were as infinitely wrinkled as his face was smooth.

"Isn't there any cake?" he inquired, after clearing his throat. "I thought we still had some of the cocoanut cake."

"Well yes, dear, but you see I thought we'd just have the plain tea today because we'll be having such an early dinner. . . ." She explained all over again about her engagement with the Wheelers, only dimly aware of having told him before, and he nodded, only dimly aware of what she was saying. As she talked she stared in absent-minded fascination at the way the dying sun shone crimson through her husband's earlobe and made his dandruff into flakes of fire, but her thoughts were hurrying ahead to the evening.

This would be no ordinary visit to the Wheelers'; it would, in fact, be the first careful step in fulfilling a plan that had come to her in a kind of vision, weeks and weeks ago. At twilight one evening, taking a stroll to calm her nerves in the blue depths of her back lawn, she had found it peopled in her mind's eye with a family gathering. April Wheeler was there, seated in a white wrought-iron chair and turning her pretty head to smile with affection at some wise and fatherly remark by Howard Givings, who sat beside her near a white wrought-iron table set with ice and cocktail mixings. Across from them, standing and leaning slightly forward with a glass in his hand, Frank Wheeler was engaged in one of his earnest conversations with John, who was reclining in dignified convalescence on a white wrought-iron chaise longue. She could see John smile, composed and courteous, begging to differ with Frank on some minor point of politics or books or baseball or whatever it was that young men talked about, and she could see him turn his head to look up at her and say:

"Mother? Won't you join us?"

The picture kept recurring for days until it was as real as a magazine illustration, and she kept improving on it. She even found a place in it for the Wheelers' children: they could be playing quietly in the shadows behind the rosebushes, dressed in white shorts and tennis shoes, catching fireflies in Mason jars. And the more vivid it grew, the less fault she was able to find with its plausibility. Wouldn't it do John a world of good to recuperate among a few sensitive, congenial people of his own age? And there need be no question of altruism on the Wheelers' part: hadn't they all but told her, time and again, how starved they were for friends of their own kind? Surely the tiresome couple on the Hill (Crandall? Campbell?) couldn't offer them much in the way of—well, of good conversation and so on. And goodness only knew that John, whatever else he might or might not be, was an intellectual.

Oh, it was the right thing for all of them; she knew it; she knew it. But she knew too that it couldn't be hurried. She had known from the start that it would have to be undertaken slowly, a step at a time.

For the past several visiting days, she and Howard had been allowed to take him for an hour's drive outside the hospital grounds on what was called a trial basis. "I don't think any home visits would be wise at this time," the doctor had said last month, hideously cracking his ink-stained knuckles, one after another, on his desk blotter. "There still does seem to be a good deal of hostility concerning the, ah, home atmosphere and whatnot. Be better just to limit him to these preliminary outings for the present. Later on, depending how things work out, you might try taking him to the home of some close friend, where he'd feel more or less on neutral ground; that would be the next logical step. You can use your own judgment on that."

She had talked it over with Howard—she had even mentioned it discreetly to John a few times, during their drives—and last week her own judgment, carefully weighing the factors, had decided that the time for this next logical step was at hand. She had arranged the conference with the doctor today simply to announce her decision, and to ask one small piece of advice. How much, in his opinion, should she tell the Wheelers about the nature of John's illness? The doctor, as she should have predicted, was no help at all— she could, he said, use her own judgment on that too—but at least he hadn't raised any objections, and all that remained now was to put the question to the Wheelers. It would have been ever so much more comfortable and gracious to have the talk here, as she'd planned, over a candlelit dinner table; but that couldn't be helped.

"I do hope it doesn't seem an imposition," she whisperingly rehearsed as she rinsed out the tea things in the kitchen, "but I was wondering if I could ask a great favor. It's about my son John. . . ." Oh, it didn't matter how she phrased it; she would find the right words when the time came, and she knew the Wheelers would understand. Bless them; bless them; she knew they would understand.

She could think of nothing else as she hurried through the preparation and the serving and the washing-up of the early dinner; and when she was ready, when she paused in the hall to freshen her lipstick and to call "I'll see you later, then, dear" before setting off, she was as excited as a girl.

But the moment she walked chatting and laughing into the Wheelers' living room her excitement changed to a kind of panic. She felt like an intruder.

She had expected to find them as tense and disorganized as ever—both talking at once, bobbing and darting around her, getting in each other's way as they sprang to remove a sharp toy from the chair she was about to sit down on—but instead their welcome was serene. April didn't have to insist that the house was in a terrible mess, because it wasn't; Frank didn't have to blurt "Get you a drink" and go lunging off to wrestle and bang at the refrigerator, because the drinks were there, nicely arranged on the coffee table. The Wheelers had, apparently, been quietly drinking and talking together here for some time before her arrival; they were cordially glad to see her, but if she hadn't come they would have gone on together in perfect self-sufficiency.

"Oh, just a tiny dollop for me, thanks, that's wonderful," Mrs. Givings heard herself saying, and "Oh, isn't it lovely to sit down," and "My, doesn't your house look nice," and a number of other things; and then: "I do hope it doesn't seem an imposition, but I was wondering if I could ask a great favor. It's about my son John."

The muscular contraction in both the Wheelers' faces was so slight that the subtlest camera in the world couldn't have caught it, but Mrs. Givings felt it like a kick. They knew! It was the one possibility she had completely overlooked. Who had told them? How much did they know? Did they know about the smashing of the house and the cutting of the phone wires and the State Police?

But she had to go through with it. Actually, her

voice was telling them now, he hadn't been at all well. What with overwork and one thing and another, he'd had what amounted to a complete nervous breakdown. Fortunately he was back in this vicinity for a time—she'd have hated the thought of his being ill so far from home—but all the same it was worrying, to his father and to her. His doctors had thought it wise for him to have a complete rest, so just for the present he was—

"—well, actually, just for the present he's at Greenacres." Her voice had become the only living thing in Mrs. Givings; all the rest was numb.

And actually, her voice assured them, they'd be surprised at what a really excellent place Greenacres was, from the standpoint of—oh, of facilities and staff and so on; much better, for instance, than most of the private rest homes and whatnot in the area.

The voice went on and on, steadily weakening, until it came at last to its point. Some Sunday soon—oh, not right away, of course, but some Sunday in the future—would the Wheelers mind very much if . . .

"Why, of course not, Helen," April Wheeler was saying. "We'd love to meet him. It's very nice of you to think of us." And Frank Wheeler, refilling her glass, said that he certainly did sound like an interesting guy.

"How about next Sunday, then?" April said. "If that suits you."

"Next Sunday?" Mrs. Givings pretended to calcu-late. "Well, let's see: I'm not sure if—All right, fine, then." She knew she ought to feel pleasure at this—it was, after all, exactly what she'd come for—but all she wanted was to get out of here and go home. "Well, of course it's nothing urgent. If next Sunday's inconven-ient or anything we can always make it some oth—"

"No, Helen. Next Sunday's fine."

"Well," she said. "Fine, then. Oh goodness, look at the time. I'm afraid I'd better be—oh, but you had something to ask *me* about, didn't you. And here I've done all the talking, as usual." When she took a sip of her drink she discovered that her mouth was very dry. It felt swollen.

"Well, actually, uh, Helen," Frank Wheeler began, "we have some pretty important news. . . ."

Half an hour later, driving home, Mrs. Givings held her eyebrows high in astonishment all the way. She could hardly wait to tell her husband about it.

She found him still in his armchair in the yellow lamplight, sitting beside the perfectly priceless grand-father clock she had picked up at an auction before the war. He had finished with the *Herald Tribune* now and was making his way through the *World-Telegram and Sun*.

"Howard," she said. "Do you know what those children told me?"

"What children, dear?"

"The Wheelers. *You* know, the people I went to see? The couple in the little Revolutionary Road place? The people I thought John might like?"

"Oh. No; what?"

"Well, first of all I happen to know they're not at all well-fixed financially; they had to borrow the whole down payment on the house, for one thing, and that was only two years ago. In the second place . . ."

Howard Givings tried to listen, but his eyes kept drifting down the newspaper in his lap. A twelve-year-old boy in South Bend, Indiana, had applied for a twenty-five-dollar bank loan to buy medicine for his dog, whose name was Spot, and the bank manager had personally co-signed the note.

". . . so I said, 'But why *sell*? Surely you'll want to have the place when you come *back*.' And do you know what he said? He looked at me in this very guarded way and said, 'Well, that's the point, you see. We won't be coming back.' I said, 'Oh, have you taken a job there?' 'Nope,' he said—just like that. 'Nope. No job.' I said, 'Will you be staying with relatives, then, or friends, or something?' 'Nope.'" And Mrs. Givings bugged her eyes to impersonate the zenith of irresponsibility. "'Nope—don't know a soul. We're just going, that's all.' Really, Howard, I can't tell how embarrassing it was. Can you imagine it? I mean, isn't it all sort of—unsavory, somehow? The whole thing?"

Howard Givings touched his hearing aid and said, "How do you mean, unsavory, dear?" He guessed he had lost the thread. It had started out to be something about somebody going to Europe, but now it was evidently about something else.

"Well, isn't it?" she asked. "People practically without a dollar to their name, with children just coming into school age? I mean people don't *do* things like that, do they? Unless they're—well, running away from something, or something? And I mean I'd hate to think there's anything—well, I don't know *what* to think; that's the point. And they always seemed such a steady, settled sort of couple. Isn't it queer? And the awkward thing, you see, is that I'd already committed myself on the John business before they came out with all this; now I suppose we'll have to go through with it, though there hardly seems much point to it any more."

"Go through with what, dear? I don't quite see what you're—"

"Well, with taking him there for a *visit*, Howard. Haven't you been listening to any of this?"

"Oh; yes, of course. What I mean is, why doesn't there seem much point to it?"

"Well, *because*," she said impatiently. "What's the

value of introducing them to John, if they're going to disappear in the fall?"

"The 'value'?"

"Well, I simply mean—*you* know. He needs *permanent* people. Oh, of course I suppose there's no harm in having him meet them, taking him there once or twice before they—it's just that I'd been thinking in terms of a much more long-range sort of thing, somehow. Oh, dear, isn't it all confusing? Why *do* you suppose people can't be more—" She wasn't quite sure what she was saying now, or what she meant to say, and she found with surprise that she'd been twisting her handkerchief into a tight, moist rope the whole time she was talking. "Still, I suppose one never—can—tell about people," she concluded, and then she turned, left the room, and fled lightly upstairs to change into something comfy.

Passing the shadowed mirror on the landing, she noticed with pride that her own image, at least when seen fleetingly from the corner of an eye, was still that of a swift, lithe girl in a well-appointed house; and on the ample carpet of her bedroom, where she quickly stripped off her jacket and stepped out of her skirt, it was almost as if she were back in her father's house, hurrying to dress for a tea dance. Her blood seemed to race with the emergency of last-minute details (Which kind of perfume? Oh, quick—which kind?) and she very nearly ran out to the banister to call, "Wait! I'm coming! I'll be right down!"

It was the sight and the feel of her old flannel shirt and baggy slacks, hanging from their peg in the closet, that steadied her. Silly, silly, she scolded herself; I *am* getting scatty. But the real shock came when she sat on the bed to take off her stockings, because she had expected her feet to be slim and white with light blue veins and straight, fragile bones. Instead, splayed on the carpet like two toads, they were tough and knuckled with bunions, curling to hide their corneous toenails. She stuffed them quickly into her bright Norwegian slipper-socks (really the nicest things in the world for knocking around the house) and sprang up to pull the rest of her simple, sensible country clothes into place, but it was too late, and for the next five minutes she had to stand there holding on to the bedpost with both hands and keeping her jaws shut very tight because she was crying.

She cried because she'd had such high, high hopes about the Wheelers tonight and now she was terribly, terribly, terribly disappointed. She cried because she was fifty-six years old and her feet were ugly and swollen and horrible; she cried because none of the girls had liked her at school and none of the boys had liked her later; she cried because Howard Givings was the only man who'd ever asked her to marry him, and because she'd done it, and because her only child was insane.

But soon it was over; all she had to do was go into the bathroom and blow her nose and wash her face and brush her hair. Then, refreshed, she walked jauntily and soundlessly downstairs in her slipper-socks and returned to sit in the ladder-back rocker across from her husband, turning out all but one of the lights in the room as she came.

"There," she said. "That's much cozier. Really, Howard, my nerves were just like *wires* after that business with the Wheelers. You can't imagine how it upset me. The point is I'd always thought they were such *solid* young people. I thought *all* the young married people today were supposed to be more settled. Wouldn't you think they ought to be, especially in a community like this? Goodness knows, all *I* hear about is young couples *dying* to come and settle here, and raise their children. . . ."

She went on talking and talking, moving around and around the room; and Howard Givings timed his nods, his smiles, and his rumblings so judiciously that she never guessed he had turned his hearing aid off for the night.

FOUR

"FLY THE COOP," Jack Ordway said, stirring his coffee. "Kick over the traces. Take off. Pretty nifty, Franklin."

They were sitting at a ketchup-stained table for two in the dark corner of the Nice place, and Frank was beginning to regret having told Ordway about Europe. A clown, a drunk, a man unable to discuss anything at all except in the elaborately derisive tone he used for talking about himself—wasn't this the desirable kind of confidant to have in a thing like this? But he'd told him, nevertheless, because in the past few weeks it had become more and more difficult to carry his secret alone through the office day. Sitting attentively in staff conferences while Bandy outlined things to be done "in the fall" or "first of the year," accepting Sales Promotion assignments that would theoretically take him months to complete, he would sometimes find his mind sliding readily into gear with the slow machinery of Bandy's projects before it occurred to him to think: No, wait a minute—I won't even be *here* then. At first these little shocks had been fun, but the fun of them had worn off and soon they had become distinctly troubling. It was getting on for the middle of June. In another two and a half months (eleven weeks!) he would be crossing the ocean, never to be concerned with Sales Promotion again, yet the reality of that fact had still to penetrate the reality of the office. It was a perfectly, inescapably real fact at home, where nobody talked of anything else; it was real on the train each morning and again on the train each night, but for the eight hours of his working day it remained as insubstantial as a half-remembered, rapidly fading dream. Everyone and everything in the office conspired against it. The stolid or tired or mildly sardonic faces of his colleagues, the sight of his IN basket and his current work pile, the sound of his phone or of the buzzer that meant he was wanted in Bandy's cubicle—all these seemed constantly to tell him he was destined to stay here forever.

The hell I am! he felt like saying twenty times a day. You just wait and see. But his defiance lacked weight. The bright, dry, torpid lake of this place had contained him too long and too peacefully to be ruffled by any silent threat of escape; it was all too willing to wait and see. This was intolerable; the only way to put an end to it was to speak out and tell somebody; and Jack Ordway was, after all, the best friend he had in the office. Today they had managed to avoid Small and Lathrop and Roscoe for lunch, and had started it off with a couple of weak but adequate martinis; and now the story was out.

"There's one small point I don't quite grasp, though," Ordway was saying. "I don't mean to be dense, but what exactly will you be doing? I don't see you languishing indefinitely at sidewalk cafés while your good frau commutes to the embassy or whatever—but that's the point, you see. I don't quite know what I *do* see you doing. Writing a book? Painting a—"

"Why does everybody think in terms of writing books and painting pictures?" Frank demanded, and then, only partly aware that he was quoting his wife, he said, "My God, are artists and writers the only people entitled to lives of their own? Look. The only reason I'm here in this half-assed job is because—well, I suppose there's a lot of reasons, but here's the point. If I started making a list of all the reasons, the one reason I damn sure couldn't put down is that I like it, because I don't. And I've got this funny feeling that people are better off doing some kind of work they like."

"Fine!" Ordway insisted. "Fine! Fine! Don't let's

get all defensive and riled up, please. My only simple-minded question is this: What kind do you like?"

"If I knew that," Frank said, "I wouldn't have to be taking a trip to find out."

Ordway thought this over, tilting his handsome head to one side, lifting his brows and curling out his underlip, which looked unpleasantly pink and slick. "Well, but don't you think," he said, "I mean to say, assuming there is a true vocation lurking in wait for you, don't you think you'd be just as apt to discover it here as there? I mean, isn't that possible?"

"No. I don't think it is. I don't think it's possible for anybody to discover anything on the fifteenth floor of the Knox Building, and I don't think you do either."

"Mm. Must say that sounds like a good point, Franklin. Yes indeed." He drank off the last of his coffee and sat back, smiling quizzically across the table. "And when did you say this noble experiment is going to begin?"

For a second Frank wanted to turn the table over on him, to see the helpless fright in his face as his chair went over backwards and the whole mess of dishes went up and over his head. "Noble experiment"! What kind of supercilious crap was that?

"We're going in September," he said. "Or October at the outside."

Ordway nodded five or six times, gazing at the con-

cealed smears of meat and potato on his plate. He
didn't look supercilious now; he looked old and beaten
and wistfully envious; and Frank, watching him, felt
his own resentment blurring into an affectionate pity.
The poor, silly old bastard, he thought. I've spoiled his
lunch; I've spoiled his day. He almost wished he could
say, "It's all right, Jack, don't worry; it may never happen"; instead he took refuge from his own confusion
in a burst of heartiness.

"Tell you what, Jack," he said. "I'll buy you a
brandy for old times."

"No, no, no, no," Ordway said, but he looked as
pleased as a stroked spaniel when the waiter cleared
the plates away and set the rich little cognac glasses in
their place; and later, when they'd paid their checks
and walked upstairs into the sunlight, he was all smiles.

It was a clear, warm day, with a sky as clean and
deep as laundry blueing above the buildings, and it was
also payday, time for the traditional after-lunch stroll
to the bank.

"Needless to say I'll keep this strictly *entre nous*, old
scout," Ordway said as they walked. "I don't suppose
you want it noised around. How much notice you
planning to give Bandy?"

"Couple of weeks, I guess. Haven't really thought
about it."

The sun was pleasingly warm. In another few days it

would be hot, but it was perfect now. In the cool marble depths of the bank, whose Muzak system was playing "Holiday for Strings," he entertained himself by pretending it was the last time he would ever stand in line here, the last time he would ever shift his feet and finger his paycheck as he and Ordway waited their turns at one of the ten tellers' windows that were reserved at lunchtime, twice a month, for Knox employees. "You ought to see us shuffling around that damned bank," he had told April years ago. "We're like a litter of suckling pigs waiting for a free tit. Oh, of course we're all very well-mannered, very refined little pigs; we all stand very suavely and try not to jostle each other too much, and when each guy gets up close to the window he takes out his check and sort of folds it in his fingers or palms it or finds some other way of hiding it without seeming to. Because it's very important to be casual, you see, but the really important thing is to make damn sure nobody else sees how much you're getting. Jesus!"

"Gentlemen," said Vince Lathrop, at Frank's shoulder. "Shall we take the air?" He and Ed Small and Sid Roscoe were pocketing their passbooks and their wallets, their tongues still sucking random shreds of Awful place food from the crevices of their teeth, and this was an invitation to join them in a digestive stroll around the block.

He pretended it was the last time he would ever do

this, too; the last time he would ever join this slow promenade of office people in the sunshine, the last time the approach of his own polished shoes would ever cause these wobbling pigeons to take fright and skitter away across the spit and peanut shells of the sidewalk, to flap and climb until they were wheeling high over the towers with alternately black and silver wings.

It was better to have told somebody; it had made a difference. He was able to glance around at the talking faces of these four men and feel truly detached from them. Ordway, Lathrop, worried little Ed Small, pretentious, boring old Sid Roscoe—he knew now that he would soon be saying goodbye to all of them and that in another year he'd have trouble remembering their names. In the meantime, and this was the best part, in the meantime it was no longer necessary to dislike them. They weren't such bad guys. He could even join happily in their laughter at some mild joke of Ordway's, and when they turned the last corner and headed back to the Knox Building he could take pleasure in the comradely way they spread out five abreast across the sidewalk, inspired by the sun to step out briskly and swing their arms with all the apparent "unit pride" of soldiers from the same platoon on pass (What *out*fit, Mac? Sales Promotion, Fifteenth Floor, Knox Business Machines).

And Goodbye, goodbye, he could say in his heart

to everyone they passed—a chattering knot of stenographers clutching packages from the dimestore, a cynical, heavy-smoking group of young clerks who leaned against a building front in their shirtsleeves—goodbye to the whole sweet, sad bunch of you. I'm leaving.

It was a splendid sense of freedom, and it lasted until he was back at his desk, where the buzzer that meant he was wanted in Bandy's cubicle was mournfully bleating.

Ted Bandy never looked his best in fine weather; he was an indoor man. His thin gray body, which seemed to have been made for no other purpose than to fill the minimum requirements of a hard-finish, double-breasted business suit, and his thin gray face were able to relax only in the safety of winter, when the office windows were shut. Once, when he'd been assigned to accompany a group of prize-winning salesmen on a trip to Bermuda, Roscoe's *Knox Knews* had carried a photograph of the whole party lined up and grinning on the beach in their swimming trunks; and Roscoe's secretly made enlargement of one section of that picture, showing Bandy doing his best to smile under the weight of two great, hairy arms that had been flung around his neck from either side, had enjoyed weeks of furtive circulation among the cubicles of the Fifteenth Floor, where everyone pronounced it the funniest damn thing they'd ever seen.

Bandy was wearing something of that same expression now, and at first Frank thought it was only because the June breeze from the window had comically dislodged some of the long side hairs that were supposed to be combed across his baldness. But he discovered with a start, on entering the cubicle, that the main cause of Bandy's uneasiness was the presence there of a rare and august visitor.

"Frank, you know Bart Pollock, of course," he said, getting to his feet, and then with an apologetic nod he said, "Frank Wheeler, Bart."

A massive figure in tan gabardine rose up before him, a big tan face smiled down, and his right hand was enveloped in a warm clinch. "Don't guess we've ever been formally introduced," said a voice deep enough to make the glassware tremble on a speaker's rostrum. "Glad to know you, Frank."

This man, who in any other corporation would have been called "Mr." rather than "Bart," was general sales manager for the Electronics Division, a man from whom Frank had never received anything more than an occasional vague nod in the elevator, and whom he had despised from a distance for years. "I mean he'd be perfect Presidential timber in the worst sense," he had told April once. "He's one of these big calm father-image bastards with a million-dollar smile and about three pounds of muscle between the ears; put him on

television and the other party'd never have a chance."
And now, feeling his own face twitch into a grimace of
servility, feeling a drop of sweat creep out of his armpit
and run down his ribs, he tried to atone for this uncontrollable reaction by planning how he would describe
it to April tonight. "And I suddenly caught myself sort
of *melting* in front of him—isn't that funny? I mean *I*
know he's a horse's ass; *I* know he's got nothing to do
with anything that matters in my life, and all the same
he almost had me cowed. Isn't that the damnedest
thing?"

"Pull up a chair, Frank," said Ted Bandy, smoothing the hairs back across his head, and when he sat
down again he shifted his weight uncomfortably from
one buttock to the other, the gesture of a man with
hemorrhoids. "Bart and I've been going over some of
the reports on the NAPE conference," he began, "and
Bart asked me to call you in on it. It seems . . ."

But Frank couldn't follow the rest of Bandy's sentence because all his attention was fixed on Bart Pollock. Leaning earnestly forward in his chair, Pollock
waited until Bandy had finished talking; then he
rapped the back of his free hand smartly across the
paper he was holding, which turned out to be a copy of
Speaking of Production Control, and said:

"Frank, this is a crackerjack. They're just tickled to
death in Toledo."

. . .

"And I mean isn't that the damnedest thing?" he demanded of April that evening, laughing and talking at the same time, following her around the kitchen with a drink in his hand while she got the dinner ready to serve. "I mean isn't it ironic? I do this dumb little piece of work to get myself off the hook with Bandy, and this is what happens. You should've heard old Pollock go on about it—all these years he hasn't known I'm alive, and suddenly I'm his favorite bright young man. Old Bandy sitting there trying to decide whether to be pleased or jealous, me sitting there trying to keep from laughing myself to death—Jesus!"

"Marvelous," she said. "Would you mind carrying these in, darling?"

"And then it turns out he's got this big—What? Oh, sure, okay." He put down his glass, took the plates she handed him and followed her into the other room, where the children were already seated at the table. "And then it turns out he's got this big idea; Pollock, that is. He wants me to do a whole series of the crazy things. *Speaking of Inventory Control, Speaking of Sales Analysis, Speaking of Cost Accounting, Speaking of Payroll*—he's got it all mapped out. I'm supposed to go out to—"

"Excuse me a sec, Frank. Michael, you sit up

straight, now, or there's going to be trouble. I mean it. And don't take such big bites. I'm sorry; go on."

"I'm supposed to go out to lunch with him next week and talk it over. Won't that be a riot? Course, if it gets too thick I'll have to tell him I'm leaving the company in the fall. No, but I mean the whole thing's pretty funny, isn't it? After all these—"

"Why not tell him anyway?"

"—years of doping along in the damn job and never—What?"

"I said why don't you tell him anyway? Why not tell the whole pack of them? What can they do?"

"Well," he said, "it's hardly a question of their 'doing' anything; it'd just be—you know, a little awkward, that's all. I mean I certainly don't see the point of saying anything until it's time to give them my formal notice, that's all." He forked a piece of pork chop into his mouth so angrily that he bit the fork as well as the meat, and as he chewed with all the strength of his jaws, exhaling a long breath through his nostrils to show how self-controlled he was, he realized that he didn't quite know what he was angry about.

"Well," she said placidly, without looking up. "Of course that's entirely up to you."

The trouble, he guessed, was that all the way home this evening he had imagined her saying "And it probably *is* the best sales promotion piece they've ever seen—what's so funny about that?"

And himself saying: "No, but you're missing the point—a thing like this just proves what a bunch of idiots they are."

And her: "I don't think it proves anything of the sort. Why do you always undervalue yourself? I think it proves you're the kind of person who can excel at anything when you want to, or when you have to."

And him: "Well, I don't know; maybe. It's just that I don't *want* to excel at crap like that."

And her: "Of course you don't, and that's why we're leaving. But in the meantime, is there anything so terrible about accepting their recognition? Maybe you don't want it or need it, but that doesn't make it contemptible, does it? I mean I think you ought to feel good about it, Frank. Really."

But she hadn't said anything even faintly like that; she hadn't even looked as if thoughts like that could enter her head. She was sitting here cutting and chewing in perfect composure, with her mind already far away on other things.

FIVE

"I'M GOING TO TAKE my dollhouse," Jennifer said that Saturday afternoon, "and my doll carriage and my bear and my three Easter rabbits and my giraffe and all my dolls and all my books and records, and my drum."

"That sounds like quite a lot, doesn't it, sweetie?" April said, frowning over her sewing machine. She had decided to spend the weekend sorting out winter clothes, discarding some things and repairing others, concentrating on the simple, sturdy kind of clothes they would need for Europe. Jennifer was sitting at her feet, playing aimlessly with torn-out linings and bits of thread.

"Oh, and my tea set too, and my rock collection and all my games, and my scooter."

"Well, but sweetie, don't you think that's quite a lot to take? Aren't you planning to leave anything behind?"

"No. Maybe I'll throw my giraffe away; I haven't quite decided."

"Your giraffe? No, I wouldn't do that. We'll have plenty of room for all the animals and dolls and the other small things. It's just some of the big things I was worried about—the dollhouse, for instance, and Mike's rocking horse. That kind of thing's very difficult to pack, you see. But you won't have to throw away the dollhouse; you could give it to Madeline."

"To keep?"

"Well, of course to keep. That's better than throwing it away, isn't it?"

" 'Kay," Jennifer said, and then, after a minute: "I know what I'll do. I'll give Madeline my dollhouse and my giraffe and my carriage and my bear and my three Easter rabbits and my—"

"Just the *big* things, I said. Didn't you understand me? I just finished explaining all that. Why can't you listen?" April's voice was rising and flattening out with exasperation, and then she sighed. "Look. Wouldn't you rather go outside and play with Michael?"

"No. I don't feel much like it."

"Oh. Well, I don't feel much like explaining everything fifteen times to somebody who's too bored and silly to pay attention, either. So that's that."

Frank was glad when their voices stopped. He was on the sofa trying to read the introduction to a book of elementary French, which he'd bought to replace the "Brighter" one, and their talking had kept him going over and over the same paragraph.

But half an hour later, when the only sound in the room for that long had been the faint irregular whir of the sewing machine, he looked up uneasily to find that Jennifer was gone.

"Where'd she go, anyway?" he said.

"Out with Michael, I guess."

"No she didn't. I know she didn't go outside."

They got up and went together to the children's room, and there she was, lying down and staring at nothing, with her thumb in her mouth.

April sat on the edge of the bed and laid her palm against Jennifer's temple, and then, apparently feeling no fever, she began stroking her hair. "What's the matter, baby?" She made her voice very gentle. "Can you tell Mommy what's the matter?"

Watching from the doorway, Frank's eyes grew as round as his daughter's. He swallowed, and so did she, first removing her thumb from her mouth.

"Nothing," she said.

April took hold of her hand to prevent the thumb from going back in, and in opening the small fist she discovered that a length of green thread had been wound tightly and many times around her index finger. She began to unwind it. It was so tight that the tip of the finger was plum-colored and the moist skin beneath it was wrinkled and bloodless.

"Is it about moving to France?" April asked, still working on the thread. "Are you feeling sort of bad about that?"

Jennifer didn't answer until the last of the thread was removed. Then she gave a small, barely discernible nod and wrenched herself awkwardly around so that her head could be buried in her mother's lap as she started to cry.

"Oh," April said. "I thought that might be it. Poor old Niffer." She stroked her shoulder. "Well, listen, baby, you know what? There isn't anything to feel bad about."

But it was impossible for Jennifer to stop, now that she'd started. Her sobs grew deeper.

"Remember when we moved out here from the city?" April asked. "Remember how sad it seemed to be leaving the park and everything? And all your friends at nursery school? And remember what happened? It wasn't more than about a week before Madeline's mommy brought her over to meet you, and then you met Doris Donaldson, and the Campbell boys, and pretty soon you started school and met all your other friends, and there wasn't anything to feel bad about any more. And that's just the way it's going to be in France. You'll see."

Jennifer raised her congested face and tried to say something, but it took her several seconds to get the words out between the convulsions of her breath. "Are we going to live there a long time?"

"Of course. Don't you worry about that."

"Forever and ever?"

"Well," April said, "maybe not forever and *ever*, but we'll certainly live there a good long time. You shouldn't worry so much, sweetie. I think it's mostly just from sitting around indoors on such a nice day. Don't you? Let's go wash your face, now, and then you run along outside and see what Michael's doing. Okay?"

When she was gone, Frank took up a slumped, standing position behind his wife at the sewing machine. "Gee," he said. "That really gave me a turn. Didn't it you?"

She didn't look up. "How do you mean?"

"I don't know. It's just that this does seem a pretty inconsiderate thing to be doing, when you think about it, from the kids' point of view. I mean, let's face it: it's going to be pretty rough on them."

"They'll get over it."

"Of course they'll 'get over it,'" he said, trying to make the phrase sound heartless. "We could trip them up and break their arms, and they'd 'get over' that too; that's hardly the point. The point is—"

"Look, Frank." She had turned to face him with

her little flat-lipped smile, her tough look. "Are you suggesting we call the whole thing off?"

"No!" He moved away from her to pace the carpet. "Of course I'm not." For all his annoyance, he found it good to be up and talking again after his long silence of faulty concentration with the French book on the sofa. "Of *course* I'm not. Why do you have to start—"

"Because if you're not, then I really don't see any point in discussing this. It's a question of deciding who's in charge and sticking to it. If the children are to be in charge, then obviously we must do what they think is best, which means staying here until we rot. On the other hand—"

"No! Wait a minute; I never said—"

"You wait a minute, please. On the other hand, if we're to be in charge—and I really think we ought to be, don't you? If only because we're about a quarter of a century older than they are? Then that means going. As a secondary thing it also means doing all we can to make the transition as easy as possible for them."

"That's all I'm saying!" He waved his arms. "What're you getting all excited about? Make the transition as easy as possible—that's absolutely all I'm saying."

"All right. The point is I think we're doing that, and I think we'll continue to do it to the best of our ability until they do get over it. In the meantime I'm afraid I don't see any point in holding our heads and moaning about how miserable they're going to be, or talking about tripping them up and breaking their arms. Frankly, I think that's a lot of emotionalistic nonsense and I wish you'd cut it out."

It was the closest thing to a fight they'd had in weeks; it left them on edge and unnecessarily polite for the rest of the day, and caused them to shy away from each other at bedtime. And in the morning they awoke to the sound of rain and the uncomfortable knowledge that this was the Sunday they had arranged to meet John Givings.

Milly Campbell had volunteered to take the children off their hands for the afternoon, "because I mean you probably won't want them around when he's there, will you? In case he turns out to be a real nut or anything?" April had declined; but this morning, as the time of the visit drew near, she had second thoughts about it.

"I think we'll take you up on that after all, Milly," she said into the telephone, "if the offer still goes. I guess you were right—it does seem a weird sort of thing to expose them to." And she drove them to the Campbells' an hour or two earlier than necessary.

"Gosh," she said, sitting down with Frank in the scrubbed kitchen when she returned. "This is sort of nervous-making, isn't it? I wonder what he'll be like? I don't think I've ever met an insane person before, have you? A real certified insane person, I mean."

He poured out two glasses of the very dry sherry he liked on Sunday afternoons. "How much you want to bet," he said, "that he turns out to be pretty much like all the uncertified insane people we know? Let's just relax and take him as he comes."

"Of course. You're right." And she favored him with a look that made yesterday's unpleasantness seem years in the past. "You always do have the right instincts about things like this. You're really a very generous, understanding person, Frank."

The rain had stopped but it was still a wet, gray day and good to be indoors. The radio was dimly playing Mozart and a gentle, sherry-scented repose settled over the kitchen. This was the way he had often wished his marriage could always be—unexcited, companionable, a mutual tenderness touched with romance—and as they sat there quietly talking, waiting for the sight of the Givingses' station wagon to appear through the dripping trees, he shivered pleasurably once or twice as a man who has been out since before dawn will shiver at the feel of the first faint warmth of sun on his neck. He felt himself at peace; and by the time the car did come, he was ready for it.

Mrs. Givings was the first one out, aiming a blind, brilliant smile toward the house before she turned back to deal with the coats and bundles in the back seat. Howard Givings emerged from the driver's side, ponderously wiping his misted spectacles, and behind him came a tall, narrow, red-faced young man wearing a cloth cap. It wasn't the kind of jaunty little back-belted cap that had lately become stylish; it was wide, flat, old-fashioned and cheap, and the rest of his drab costume was equally suggestive of orphanage or prison: shapeless twill work pants and a dark brown button-front sweater that was too small for him. From a distance of fifty feet, if not fifty yards, you could tell he was dressed in items drawn from state institutional clothing supplies.

He didn't look up at the house or at anything else. Lagging behind his parents, he stood with his feet planted wide apart on the wet gravel, slightly pigeon-toed, and gave himself wholly to the business of lighting a cigarette—tamping it methodically on his thumbnail, inspecting it with a frown, fixing it carefully in his lips, hunching and cupping the match to it, and then taking the first deep pulls as intently as if the smoke of this particular cigarette were all he would ever have or expect of sensual gratification.

Mrs. Givings had time to chatter several whole sentences of greeting and apology, and even her husband was able to get a few words in, before John moved from his cigarette-lighting place in the driveway. When he did, he was very quick: he walked springingly on the balls of his feet. Seen at close range, his face proved to be big and lean, with small eyes and thin lips, and its frown was the look of a man worn down by chronic physical pain.

"April . . . Frank," he said in reply to his mother's introduction, almost visibly committing both names to memory. "Glad to meetcha. Heard a lot aboutcha." Then his face burst into an astonishing grin. His cheeks drew back in vertical folds, two perfect rows of big, tobacco-stained teeth sprang out between his whitening lips, and his eyes seemed to lose their power of sight. For a few seconds it seemed that his face might be permanently locked in this monstrous parody of a friend-winning, people-influencing smile, but it dwindled as the party moved deferentially into the house.

April explained (too pointedly, Frank thought) that the children were away at a birthday party, and Mrs. Givings began telling of how perfectly frightful the traffic had been on Route Twelve, but her voice trailed off when she found that John had claimed the Wheelers' whole attention. He was making a slow, stiff-legged circuit of the living room, still wearing his cap, examining everything.

"Not bad," he said, nodding. "Not bad. Very adequate little house you got here."

"Won't you all sit down?" April asked, and the

elder Givingses obeyed her. John removed his cap and laid it on one of the bookshelves; then he spread his feet and dropped to a squat, sitting on his heels like a farmhand, bouncing a little, reaching down between his knees to flick a cigarette ash neatly into the cuff of his work pants. When he looked up at them now his face was free of tension; he had assumed a kind of pawky, Will Rogers expression that made him look intelligent and humorous.

"Old Helen here's been talking it up about you people for months," he told them. "The nice young Wheelers on Revolutionary Road, the nice young revolutionaries on Wheeler Road—got so I didn't know what she was talking about half the time. Course, that's partly because I didn't listen. You know how she is? How she talks and talks and talks and never says anything? Kind of get so you quit listening after a while. No, but I got to hand it to her this time; this isn't what I pictured at all. This is nice. I don't mean 'nice' the way she means 'nice,' either; don't worry. I mean nice. I like it here. Looks like a place where people live."

"Well," Frank said. "Thank you."

"Would anyone like some sherry?" April inquired, twisting her fingers at her waist.

"Oh no, please don't bother, April," Mrs. Givings was saying. "We're fine; please don't go to any trouble. Actually, we can only stay a min—"

"Ma, how about doing everybody a favor," John said. "How about shutting up a little while. Yes, I'd like some sherry, thanks. Bring some for the folks too, and I'll drink Helen's if she doesn't beat me to it. Oh, hey, listen, though." All the wit vanished from his face as he leaned forward in his squat and extended one gesturing hand toward April like a baseball coach wagging instructions to the infield. "You got a highball glass? Well, look. Take a highball glass, put a couple-three ice cubes in it, and pour the sherry up to the brim. That's the way I like it."

Mrs. Givings, sitting tense as a coiled snake on the edge of the sofa, gently closed her eyes and wanted to die. Sherry in a highball glass! His cap on the bookshelf—oh, and those *clothes*. Week after week she brought him clothes of his own to wear—good shirts and trousers, his fine old tweed jacket with the leather elbows, his cashmere sweater—and still he insisted on dressing up in these hospital things. He did it for spite. And this dreadful rudeness! And why was Howard always, always so useless at times like this? Sitting there smiling and blinking in the corner like an old— oh God, why didn't he *help*? "Oh, this is lovely, April, thanks so much," she said, tremulously lifting a sherry glass from the tray. "Oh, and look at this magnificent *food*!" She drew back in mock disbelief at the platter of small, crustless sandwiches that April had made and cut that morning. "You *really* shouldn't have gone to all this bother for us." John Givings took two sips of his drink and left it standing on the bookcase for the rest of the visit. But he ate half the plate of sandwiches as he restlessly patrolled the room, taking three or four at a time and wolfing them down while breathing audibly through his nose. Mrs. Givings managed to hold the floor for a few minutes, talking steadily, making such smooth elisions between one sentence and the next as to leave no opening for interruption. She was trying to filibuster the afternoon away. Had the Wheelers heard the latest ruling of the zoning board? Personally she considered it an outrage; still, she supposed it would ultimately bring the tax rate down, and that was always a blessing. . . .

Howard Givings, sleepily nibbling a sandwich, kept a watchful eye on his son's every action during this monologue; he might have been a benign old nursemaid in the park, making sure the youngster stayed out of mischief.

John watched his mother, head cocked to one side, and when he had swallowed his last mouthful he cut her off in mid-sentence.

"You a lawyer, Frank?"

"Me? A lawyer? No. Why?"

"Hoping you might be, is all. I could use a lawyer. Whaddya do, then? Advertising man, or what?"

"No. I work for Knox Business Machines."

"Whaddya do there? You design the machines, or make them, or sell them, or repair them, or what?"

"Sort of help sell them, I guess. I don't really have much to do with the machines themselves; I work in the office. Actually it's sort of a stupid job. I mean there's nothing—you know, interesting about it, or anything."

"'Interesting'?" John Givings seemed offended by the word. "You worry about whether a job is 'interesting' or not? I thought only women did that. Women and boys. Didn't have you figured that way."

"Oh, *look*, the sun's coming out!" Mrs. Givings cried. She jumped up, went to the picture window and peered through it, her back very rigid. "Maybe we'll see a rainbow. Wouldn't that be lovely?"

The skin at the back of Frank's neck was prickling with annoyance. "All I meant," he explained, "is that I don't like the job and never have."

"Whaddya do it for, then? Oh, okay, okay—" John Givings ducked his head and weakly raised one hand as if in a hopeless attempt to ward off the bludgeon of public chastisement. "Okay; I know; it's none of my business. This is what old Helen calls Being Tactless, Dear. That's my trouble, you see; always has been. Forget I said it. You want to play house, you got to have a job. You want to play very *nice* house, very *sweet* house, then you got to have a job you don't like. Great.

This is the way ninety-eight-point-nine per cent of the people work things out, so believe me buddy you've got nothing to apologize for. Anybody comes along and says 'Whaddya do it for?' you can be pretty sure he's on a four-hour pass from the State funny-farm; all agreed. Are we all agreed there, Helen?"

"Oh look, there *is* a rainbow," Mrs. Givings said, "—or no, wait, I guess it isn't—oh, but it's perfectly lovely in the sunshine. Why don't we all take a walk?"

"As a matter of fact," Frank said, "you've pretty well put your finger on it, John. I agree with everything you said just now. We both do. That's why I'm quitting the job in the fall and that's why we're taking off."

John Givings looked incredulously from Frank to April and back again. "Yeah? Taking off where? Oh, hey, yeah, wait a minute—she did say something about that. You're going to Europe, right? Yeah, I remember. She didn't say why, though; she just said it was 'very strange.'" And all at once he split the air—very nearly split the house, it seemed—with a bray of laughter. "Hey, how about that, Ma? Still seem 'very strange' to you? Huh?"

"Steady down, now," Howard Givings said gently from his corner. "Steady down, son."

But John ignored him.

"Boy!" he shouted. "Boy, I bet this whole conversation seems very, *very* strange to you, huh, Ma?"

They had grown so used to the bright, chirping sound of Mrs. Givings's voice that day that her next words came as a shock, addressed to the picture window and spoken in a wretchedly tight, moist whimper: "Oh John, please stop."

Howard Givings got up and shuffled across the room to her. One of his white, liver-spotted hands made a motion as if to touch her, but he seemed to think better of it and the hand dropped again. They stood close together, looking out the window; it was hard to tell whether they were whispering together or not. Watching them, John's face was still ebullient with the remnants of his laughter.

"Look," Frank said uneasily, "maybe we *ought* to take a walk or something." And April said, "Yes, let's."

"Tell you what," John Givings said. "Why don't the three of us take a walk, and the folks can stay here and wait for their rainbow. Ease the old tension all around."

He loped across the carpet to retrieve his cap, and on the way back he veered sharply with an almost spastic movement to the place where his parents stood, his right fist describing a wide, rapid arc toward his mother's shoulder. Howard Givings saw it coming and his glasses flashed in fright for an instant, but there was no time to interfere before the fist landed—not in a blow but in a pulled-back, soft, affectionate cuffing against the cloth of her dress.

"See you later, then, Ma," he said. "Stay as sweet as you are."

Up in the woods behind the house, steaming in the sun, the newly rainwashed earth gave off an invigorating fragrance. The Wheelers and their guest, relaxing in an unexpected sense of cameraderie, had to walk single file on the hill and pick their way carefully among the trees; the slightest nudge of an overhanging branch brought down a shower of raindrops, and the glistening bark of passing twigs was apt to leave grainy black smears on their clothing. After a while they quit the woods and walked slowly around the back yard. The men did most of the talking; April listened, staying close to Frank's arm, and more than once he noticed, glancing down at her, that her eyes were bright with what looked like admiration for the things he was saying.

The practical side of the Europe plan didn't seem to interest John Givings, but he was full of persistent questions about their reasons for going; and once, when Frank said something about "the hopeless emptiness of everything in this country," he came to a stop on the grass and looked thunderstruck.

"Wow," he said. "Now you've said it. The hopeless emptiness. Hell, plenty of people are on to the emptiness part; out where I used to work, on the Coast, that's all we ever talked about. We'd sit around talking about emptiness all night. Nobody ever said 'hopeless,' though; that's where we'd chicken out. Because maybe it does take a certain amount of guts to see the emptiness, but it takes a whole hell of a lot more to see the hopelessness. And I guess when you do see the hopelessness, that's when there's nothing to do but take off. If you can."

"Maybe so," Frank said. But he was beginning to feel uncomfortable again; it was time to change the subject. "I hear you're a mathematician."

"You hear wrong. Taught it for a while, that's all. Anyway, it's all gone now. You know what electrical shock treatments are? Because you see, the past couple months I've had thirty-five—or no, wait—thirty-seven—" He squinted at the sky with a vacant look, trying to remember the number. In the sunlight, Frank noticed for the first time that the creases in his cheeks were really the scars of a surgeon's lancet, and that other areas of his face were blotched and tough with scar tissue. At one time in his life his face had probably been a mass of boils or cysts. "—thirty-seven electrical shock treatments. The idea is to jolt all the emotional problems out of your mind, you see, but in my case they had a different effect. Jolted out all the God damned mathematics. Whole subject's a total blank."

"How awful," April said.

"'*How awful.*'" John Givings mimicked her in a

mincing, effeminate voice and then turned on her with a challenging smirk. "Why?" he demanded. "Because mathematics is so 'interesting'?"

"No," she said. "Because the shocks must be awful and because it's awful for anybody to forget something they want to remember. As a matter of fact I think mathematics must be very dull."

He stared at her for a long time, and nodded with approval. "I like your girl, Wheeler," he announced at last. "I get the feeling she's female. You know what the difference between female and feminine is? Huh? Well, here's a hint: a feminine woman never laughs out loud and always shaves her armpits. Old Helen in there is feminine as hell. I've only met about half a dozen females in my life, and I think you got one of them here. Course, come to think of it, that figures. I get the feeling you're male. There aren't too many males around, either."

Mrs. Givings, covertly watching them from the house, didn't quite know what to think. She was still shaken—the beginning of the afternoon had been worse than the worst of her fears—but she had to admit that John had seldom looked happier and more relaxed than he did now, strolling and chatting in the Wheelers' back yard. And the Wheelers looked comfortable too, which was even more surprising.

"They do seem to—to like him, don't they?" she

said to Howard, who was picking through the Wheelers' Sunday *Times*.

"Mm," he said. "You shouldn't get so nervous about these things, Helen. Why don't you just relax when they come back, and let them do the talking?"

"Oh, I know," she said. "I know, you're right. That's what I ought to do."

And she did, and it worked. For the last hour of the visit, while everyone but John had another glass of wine, she scarcely said a word. She and Howard sat benignly in the background of the young people's conversation, a peaceful medley of voices in which John's voice was never once more raucous than the others. They were reminiscing about the children's radio programs of the nineteen-thirties.

"'Bobby Benson,'" Frank was saying. "Bobby Benson of the H-Bar-O Ranch; I always liked him. I think he came on just before 'Little Orphan Annie.'"

"Oh, and 'Jack Armstrong,' of course," April said, "and 'The Shadow,' and that other mystery one— something about a bee? 'The Green Hornet.'"

"No, but 'The Green Hornet' was later," John said. "That was still going in the forties. I mean the real way-back ones; thirty-five and -six, along in there. Remember the one about the naval officer? What was his name? Used to come on right about this time? On week days?"

"Oh yes," April said. "Wait a minute—'Don Winslow.'"

"Right! 'Don Winslow of the United States Navy.'"

It wasn't at all the kind of topic Mrs. Givings would have thought they'd discuss, but they all seemed to enjoy it; the sound of their easy, nostalgic laughter filled her with pleasure, and so did the taste of her sherry, and so did the sherry-colored squares of sunset on the wall, each square alive with the nodding shadows of leaves and branches stirred by the wind.

"Oh, this has been such fun," she said when it was time to go, and for a second she was afraid John might turn on her and say something awful, but he didn't. He was talking and shaking hands with Frank, and the party broke up in the driveway with a chorus of regrets and good wishes and promises to see each other soon.

"You were wonderful," April said when the car had disappeared. "The way you handled him! I don't know what I'd ever have done if you hadn't been here."

Frank reached for the sherry bottle, but changed his mind and got out the whiskey instead. He felt he deserved it. "Hell, it wasn't a question of 'handling' him," he said. "I just treated him like anyone else, is all."

"But that's what I mean—that's what was so wonderful. I would've treated him like an animal in the zoo or something, the way Helen does. Wasn't it funny how much more sane he seemed once we got him away from her? And he's sort of nice, isn't he? *And* intelligent. I thought some of the things he said were sort of brilliant."

"Mm."

"He certainly did seem to sort of approve of us, didn't he? Wasn't that nice about 'male' and 'female'? And do you know something, Frank? He's the first person who's really seemed to know what we're talking about."

"That's true." He took a deep drink, standing at the picture window and watching the last of the sunset. "I guess that means we're as crazy as he is."

She came up close behind him and put her arms around his chest, nestling her head against his shoulder blade. "I don't care if we are," she said. "Do you?"

"No."

But he had begun to feel depressed in a way that couldn't be attributed to ordinary Sunday-evening sadness. This odd, exhilarating day was over, and now in the fading light he could see that it had only been a momentary respite from the tension that had harried him all week. He could feel the resumption of it now, despite the reassurance of her clinging at his back—a dread, a constricting heaviness of spirit, a foreboding of some imminent, unavoidable loss.

And he was gradually aware that she felt it too: there was a certain stiffness in the way she was holding him, a suggestion of effort to achieve the effect of spontaneity, as though she knew that a nestling of the shoulder blade was in order and was doing her best to meet the specifications. They stood that way for a long time.

"Wish I didn't have to go to work tomorrow," he said.

"Don't, then. Stay home."

"No. I guess I've got to."

SIX

"NOW TED BANDY'S a nice fella," Bart Pollock said as they walked rapidly uptown, "and he's a good department head, but I'll tell you something." He smiled down along his gabardine shoulder into Frank's attentive face. "I'll tell you something. I'm a little sore at him for the way he's kept you under a bushel all these years."

"Well, I wouldn't say that, Mr.—Bart." Frank felt his features jump into a bashful smile. "But thanks anyway." ("I mean what the hell else could I say?" he would explain to April later, if necessary. "What else can you *say* to a thing like that?") He had to skip and quicken his step to keep up with Pollock's long stride, and he was uncomfortably aware that these little hurrying motions, combined with the way his fingers were fussing to keep his tie from slipping out of his jacket, must make him look the picture of an underling.

"This place okay with you?" Pollock swept him into the lobby and then into the restaurant of a big hotel, a place that bustled with heavy-laden, rubber-heeled waiters and throbbed with executive shoptalk under the clash of knives and forks. When they were settled at a table Frank took a sip of ice water and glanced around the room, wondering if this was the same place he had come with his father that other day for the lunch—the luncheon—with Mr. Oat Fields. He couldn't be sure—there were several hotels of this size and kind in the neighborhood—but the possibility was strong enough to please his sense of ironic coincidence. "Isn't that the damnedest thing?" he would demand of April tonight. "Exactly the same room. Same potted palms, same little bowls of oyster crackers— Jesus, it was like something in a dream. I sat there feeling ten years old."

It was a relief, at any rate, to be sitting down. It made Pollock less tall and allowed Frank to conceal, under the table, the fact that he was picking and tearing at a loose strip of skin along his left thumbnail while Pollock talked. Was Frank married? Children? Where did he live? Well, it certainly was wise to live in the country when you had kids; but how did Frank feel about commuting? It was almost exactly like Oat Fields wishing to know how he felt about school and baseball.

"You know what impressed me most about that piece of yours?" Pollock asked over his martini, the stemmed glass of which looked very fragile in his hand. "The logic and the clarity of it. You hit each point in the right place and you drove it home. To me it wasn't like a piece of reading matter at all. It was like a man talking."

Frank ducked his head. "Well, as a matter of fact, that's what it was. I just talked it into the Dictaphone, you see. Actually the whole thing was more or less an accident. Our department isn't supposed to handle the creative end or the production end of these things, you see; that's the agency's job. All we're supposed to do is control the distribution of their stuff to the field."

Pollock nodded, chewing on his gin-soaked olive. "Let me tell you something. I'm having another of these, you with me? Good. Let me tell you something, Frank. I'm not interested in creative ends or production ends or who's supposed to control the distribution of what. I'm interested in one thing, and one thing only: selling the electronic computer to the American businessman. Frank, a lot of people tend to look down on plain old-fashioned selling today, but I want to tell you something. Back when I was first breaking into the selling field a very wise and wonderful older man told me something I've never forgotten. He said to me, 'Bart, *everything* is selling.' He said, 'Nothing happens in this world, nothing comes *into* this world, until somebody makes a sale.' He said, 'You don't believe me? All right, look at it this way.' He said, 'Bart, where the hell do you think *you'd* be if your father hadn't sold your mother a bill of goods?'"

"And I kept sitting there getting drunk and thinking 'What the hell does this guy *want* from me?'" he would tell April tonight. "Of course I kept thinking none of it matters a damn, but still; he really had me guessing. And it's true about these big, bluff, rough-diamond types, you know it? They do have a certain personal magnetism. He does, anyway."

"Now of course, good selling today consists of many things, the combining of many forces, and as you know this is particularly true when you've got an idea to sell instead of just a product. Take a job like ours, introducing a whole new concept of business control, and hell, it gets so you can't hardly see the woods for the trees. You got your market research people, you got your advertising and your whaddyacallit, your public relations people; you got to coordinate all these forces into one basic, overall selling effort. I like to think of it as building a bridge." He squinted and used one forefinger to describe a slow aerial arc between the ash tray and the celery-and-olives dish. "A bridge of understanding, a bridge of communication between the science of electrox"— he hiccupped—"Excuse me.

The science of electronics and the practical, everyday world of commercial management. Now, you take a company like Knox." He looked regretfully into the empty glass of his second, or possibly his third, martini. "Very old, very slow, very conservative—hell, you know this as well as I do: our whole operation's geared to selling typewriters and file cabinets and clankety-clank old punched-card machines, and half the old farts on the payroll think McKinley's in the White House. On the other hand—you want to order now, or wait a while? All right, sir, let's have a look. The ragout's very tasty here and so's the smoked salmon and so's the mushroom omelet and so's the lemon sole. Fine and dandy, make it two. Couple more of these things too, while you're at it. Right. Now, you might say this company's like some real old, tired old man. On the other hand—" He shot his cuffs and leaned massively on the table, eyes bulging. Beads of sweat had begun to appear among the big tan freckles of his head. "On the other hand, here comes this whole revolutionary concept of electronic data processing, and Frank, let's face it: this is a newborn baby." He cradled an imaginary infant in both hands, and then he shook them quickly as if to rid his fingers of a glutinous fluid. "I mean it's still *wet*! I mean they just now hauled it out and turned it over and slapped its ass and by Jesus its belly button's still hangin' out sore as a boil! You follow me? All right; you take this little-biddy newborn baby and you give it to this old, old man, or this old woman, let's say, these old married folks, and whaddya think's gunna happen? Why, they're gunna let it shrivel up and die, that's what. They're gunna take it and lay it away in a dresser drawer someplace and give it sour old milk to suck and never change its pants, and are you tryna tell me that baby'll ever grow up healthy and strong? Why hell that baby's got no more chance 'n a fiddler's bitch. Let me give an example."

And he gave one example after another, while Frank did his best to follow him. After a while he stopped to blot his head with a handkerchief, looking bewildered. "And that's the problem," he said. "That's pretty much what we're up against." Sighting grimly and carefully on the last of his drink, he downed it in a swallow and fell to work on his cooling food, which seemed to sober him. He went on talking as he ate but he was quieter now and more dignified, using words like "obviously" and "furthermore" instead of "fart" and "belly button." His eyes no longer protruded; he had left off being the backwoods tycoon and was resuming his customary role as balanced, moderate executive. Had Frank considered the tremendous effect of the computer on the business life of the future? It was, Bart Pollock could assure him, food for thought. And he went on and on, modestly confessing his ignorance of technicalities, disparaging his right to speak as a prophet, earnestly losing his way in the labyrinthine structure of his sentences.

Watching him and trying to listen, Frank found that his own three martinis (or was it four?) had amplified the sounds of the restaurant into a sea of noise that jammed his eardrums, and had caused a dark mist to close in on all four sides of his vision so that only the things coming directly before him could be seen at all, and they with a terrible clarity: his food, the bubbles in his glass of ice water, Bart Pollock's tirelessly moving mouth. He used the full power of this pinpoint scrutiny to watch Bart Pollock's table manners, to see if he would leave white curds on the rim of his glass or soak his roll in the gravy boat, and he felt enormously, drunkenly gratified on being able to establish that Bart Pollock did neither of those things. Before long Pollock subsided, with visible relief, into a conversational vein that had less to do with abstractions than with company personalities, and that was when Frank felt it safe to bring up the topic nearest his heart.

"Bart," he said. "Do you happen to remember a man here in the Home Office named Otis Fields?"

Pollock blew a long jet of cigarette smoke and watched it fade. "No, I don't believe I—" he began, but then he blinked happily to attention. "Oh, *Oat* Fields. Oh, hell, yes, many years ago. Oat Fields was one of our general sales managers back in—Lord, this goes back a good many—hey, hold on, though. You couldn't 've been around then."

And Frank, surprised at the fluency of his own voice, gave a brief account of the last time he'd sat at a luncheon table very much like this one.

"Earl Wheeler," Pollock said, leaning back to squint in the effort of memory. "Earl Wheeler. Newark, you said? Wait a second. I do remember a Wheeler and I *think* he had a name like Earl—no, but that was in Harrisburg, or Wilmington, and anyway, he was a much older man."

"Harrisburg, that's right. That was later, though. Harrisburg was the last place he worked. The Newark job was earlier, back around 'thirty-five or -six. Then he also worked in Philadelphia a while, and Providence— pretty much all over the Eastern Region. That's why I grew up in about fourteen different places, you see." And he was startled to hear a note of self-pity creeping into his voice: "Never did get much of a chance to feel at home anywhere."

"Earl Wheeler," Pollock was saying. "Why hell, of course I remember him. And you see the reason I didn't connect him with Newark is because that was before *my* time. But I do recall Earl Wheeler very clearly in Harrisburg; only thing is I had the impression he was more of an elderly man. I'm probably—"

"You're right. He was. He already had two full-grown kids by the time I was born, you see—" and he almost caught himself saying, "I was the accident, you see; I was the one they didn't want." Hours later, sobering up and trying to remember this part of the talk, he couldn't be sure that he *hadn't* said that; he couldn't even be sure that he hadn't broken into a wild shout of laughter and said, "You see? You see, Bart? They laid me away in a dresser drawer and gave me sour old milk to suck—" and that he and Bart Pollock hadn't risen up to punch each other's arms at the hilarity of this joke and laughed and laughed until they cried and fell into the coffee cups.

But that didn't happen. What happened instead was Bart Pollock's shaking his head in wonderment and saying, "Isn't that something? And imagine your remembering this restaurant all these years; even remembering old Oat Fields's name."

"Well, it's not too surprising. It was the only time my father ever took me to New York, for one thing; besides, a hell of a lot depended on that day. He really thought Fields was going to give him a Home Office job, you see. He and my mother had the whole thing planned, the house in Westchester and all the rest of it. I don't think he ever did get over it."

Pollock respectfully lowered his eyes. "Well, of course that's—that's the breaks in this business." And then he hurried on to more cheerful aspects of the story. "No, but this is really interesting, Frank. I had no idea you were the son of a Knox man. Funny Ted didn't mention it."

"I don't think Ted knows it. It wasn't a thing I featured when I took the job."

And now Bart Pollock was frowning and smiling at the same time. "Hold on here a second. You mean to say your dad sold for us all his life and you never even let on?"

"Well yes, actually, that's right. I didn't. He was retired then, and I just—I don't know; anyway, I didn't. It seemed important not to at the time."

"I'll tell you something, Frank. I admire that. You didn't want anybody giving you a special break here and a special break there; you wanted to make good on your own. Right?"

Frank shifted uncomfortably in his chair. "No, it wasn't exactly that. I don't know. It was pretty complicated."

"A thing like that *is* complicated," Bart Pollock said with solemnity. "Many people wouldn't understand a thing like that, Frank, but I'll tell you something. I admire it. I bet your dad did too. Didn't he? Or no, wait a minute." He leaned back, smiling and cannily narrowing his eyes. "Wait a minute. Let me see how good a judge of character I am. I bet I know what hap-

pened. This is just a guess, now." He winked. "An edu-
cated guess. I bet you went ahead and let your dad
think his name had helped you get the job, just to
please him. Am I right?"

And the disturbing fact of the matter was that he
was. On an autumn day of that year, feeling stiff and
formal in a new serge suit, Frank had taken his wife to
visit his parents; and all the way out to Harrisburg he'd
planned to be elaborately, sophisticatedly offhand in
the announcing of his double piece of news, the baby
and the job. "Oh, and by the way, I've got a steadier
kind of job now, too," he had planned to say, "kind of a
stupid job, nothing I'm interested in, but the money's
nice." And then he would let the old man have it.

But when the moment came, in that overstuffed
Harrisburg living room with its smell of weakness and
medicine and approaching death, with his father doing
his best to be benign, his mother doing her best to be
tearfully pleased about the baby and April doing her
best to be sweetly and shyly proud—when all the lying
tenderness of that moment came it had robbed him of
his nerve, and he'd blurted it out—a job in the Home
Office!—like a little boy come home with a good
report card.

"Who'd you see there?" Earl Wheeler had
demanded, looking ten years younger than he'd looked
ten minutes before. "Ted who? Bandy? Don't believe I

know him; course, I've forgotten a lot of the names. He knew me, though, I guess, didn't he?"

And "*Oh* yes," Frank had heard himself saying over a preposterous swelling in his throat. "*Oh* yes, certainly. He spoke very highly of you, Dad."

And it wasn't until they were on the train again, going back to New York, that he'd regained enough composure to pound his fist on his knee and say, "He beat me! Isn't that the damnedest thing? The old bastard beat me again."

"I knew it," Bart Pollock was saying now, his eyes twinkling and suffused with heart-warmth. "I'll tell you something, Frank: I'm seldom wrong in my hunches about people. Care for a little cordial or a little B and B or something with your dessert?"

"And do you mean to say you sat through the whole lunch," April might well ask tonight, "and told him your whole life story, and never even got around to telling him you're leaving the company in the fall? Whatever was the point of that?"

But Pollock was making it impossible, now, to get a word in edgewise. He was getting down, at last, to business. Who was going to nurse that baby? Who was going to build that bridge?

". . . Your public relations expert? Your electronics engineer? Your management consultant? Well, now, certainly, all of them are going to play important roles in the overall picture; each of them is going to offer very valuable specialized knowledge in their respective fields. But here's the point. No single one of them has the right background or the right qualifications for the job. Frank, I've talked to some of the top advertising and promotion men in the business. I've talked to some of the top technical men in the computer field and I've talked to some of the top business administration men in the country, and we've all of us pretty much come to this conclusion: it's a completely new kind of job, and we're going to have to develop a completely new kind of talent to do it.

"Now, the past six months or so I've been going around sounding men out, inside the company and outside too. So far I've got my eye on half a dozen young men with various backgrounds, and I hope to line up half a dozen more. You see what I'm doing? I'm recruiting myself a team. Now let me"—he held up a thick hand to ward off any interruptions—"let me be more specific. These little pieces you're doing for us now are only the beginning. I want you to finish that series the way we mapped it out the other day in Ted's office; that's fine; but what I'm driving at now goes way beyond that. As I say, this whole project's still taking shape, nothing's definite yet, but this'll show you the direction of my thinking. I've got a hunch you're the kind of a fella I could send out to groups of people all over the country—civic groups, business seminars, groups of our own field sales people as well as customers and prospects, and all you'd do is stand up in front of those groups and talk. You'd talk computers, chapter and verse; you'd answer questions; you'd put the electronic data processing story over in the kind of language a businessman can understand. Frank, maybe it's the old-time salesman in me, but I've always had one conviction, and that's this: when you're trying to sell an idea, I don't care how complicated or what it may be, you'll never find a more effective instrument of persuasion than the living human voice."

"Well, Bart, before you go any further, there's something I—" He felt tight in the chest and short of breath. "I mean I couldn't very well say this in Ted's office the other day because I haven't told him about it yet, but the thing is I'm planning to leave the company in the fall. I guess I should've made that clear earlier; now I feel sort of—I mean I really am sorry if this conflicts with your—"

"You mean to say you *apologized* to him?" April might ask. "As if you had to ask his permission to leave, or something?"

"No!" he would insist. "Of course I didn't apologize to him. Will you give me a chance? I *told* him, that's all. Naturally it was a little awkward; it was bound to be awkward after the way he'd been talking; can't you see that?"

"Well, now I *am* sore at Bandy," Pollock was saying. "Let a man of your caliber go to waste for seven years and then lose you to another outfit." He shook his head.

"Oh, it's not to another *outfit*—I mean *you* know; it's not anything else in the business machine field."

"Well, I'm glad of that, anyway. Frank, you've been aboveboard with me and I appreciate it; now I'll be aboveboard with you. I don't want to pry into things that're none of my business, but can you tell me this? Can you tell me how definite a commitment you've made on this other thing?"

"Well—pretty definite, I'm afraid, Bart. It's kind of hard to—well, yes. Quite definite."

"Because here's my point. If it's a question of money, there's certainly no reason why we can't get together on a satisfactory . . ."

"No. I mean I appreciate your saying that, but it's not really a question of money at all. It's more of a personal thing."

And that seemed to settle it. Pollock began to nod slowly and steadily, to show his infinite understanding of personal things.

"I mean it won't affect the series I'm working on

now," Frank told him. "I'll have plenty of time to finish that; it's just that anything beyond that is—*you* know, pretty much out of the question."

Pollock's nodding continued for a while. Then he said, "Frank, let me put it to you this way. Nothing's ever so definite a man can't change his mind. All I'm asking is, I'd like you to give a little thought to this chat we've had today. Sleep on it a while; talk it over with your wife—and that's always the main thing, isn't it? Talking it over with your wife? Where the hell would any of us be without 'em? And I'd like you to feel free to come to me at any time and say, 'Bart, let's have another chat.' Will you do that? Can we leave it that way? Fine. And remember, this thing I'm talking about would amount to a brand-new job for you. Something that could turn into a very challenging, very satisfying career for any man. Now I'm sure this other thing looks very desirable to you right now"—he winked—"you'll never catch me knocking a competitor; and of course it's entirely your decision. But Frank, in all sincerity, if you do decide for Knox I believe it'll be a thing you'll never regret. And I believe something else, too. I believe—" He lowered his voice. "I believe it'd be a fine memorial and tribute to your dad."

And how could he ever tell April that these abysmally sentimental words had sent an instantaneous rush of blood to the walls of his throat? How could he ever explain, without bringing down her everlasting scorn, that for a minute he was afraid he might weep into his melting chocolate ice cream?

Fortunately, there was no chance to tell her anything that night. She had spent the day at a kind of work she had always hated and lately allowed herself to neglect: cleaning the parts of the house that didn't show. Breathing dust and spitting cobwebs, she had hauled and bumped the screaming vacuum cleaner into all the corners of all the rooms and crawled with it under all the beds; she had cleaned each tile and fixture in the bathroom with a scouring powder whose scent gave her a headache, and she had thrust herself head and shoulders into the oven to swab with ammonia at its clinging black scum. She had torn up a loose flap of linoleum near the stove to reveal what looked like a long brown stain until it came alive—a swarm of ants that seemed still to be crawling inside her clothes for hours afterwards—and she'd even tried to straighten up the dripping disorder of the cellar, where a wet corrugated-paper box of rubbish fell apart in her hands as she lifted it out of a puddle, releasing all its mildewed contents in a splash from which an orange-spotted lizard emerged and sped away across her shoe.

By the time Frank came home she was too tired to feel like talking.

She didn't feel like talking the next night, either. Instead they watched a television drama which he found wholly absorbing and she declared was trash.

And it was the next night, or the next—he could never afterwards remember which—that he found her pacing the kitchen in the same tense, high-shouldered way she had paced the stage in the second act of *The Petrified Forest*. From the living room came the muffled strains of horn and xylophone, interspersed with the shrieks of midget voices; the children were watching an animated cartoon on television.

"What's the matter?"

"Nothing."

"I don't believe you. Did something happen today, or what?"

"No." Then the perfection of her curtain-call smile began to blur and moisten into a wrinkled grimace of despair and her breathing became as loud as the boiling vegetables on the stove. "Nothing happened today that I haven't known about for days and days—and oh God, Frank, please don't look so dense; do you really mean you haven't known it too, or guessed it or anything? I'm pregnant, that's all."

"Jesus." His face obediently paled and gaped into the look of a man stunned by bad news, but he knew he

wouldn't be able to keep it that way for long: an exultant smile was already struggling up for freedom from
his chest; he had to take hold of his mouth to stop it.
"Wow," he said quietly through his fingers. "Are you
sure?"

"Yes." And she came heavily into his arms as if the
act of telling him had taken all her strength away.
"Frank, I didn't want to clobber you with it before
you've even had a drink or anything; I meant to wait
until after dinner but I just—the thing is, I've really
been pretty sure all week and today I finally saw the
doctor and now I can't even *pretend* it's not true any
more."

"Wow." He gave up trying to control his face,
which now hung aching with joy over her shoulder as
he pressed and stroked her with both hands, muttering
mindless words into her hair. "Oh, listen, it doesn't
mean we can't go; listen, it just means we'll have to figure out some other *way* of going, is all."

The pressure was off; life had come mercifully back
to normal.

"There isn't any other way," she said. "Do you
think I've thought about anything else all week? There
isn't any other way. The whole *point* of going was to
give you a chance to find yourself, and now it's ruined.
And it's my fault! My own dumb, careless . . ."

"No, listen to me; nothing's ruined. You're all

upset. At the very worst it only means waiting a little while until we can work out some—"

"A little *while*! Two years? Three years? Four? How long do you think it'll *be* before I can take a full-time job? Darling, *think* about it a minute. It's hopeless."

"No, it's not. Listen."

"Not now; don't let's try to talk about it now, okay? Let's at least wait'll the kids are asleep." And she turned back to the stove, wiping the inside of her wrist against one dribbling eye in a childish gesture of shame at being seen in tears.

"Okay."

In the living room, hugging their knees, the children were staring blankly at a cartoon bulldog who brandished a spiked club as he chased a cartoon cat through the wreckage of a cartoon house. "Hi," Frank said, and made his way past them to the bathroom to wash up for dinner, allowing his mind to fill with the rhythm and the song of all the things he would say as soon as he and April were alone. "Listen," he would begin. "Suppose it does take time. Look at it this way . . ." And he would begin to draw the picture of a new life. If there was indeed a two- or three-year span of waiting to be done, wouldn't it be made more endurable by the money from Pollock's job? "Oh, of course it'll be a nothing-job, but the money! Think of the money!" They could get a better house—or better still, if they continued to find the suburbs intolerable, they could move back to town. Oh, not to the dark, roach-infested, subway-rumbling city of the old days, but to a brisk, stimulating, new New York that only money could discover. Who knew how much broader and more interesting their lives might become? And besides . . . besides . . .

He was washing his hands, breathing the good smell of soap and the aromatic fumes of April's scouring powder, noticing that his face in the mirror looked ruddier and better than he'd seen it look in months—he was thus engaged when the full implication, the full meaning of his "besides" clause broke over him. Besides: why *think* of accepting Pollock's money as a mere compromise solution, an enforced making-the-best-of-things until the renewal of her ability to support him in Paris? Didn't it have the weight and dignity of a plan in its own right? It might lead to almost anything—new people, new places—why, it might even take them to Europe in due time. Wasn't there a good chance that Knox, through Knox International, might soon be expanding its promotion of computers abroad? ("You and Mrs. Wheeler are so very unlike one's preconceived idea of American business people," a Henry James sort of Venetian countess might say as they leaned attractively on a balustrade above the Grand Canal, sipping sweet vermouth. . . .)

"Well, but what about you?" April would say. "How are you *ever* going to find yourself now?" But as he firmly shut off the hot-water faucet he knew he would have the answer for her:

"Suppose we let that be my business."

And there was a new maturity and manliness in the kindly, resolute face that nodded back at him in the mirror.

When he reached for a towel he found she had forgotten to put one on the rack, and when he went to the linen closet to get one he saw, on the top shelf, a small square package freshly wrapped in drugstore paper. Its newness and the incongruity of its being there among the folded sheets and towels gave it a potent, secret look, like that of a hidden Christmas gift, and it was this as much as his unaccountable, rising fear that made him take it down and open it. Inside the wrapping was a blue cardboard box bearing the Good Housekeeping Seal of Approval, and inside the box was the dark pink bulb of a rubber syringe.

Without giving himself time to think, without even wondering if it mightn't be better to wait till after dinner, he carried the package back through the living room, swiftly past the place where the children watched their cartoon (the cat had turned now and was chasing the dog over acres of cartoon countryside), and into the kitchen. And the way her startled face began to harden when she looked at it, and then up into his eyes, left no doubt at all of her intentions.

"Listen," he said. "Just what the hell do you think you're going to do with this?"

She was backing away through the vegetable steam, not in retreat but in defiant readiness, her hands sliding tensely up and down her hips. "And what do you think *you're* going to do?" she said. "Do you think you're going to stop me?"

PART THREE

ONE

OUR ABILITY TO MEASURE and apportion time affords an almost endless source of comfort.

"Synchronize watches at oh six hundred," says the infantry captain, and each of his huddled lieutenants finds a respite from fear in the act of bringing two tiny pointers into jeweled alignment while tons of heavy artillery go fluttering overhead: the prosaic, civilian-looking dial of the watch has restored, however briefly, an illusion of personal control. Good, it counsels, looking tidily up from the hairs and veins of each terribly vulnerable wrist; fine: so far, everything's happening right on time.

"I'm afraid I'm booked solid through the end of the month," says the executive, voluptuously nestling the phone at his cheek as he thumbs the leaves of his appointment calendar, and his mouth and eyes at that moment betray a sense of deep security. The crisp, plentiful, day-sized pages before him prove that nothing unforseen, no calamity of chance or fate can overtake him between now and the end of the month. Ruin and pestilence have been held at bay, and death itself will have to wait; he is booked solid.

"Oh, let me see now," says the ancient man, tilting his withered head to wince and blink at the sun in bewildered reminiscence, "my first wife passed away in the spring of—" and for a moment he is touched with terror. The spring of what? Past? Future? What is any spring but a mindless rearrangement of cells in the crust of the spinning earth as it floats in endless circuit of its sun? What is the sun itself but one of a billion insensible stars forever going nowhere into nothingness? Infinity! But soon the merciful valves and switches of his brain begin to do their tired work, and "The spring of Nineteen-Ought-Six," he is able to say. "Or no, wait—" and his blood runs cold again as the galaxies revolve. "Wait! Nineteen-Ought—Four." Now he is sure of it, and a restorative flood of well-being brings his hand involuntarily up to slap his thigh in satisfaction. He may have forgotten the shape of his first wife's smile and the sound of her voice in tears, but by imposing a set of numerals on her death he has imposed coherence on his own life, and on life itself. Now all the other years can fall obediently into place, each with its orderly contribution to the whole. Nineteen-Ten, Nineteen-Twenty—Why, of course he remembers!—Nineteen-Thirty, Nineteen-Forty, right on up to the well-deserved peace of his present and on into the gentle promise of his future. The earth can safely resume its benevolent stillness—Smell that new grass!—and it's the same grand old sun that has hung there smiling on him all these years. "Yes sir," he can say with authority, "Nineteen-Ought-Four," and the stars tonight will please him as tokens of his ultimate heavenly rest. He has brought order out of chaos.

The early summer of 1955 might well have been intolerable for both the Wheelers, and might in the end have turned out very differently, if it hadn't been for the calendar that hung on their kitchen wall. A New Year's gift of A. J. Stolper and Sons, Hardware and Home Furnishings, illustrated with scenes of Rural New England, it was the kind of calendar whose page for each month displays two smaller charts as well, last month and next, so that a quarter of the year can be comprehended in a single searching glance.

The Wheelers were able to fix their date of conception in the latter part of the first week in May—the week after his birthday when they could both remember his whispering, "It feels sort of loose," and her whispering, "Oh no, I'm sure it's all right; don't stop . . ." (she had bought a new diaphragm the following week, just to be sure), and this placed the first week in August, more than four weeks away and clear over on the next page, as the mysterious time "right at the end of the third month" when the school friend, long ago, had said it would be safe to apply the rubber syringe.

Panic had sent her straight to the drugstore the minute she was free of the doctor's office that afternoon; panic had driven him down the hall to confront her with the thing the minute he found it in the closet that evening, and it was panic that held them locked and staring at each other in the vegetable steam, brutally silent, while the cartoon music floated in from the next room. But much later that same night, after each of them furtively and in turn had made studies of the calendar, their panic was drowned in the discovery that row on row of logical, orderly days lay waiting for intelligent use between now and the deadline. There was plenty of time for coming to the right decision on this thing, for working this thing out.

"Darling, I didn't mean to be so awful about it; I wouldn't have been if you hadn't come *at* me with it like that, before either of us had a chance to discuss it in any kind of a rational way."

"I know; I know." And he patted her softly weeping

shoulder. These tears didn't mean she was capitulating; he knew that. At best they meant what he'd hopefully suspected from the start, that she halfway wanted to be talked out of it; at worst they meant only that she didn't want to antagonize him, that in drawing her own kind of reassurance from the calendar she had seen the four weeks as a generous opportunity for gradually winning him over. But either way, and this was what filled him with gratitude as he held and stroked her, either way it meant she was considering him; she cared about him. For the time being, that was all that mattered.

"Because I mean we've got to be together in this thing, haven't we?" she asked, drawing back a little in his grip. "Otherwise nothing's going to make any sense. Isn't that right?"

"Of course it is. Can we talk a little now? Because I do have a few things to say."

"Yes. I want to talk too. Only let's both promise not to fight, all right? It's just not a thing we can afford to fight about."

"I know. Listen. . . ."

And so the way was cleared for the quiet, controlled, dead-serious debate with which they began to fill one after another of the calendar's days, a debate that kept them both in a fine-drawn state of nerves that was not at all unpleasant. It was very like a courtship.

Like a courtship too it took place in a skillfully

arranged variety of settings; Frank saw to that. Their numberless hundreds of thousands of words were spoken indoors and out, on long drives through the hills at night, in expensive country restaurants, and in New York. They had as many evenings out in two weeks as they'd had in the whole previous year, and one of the ways he began to suspect he was winning, early in the second week, was that she didn't object to spending so much money; she almost certainly would have done so if she'd still been wholly committed to Europe in the fall.

But by then he was in little need of such minor indications. Almost from the start he had seized the initiative, and he was reasonably confident of victory. The idea he had to sell, after all, was clearly on the side of the angels. It was unselfish, mature, and (though he tried to avoid moralizing) morally unassailable. The other idea, however she might try to romanticize its bravery, was repugnant.

"But Frank, don't you see I only want to *do* it for your sake? Won't you please believe that, or try to believe it?"

And he would smile sadly down at her from his fortress of conviction. "How can it be for my sake," he would ask, "when the very thought of it makes my stomach turn over? Just think a little, April. Please."

His main tactical problem, in this initial phase of the campaign, was to find ways of making his position

attractive, as well as commendable. The visits to town
and country restaurants were helpful in this connection; she had only to glance around her in such places
to discover a world of handsome, graceful, unquestionably worthwhile men and women who had somehow
managed to transcend their environment—people who
had turned dull jobs to their own advantage, who had
exploited the system without knuckling under to it,
who would certainly tend, if they knew the facts of the
Wheelers' case, to agree with him.

"All right," she would say after hearing him out.
"Supposing all this does happen. Supposing a couple
of years from now we're both terribly sleek and stimu-
lated and all that, and we have loads of fascinating
friends and long vacations in Europe every summer.
Do you really think you'd be any happier? Wouldn't
you still be wasting the prime of your manhood in a
completely empty, meaningless kind of—"

And so she would play straight into his snare:

"Suppose we let that be my business." How much,
he would ask her, would his prime of manhood be
worth if it had to be made conditional on allowing her
to commit a criminal mutilation of herself? "Because
that's what you'd be doing, April; there's no getting
around it. You'd be committing a crime against your
own substance. And mine."

Sometimes, gently, she would charge him with

overdramatizing the whole thing. It was a thing women did every day in perfect safety; the girl at school had done it twice at least. Oh, doing it after the third month would be a different story, she granted him that—"I mean it certainly *would* be legitimate to worry, if that were the case. This way, though, being able to time it so closely and everything, it's the safest thing in the world."

But at her every mention of how safe it was he would puff out his cheeks and blow, frowning and shaking his head, as if he'd been asked to agree that an ethical justification could be found for genocide. No. He wouldn't buy it.

Soon there began to be a slight embarrassed hesitation in her voice and a distinct averting of her eyes whenever she spoke of the abortion as "doing this thing," even in the context of a heartfelt statement on how absolutely essential it was that the thing be done, as if the presence of his loving, troubled face had put the matter beyond the limits of conversational decency. Soon too—and this was the most encouraging sign of all—he began to be aware at odd moments that she was covertly watching him through a mist of romantic admiration.

These moments were not always quite spontaneous; as often as not they followed a subtle effort of vanity on his part, a form of masculine flirtation that was as skillful as any girl's. Walking toward or away from her across a restaurant floor, for example, he remembered always to do it in the old "terrifically sexy" way, and when they walked together he fell into another old habit of holding his head unnaturally erect and carrying his inside shoulder an inch or two higher than the other, to give himself more loftiness from where she clung at his arm. When he lit a cigarette in the dark he was careful to arrange his features in a virile frown before striking and cupping the flame (he knew, from having practiced this at the mirror of a blacked-out bathroom years ago, that it made a swift, intensely dramatic portrait), and he paid scrupulous attention to endless details: keeping his voice low and resonant, keeping his hair brushed and his bitten fingernails out of sight; being always the first one athletically up and out of bed in the morning, so that she might never see his face lying swollen and helpless in sleep.

Sometimes after a particularly conscious display of this kind, as when he found he had made all his molars ache by holding them clamped too long for an effect of grim-jawed determination by candlelight, he would feel a certain distaste with himself for having to resort to such methods—and, very obscurely, with her as well, for being so easily swayed by them. What kind of kid stuff was this? But these attacks of conscience were quickly allayed: all was fair in love and war; and besides, wasn't she all too capable of playing the same game? Hadn't she pulled out everything in her own bag of tricks last month, to seduce him into the Europe plan? All right, then. Maybe it was sort of ludicrous; maybe it wasn't the healthiest way for grown people to behave, but that was a question they could take up later. There was too much at stake to worry about such things now.

And so he freed himself to concentrate on the refinements of his role. He was particularly careful never to mention his day at the office or confess to being tired after the train, he assumed a quiet, almost Continental air of mastery in dealing with waiters and gas station attendants, he salted his after-theater critiques with obscure literary references—all to demonstrate that a man condemned to a life at Knox could still be interesting ("You're the most interesting person I've ever met"); he enthusiastically romped with the children, disdainfully mowed the lawn in record time, and once spent the whole of a midnight's drive in an impersonation of Eddie Cantor singing "That's the Kind of a Baby for Me" because it made her laugh—all to demonstrate that a man confronted with this bleakest and most unnatural of conjugal problems, a wife unwilling to bear his child, could still be nice ("I love you when you're nice").

His campaign might have been quickly and easily won if he could have arranged for all the hours of the four weeks to be lived at the same pitch of intensity; the trouble was that ordinary life still had to go on.

It was still necessary for him to kill most of each day at the office, where Jack Ordway kept congratulating him on the niftiness of his flying the coop, and for her to spend it imprisoned in the reality of their home.

It was also necessary to deal with Mrs. Givings, who lately had found one excuse after another for calling up and dropping in. Her ostensible purpose was business, which in itself was very trying—there were many details to discuss about putting the house on the market, to which the Wheelers had to listen poker-faced—but her talk kept coming back to John and to "the lovely time we all had that day." Almost before they knew it, they had agreed to a tentative program of future Sunday afternoons "whenever it's convenient, whatever Sundays you're not too busy, between now and the time you leave."

It was necessary to deal with the Campbells, too. One whole Saturday was consumed that way, a picnic and outing at the beach undertaken at the Campbells' insistence—a day of hot dogs and children's tears, of sand and sweat and dazzling confusion—and it left them on the brink of hysteria that night. It was that night, in fact, that the courtship, or the sales campaign, or whatever it was, passed abruptly into its second, nonromantic phase.

"*God*, what a day," April said as soon as she'd shut the children's door, and then she began to move stiffly around the living room in a way that always meant trouble. He had learned early in the courtship, or the campaign, that this room was the worst possible place for getting his points across. All the objects revealed in the merciless stare of its hundred-watt light bulbs seemed to support her argument; and more than once, on hot nights like this, their cumulative effect had threatened to topple the whole intricate structure of his advantage: the furniture that had never settled down and never would, the shelves on shelves of unread or half-read or read-and-forgotten books that had always been supposed to make such a difference and never had; the loathsome, gloating maw of the television set; the forlorn, grubby little heap of toys that might have been steeped in ammonia, so quick was their power to attack the eyes and throat with an acrid pain of guilt and self-reproach ("But I don't think we were ever *meant* to be parents. We're not even *adequate* as parents. . . .").

Tonight her forehead, cheekbones, and nose were sorely pink with sunburn, and the fact that she'd worn sunglasses all day gave her eyes a white, astonished look. Her hair hung in disorderly strings—she kept

having to push out her lower lip to blow it away from
her eyes—and her body looked uncomfortable too.
She was wearing a damp blouse and a pair of wrinkled
blue shorts that were just beginning to be tight across
the abdomen. She hated to wear shorts anyway
because they called attention to how heavy and soft
and vein-shot her thighs had grown in the past few
years, though Frank had often told her not to be silly
about it ("They're lovely; I like them even better this
way; they're a woman's legs now"), and now she
seemed almost to be parading them in a kind of spite.
All right, look at them, she seemed to be saying. Are
they "womanly" enough for you? Is this what you
want?

He couldn't, at any rate, take his eyes off them as
they ponderously lifted and settled in her walk around
the room. He made himself a powerful drink and stood
sipping it near the kitchen door, bracing himself.

After a while she sat heavily on the sofa and began a
lethargic picking-over of old magazines. Then she
dropped them and lay back, setting her sneakered feet
on the coffee table, and said, "You really are a much
more moral person than I am, Frank. I suppose that's
why I admire you." But she didn't look or sound
admiring.

He tried to dismiss it with a careful shrug as he
took a seat across from her. "I don't know about that. I

don't see what any of this has to do with being 'moral.'
I mean—*you* know, not in any sense of conventional
morality."

She seemed to think this over for a long time as she
lay back allowing one knee to sway from side to side,
rocking it on the swivel of her ankle. Then: "Is there
any other kind?" she asked. "Don't 'moral' and 'conventional' really mean the same thing?"

He could have hit her in the face. Of all the insinu-
ating, treacherous little—Christ! And in any other
month of his married life he would have been on his
feet and shouting: "*Christ*, when are you going to get
over this damn Noël Coward, nineteen-twenties way
of denigrating every halfway decent human value with
some cute, brittle, snobbish little thing to say? Listen!"
he would have raged at her. "Listen! Maybe that's the
way *your* parents lived; maybe that's the kind of chic,
titillating crap *you* were raised on, but it's about time
you figured out it doesn't have a God damned thing to
do with the real world." It was his knowledge of the
calendar that stopped his mouth. There were twelve
days to go. He couldn't afford to take any chances now,
and so instead of shouting those things he held his jaws
shut and stared at his glass, which he gripped until it
nearly spilled with trembling. Without even trying, he
had given his most memorable facial performance to
date. When the spasm was over he said, very quietly:

"Baby, I know you're tired. We shouldn't be talking about it now. I know you know better than that. Let's skip it."

"Skip what? You know I know better than what?"

"You know. This business about 'moral' and 'conventional.'"

"But I *don't* know the difference." She had come earnestly forward on the sofa, had drawn her sneakers back under it and was leaning toward him with both tense forearms on her knees. Her face was so innocently confused that he couldn't look at it. "Don't you see, Frank? I really *don't* know the difference. Other people seem to; you do; I just don't, that's all, and I don't think I ever really have."

"Look," he said. "First place, 'moral' was your word, not mine. I don't think I've ever held any brief for this thing on moral grounds, conventional or otherwise. I've simply said that under these particular circumstances, it seems pretty obvious that the only mature thing to do is go ahead and have the—"

"But there we are again," she said. "You see? I don't know what 'mature' means, either, and you could talk all night and I still wouldn't know. It's all just *words* to me, Frank. I watch you talking and I think: Isn't that amazing? He really does *think* that way; these words really do *mean* something to him. Sometimes it seems I've been watching people talk and thinking that all my life"—her voice was becoming unsteady—"and maybe it means there's something awful the matter with me, but it's true. Oh no, stay there. Please don't come and kiss me or anything, or we'll just end up in a big steaming heap and we won't get anything settled. Please stay sitting there, and let's just sort of try to talk. Okay?"

"Okay." And he stayed sitting there. But trying to talk was something else again; all they could do was look at each other, heavy and weak and bright-eyed in the heat.

"All I know," she said at last, "is what I feel, and I know what I feel I've got to do."

He got up and turned off all the lights, murmuring "Cool the place off a little," but the darkness didn't help. This was deadlock. If everything he said was "just words," what was the point of talking? How could any possibility of speech prevail against the weight of a stubbornness as deep as this?

But before long his voice had started to work again; almost independent of his will, it had fallen back and begun to employ his final tactic, the dangerous last-ditch maneuver he had hoped to hold in reserve against the possibility of defeat. It was reckless—there were still twelve days to go—but once he had started he couldn't stop.

"Look," he was saying, "this may sound as if I think there *is* something 'awful' the matter with you; the fact is I don't. I do think, though, that there's one or two aspects to this thing we haven't really touched on yet, and I think we ought to. For instance, I wonder if your real motives here are quite as simple as you think. I mean isn't it possible there are forces at work here that you're not entirely aware of? That you're not recognizing?"

She didn't answer, and in the darkness he could only guess at whether she was listening or not. He took a deep breath. "I mean things that have nothing to do with Europe," he said, "or with me. I mean things within yourself, things that have their origin in your own childhood—your own upbringing and so on. Emotional things."

There was a long silence before she said, in a pointedly neutral tone: "You mean I'm emotionally disturbed."

"I didn't say that!" But in the next hour, as his voice went on and on, he managed to say it several times in several different ways. Wasn't it likely, after all, that a girl who'd known nothing but parental rejection from the time of her birth might develop an abiding reluctance to bear children?

"I mean it's always been a wonder to me that you could *survive* a childhood like that," he said at one point, "let alone come out of it without any damage to your— you know, your ego and everything." She herself, he reminded her, had suggested the presence of something "neurotic" in her wish to abort the first pregnancy, on Bethune Street—and all right, all right, of *course* the circumstances were different this time. But wasn't it just possible that something of the same confusion might still exist in her attitude? Oh, he wasn't saying this was the whole story—"I'm not *qualified* to say that"—but he did feel it was a line of reasoning that ought to be very carefully explored.

"But I've *had* two children," she said. "Doesn't that count in my favor?"

He let these words reverberate in the darkness for a while. "The very fact that you put it that way is kind of significant," he said quietly, "don't you think? As if having children were a kind of punishment? As if having two of them could 'count in your favor' as a credit against any obligation to have another? And the way you said it, too—all defensive, all ready to fight. Jesus, April, if you want to talk that way I can come right back at you with another statistic: you've had three pregnancies and you've wanted to abort two of them. What kind of a record is that? Oh, look." He made his voice very gentle, as if he were talking to Jennifer. "Look, baby. All I'm trying to suggest is that you don't seem to be entirely rational about this thing. I just wish you'd think about it a little, that's all."

"All right," her voice said bleakly. "All right, sup-

pose all this is true. Suppose I'm acting out a compul-
sive behavior pattern, or whatever they call it. So
what? I still can't help what I feel, can I? I mean
what're we supposed to *do* about it? How am I supposed to get over it? Am I just supposed to Face Up to
my Problems and start being a different person tomorrow morning, or what?"

"Oh, baby," he said. "It's so simple. I mean assuming you *are* in some kind of emotional difficulty,
assuming there *is* a problem of this sort, don't you see
there *is* something we can do about it? Something very
logical and sensible that we ought to do about it?" He
was weary of the sound of his own voice; he felt he had
been talking for years. He licked his lips, which tasted
as foreign as the flesh of a dentist's finger in his mouth
("Open wide, now!"), and then he said it. "We ought to
have you see a psychoanalyst."

He couldn't see her, but he could guess that her
mouth was flattening out and drawing a little to one
side, her tough look. "And is Bart Pollock's job going
to pay for that too?" she asked.

He issued a sigh. "You see what you're doing, when
you say a thing like that? You're fighting with me."

"No, I'm not."

"Yes you are. And what's worse, you're fighting
with yourself. This is exactly the kind of thing we've
both been doing for years, and it's about time we grew

up enough to cut it out. *I* don't know if Pollock's job is going to pay for it; frankly, I couldn't care less whose job pays for what. We're two supposedly adult human beings, and if one or the other of us needs this kind of help we ought to be able to talk it over in an adult way. The question of how it's going to be 'paid for' is the very least important part of it. If it's needed, it'll be paid for. I promise you."

"How nice." It was only by a dim shifting of shadows and a rustling of upholstery that he could tell she was standing up. "Could we sort of stop talking about it now? I'm dead tired."

As he listened to her receding footsteps down the hall, and then to the sounds of her brief preparations for bed, and then to the silence, he finished his drink with a foretaste of defeat. He felt that he had played his last chance, and had almost certainly lost.

But the next day brought fresh reserves of strength to his position from an unexpected source: it was the Sunday of John Givings's second visit.

"Hi!" he called, getting out of the car, and from the moment he ambled pigeon-toed across the driveway with his parents twitching and apologizing around him, it was clear that this would be a different and more difficult afternoon than the last. There would be no strolling companionship today, no fond remembrance of radio shows; he was in a highly agitated state. The sight and the sound of him was so unnerving, at first, that it was some time before Frank began to see how this visit might have a certain beneficial, cautionary effect. Here, after all, was a full-fledged mental case for April to observe and contemplate. Could she still say, after this, that she didn't care if she was crazy too?

"How soon you people taking off?" he demanded, interrupting his mother in the midst of a rapturous sentence about the magnificence of the day. They were sitting out on the back lawn, where April was serving iced tea—or rather, everyone but John was sitting. He was up and walking around, occasionally pausing to stare with narrowed eyes at some point far away in the woods or past the house and down across the road; he looked as if he were turning over grave and secret issues in his mind. "September, did you say? I don't remember."

"It isn't really definite yet," Frank said.

"You'll be around another month or so, though, anyway; right? Because the thing is, I need to ask somebody for a—" He broke off and glanced around the lawn with a puzzled look. "Hey, by the way, where do you people keep your kids? Old Helen keeps telling me about your kids, and I never see 'em. They go to birthday parties every Sunday, or what?"

"They're visiting friends this afternoon," April said.

John Givings looked at her steadily and long, and then at Frank; then he lowered his eyes, squatted, and began to pull blades of grass out of the lawn. "Well, that figures," he said. "I had a paranoid schizophrenic coming to my house, I'd probably get the kids out of the way too. If I had any kids, that is. If I had any house."

"Oh, this is the most wonderful egg *salad*, April," Mrs. Givings said. "You must tell me how you fix it."

"Save it, Ma, okay? She can tell you later. Listen, though, Wheeler. This is important. The thing is, I need to ask somebody for a favor, and as long as you're going to be around for a month I figure I'd like it to be you. Shouldn't take much of your time, and it won't take any of your money. I wonder if you could get me a lawyer."

Howard Givings cleared his throat. "John, don't let's get started again about the lawyer. Steady down, now."

The look on John's face now was that of reasonable patience tried to the breaking point. "Pop," he said, "couldn't you just sit there and eat your wonderful egg salad, and quit horning in? Turn off your hearing aid or something. Come on," he said to Frank. "I guess we'd better make this a private talk. Oh, and bring your wife too." And with an air of tense conspiracy he led them both away to a far corner of the yard. "There isn't any reason why they shouldn't hear this," he explained; "it's just that they'd keep interrupting all the time. Here's the deal. I want to find out if inmates of mental hospitals have any legal rights. You suppose you could find that out for me?"

"Well," Frank said, "offhand, I'm afraid I don't know how I'd—"

"Okay, okay, forget that part of it. In order to find that out you'd probably have to spend money. All I'm asking you to spend is time. Get me the name and address of a good lawyer, and I'll take it from there. The thing is, you see, I've got a good many questions to ask, and I'm willing to pay for the answers. I think I've got a pretty good case, if we can get around this business of the legal rights. . . ."

It might have been only that his gaze kept switching back and forth between the Wheelers' faces, with intermittent glances over their shoulders to check on what his parents were doing across the lawn—it might have been only that, in combination with the pallor and dryness of his lips and the fact that his hair stood up and out from his scalp in stiff bristles (he hadn't worn his cap today), but as his monologue in the sun progressed he began to look more and more like the picture of a racked, wild-eyed madman.

". . . Now, I don't need to be told that a man who

goes after his mother with a coffee table is putting himself in a weak position legally; that's obvious. If he hits her with it and kills her, that's a criminal case. If all he does is break the coffee table and give her a certain amount of aggravation and she decides to go to court over it, that's a civil case. All right. Either way the man's in a weak position, but here's the point: in neither case is there any question of his own legal rights being jeopardized. Now, supposing the second of these two possibilities takes place. The guy doesn't hit her, does break the coffee table, does give her the aggravation—but the woman, the mother, doesn't exercise her option to take it to court. Supposing what she does instead is to call out the State Troopers. Supposing when she gets hold of the State Troopers she—*Pop!*"

At this apparently meaningless shout he began backing away from them like a cornered fugitive, his face distorted in a mixture of menace and fear; when Frank turned around he saw the reason for this outburst was the slow approach of Howard Givings across the grass.

"*Pop!* I *told* you not to interrupt me, didn't I? Didn't I? I mean it now, Pop. Don't *interrupt* me when I'm *talking*."

"Steady down, boy," Howard Givings said. "Let's steady down, now. It's time to go."

"I *mean* it, Pop—" He had backed himself up

against the stone wall; he was looking desperately around as if for a weapon, and for a second Frank was afraid he might pick a rock out of the wall and throw it; but Howard Givings continued his steady, mollifying advance. He had only to touch his son softly on the elbow to restore a kind of order: John continued to shout, but he was more like a child in a tantrum now than a maniac. "Don't inter*rupt* me, that's all. You got something to say, you can *save* it till I finish *talk*ing."

"All right, John," Howard Givings murmured, turning and leading him away for a quieting stroll along the edge of the lawn. "All right, now, boy."

"Oh, dear," Mrs. Givings said. "I'm terribly sorry about this. It's his nerves, you see." She was looking up at the Wheelers in an agony of embarrassment, unable to decide what to do with the egg salad sandwich in her hand. "I'm afraid you'll have to—excuse us. We shouldn't have come today."

"Lord," April said, washing out the iced-tea glasses when the visitors had gone. "I wonder what *his* childhood was like."

"Couldn't have been very great, I guess, with a pair of parents like that."

She didn't say anything until she had finished at the sink and hung up the dish towel. Then: "But at least he *had* a pair of parents, so at the very least he must have had more emotional security than me. Is that what you're saying?"

"What *I'm* saying? Jesus, take it easy, will you?"

But she had already gone, banging the screen door behind her, to retrieve the children from the Campbells' house. She seemed calm and aloof through the rest of the evening, moving efficiently through the tasks of the dinner and the children's bedtime, and Frank was careful to keep out of her way. It began to appear that this was to be one of their silent nights, one of the times when they would read the papers in different parts of the room like two discreet, courteous strangers in a hotel lobby; but at ten o'clock, without warning, she broke the truce.

"Sort of a denial of womanhood," she said. "Is that how you'd put it?"

"Is that how I'd put what? What're you talking about?"

She looked faintly annoyed, as if impatient with him for having failed to follow the thread of a continuous discussion. "You know. The psychological thing behind this abortion business. Is that what women are supposed to be expressing when they don't want to have children? That they're not really women, or don't want to be women, or something?"

"Baby, I don't know," he said kindly, while his heart

thickened in gratitude. "Believe me, it's a thing about
which your guess is as good as mine. It does sound sort
of logical, though, doesn't it? I do remember reading
somewhere—oh, in Freud or Krafft-Ebing or one of
those people; this was back in college—I do remember
reading something about a woman with a sort of infan-
tile penis-envy thing that carried over into her adult
life; I guess this is supposed to be fairly common
among women; I don't know. Anyway, she kept trying
to get rid of her pregnancies, and what this particular
guy figured out was that she was really trying to sort of
open herself up so that the—you know—so that the
penis could come out and hang down where it
belonged. I'm not sure if I have that right; I read it a
long time ago, but that was the general idea." He wasn't,
in fact, quite sure if he'd read it at all (though where
could it have come from if he hadn't?), and he was not
at all sure it had been a wise thing to relate at this particular time.

But she seemed able to absorb the information
with no particular surprise. She was looking off into
space with her chin in her two cupped hands and
both elbows on her knees. She looked perplexed; that
was all.

"In any case," he went on, "I'm sure it's probably a
mistake to try and draw your own conclusions from the
things you read in books. Who knows?" He decided he

ought to stop there and let her talk for a while, but she didn't say anything, and the silence seemed to demand to be filled.

"I think we *can* assume, though," he said, "just on the basis of common sense, that if most little girls do have this thing about wanting to be boys, they probably get over it in time by observing and admiring and wanting to emulate their mothers—I mean *you* know, attract a man, establish a home, have children, and so on. And in your case, you see, that whole side of life, that whole dimension of experience was denied you from the start. I don't know; all these things are very obscure and hard to—hard to get hold of, I guess."

She got up and walked away to stand near the bookcase, with her back to him, and he was reminded of the way he had first seen her, long ago, across that roomful of forgotten talkers in Morningside Heights—a tall, proud, exceptionally first-rate girl.

"How do you suppose we'd go about finding one?" she asked. "A psychiatrist, I mean. Aren't a lot of them supposed to be quacks? Well, but still, I guess that isn't really much of a problem, is it."

He held his breath.

"Okay," she said. Her eyes were bright with tears as she turned around. "I guess you're right. I guess there isn't much more to say, then, is there?"

He knew, as he lay awake between fitful spells of

sleep beside her, later in the night, that the campaign was by no means over. There were still eleven days before the deadline, in any one of which she might violently change her mind. For eleven more days, whenever he was with her, he would have to keep all the forces of his argument marshaled and ready for instant, skillful use.

His job now was to consolidate this delicate victory in as many ways as possible, to hold the line. It would be best, he decided, to lose no time in letting everyone know about their change of plans—the Campbells, everyone—so that the whole question of the Wheelers going to Europe could quickly be relegated to the past tense; and meanwhile he must allow no hint of complacency to undermine his position. He would have to be constantly on hand as a source of reassurance until the danger period was over. For a start, he decided he would stay home from work today.

TWO

"WE'RE NOT?" Jennifer said that afternoon. She and Michael were standing in their bathing suits on the living room carpet, with towels drawn around their shoulders like cloaks. They'd been playing in the lawn sprinkler, and their mother had called them indoors ostensibly to "dry off for a minute and have some milk and cookies," but also, as it turned out, to hear a formal announcement, from both parents, that they weren't going to France after all. "We're not? How come?"

"Because Daddy and Mommy have decided it would be better not to just now," April said. They had settled on this answer a few minutes before (there was no point in telling them about the baby yet) and the words had a stiff, made-up sound which she tried to counteract by adding, very gently, "That's how come."

"Oh." The total neutrality of expression on both

children's faces was emphasized by the fact that their eyes were still sun-dazed and their lips, under smiling spoors of milk, were blue from having stayed in the water too long. Jennifer lifted one bare foot and used it to scratch a mosquito bite on the ankle of her other leg.

"Is that all you've got to say?" Frank demanded, with a little more heartiness than he'd planned. "Not even 'Hurray' or anything? We thought you'd be pleased."

The children looked briefly at one another and performed bashful smiles. It had become increasingly hard, lately, for either of them to know what was expected. Jennifer wiped away her milk mustache. "Are we going to France later, then, or what?"

"Well," her mother said. "Maybe. We'll see. But we certainly won't be going for a long time, so it's nothing you need to be thinking about any more."

"So we'll be staying here," Jennifer said helpfully, "but not forever and ever."

"That's about right, Niffer. Give Mommy a kiss now, and then how about both of you going out and getting some sun? And try staying out of the water for a while, okay? Your lips are all blue. You can each have a couple more cookies, if you want."

"Know what we can do, Niffer?" Michael said as soon as they were outside again. "Know that place up in the woods where the big tree's fallen over and it's got this little branch you can sit on and make a pretend soda fountain? We can take our cookies up there and you can be the lady coming into the soda fountain and I can be the soda fountain man."

"I don't feel like it."

"Come on. And I'll say 'What would you like to eat today?' And you'll say 'A cookie, please,' and I'll say—"

"I don't *feel* like it, I said. It's too hot." And she sat well away from him on the scorched grass. Why was it "better not to just now"? And why had her mother looked so funny and sad when she said "That's about right"? And why had her father stayed home from work when he wasn't even sick?

When Michael finished eating he ran crazily out along the crest of the front-yard slope, flailing his arms. "Look at me, Niffer, look at me, look at me—I'm falling down dead!" He wobbled and fell, rolled over a few times and lay very flat and still in the grass, giggling to himself at how funny it must have looked. But she wasn't watching. She had walked up close to the picture window and was peeking inside.

They were still sitting on the sofa, leaning a little toward each other, and her mother was nodding and her father was talking. It was funny to see his hands making little gestures in the air and his mouth, moving and moving, with no sound coming out. After a while her mother went away to the kitchen and her father went on sitting there alone. Then he got up and went down to the cellar and came outdoors with his shovel, to work on the stone path.

"Oh, I don't know whether to be sad or glad," said Milly Campbell a few nights later, squirming deep into the sofa cushions. "I mean it's a darn shame and everything for *you* folks, I guess you're awfully disappointed, but I mean personally I'm just as pleased as I can be. Aren't you, sweetie?"

And Shep, after a tremulous sip of gin and tonic that brought the ice cubes clicking painfully against his front teeth, said he sure was.

But the truth was that he wasn't sure of anything. For weeks now, in an effort to put April Wheeler out of his mind, he had drawn solace from a daydream in which ten years had passed: the Wheelers were coming back from Europe, the Campbells were meeting the boat, and from the moment April came down the gang-plank he saw that she'd grown thick and stumpy from her decade of breadwinning. Her cheeks had sagged into jowls, she stood and moved like a man and talked in a sarcastic, squint-eyed way with a cigarette wagging in her lips. Whenever this vision faltered he contented himself with a single-minded cataloguing of her present imperfections (She *was* too heavy across the beam;

her voice *did* get too shrill when she was tense; there *was* something nervous and artificial about her smile), and every time he saw a pretty girl, on the beach or at traffic lights on his daily drive to Stamford and back, he would use her to strengthen his belief that the world was full of better-looking, more intelligent, finer, and more desirable women than April Wheeler. Throughout this period too he had schooled himself to be more than ordinarily fond of Milly. He had paid her numberless little courtly attentions; once he had picked out an expensive blouse at the best shop in Stamford and brought it home to her ("What do you mean, what for? Because you're my girl, that's what for . . ."), and he had enjoyed the impression that she was flowering into a new serenity at his touch.

And now it was all shot to hell. The Wheelers weren't going anywhere. Milly was sitting here chattering about pregnancy and babies, with her new blouse already missing a button and gray around the armpits; April Wheeler was as cool and beautiful as ever. He cleared his throat. "So you figure you'll be staying on here indefinitely, then?" he asked. "Or will you be getting a bigger house, or what?"

"Ah," said Jack Ordway. "So. Foiled by faulty contraception. Well, Franklin, I can't say I'm sorry. You'd have been sorely missed here in the old cubicle, I can promise you that. Besides which"—he leaned elegantly back in his creaking swivel chair and threw one ankle over his knee—"apart from which, if you'll forgive me, the whole European scheme did sound a bit—a tiny bit unrealistic, sort of. None of my business, I'm sure."

"Pull up a chair, uh, Frank," said Bart Pollock. "What's on your mind?"

It was the hottest day of the year, the kind of a day when everyone on the Fifteenth Floor discussed how scandalous it was that a company the size of Knox did not have air conditioning, yet Frank had expected that Pollock's private office, here on the Twentieth, would somehow be cooler. He had imagined too that Pollock would greet him standing up, perhaps striding across the carpet with hand outstretched, and that as soon as the formalities were out of the way ("Frank, I'm tickled to death. . . .") they might adjourn to do business over a brace of Tom Collinses in some air-conditioned cocktail lounge. Instead they were sitting stiff and damp under the irritating buzz of an electric fan. The room was smaller than it looked from the outside, and Pollock, wearing a surprisingly cheap summer shirt through which the outlines of his soaked undershirt were clearly visible, looked more like an exhausted salesman than a top executive. His desk, though appropriately wide and glass-topped, bore as many disorderly piles of paper as Frank's own. Its only ornament suggesting the luxury of rank was a cork-and-silver tray that held a stout little thermos jug for ice water and a tumbler, and a careful inspection of this display revealed that all its elements were finely coated with dust.

"Mm," he said when Frank had finished. "Well, that's fine. I'm personally very glad you've come to this decision. Now of course, as I've told you—" He closed his bulbous eyes and tenderly rubbed their lids. This didn't mean he had forgotten anything; Frank could see that. Everything was all right. It was just that no man could be jubilant in a room like this, on a day like this; and besides, what they were talking about was, after all, a matter of business. "As I mentioned that day at lunch, this whole project's still in the development stage. I'll be calling you in for conferences from time to time as the thing shapes up; meanwhile I'd suggest you keep on with these whaddyacallits, these promotion pieces of yours. I'll give Ted a buzz and tell him you're working on something for me. That's all he'll need to know for the time being. Right?"

"Changed your what?" said Mrs. Givings, frowning fearfully into the black perforations of her telephone.

She was nearing the end of a bleak and very trying day, the whole afternoon of which had been spent at Greenacres—first sitting for unendurable lengths of time on various benches in the waxed and disinfected corridor, waiting for an appointment with John's doctor, then sitting in wretched politeness beside the doctor's desk while he told her that John's behavior in the past several weeks had been "not very encouraging, I'm afraid," and that "I think we'd better call a halt to these outings of his for a while, say five or six weeks."

"But he's been perfectly fine with us," she had lied. "That's what I was going to tell you. Oh, things did get a little out of hand this last time, as I said, but in general he's seemed *very* relaxed. *Very* cheerful."

"Yes. Unfortunately, we can only proceed on the basis of our own, ah, our own observations here in the ward. Tell me, what does his attitude seem to be at the conclusion of the visits? How does he seem to feel about coming back to the hospital each time?"

"He *couldn't* be sweeter about it. Really, Doctor, he's just as willing and cooperative as a lamb."

"Yes." And the doctor had fingered his loathsome tie clasp. "Well, actually, you see, it would probably be a healthier sign if he showed some reluctance. Let's say"—he frowned at his calendar—"let's say at least until the first Sunday in September. Then we might try again."

He might as well have said never. By the first Sunday in September, in all probability, the Wheelers would be on their way to the other side of the world. Now, feeling enormously tired, she had called the Wheelers to cancel the next date they had made—she would have to find other excuses for the other Sundays from now on—and April Wheeler, whose voice sounded small and very far away, was trying to tell her that something was changed. Why did everything always change, when all you wanted, all you had ever humbly asked of whatever God there might be, was that certain things be allowed to remain the same?

"Changed your what? . . ." Then all at once Mrs. Givings was aware of the blood in her veins. ". . . Oh, changed your *plans*. Oh, then you're *not* ready to sell. . . ." and her pencil began to draw a row of black, five-pointed stars across the top of her scratch pad—to draw them with such furious pressure that their joyful shapes were embossed on all the pages underneath. "Oh, I *am* so glad to hear that, April. Really, this is the best news I've had in I don't know how long. So you'll be staying here with us, then. . . ." She was afraid she might begin to cry; but luckily April was apologizing now for "all the trouble you've gone to about putting the house on the market," which allowed her to retreat into the protection of a cool, tolerant businesswoman's chuckle. "Oh, no, please don't mention that. Really, it's been no trouble at all. . . . All right, then. . . . Fine, then, April. . . . Good. We'll be in touch."

When she put the receiver back it was as if she were returning a rare and exquisite jewel to its velvet case.

A bad dream or a shrill bird, or both, woke him much too early in the morning and filled him with a sense of dread—a feeling that his next breath and blink of wakefulness would recall him to the knowledge of a grief, a burden of bad news from yesterday that sleep had only temporarily eased. It took him at least a minute to remember that it was good news, not bad: yesterday had been the last of the first week in August. The deadline had come and gone. The debate was over, and he had won.

He raised himself on one elbow to look at her in the blue light—she was turned away from him with her face hidden under a tangle of hair—and nestled close to her back with his arm around her. He arranged his face in a smile of contentment and his limbs in an attitude of total peace, but it didn't work. Half an hour later he was still awake, wanting a cigarette and watching the sky turn to morning.

The peculiar thing was that in the past week or so they hadn't mentioned it. Each afternoon he had come home ready to intercept whatever last-minute points of argument she might raise—he had even cut down on his drinking, so that his head would be clear for discussion— but each evening they had either talked of other things or hadn't talked at all. Last night she had set up the ironing board in front of the television set and worked there, glancing up every few seconds from the steaming whisk and glide of the iron to peer, frowning, at whatever mottled image was cavorting on the screen.

What do you want to talk for? her profile seemed to be saying, in reply to his uneasy gaze from across the room. What is there to talk about? Haven't we done enough talking?

When she turned off the television and folded up the ironing board at last, he went over and touched her arm.

"You know what this is?"

"What what is? What do you mean?"

"Today. It's the last day of the—you know. If you'd gone ahead with that business, this would've been your last day for doing it."

"Oh. Yes, I suppose that's true."

He patted her shoulder, feeling clumsy. "No regrets?"

"Well," she said, "I guess I'd better not have any, had I? Be a little late for them now, wouldn't it?" She carried the ironing board awkwardly away, one of its legs dangling, and she was all the way to the kitchen door before it occurred to him to help her. He sprang to her side.

"Here, let me take that."

"Oh. Thank you."

And in bed, without a word, they made a sensible, temperate, mature kind of love. The last thing he said before falling asleep was "Listen. We're going to be all right."

"I hope so," she whispered. "I hope so; very much."

Then he had slept, and now he was awake.

He got up and went padding through the silent house. The kitchen was alight with all the colors of the sunrise—it was a beautiful morning—and the calendar had lost its power. There it hung, through the courtesy of A. J. Stolper and Sons, a document useful only in the paying of bills and the making of dental appointments. Days and weeks could pass now without anyone's caring; a month might vanish before anyone thought to tear away the page for the month before.

Franklin H. Wheeler poured himself a glass of ice-cold orange juice, the color of the sun, and sipped it slowly at the kitchen table, afraid it would sicken him to take it all at once. He had won but he didn't feel like a winner. He had successfully righted the course of his life but he felt himself more than ever a victim of the world's indifference. It didn't seem fair.

Only very gradually, there at the table, was he able to sort out and identify what it was that had haunted him on waking, that had threatened to make him gag on his orange juice and now prevented his enjoyment of the brilliant grass and trees and sky beyond the window.

It was that he was going to have another child, and he wasn't at all sure that he wanted one.

"Knowing what you've got, comma," said the living human voice in the playback of the Dictaphone, "knowing what you need, comma, knowing what you can do without, dash. That's inventory control.

"Paragraph . . ."

It was suddenly past the middle of August, and two weeks had elapsed since his last talk with Pollock, or possibly three; time, now that he'd overcome the need to measure and apportion it, had again begun to slip away from him. "You mean to say it's Friday already?" he was apt to demand on what he'd thought was Tuesday or Wednesday, and it wasn't until lunchtime today, when he passed a store window featuring a display of autumn leaves and the words BACK TO SCHOOL, that he realized the summer was over. Very soon now it would be time for topcoats, and then it would be Christmas.

"The main thing I have to do now," he had recently explained to April, "is to finish this Speaking-of series.

I mean I can't very well expect to talk money with him
until I've done that, can I?"

"No; I suppose not. You know best."

"Well, I can't. I mean we can't expect any miraculous changes overnight in a thing like this; it's the kind
of a thing that can't be rushed."

"Do I seem to be rushing you? Really, Frank; how
many ways can I say it? It's entirely up to you."

"I know," he said. "I know, of course I know that.
Anyway, I do want to get the damn series done as soon
as possible. I'll probably stay in late a couple of nights
this week to work on it."

And he'd taken to staying in late nearly every night
since then. He rather enjoyed having dinner alone in
town and taking walks through the city at evening
before catching the late train. It gave him a pleasant
sense of independence, of freedom from the com-
muter's round; and besides, it seemed a suitable practice for the new, mature, non-sentimental kind of
marriage that was evidently going to be their way from
now on.

The only trouble was that this second Speaking-of
piece had turned out to be much harder than the first.
He had finished it twice now, and each time had
discovered gaping errors of logic or emphasis that
seemed to demand a total revision.

The office clock read five-forty-five as he listened to the playback of his third and final revision, and the silence beyond his cubicle proved that even the last and most drearily conscientious people on the Fifteenth Floor had gone home; soon the platoons of scrubwomen would arrive with mops and buckets. When the recording had droned to its conclusion he felt nicely exhilarated. It wasn't very good, but it would do. Now he could take off uptown and have a couple of drinks before dinner.

He was in the act of leaning over to shut off the machine when the click, click, click of a woman's heels came delicately up the aisle outside. He knew at once that it was Maureen Grube, that she had purposely stayed late in order to be alone with him, and that he was going to take her out tonight. It seemed important not to look openly into the aisle as she passed; instead he remained hunched over the Dictaphone, peeking at the doorway from cover. It was Maureen, all right; the quick glimpse he caught of her was more than enough to confirm that. It was enough to show him that an inch of petticoat was switching nicely through a vent in the hem of her skirt with every step and that her face, as subtly averted as his own, had not quite dared to glance in at him.

Her footsteps receded, and as he waited confidently for their return he reset the machine to the "start" position and leaned back in his chair to listen. That way he could be staring frankly into the aisle, yet quite legitimately occupied with business, when she came by again.

"Copy for Veritype," the Dictaphone said. "Title: Speaking of Inventory Control, parenthesis, revision three. Paragraph. Knowing what you've got, comma, knowing what you need, comma, knowing what you can do without, dash. That's—"

"Oh." She had stopped directly in his line of vision, and her careful expression of surprise was somewhat vitiated by the deep, permanent-looking blush that had suffused her face and neck. "Hello, Frank. Working late?"

He shut off the machine and got slowly to his feet, moving toward her with the loose, almost sleepy gait of a man who knows exactly what he's doing.

"Hi," he said.

THREE

EVERY FRIDAY AND SATURDAY NIGHT, "For Your Dancing Pleasure," the Steve Kovick Quartet played at Vito's Log Cabin, on Route Twelve, and on those two nights (as Steve himself liked to say, winking over the rim of his rye-and-ginger) the joint really jumped.

Piano, bass, tenor sax, and drums, they prided themselves on versatility. They could play anything, in any style you wanted to name, and to judge from the delight that swam in their eyes they had no idea of what inferior musicians they were. In the three supporting members of the Quartet this lack of discernment could be excused on the grounds of inexperience or amateurism or both, but it was harder to condone in their leader, who played the drums. A thick, blunt, blue-jawed man, getting on for forty now, he had been a professional for twenty years without ever quite learning his craft. Artistically awakened and nourished by the early recordings and movies of Gene Krupa, he had spent the only happy hours of his youth in a trance of hero-worshiping imitation—first intently slapping telephone books and overturned dishpans, later using a real set of drums in the sweat and liniment smells of the high-school gym—until one June night in his senior year when the rest of the band stopped playing, the hundreds of couples stood still, and Steve Kovick felt the weight of all their rapture on his wagging, chewing head while he beat it out for three solid minutes. But the splendid crash of cymbals with which he ended that performance marked the pinnacle and ruin of his talent. He would never drum that well again, he would never again kindle that much admiration, nor would he ever again lose his frantic grip on the conviction that he was great and getting better all the time. Even now, at a rundown beer-and-pizza joint like Vito's Log Cabin, there was a negligent grandeur in the way he took the stand, the way he frowned over the arrangement of sticks and brushes and hi-hat cymbals and then peered out, beetle-browed, to ask if the spotlight could be adjusted a fraction of an inch before he settled down; and there was elaborate condescension in the way he whisked and thumped through preliminary fox trots or handled the gourds for Latin-American interludes; anyone could tell he was only marking time, waiting for the moment when he could tell the boys to cut loose on one of the old-time Benny Goodman jump numbers.

Only then, once or twice an hour, did he give himself wholly to his work. Socking the bass drum as if to box the ears of every customer in the house, doing his damnedest on snare and tom-tom, he would take off in a triumph of misplaced virtuosity that went relentlessly on and on until it drenched his hair with sweat and left him weak and happy as a child.

The patrons of the Log Cabin on dance nights were mostly high-school seniors (it was the corniest band in the world but the only live music for miles around; besides, there wasn't any cover and they'd serve you without proof of age and the big parking lot was nice and dark) and a smattering of local storekeepers and contractors who sat in a state of constant laughter with their arms around their wives, remarking on how young it made them feel to watch these kids enjoying themselves. There was an occasional tough element, too, boys in black leather jackets and boots who slouched in the urine-smelling corner near the men's room with their thumbs in their jeans, watching the girls with menacingly narrow eyes and taking repeated trips to the toilet to comb and recomb their hair; and there were the regulars, lonely and middle-aged and apparently homeless, the single or inadequately married people who came to the Log

Cabin every night, music or not, to drink and sentimentalize under the fly-blown, joke-hung mirror of its
rustic bar.

Not infrequently, over the past two years, the
dance night crowd had included a party of four
intensely humorous young adults who belonged to no
discernible group at all: the Campbells and the Wheelers. Frank had discovered the place soon after moving
to the country—had discovered it in search of drunk-
enness one night after a quarrel with his wife, and been
quick to bring her back for dancing as soon as things
were happier.

"You people ever been to the Log Cabin?" he had
asked the Campbells early in their acquaintance, and
April had said, "Oh *no*, darling; they'd hate it. It's terrible." The Campbells had looked from one to the other
of their faces with uncertain smiles, ready to hate it or
love it or espouse whatever other opinion of it might
please the Wheelers most.

"No, I don't think they'd hate it," Frank had
insisted. "I bet they'd like it. It takes a special kind of
taste, is all. I mean the thing about the Log Cabin, you
see," he explained to them at last, "is that it's so awful
it's kind of nice."

At first, through the spring and summer of 1953,
the four of them had come here only once in a while,
as a kind of comic relief from more ambitious forms of

entertainment; but by the following summer they had
fallen into it like a cheap, bad habit, and it was their
awareness of this particular degeneration, as much as
any other, that had made the idea of the Laurel Players
uncommonly attractive last winter. When *The Petrified
Forest* went into rehearsal their attendance at the Log
Cabin dwindled sharply (there were other, quieter
places to stop for drinks on the way home from the
school), and in the long uneasy time since the failure of
the play they had not come here at all—almost as if to
do so would have constituted an admission of moral
defeat.

But "What the hell," Frank had said this evening,
after every conversational attempt in the Campbells'
living room had petered out and died, "why don't we
all break down and go to the Log Cabin?"

And here they were, a quiet foursome ordering
round after round of drinks, getting up and coupling
off to dance, coming back and sitting silent under the
blast of the jump numbers. But for all its awkwardness
the evening was oddly free of tension, or so at least it
seemed to Frank. April was as aloof and enigmatic, as
far away from the party as she'd ever been in the worst
of the old days, but the difference was that now he
refused to worry about it. In the old days he might
have talked and laughed himself sick trying to win an
affectionate smile from her, or trying by sheer vivacity

to make up for her rudeness to the Campbells (because that was what it did amount to, sitting there like some long-necked, heavy-lidded queen among commoners—plain damn rudeness); instead he was content to relax in his chair, one hand lightly tapping the table to Steve Kovick's beat, and perform the minimal pleasantries while thinking his own thoughts.

Was his wife unhappy? That was unfortunate, but it was, after all, her problem. He had a few problems too. This crisp way of thinking, unencumbered by guilt or confusion, was as new and as comfortable as his lightweight autumn suit (a wool gabardine in a pleasingly dark shade of tan, a younger and more taste-ful, junior-executive version of the suit Bart Pollock wore). The resumption of the business with Maureen had helped him toward a renewal of self-esteem, so that the face he saw in passing mirrors these days gave him back a level, unembarrassed glance. It was hardly a hero's face but neither was it a self-pitying boy's or a wretchedly anxious husband's; it was the steady, con-trolled face of a man with a few things on his mind, and he rather liked it. The business with Maureen would have to be brought to a graceful conclusion soon—it had served its purpose—but in the meantime he felt he was entitled to savor it. That, in fact, was what he was doing now, allowing the erotic thump of Steve Kovick's tom-tom to remind him of her hips, gazing wryly off into the swirl of dancers as he gave in to voluptuous memories.

For the last three times, evenings when they couldn't use her apartment because her roommate was home, she had agreed with surprising alacrity to let him take her to a hotel. Anonymous and safe behind a double-locked door in an air-conditioned tower, they had dined on room-service lamb chops and wine while the sound of midtown traffic floated up from twenty stories below; they had reveled in the depths of a long, wide bed and lathered themselves clean in a steaming palace of a bathroom stocked with acres of towels; and each time, when he'd handed her into a taxi at last and turned alone toward Grand Central, he had wanted to laugh aloud at having so perfectly fulfilled the standard daydream of the married man. No fuss, no complications, everything left behind in a tumbled room under somebody else's name, and all of it wound up in time to catch the ten-seventeen. It was too good to be true, like the improbable stories that older, more experienced soldiers had once told him of three-day passes with Red Cross girls. It couldn't go on much longer, of course, and it wouldn't. In the meantime . . .

In the meantime, all during the next slow tune and the one after that, he cordially danced with Milly Campbell. She made a damp, untidy package in his arms and she talked inanely ("Gosh, you know something, Frank? I don't think I've had this much to drink in years and years and years . . ."), but he was afraid that if he danced with April now she would only say, "This is horrible; please let's go home," and he didn't feel like it. He wouldn't have minded going home alone, if such a thing were possible (he had a pleasant vision of himself preparing neatly for bed with book and nightcap, bachelor style); otherwise he was happy enough to stay in this jumbled, lively place where the drinks were cheap and the band was loud and he could feel the inner peace that comes from knowing that all your clothes are new and perfectly fitted.

"Gosh. Gee, Frank, I'm afraid I'm not very— excuse me a second." Milly lurched pathetically away toward the ladies' room, which gave him an opportunity to have a dignified drink alone at the bar. When she came out, a long time later, she looked exhausted and gray under the blue lights. "Gosh." She tried to smile, giving off a faint scent of vomit. "I guess Shep and I'd better sort of go home, Frank. I think I must be sick or something. I guess I'm being an awful party-poop; you must think I'm—"

"No, don't be silly. Just hold on a second and I'll get Shep." He peered dizzily into the swaying roomful of dancers until he picked out Campbell's big red neck and April's small head moving along the far wall; he gave them an urgent beckoning signal, and soon they were all four crunching in the gravel outside, wandering lost in a dark sea of automobiles.

"Which way . . . ?"

"This way. . . . Over here. . . ."

"You okay, honey?"

"It's so *dark*. . . ."

The slick, chin-high tops of the cars made an undulating surface that stretched away into the darkness in all directions; beneath it stood endless shadowy ranks of fenders and fins, of intricately bulbous bumpers and grills alive with numberless points of reflected neon. Once, when Frank bent over to strike a match for guidance, the flame caused a writhing recoil of human flesh only inches away from his face—he had startled a pair of lovers in one of the cars—and he hurried into the darkness of the next aisle, saying, "Where the hell *did* we leave the damn cars, then? Does anybody remember?"

"Here," Shep called. "Over here in the last row. Oh, but Jesus, look. Mine's blocked in." He had backed his big Pontiac against a tree, hours before. Now two other cars stood directly in front of it and there was no room for maneuvering on either side.

"Lord, what a mess. . . ."

"Of all the inconsiderate . . ."

"Damn that tree. . . ."

"Well, look, though," Frank said. "We've still got

one car free; we could run Milly home and bring Shep back, and maybe by that time the car'll be—"

"But it might take *hours*," Milly said weakly, "and meantime your sitter'll be costing you a fortune. Oh dear."

"No, hold it," Shep said. "We can all go home in your car; then I'll borrow your car and come back and—or no, wait—"

"Oh, look." April's voice cut through the confusion with such sober authority that they all stopped talking. "It's perfectly simple. You take Milly home, Frank, and go on home yourself—that takes care of both sitters— and Shep and I can wait till the other car's free. That's the only logical way."

"Fine," Frank said, moving away with his car keys out and ready. "All agreed, then?"

The next thing Shep Campbell knew, the taillights of the Wheelers' car were winking away down Route Twelve and he was walking back toward the Log Cabin (which throbbed now to a slow, sentimental waltz) with April's slender elbow in his hand. In all his guilty fantasies he could never have plotted a better way of finding himself alone with her, and the funny part was that he hadn't even had to arrange it: it had happened because it was the only logical—or no, wait a minute.

His fuddled mind worked hard to sort it out as they mounted the steps under red and blue lights. Wait a minute—why couldn't *she* have taken Milly home, and left Frank behind? Wouldn't that have been logical too?

By the time he'd worked it out that far they were back on the brink of the dance floor; she had turned to him gravely with her eyes fixed on his right lapel, and the only thing to do was take her lightly around the waist and go on dancing. He couldn't ask her if she'd planned it this way without being a fool, and he couldn't assume she had without being a bigger one. Allowing his fingers to spread out very shyly on the small of her back and his hot cheek to rest against her hair, he moved to the music and was humbly grateful that the thing had happened; never mind how.

It was like the other time here last summer, but it was much, much better. The other time she'd been drunk, for one thing, and he had known even as he miserably pressed and mauled her that it was strictly a one-way deal: she'd been too far gone to know how much she was giving him, and the proof of it was the way she'd kept arching back her neck to talk and chatter in his face as if they were sitting across a bridge table or some damn thing, instead of locked as tight as lovers from the collarbone down. This time she was sober, she hardly talked at all, and she seemed as sensitive as he was to every tactile subtlety, every tentative seeking and granting and shy withdrawal and seeking again; it was almost more than his bashful heart could stand.

"Feel like another drink?"

"All right."

But as they stood at the bar, self-consciously sipping and puffing cigarettes among the regulars, he couldn't think of anything to say. He felt like a boy on his first date, crippled by the secret, ignorant desire of virginity; he was sweating.

"Tell you what," he said at last, almost roughly. "I'll go check the car." And he promised himself that if she gave the slightest hint, if she smiled and said "What's your hurry, Shep?" or anything like that, he would forget everything—his wife, his fear, everything—and go for her all the way.

There was nothing in her gray eyes to suggest complicity: they were the eyes of a pleasant, tired young suburban matron who'd been kept up past her bedtime, that was all. "Yes, all right," she said. "Why don't you?"

Stumbling down the wooden steps and out into the darkness, grinding the pebbles fiercely under his heels, he felt all the forces of the plausible, the predictable, and the ordinary envelop him like ropes. Nothing was going to happen; and the hell with her. Why wasn't she home where she belonged? Why couldn't she go to Europe or disappear or die? The hell with this aching, suffering, callow, half-assed delusion that he was in "love" with her. The hell with "love" anyway, and with every other phony, time-wasting, half-assed emotion in the world. But by the time he'd reached the last row he was jelly-kneed and trembling in a silent prayer: Oh God, please don't let the car be free.

And it wasn't. The other cars still held it fast against the tree. As he whirled back to face the building its lights careened in his head and he nearly keeled over. He was loaded. That last drink must have really—Wow. His lungs felt very shallow, and he knew that unless something could be done at once to stop the lights from sliding around that way he would be sick. He began running in place, pumping his fists and bringing his knees up high, his shoes making brisk, athletic sounds in the gravel. He did that until he'd counted a hundred, taking deep breaths, and when he was finished the lights held still. He felt chastened and full of blood as he walked back to the Log Cabin, where the Quartet had broken into its own crude version of one of the old-time, big-band numbers—"One O'Clock Jump" or "String of Pearls" or something, the kind of music that always took him back to basic training.

She had left the bar for one of the dark leatherette

booths nearby; she was sitting very straight in its deep seat, partly turned around to watch for him through the smoke, and she greeted him with a shyly welcoming smile.

"Still blocked in, I'm afraid," he said.

"Oh, well. Come and sit a minute. I don't really mind, do you?"

He could have crawled across the leatherette seat and buried his head in her lap. What he did instead was to slide in as close beside her as he dared and begin to tear up a cardboard match in the ash tray, splitting it at the base with his thumbnail and carefully peeling it down in strips, frowning as intently as a watchmaker over his work.

She was gazing off into the blur of the dance floor, moving her uptilted head very slightly to the rhythm of the band. "This is the kind of music that's supposed to make everybody our age very nostalgic," she said. "Does it you?"

"I don't know. Not really, I guess."

"It doesn't me, either. I'd like it to, but it doesn't. It's supposed to remind you of all your careless teen-age raptures, and the trouble is I never had any. I never even had a real date until after the war, and by then nobody played this kind of music any more, or if they did I was too busy being blasé to notice it. That whole big-band swing period was a thing I missed out on.

Jitterbugging. Trucking on down. Or no, that was earlier, wasn't it? I think people talked about trucking on down when I was in about the sixth grade, at Rye Country Day. At least I remember writing 'Artie Shaw' and 'Benny Goodman' all over the sides of my schoolbooks without quite being sure who they were, because some of the older girls used to have those names on their books and it seemed a terribly sophisticated thing to do, like putting dabs of nail polish on your ankles to hold your bobby socks up. God, how I wanted to be seventeen when I was twelve. I used to watch the seventeen-year-olds getting into cars and riding away with boys after school, and I was absolutely certain they had the answers to everything."

Shep was watching her face so closely that everything else vanished from his consciousness. It didn't even matter what she was saying, nor did he care that she was talking to herself as much as to him.

"And then by the time *I* turned seventeen I was shut up in this very grim boarding school, and the only times I ever really jitterbugged were with another girl, in the locker room. We'd play Glenn Miller records on this old portable Victrola she had, and we'd practice and practice by the hour. And that's all this kind of music can ever really remind me of—bouncing around in my horrible gym suit in that sweaty old locker room and being convinced that life had passed me by."

"That's hard to believe."

"What is?"

"That you never had any dates or anything, all that time."

"Why?"

He wanted to say, "Oh God, April, you know why. Because you're lovely; because everyone must have loved you, always," but he lacked the courage. Instead he said, "Well, I mean, hell; didn't you ever have fun on vacations?"

"Fun on vacations," she repeated dully. "No. I never did. And now you see you've put your finger on it, Shep. I can't very well blame boarding school for that, can I? No, all I ever did on vacations was read and go to movies by myself and quarrel with whichever aunt or cousin or friend of my mother's it was who happened to be stuck with me that summer, or that Christmas. It all does tend to sound pretty malad-justed, doesn't it? So you're quite right. It wasn't boarding school's fault and it wasn't anyone else's fault, it was my own Emotional Problem. And there's a fairly good rule-of-thumb for you, Shep: take somebody who worries about life passing them by, and the chances are about a hundred-and-eight to one that it's their own Emotional Problem."

"I didn't mean anything like that," Shep said uncomfortably. He didn't like the sardonic lines that had appeared at the pulled-down corner of her mouth, or the way her voice had flattened out, or the way she clawed a cigarette out of the pack and stuck it in her lips—these things were too close to the cruel image he had projected of her ten years from now. "I just meant, I never would've pictured you being that lonely."

"Good," she said. "Bless you, Shep. I always hoped people wouldn't picture me being that lonely. That was really the best thing about being in New York after the war, you see. People didn't."

Now that she'd mentioned her life in New York he was yearning to ask a question that had morbidly haunted him as long as he'd known her: had she still been a virgin when she met Frank? If not, it would somehow lessen his envy; if so, if he had to think of Frank Wheeler as her first lover as well as her husband, he felt it would make his envy too great to be borne. This was the closest he had ever come to an opportunity for finding out, but if words existed to make the question possible they had hopelessly eluded him. He would never know.

". . . Oh, it was fun, I suppose, those years," she was saying. "I always think of that as a happy, stimulating time, and I suppose it was, but even so." Her voice wasn't flat any more. "I still felt—I don't know."

"You still felt that life was passing you by?"

"Sort of. I still had this idea that there was a whole

world of marvelous golden people somewhere, as far ahead of me as the seniors at Rye when I was in sixth grade; people who knew everything instinctively, who made their lives work out the way they wanted without even trying, who never had to make the best of a bad job because it never occurred to them to do anything less than perfectly the first time. Sort of heroic super-people, all of them beautiful and witty and calm and kind, and I always imagined that when I did find them I'd suddenly know that I belonged among them, that I was one of them, that I'd been meant to be one of them all along, and everything in the meantime had been a mistake; and they'd know it too. I'd be like the ugly duckling among the swans."

Shep was looking steadily at her profile, hoping the silent force of his love would move her to turn and face him. "I think I know that feeling," he said.

"I doubt it." She didn't look at him, and the little lines had appeared again around her mouth. "At least I hope you don't, for your sake. It's a thing I wouldn't wish on anybody. It's the most stupid, ruinous kind of self-deception there is, and it gets you into nothing but trouble."

He let all the air out of his lungs and subsided against the back of the seat. She didn't really want to talk; not to him, anyway. All she wanted was to sound off, to make herself feel better by playing at being

wistful and jaded, and she had elected him as her audience. He wasn't expected to participate in this discussion, and he certainly wasn't to go getting any ideas;
his role was to be big, dumb, steady old Shep until the
car was free, or until she'd gotten all the gratification
there was to be had from the sound of her own voice.
Then he'd drive her home and she'd make a few more
worldly-wise pronouncements on the way; she might
even lean over and give him a sisterly peck on the
cheek before she slithered out of the car and slammed
the door and went inside to get into bed with Frank
Wheeler. And what the hell else did he expect? When
the hell was he ever going to grow up?

"Shep?" Both of her slim, cool hands had reached
out and grasped one of his on the table, and her face,
pressing toward him, was transformed into a mischie-
vous smile. "Oh, Shep—let's do it."

He thought he was going to faint. "Do what?"

"Jitterbug. Come on."

Steve Kovick was nearing the climax of his evening. It was almost closing time; most of the people had
gone home, the manager was counting his money, and
Steve, no less than the hero of every Hollywood movie
ever made about jazz, knew that this was the approach
of what was supposed to be his finest hour.

Shep had never really learned to dance, let alone to

abandon himself to this kind of dancing, but no power
on earth could have stopped him now. Turning, clumsily hopping and shuffling in the enchanted center of
that dizzy room, he allowed the noise and the smoke
and the lights to revolve and revolve around him
because he was wholly certain of her now. As long as
he lived he would never see anything more beautiful
than the way she reeled away as far as their joined
hands would allow and did a quick little bobbing, hip-
switching curtsy out there before she came twisting
back. Oh, look at her! his heart sang, Look at her!
Look at her! He knew that when the music stopped
she would fall laughing in his arms, and she did. He
knew, leading her tenderly away to the bar, that she
would allow his arm to stay close around her while
they had another drink, and she did that too. As they
talked there in suggestively low voices he no longer
cared what he was saying—what did it matter? What
did words amount to, anyway?—because he was full of
delirious plans. A motel sprang up in his mind's eye: he
saw himself filling out the registry form in the glare of
its clapboard office ("Thank *you*, sir. That'll be six-
fifty, Number Twelve . . .") while she sat waiting in the
car outside; he pictured the abrupt, shockingly total
privacy of the cabin with its maple chair and desk and
staring double bed, and here he was briefly troubled:

Could you really take a girl like April Wheeler to a
motel? But why not? And besides, a motel wasn't the
only possibility. Miles and miles of open country lay
waiting in all directions; the night was warm and he
had an old army poncho in the car; they could climb to
some gentle pasture high out of sight and sound and
make their bed among the stars.

It started in the parking lot, in the darkness less than
ten yards away from the red- and blue-lighted steps. He
stopped and let her turn against him in his arms, and
then her crushed lips were opening under his mouth
and her hands slid up and around his neck as he pressed
her back against the fender of a parked car. They broke
apart and came together again; then he led her swaying
and stumbling out across the lot—it was nearly empty
now—to the place where the chromework of his Pontiac, all alone, caught faint glimmers of starlight under
the whispering black trees. He found the right-hand
door and helped her in; then he walked in a correct,
unhurried way around the hood to the driver's side. The
door slammed behind him and there were her arms and
her mouth again, there was the feel and the taste of her,
and his fingers were finding miraculous ways to unfas-
ten her clothing, and there was her rising breast in his
hand. "Oh, April. Oh My God, I—Oh, April . . ."

The noise of their breathing had deafened them to
all other sounds: the loud insects that sang near the car,

the drone of traffic on Route Twelve and the fainter sounds from the Log Cabin—a woman's shrieking laugh dissolving into the music of horn and piano and drums.

"Honey, wait. Let me take you somewhere—we've got to get out of—"

"No. Please," she whispered. "Here. Now. In the back seat."

And the back seat was where it happened. Cramped and struggling for purchase in the darkness, deep in the mingled scents of gasoline and children's overshoes and Pontiac upholstery, while a delicate breeze brought wave on wave of Steve Kovick's final drum solo of the night, Shep Campbell found and claimed the fulfillment of his love at last.

"Oh, April," he said when he was finished, when he had tenderly disengaged and rearranged her, when he had helped her to lie small and alone on the seat with his wadded coat for a pillow and bunched himself into an awkward squat on the floor boards, holding both her hands, "Oh, April, this isn't just a thing that happened. Listen. This is what I've always—I love you."

"No. Don't say that."

"But it's true. I've always loved you. I'm not just being—listen."

"Please, Shep. Let's just be quiet for a minute, and then you can take me home."

With a little shock he thought of what he'd steadfastly put out of his mind all evening, what had occurred to him briefly and not at all as a deterrent in the heat of his desire, and now for the first time began to take on an oppressive moral weight: she was pregnant. "Okay," he said, "I'm not forgetting anything." He freed one of his hands to rub his eyes and his mouth with vigor, and then he sighed. "I guess you must think I'm kind of an idiot or something."

"Shep, it's not that."

There was just enough light to show him where her face was, not enough for him to see its expression or even to tell whether it had any expression at all.

"It's not that. Honestly. It's just that I don't know who you are."

There was a silence. "Don't talk riddles," he whispered.

"I'm not. I really don't know who you are."

If he couldn't see her face, at least he could touch it. He did so with a blind man's delicacy, drawing his fingertips from her temple down into the hollow of her cheek.

"And even if I did," she said, "I'm afraid it wouldn't help, because you see I don't know who I am, either."

FOUR

WALKING AWAY FROM THE HISS and whine of a Sixth
Avenue bus, three or four days later, Frank Wheeler
moved with a jaunty resignation toward Maureen
Grube's street. He didn't especially feel like seeing her
tonight, and this, he knew, was as it should be. The purpose of this visit was to break the thing off, and any
impulsive eagerness for the sight of her would have been
disconcerting. It always surprised and pleased him when
his mood coincided with the nature of the thing he had
to do, and this rare state had lately become almost habitual. He had been able, for instance, to wrap up all the
rest of his Speaking-of series in little more than a day's
work apiece. *Speaking of Sales Analysis*, *Speaking of Cost
Accounting*, and *Speaking of Payroll*—all now lay safely
finished along with *Production* and *Inventory Control*, in a
handsome cardboard folder on Bart Pollock's desk.

"Well, Frank, these are fine," Pollock had said yesterday, riffling the folder with his thumb. "And fortunately, I've got some good news for you this morning." The good news, which Frank was able to receive with perfect composure, was that plans for Pollock's project had now been "finalized." There would be an "informal shakedown conference" next Monday, at which Frank would join his new colleagues in helping to "block out a few objectives," and after which he could consider himself no longer a member of Bandy's staff. Meanwhile, it was now "time for the two of us to get together here on the matter of salary." No nervous sweat broke out inside Frank's shirt as they got together on it, and no ludicrous ghost of Earl Wheeler hung over the proceedings. His eyes never strayed in dismal aesthetic searching among Pollock's office fixtures, nor was he plagued with cautionary thoughts of what April might say. It was strictly business. He was richer by three thousand a year after shaking Pollock's thick hand that morning—a sound, satisfactory amount that would provide, among other things, a comfortable fund against which to draw for the costs of obstetrics and psychoanalysis.

"Good," April said on hearing the figure. "That's about what you expected, isn't it?"

"Just about, yes. Anyway, it's nice to have the thing settled."

"Yes. I imagine it must be."

And now, having so competently arranged his business affairs, he could give his full attention to personal matters—which did, at the moment, need considerable straightening out. For the past two nights, or three, his marriage had taken that technical turn for the worse which, in the old days, would have filled him with anguish: April had begun to sleep in the living room again. But these, thank God, were not the old days. This time it hadn't come about as the result of a fight, for one thing, and it wasn't accompanied by any apparent rancor on her part.

"I haven't been sleeping at all well," she had announced the first night, "and I think I'd be more comfortable alone."

"Okay." He had assumed, though, that it was an arrangement for that night only, and he was nettled the following evening, when she again came trudging from the linen closet with an armload of bedclothes and began making the sofa into a bed.

"What's the deal?" he asked mildly, leaning against the kitchen doorjamb with a drink in his hand while she flapped and spread the sheets. "You sore at me, or what?"

"No. Of course I'm not 'sore' at you."

"You planning to go on doing this indefinitely, or what?"

"I don't know. I'm sorry if it upsets you."

He took his time in replying, first lazily dunking the ice cubes in his glass with a forefinger, then licking the finger, then moving away from the door with a luxuriantly tired shrug. "No," he said. "It doesn't upset me. I'm sorry you're not sleeping well."

And that, of course, was the other, the really important difference: it *didn't* upset him. It annoyed him slightly, but it didn't upset him. Why should it? It was her problem. What boundless reaches of good health, what a wealth of peace there was in this new-found ability to sort out and identify the facts of their separate personalities—this is my problem, that's your problem. The pressures of the past few months had brought them each through a kind of crisis; he could see that now. This was their time of convalescence, during which a certain remoteness from each other's concerns was certainly natural enough, and probably a good sign. He knew, sympathetically, that in her case the adjustment must be especially hard; if it caused her periods of moodiness and insomnia, that was perfectly understandable. In any case, the time was now at hand when he could, in the only mature sense, be of help to her. Next week, or as soon as possible, he would take whatever steps were necessary in lining up a reputable analyst; and he could already foresee his preliminary discussions with the man, whom he pictured as owlish and slow-spoken, possibly Viennese ("I think your own evaluation of the difficulty is essentially correct, Mr. Wheeler. We can't as yet predict how extensive a course of therapy will be indicated, but I can assure you of this: with your continued cooperation and understanding, there is every reason to hope for rapid . . .").

In the meantime, the main task before him was to put an end to the business with Maureen. He would much rather have been able to do it in a bar or a coffee shop uptown; that was what he'd had in mind this morning, when he'd cornered her in an alcove of the central file to make this date, but, "No, come to my place," she had whispered over the spread folder they were using as camouflage. "Norma's leaving early, and I'll fix supper for us."

"No, really," he said. "I'd rather not. The thing is—" He would have said, "The thing is I want to have a talk with you," but her eyes frightened him. What if she should begin to cry or something, right here in the office? Instead he said, "I don't want you to go to any trouble," which was true too; but in the end he had agreed.

The scene of the talk probably didn't matter; the important thing was the talk itself, and the only really important thing about that was to make it definite and final. There was, he assured himself for the hundredth time, nothing to be apologetic about. It depressed him to consider how much energy he had wasted, over the years, in the self-denying posture of apology. From now on, whatever else his life might hold, there would be no more apologies.

"Excuse me," called a woman's voice from the curb. "You're Mr. Frank Wheeler, aren't you?" She was coming toward him across the sidewalk, carrying a small suitcase, and he knew at once who she was from the predatory quality of her smile. She had caught him with his foot on the first of the pink stone steps of Maureen's building.

"I'm Norma Townsend, Maureen's roommate. I wonder if I could have a word with you."

"Sure." He didn't budge. "What can I do for you?"

"Please." She tilted her head slightly to one side as if to reprove a sullen child. "Not here." And she moved past him toward an arty little espresso lounge two doors away. There was nothing to do but follow her, but he atoned for his meekness by staring critically at her tense, quivering buttocks. She was solid and duck-footed, wearing a modishly tubular dress, a "sheath," in defiance of the fact that it emphasized her breadth and muscularity, and she trailed a perfume that had probably been described as Dark and Exciting in its point-of-sale display at Lord and Taylor's.

"I won't keep you a minute," she said when she had

him cornered at a small marble-topped table, when she'd arranged the suitcase at her feet, ordered a sweet vermouth, and put her hands through the series of clicking, snapping, and organizing motions required in the job of removing a pack of cigarettes from her complicated handbag. "I've just time for an *apéritif*, and then I must run. I'm off to the Cape for two weeks. Maureen *was* coming with me, but she's changed her plans. She now intends to spend her entire vacation here, as I expect you know. *I* didn't know until last night, which I'm afraid does put me in a rather awkward position with the friends we were to visit. Are you sure you won't have a drink?"

"No thanks." He had to admit, watching her, that she wasn't unattractive. If she could loosen her hair instead of skinning it back, if she could take off a little weight through the cheeks . . . but then he decided she would have to do more than that. She would have to learn not to move her eyebrows so much when she talked, and she would certainly have to get over saying things like "I've just time for an *apéritif*" and "I'm off to the Cape."

"I happen to be very annoyed with Maureen at the moment," she was saying. "This vacation mix-up is only the latest in a long line of foolishness, but that's beside the point. The main thing"—and here she looked at him keenly—"the important thing, is that

I'm very deeply concerned about her too. I've known her a good deal longer and I believe I know her better than you do, Mr. Wheeler. She's a very young, very insecure, very sweet kid, and she's gone through a lot of hell in the past few years. Right now she needs guidance and she needs friendship. On the face of it—and I hope you'll forgive my speaking plainly—on the face of it, the one thing she definitely does not need is to get involved in a pointless affair with a married man. Mind you, I'm not—please don't interrupt. I'm not interested in moralizing. I'd much rather feel that you and I can discuss this thing as civilized adults. But I'm afraid I must begin with an awkward question. Maureen appears to be under the impression that you're in love with her. Is this true?"

The answer was so classically simple that the framing of it filled him with pleasure. "I'm afraid I don't think that's any of your business."

She leaned back and smiled at him in a canny, speculative way, letting little curls of smoke dribble out of her nostrils, picking a flake of cigarette paper from her lip with the lacquered nails of little-finger and thumb. He was reminded of Bart Pollock at lunch saying, "Let me see how good a judge of character I am," and he wanted to reach across the table and strangle her.

"I think I like you, Frank," she said at last. "May I call you that? I think I even like your getting angry; it shows integrity." She came forward again, took a coquettish sip of her drink, and propped one elbow on the table. "Oh, look, Frank," she said. "Let's try to understand each other. I think you're probably a very good, serious boy with a nice wife and a couple of nice kids out there in Connecticut, and I think possibly all that's happened here is that you've gone and gotten yourself involved in a very human, very understandable situation. Doesn't that about sum it up?"

"No," he said. "It doesn't even come close. Now I'll try, okay?"

"Okay."

"Okay. I think you're probably a meddling, tiresome woman, possibly a latent lesbian, and very definitely"—he laid a dollar bill on the table—"very definitely a pain in the ass. Have a nice vacation."

And in four headlong strides, one of which nearly sent an effeminate waiter sprawling with a tray of demi-tasse cups, he was out of the place. All the way up the pink stone steps he felt he couldn't contain the giant sobs of laughter that heaved in his chest—the look on her face!—but in the vestibule, where he leaned against a row of polished brass mailboxes to let it all come out of him, he found that instead of guffaws he was capable only of a self-stifling, whimpering giggle that came in uncontrollable spasms, using only the top part of his lungs and making his diaphragm ache. He couldn't breathe.

When it was over, or nearly over, he crept back to the front door, pushed aside the dusty net curtain that covered its glass and peered down, just in time for a rear view of Norma out on the curb, wagging her handbag for a taxi. Her back was stiff with anger and there was something extremely pathetic about her suitcase, which looked expensive and brand-new. She had probably spent days buying it and weeks shopping for the things that would ride in its silken depths today—new bathing suits, slacks, sun lotion, a new camera—all the fussy, careful apparatus of a girlish good time. With the odd whimpering sounds still bubbling up from his rib cage he felt an incongruous wave of tenderness go out to her, as she climbed into the cab and rolled away.

He was sorry. But he would have to pull himself together now; it was time to deal with Maureen. He took several deep breaths and pressed the bell, and when the answering buzzer let him into the hallway he was careful not to take the stairs too fast. He didn't want to be short of breath when he got there; everything depended on his being calm.

The door was on the latch. He knocked once or twice and then heard her voice, apparently coming from the bedroom. "Frank? Is that you? Come on in. I'll be right out."

The apartment was scrupulously clean, as if in readiness for a party, and a faint scent of simmering meat came from the kitchenette. Only now, strolling around the carpet, did he notice that a phonograph was playing the music he was dimly aware of having heard all the way upstairs, a smooth Viennese waltz done with many violins, the kind of thing known as cocktail music.

"There's some drinks and stuff on the coffee table," Maureen's voice called. "Help yourself."

He did, gratefully making a stiff one, and tried to relax by sitting well back in the deep sofa.

"Did you close the door?" she called. "And lock it?"

"I think so, yes. What's all the—"

"And are you sure you're alone?"

"Sure I'm sure. What's all the mystery about?"

She threw open the bedroom door and stood smiling there on tiptoe, nude. Then she began an undulant dance around the room, in waltz time, waving and rippling her wrists like an amateur ballerina, blushing and trying mightily not to giggle as she whirled for him to the soaring strings. He barely managed to put his drink on the table, spilling part of it, before she came falling heavily into his arms and knocked the wind out of him. She was drenched in the same perfume as Norma's, and when she enveloped his head in a welcoming kiss he saw, at startlingly close range, that she was wearing even more eye make-up than usual. Each of her lashes was as thick and ragged as a spider's leg on her cheek. Released from her mouth at last, he tried to ease himself into a more upright sitting position, to shift her weight off his belly, but it wasn't easy because her arms were still locked around his neck, and in the effort his coat and shirt were dragged painfully tight across his back and chest. Finally he was able to free one hand to tear open his choking collar, and he tried to smile.

"Hello," she murmured huskily, and kissed him again, filling his mouth with her tongue.

This time there was the desperation of a drowning man in his upward struggle; when he'd made it, she drew back and looked at him in dismay, her breasts wagging like little startled faces. He couldn't speak for a minute until he'd regained his breath; then instead of looking at her he gazed down at his own hands, which were clasping the heavy sprawl of her thighs across his lap. He released his grip, spread his fingers and lightly tapped the upper thigh, as if it were the edge of a conference table.

"Look, Maureen," he said. "I think we ought to have a talk."

What happened after that, even while it was happening, was less like reality than a dream. Only a part of his consciousness was involved; the rest of him was a detached observer of the scene, embarrassed and helpless but relatively confident that he would soon wake up. The way her face clouded over when he began to talk, the way she sprang off his lap and fled for her dressing gown, which she clutched around her throat as tightly as a raincoat in a downpour as she paced the carpet—"Well; in that case there really isn't anything more to say, is there? There really wasn't any point in your coming over today, was there?"—these seemed to exist as rankling memories even before they were events: so did the way he followed her around the room, abjectly twisting one hand in the other as he apologized and apologized.

"Maureen, look; try to be reasonable about this. If I've ever given you cause to believe that I—that we— that I'm not happily married or anything, well, I'm sorry. I'm sorry."

"And what about me? How am I supposed to feel? Have you thought about what kind of position this puts me in?"

"I'm sorry. I—"

And this was the final vignette: Maureen hunched in the belching black smoke of the kitchenette while her veal scallopini burned to a crisp.

"It's not too bad, Maureen. I mean we can still eat it, if you like."

"No. It's ruined. Everything's ruined. You'd better go now."

"Oh, look. There's no reason why we have to be—"

"I said please *go*."

No amount of drink in the Grand Central bars was able to blur those images, and all the way home, hungry and drunk and exhausted on the train, he sat with round, imploring eyes and moving lips, still trying to reason with her.

His dread of seeing her in the office the next day was so intense that he was in the act of stepping off the elevator before he remembered that she wouldn't be there. She was on vacation. Would she follow Norma to the Cape? No; more likely she would use her two weeks to look for another job; in either case he could be fairly certain he would never see her again. And his relief on realizing this soon turned, perversely, into a worried kind of dismay. If he never saw her again, how would he ever have a chance to—well, to explain things to her? To tell her, in a level, unapologetic voice, all the level, unapologetic things he had to say?

Anxious thoughts of Maureen (Should he call her up? Should he write her a letter?) still preoccupied him on Saturday, while he labored at his stone path in the dizzying heat or invented little errands that would take him away from home, allowing him to cruise aimlessly down back roads in his station car, mumbling to himself. It wasn't until early Sunday afternoon, when he'd gone out in the station car to get the papers and ended up driving for miles, that the words "Forget it" rose to his lips.

It was a beautiful day. He was driving over the sunny crest of a long hill, past a thicket of elms whose leaves were just beginning to turn, when he suddenly began to laugh and to pound the old cracked plastic of the steering wheel with his fist. Forget it! What the hell was the point of thinking about it? The whole episode could now be dismissed as something separate and distinct from the main narrative flow of his life—something brief and minor and essentially comic. Norma humping out to the curb with her suitcase, Maureen leaping naked from his lap, himself padding after her through the smoke of the burning meat, wringing his hands—all now seemed as foolish as the distorted figures in an animated cartoon at the moment when the bouncing, tinny music swells up and the big circle begins to close in from all sides, rapidly enclosing the action within a smaller and smaller ring, swallowing it up until it's nothing more than a point of jiggling light that blinks out altogether as the legend "That's All, Folks!" comes sprawling happily out across the screen.

He stopped the car on the side of the road until his laughter had subsided; then, feeling much better, he made a U-turn and headed for home. Forget it! On the

way back to Revolutionary Road he allowed his mind
to dwell only on good things: the beauty of the day, the
finished job of work on Pollock's desk, the three thousand a year, even the "shakedown conference" that was
scheduled for tomorrow morning. It hadn't been such
a bad summer after all. Now, rolling home, he could
look forward to the refreshment of taking a shower
and getting into clean clothes; then he would sip
sherry (his lips puckered pleasurably at the thought of
it) and drowse over the *Times* for the rest of the afternoon. And tonight, if everything went well, would be
the perfect time for a rational, common-sense discussion with April about this annoying business of the
sofa. Whatever was bothering her could be fixed,
could probably have been fixed days ago, if he'd taken
the trouble to sit down with her and talk things out.

"Look," he would begin. "This has been kind of a
crazy summer, and I know we've both been under a
strain. I know you're feeling sort of lonely and confused just now; I know things look pretty bleak, and
believe me I—"

The house looked very neat and white as it
emerged through the green and yellow leaves; it wasn't
such a bad house after all. It looked, as John Givings
had once said, like a place where people lived—a place
where the difficult, intricate process of living could
sometimes give rise to incredible harmonies of happi-

ness and sometimes to near-tragic disorder, as well as to ludicrous minor interludes ("That's All, Folks!"); a place where it was possible for whole summers to be kind of crazy, where it was possible to feel lonely and confused in many ways and for things to look pretty bleak from time to time, but where everything, in the final analysis, was going to be all right.

April was working in the kitchen, where the radio was blaring.

"Wow," he said, laying the heavy Sunday papers on the table. "Is this ever a beautiful day."

"Yes; it's lovely."

He took a long, voluptuously warm shower and spent a long time brushing and combing his hair. In the bedroom, he inspected three shirts before deciding on the one he would wear with his tight, clean khakis—an expensive cotton flannel in a dark green-and-black plaid—and he tried several ways of wearing it before he settled on folding its cuffs back twice, turning its collar up in back and leaving it unbuttoned halfway down his chest. Crouching at the mirror of April's dressing table, he used her hand mirror to check the way the collar looked from the side and to test the effect, in profile, of his tightening jaw muscle.

Back in the kitchen, looking over the papers and loosely snapping his fingers in time to the jazz on the radio, he had to glance at April twice before he realized what was different about her: she was wearing one of her old maternity dresses.

"That looks nice," he said.

"Thank you."

"Is there any sherry?"

"I don't think so, no. I think we've used it up."

"Damn. Guess there isn't any beer either, is there." He considered having whiskey instead, but it was too early in the day.

"I've made some iced tea, if you'd like that. It's in the icebox."

"Okay." And he poured himself a glass without really wanting it. "Where are the kids, anyway?"

"Over at the Campbells'."

"Oh; too bad. I thought I'd read them the funnies."

He continued to finger through the papers for a few minutes, while she worked at the sink; then, because there was nothing else to do, he moved up close behind her and took hold of her arm, which caused her to stiffen.

"Look," he began. "This has been kind of a crazy summer, and I know you're—I know we've both been under a strain. I mean I know you're—"

"You know I'm not sleeping with you and you want to know why," she said, pulling away from his hand. "Well, I'm sorry, Frank, I don't feel like talking about it."

He hesitated, and then, to establish a better mood for communication, he kissed the back of her head with reverence. "Okay," he said. "What do you feel like talking about, then?"

She had finished with the dishes and let the water out of the sink; now she was rinsing the dishrag, and she didn't speak again until she had wrung it out, hung it on its hook, and moved away from the sink to turn and look at him, for the first time. She looked frightened. "Would it be all right if we sort of didn't talk about anything?" she asked. "I mean couldn't we just sort of take each day as it comes, and do the best we can, and not feel we have to talk about everything all the time?"

He smiled at her like a patient psychiatrist. "I don't think I suggested that we 'talk about everything all the time,'" he said. "I certainly didn't mean to. All I meant to sug—"

"All right," she said, backing away another step. "It's because I don't love you. How's that?"

Luckily the bland psychiatrist's smile was still on his face; it saved him from taking her seriously. "That isn't much of an answer," he said kindly. "I wonder what you really feel. I wonder if what you're really doing here isn't sort of trying to evade everything until you're—well, until you're in analysis. Sort of trying to resign from personal responsibility between now and the time you begin your treatment. Do you suppose that might be it?"

"No." She had turned away from him. "Oh, I don't know; yes. Whatever you like. Put it whichever way makes you the most comfortable."

"Well," he said, "it's hardly a question of making me comfortable. All I'm saying is that life does have to go on, analysis or not. Hell, *I* know you're having a bad time just now; it *has* been a tough summer. The point is we've both been under a strain, and we ought to be trying to help each other as much as we can. I mean God knows my own behavior has been pretty weird lately; matter of fact I've been thinking it might be a good idea for me to see the headshrinker myself. Actually—" He turned and stood looking out the window, tightening his jaw. "Actually, one of the reasons I've been hoping we could get together again is because there's something I'd like to tell you about: something kind of—well, kind of neurotic and irrational that happened to me a few weeks ago."

And almost, if not quite, before he knew what his voice was up to, he was telling her about Maureen Grube. He did it with automatic artfulness, identifying her only as "a girl in New York, a girl I hardly even know," rather than as a typist at the office, careful to stress that there had been no emotional involvement on his part while managing to imply that her need for him had been deep and ungovernable. His voice, soft and strong with an occasional husky falter or hesitation that only enhanced its rhythm, combined the power of confession with the narrative grace of romantic storytelling.

"And I think the main thing was simply a case of feeling that my—well, that my masculinity'd been threatened somehow by all that abortion business; wanting to prove something; I don't know. Anyway, I broke it off last week; the whole stupid business. It's over now; really over. If I weren't sure of that I guess I could never've brought myself to tell you about it."

For half a minute, the only sound in the room was the music on the radio.

"Why did you?" she asked.

He shook his head, still looking out the window. "Baby, I don't know. I've tried to explain it to you; I'm still trying to explain it to myself. That's what I meant about its being a neurotic, irrational kind of thing. I—"

"No," she said. "I don't mean why did you have the girl; I mean why did you tell me about it? What's the point? Is it supposed to make me jealous, or something? Is it supposed to make me fall in love with you, or back into bed with you, or what? I mean what am I supposed to say?"

He looked at her, feeling his face blush and twitch into an embarrassed simper that he tried, unsuccessfully, to make over into the psychiatric smile. "Why don't you say what you feel?"

She seemed to think this over for a few seconds, and then she shrugged. "I have. I don't feel anything."

"In other words you don't care what I do or who I go to bed with or anything. Right?"

"No; I guess that's right; I don't."

"But I *want* you to care!"

"I know you do. And I suppose I would, if I loved you; but you see I don't. I don't love you and I never really have, and I never really figured it out until this week, and that's why I'd just as soon not do any talking right now. Do you see?" She picked up a dust cloth and went into the living room, a tired, competent house-wife with chores to do.

"And listen to this," said an urgent voice on the radio. "Now, during the big Fall Clearance, you'll find Robert Hall's *entire stock* of men's walk shorts and sport jeans drastically reduced!"

Standing foursquare and staring down at his untouched glass of iced tea on the table, he felt his head fill with such a dense morass of confusion that only one consecutive line of thought came through: an abrupt remembrance of what Sunday this was, which explained why the kids were over at the Campbells', and which also meant there wasn't much time left for talking.

"Oh, now listen," he said, wheeling and following her into the living room with decisive, headlong strides. "You just put down that God damn rag a minute and listen. *Listen* to me. In the first place, you know God damn well you love me."

FIVE

"OH, IT'S SUCH A LOVELY LUXURY just to ride instead of driving," Mrs. Givings said, holding fast to the handle of the passenger's door. Her husband always drove on these trips to the hospital, and she never failed to remark on how relaxing a change it made for her. When one drove a car all day and every day, she would point out, there was no more marvelous vacation in the world than sitting back and letting someone else take over. But the force of habit was strong: she continued to watch the road as attentively as if she were holding the wheel, and her right foot would reach out and press the rubber floor mat at the approach of every turn or stop signal. Sometimes, catching herself at this, she would force her eyes to observe the passing countryside and will the sinews of her back to loosen and subside into the upholstery. As a final demonstration of self-control she might even uncoil her hand from the door handle and put it in her lap.

"My, isn't this a marvelous day?" she asked. "Oh, and look at the beautiful leaves, just beginning to turn. Is there anything nicer than the beginning of fall? All the wonderful colors and the crispness in the air; it always takes me back to dear look OUT!"

Her shoe slapped the floor mat and her body arched into a frantic posture of bracing against the impact of collision: a red truck was turning out of a side road, straight ahead.

"I see it, dear," Howard Givings said, smoothly applying the brakes so that the truck had ample room to pass, and afterwards, easing down on the accelerator again, he said: "You just relax, now, and let me worry about the driving."

"Oh, I know; I will. I'm sorry. I know I'm being silly." She took several deep breaths and folded her hands on her thigh, where they rested as tentatively as frightened birds. "It's just that I always do get such awful butterflies in my stomach on these visiting days, especially when it's been so long."

"Patient's name?" asked the painfully thin girl at the visitors' desk.

"John Givings," Mrs. Givings said with a polite dip

of her head, and she watched the girl's chewed pencil proceed down a mimeographed list of names until it stopped at Givings, John.

"Relationship?"

"Parents."

"Sign here please and take this slip. Ward Two A, upstairs and to your right. Have the patient back by five P.M."

In the outer waiting room of Ward Two A, after they had pressed the bell marked RING FOR ATTENDANT, Mr. and Mrs. Givings shyly joined a group of other visitors who were inspecting an exhibition of patients' artwork. The pictures included a faithfully rendered likeness of Donald Duck, in crayon, and an elaborate purple-and-brown crucifixion scene in which the sun, or moon, was done in the same crimson paint as the drops of blood that fell at precisely measured intervals from the wound in the Savior's ribs.

In a minute they heard a dim thudding of rubber heels and a jingle of keys behind the locked door; then it opened on a heavy, bespectacled young man in white who said, "May I have your slips, please?" and allowed them to pass, two at a time, into the inner waiting room. This was a large, dimly lighted place containing bright plastic-topped tables and chairs for the visitors of patients not on the privilege list. Most of the tables

were occupied, but there was very little sound of conversation. At the table nearest the door a young Negro
couple sat holding hands, and it wasn't easy to identify
the man as a patient until you noticed that his other
hand was holding the chromium leg of the table in a
yellow-knuckled grip of desperation, as if it were the
rail of a heaving ship. Farther away, an old woman was
combing the tangled hair of her son, whose age could
have been anything between twenty-five and forty; his
head wobbled submissively under her strokes as he ate
a peeled banana.

The attendant, hooking his ring of keys to a clip
against his hip pocket, struck off down the corridor of
the ward and began sonorously calling out names from
the slips he had collected. Looking after him down the
mouth of the corridor, which was filled with the sound
of many radios tuned to different stations, all you
could see was a long expanse of waxed linoleum and
the corners of several steel hospital beds.

After a while the attendant came back, walking
neat and white at the head of a small, shabby parade.
John Givings brought up the rear, tall and pigeon-
toed, buttoning his sweater with one hand and carrying the twill workman's cap in the other.

"Well," he said, greeting his parents. "They letting
the prisoners out in the sunshine today? Big deal." He

carefully placed the cap dead-center on his head, and the picture of the public charge was complete. "Let's go."

No one spoke in the car until they were clear of the hospital grounds, past the ranks of long brick ward buildings, past the administration building and the softball diamond, out around the well-tended circle of grass that enclosed the twin white shafts of the State and American flags, and on up the long blacktop road that led to the highway. Mrs. Givings, riding in the back seat (she usually found it more comfortable there when John was in front), tried to gauge his mood by studying the back of his neck. Then she said: "John?"

"Mm?"

"We have some good news. You know the Wheelers, that you liked so much? They've very kindly asked us to drop by again today, by the way, if you'd like to; that's one thing; but the really good news is that they've decided to stay. They're not going to Europe after all. Isn't that lovely?" And with an uneasy smile she watched him slowly turn around to face her over the seat back.

"What happened?" he said.

"Well, I'm sure I don't—how do you mean, what happened, dear? I don't suppose anything necessarily 'happened'; I imagine they simply talked it over and changed their minds."

"You mean you didn't even ask? People're all set to do something as big as that and then they drop the whole idea, and you don't even ask what the deal is? Why?"

"Well, John, I suppose because I didn't feel it was my *business* to ask. One doesn't in*quire* into these things, dear, unless the other person wishes to volunteer the infor*mation*." In an effort to still the rising cautionary note in her voice, which was almost certain to antagonize him, she forced the skin of her forehead and mouth to assume the shape of a jolly smile. "Can't we just be pleased that they're staying, without inquiring into the why of it? Oh, look at that lovely old red silo. I've never noticed that one before, have you? That must be the tallest silo for miles around."

"It's a lovely old silo, Ma," John said. "And it's lovely news about the Wheelers, and you're a lovely person. Isn't she, Pop? Isn't she a lovely person?"

"All right, John," Howard Givings said. "Let's steady down, now."

Mrs. Givings, whose fingers were grinding and tearing a book of matches into moist shreds, closed her eyes and tried to fortify herself for what would almost certainly be an awkward afternoon.

Her anxiety was compounded at the Wheelers' kitchen door. They were home—both cars were there—but the house had a strangely unwelcoming look, as if they weren't expecting visitors. There was no answer to her very light knock on the glass pane of the door, which gave back a vivid reflection of sky and trees, of her own craning face and the faces of Howard and John behind her. She knocked again, and this time she made a visor of one hand and pressed it to the pane, to see inside. The kitchen was empty (she could see what looked like a glass of iced tea on the table) but just then Frank Wheeler came lunging in from the living room, looking awful—looking as if he were about to scream or to weep or to commit violence. She saw at once that he hadn't heard her knock and didn't know she was there: he hadn't come to answer the door but in desperate escape from the living room, possibly from the house itself. And there wasn't time for her to step back before he saw her—caught her crouched and peering into his very eyes—which made him start, stop, and arrange his features into a smile that matched her own.

"Well," he said, opening the door. "Hi, there. Come on in."

Then they were moving sociably into the living room, where April was, and April looked awful too: pale and haggard, twisting her fingers at her waist. "Nice to see you all," she was saying faintly. "Won't you sit down? I'm afraid the house is in a terrible mess."

"Are we awfully early?" Mrs. Givings asked.

"Early? No, no; we were just—would anyone like a drink? Or some—iced tea, or something?"

"Oh, nothing at all, thanks. Actually we can only stay a minute; we just dropped by to say hello."

The party fell into an odd, uncomfortable grouping: the three Givingses seated in a row; the two Wheelers standing backed up against the bookcase, restlessly shifting toward and then apart from each other as they made conversation. Only now, watching them, was Mrs. Givings able to hazard a guess at the cause of their constraint: they must have been quarreling.

"Listen," John said, and all the other talk stopped dead. "What's the deal, anyway? I mean I hear you people changed your minds. How come?"

"Well," Frank said, and chuckled in embarrassment. "Well, not exactly. You might say our minds were sort of—forcibly changed for us."

"How come?"

Frank made a little sidling skip to stand close to his wife, edging behind her. "Well," he said. "I should've thought that was fairly obvious by now." And Mrs. Givings's eyes were drawn, for the first time, to notice what April was wearing. Maternity clothes!

"Oh, *April*!" she cried. "Why, this is perfectly marvelous!" She wondered what one was expected to do on such occasions: should she get up and—well, kiss her, or something? But April didn't look like a girl who wanted to be kissed. "Oh, I think this is terribly exciting," Mrs. Givings went on, and "I can't tell you how pleased I am," and "Oh, but I expect you'll be needing a bigger house, now, won't you?" and through it all she hoped against hope that John would keep still. But:

"Hold it a second, Ma," he said, standing up. "Hold it a second. I don't get this." And he fixed on Frank the stare of a prosecuting attorney. "What's so obvious about it? I mean okay, she's pregnant; so what? Don't people have babies in Europe?"

"Oh John, really," said Mrs. Givings. "I don't think we need to—"

"Ma, will you keep out of this? I'm asking the man a question. If he doesn't want to give me the answer, I'm assuming he'll have sense enough to tell me so."

"Of course," Frank said, smiling down at his shoes. "Suppose we just say that people anywhere aren't very well advised to have babies unless they can afford them. As it happens, the only way we can afford this one is by staying here. It's a question of money, you see."

"Okay." John nodded in apparent satisfaction, looking from one of the Wheelers to the other. "Okay; that's a good reason." They both looked relieved, but Mrs. Givings went tight all over because she knew, from long experience, that something perfectly awful was coming next.

"Money's always a good reason," John said. He began to move around the carpet, hands in his pockets. "But it's hardly ever the real reason. What's the real reason? Wife talk you out of it, or what?" And he turned the full force of his dazzling smile on April, who had moved across the room to stab out her cigarette in an ash tray. Her eyes looked briefly up at him and then down again.

"Huh?" he persisted. "Little woman decide she isn't quite ready to quit playing house? Nah, nah, that's not it. I can tell. She looks too tough. Tough and female and adequate as hell. Okay, then; it must've been you." And he swung around to Frank. "What happened?"

"John, please," Mrs. Givings said. "You're being very—" But there was no stopping him now.

"What happened? You get cold feet, or what? You decide you like it here after all? You figure it's more comfy here in the old Hopeless Emptiness after all, or—Wow, that did it! Look at his face! What's the matter, Wheeler? Am I getting warm?"

"John, you're being impossibly rude. Howard, please—"

"All right, son," Howard Givings said, getting to his feet. "I think we'd better be—"

"Boy!" John broke into his braying laugh. "Boy! You know something? I wouldn't be surprised if you knocked her up on purpose, just so you could spend the rest of your life hiding behind that maternity dress."

"Now, *look*," said Frank Wheeler, and to Mrs. Givings's shocked surprise his fists were clenched and he was trembling from head to foot. "I think that's just about *enough* outa you. I mean who the hell do you think you are? You come in here and say whatever crazy God damn thing comes into your head, and I think it's about time somebody told you to keep your God damn—"

"He's not *well*, Frank," Mrs. Givings managed to say, and then she bit the inside of her lip in consternation.

"Oh, not well my ass. I'm sorry, Mrs. Givings, but I don't give a damn if he's well or sick or dead or alive, I just wish he'd keep his God damn opinions in the God damn insane asylum where they belong."

During the painful silence that followed this, while Mrs. Givings continued to chew her lip, they all stood grouped in the middle of the room: Howard intently folding a light raincoat over his arm; April staring red-faced at the floor; Frank still trembling and audibly breathing, with a terrible mixture of defiance and humiliation in his eyes. John, whose smile was now serene, was the only one of them who seemed at peace.

"Big man you got here, April," he said, winking at her as he fitted the workman's cap on his head. "Big family man, solid citizen. I feel sorry for you. Still, maybe you deserve each other. Matter of fact, the way you look right now, I'm beginning to feel sorry for him, too. I mean come to think of it, you must give him a pretty bad time, if making babies is the only way he can prove he's got a pair of balls."

"All right, John," Howard was murmuring. "Let's get on out to the car now."

"April," Mrs. Givings whispered. "I can't tell you how sorry I—"

"Right," John said, moving away with his father. "Sorry, sorry, sorry. Okay Ma? Have I said 'Sorry' enough times? I *am* sorry, too. Damn; I bet I'm just about the sorriest bastard I know. Course, get right down to it, I don't have a whole hell of a lot to be glad about, do I?"

And at least, Mrs. Givings thought, if nothing else could be salvaged from this horrible day, at least he was allowing Howard to lead him away quietly. All she had to do now was to follow them, to find some way of getting across this floor and out of this house, and then it would all be over.

But John wasn't finished yet. "Hey, I'm glad of one thing, though," he said, stopping near the door and turning back, beginning to laugh again, and Mrs. Givings thought she would die as he extended a long yellow-stained index finger and pointed it at the slight mound of April's pregnancy. "You know what I'm glad of? I'm glad I'm not gonna be that kid."

SIX

THE FIRST THING FRANK DID when the Givingses were out of the house was to pour himself three fingers of bourbon and drink it down.

"Okay," he said, turning on his wife. "Okay, don't tell me." The ball of whiskey in his stomach made him cough with a convulsive shudder. "Don't tell me; let me guess. I made a Disgusting Spectacle of Myself. Right? Oh, and another thing." He followed her closely through the kitchen and into the living room, glaring in shame and anger and miserable supplication at the smooth back of her head. "Another thing: Everything That Man Said Is True. Right? Isn't that what you're going to say?"

"Apparently I don't have to. You're saying it for me."

"Oh, but April, don't you see how wrong that is?

Don't you see how terribly, God-awfully wrong it is, if that's what you think?"

She turned around and faced him. "No. Why is it wrong?"

"Because the man is insane." He put down his drink on the window sill, to free both hands, and used them to make a gesture of impassioned earnestness, clawing upward and outward from his chest with all ten of his spread fingers and gathering them into quivering fists, which he shook beneath his chin. "The man," he said again, "is insane. Do you know what the definition of insanity is?"

"No. Do you?"

"Yes. It's the inability to relate to another human being. It's the inability to love."

She began to laugh. Her head went back, the two perfect rows of her teeth sprang forth, and her eyes were brilliantly narrowed as peal after peal of her laughter rang in the room. "The in," she said; "the in; the inabil; the inability to—"

She was hysterical. Watching her as she swayed and staggered from the support of one piece of furniture to another and then to the wall and back again, laughing and laughing, he wondered what he ought to do. In the movies, when women got hysterical like this, men slapped them until they stopped; but the men in the movies were always calm enough themselves to make it clear what the slapping was for. He wasn't. He wasn't, in fact, able to do anything at all but stand there and watch, foolishly opening and shutting his mouth.

Finally she sank into a chair, still laughing, and he waited for what he guessed would be a transition from laughter to weeping—that was what usually happened in the movies—but instead her subsiding was oddly normal, more like a recovery from a funny joke than from hysteria.

"Oh," she said. "Oh, Frank, you really are a wonderful talker. If black could be made into white by talking, you'd be the man for the job. So now I'm crazy because I don't love you—right? Is that the point?"

"No. Wrong. You're not crazy, and you do love me; *that's* the point."

She got to her feet and backed away from him, her eyes flashing. "But I don't," she said. "In fact I loathe the sight of you. In fact if you come any closer, if you touch me or anything I think I'll scream."

Then he did touch her, saying, "Oh baby, lis—" and she did scream.

It was plainly a false scream, done while she looked coldly into his eyes, but it was high, shrill, and loud enough to shake the house. When the noise of it was over he said:

"God damn you. God damn all your snotty, hateful little—Come *here*, God damn it—"

She switched nimbly past him and pulled a straight chair around to block his path; he grabbed it and slung it against the wall and one of its legs broke off.

"And what're you going to do now?" she taunted him. "Are you going to hit me? To show how much you love me?"

"No." All at once he felt massively strong. "Oh, no. Don't worry. I couldn't be bothered. You're not worth the trouble it'd *take* to hit you. You're not worth the powder it'd take to blow you *up*. You're an *emp*ty—" He was aware, as his voice filled out, of a sense of luxurious freedom because the children weren't here. Nobody was here, and nobody was coming; they had this whole reverberating house to themselves. "You're an *emp*ty, *hol*low fucking *shell* of a woman. . . ." It was the first opportunity for a wide-open, all-out fight they'd had in months, and he made the most of it, stalking and circling her as he shouted, trembling and gasping for breath. "What the hell are you living in my *house* for, if you hate me so much? *Huh?* Will you answer me that? What the hell are you carrying my *child* for?" Like John Givings, he pointed at her belly. "Why the hell *didn't* you get rid of it, when you had the chance? Because listen. Listen: I got news for you." The great pressure that began to be eased inside him now, as he slowly and quietly intoned his next words, made it seem that this was a cleaner breakthrough into truth than any he had ever made before: "I wish to God you'd done it."

It was the perfect exit line. He lunged past her and out of the room, down the swaying, tilting hall and into the bedroom, where he kicked the door shut behind him, sat bouncingly on the bed and drove his right fist into the palm of his left hand. Wow!

What a thing to say! But wasn't it true? Didn't he wish she'd done it? "Yes," he whispered aloud. "Yes, I do. I do. I do." He was breathing fast and heavily through his mouth, and his heart was going like a drum; after a while he closed his dry lips and swallowed, so that the only sound in the room was the rasp of air going in and out of his nose. Then this subsided, very gradually, as his blood slowed down, and his eyes began to take in some of the things around him: the window, whose glass and curtains were ablaze with the colors of the setting sun; the bright, scented jars and bottles on April's dressing table; her white nightgown hanging from a hook inside the open closet, and her shoes lined up neatly along the closet floor: three-inch heels, ballet shoes, soiled blue bedroom slippers.

Everything was quiet now; he was beginning to wish he hadn't shut himself in here. For one thing, he wanted another drink. Then he heard the kitchen door being closed and the screen being clapped behind it, and the old panic rose up: she was leaving him.

He was up and running soundlessly back through the house, intent on catching her and saying something—anything—before she got the car started; but she wasn't in the car, or anywhere near it. She was nowhere. She had disappeared. He ran all the way around the outside of the house, looking for her, his loose cheeks jogging, and he had started mindlessly to run around it again when he caught sight of her up in the woods. She was climbing unsteadily up the hill, looking very small among the rocks and trees. He sprinted out across the lawn, took the low stone wall in a leap and went stumbling up through the brush, after her, wondering if she really had gone crazy this time. What the hell was she wandering around up there for? Would she, when he caught up with her and took hold of her arm and turned her around, would she have the vacant, smiling stare of lunacy?

"Don't come any closer," she called.

"April, listen, I—"

"Don't come any *closer*. Can't I even get away from you in the *woods*?"

He stopped, panting, ten yards below her. At least she was all right; her face was clear. But they couldn't fight up here—they were well within sight and earshot of houses down on the road.

"April, listen, I didn't mean that. Honestly; I didn't mean that about wishing you'd done it."

"Are you still talking? Isn't there any way to stop your talking?" She was bracing herself against a tree trunk, looking down at him.

"Please come down. What're you doing up—"

"Do you want me to scream again, Frank? Because I will, if you say another word. I mean it."

And if she screamed here on the hillside they would hear her in every house on Revolutionary Road. They would hear her all over the top of the Hill, too, and in the Campbells' house. There was nothing for him to do but to go back alone, down through the woods to the lawn, and then indoors.

Once he was back in the kitchen he gave all his attention to the grim business of keeping watch on her through the window, standing—or crouching, and finally sitting on a chair—far enough back in the shadows so that she wouldn't be able to see him.

She didn't seem to be doing anything up there: she continued to stand leaning against the tree, and as twilight closed in it became difficult to make her out. Once there was a yellow flare as she lit a cigarette, and then he watched the tiny red coal of it move in the slow arcs of her smoking; by the time it went out the woods were in total darkness.

He went on doggedly watching the same place in the trees until the pale shape of her surprised him at much closer range: she was walking home across the lawn. He barely managed to get out of the kitchen before she came in. Then, hiding in the living room, he listened to her pick up the phone and dial a number.

Her voice was normal and calm. "Hello, Milly? Hi. . . . Oh yes, they left a little while ago. Listen, though, I was wondering if I could ask a favor. The thing is, I'm not feeling very well; I think I may be getting the flu or something, and Frank's tired out. Would you awfully much mind keeping the kids for the night? . . . Oh, that's wonderful, Milly, thanks. . . . No, don't bother, they both had their baths last night. . . . Well, I know they'll enjoy it too. They always have a wonderful time at your place. . . . All right, fine, then. I'll call you in the morning."

Then she came into the living room and turned on the lights, and the exploding glare caused them both to blink and squint. What he felt, above all, was embarrassment. She looked embarrassed too, until she walked across the room and lay down on the sofa with her face out of sight.

It was at times something like this, in the past, that he'd gone out and wrenched the car into gear and driven for miles, stopping at one blue- and red-lighted bar after another, spilling his money on wet counters, morosely listening to the long, fuddled conversations of waitresses and construction workers, playing clangorous jukebox records and then driving again, speeding, eating up the night until he could sleep.

But he wasn't up to that tonight. The trouble was that there had never, in the past, been a time exactly like this. He was physically incapable of going out and starting the car, let alone of driving. His knees had turned to jelly and his head rang, and he was meekly grateful for the protective shell of the house around him; it was all he could do to make his way to the bedroom again and shut himself inside it, though this time, for all his despair, he was sensible enough to take the bottle of whiskey along with him.

There followed a night of vivid and horrible dreams, while he sprawled sweating on the bed in his clothes. Sometimes, either waking or dreaming that he was awake, he thought he heard April moving around the house; then once, toward morning, he could have sworn he opened his eyes and found her sitting close beside him on the edge of the bed. Was it a dream, or not?

"Oh, baby," he whispered through cracked and swollen lips. "Oh, my baby, don't go away." He reached for her hand and held it. "Oh, please stay."

"Sh-sh-sh. It's all right," she said, and squeezed his fingers. "It's all right, Frank. Go to sleep." The sound of her voice and the cool feel of her hand conveyed such a miracle of peace that he didn't care if it was a dream; it was enough to let him sink back into a sleep that was mercifully dreamless.

Then came the bright yellow pain of his real awakening, alone; and he'd scarcely had time to decide that he couldn't possibly go to work today before he remembered that he had to. It was the day of the shakedown conference. Trembling, he forced himself up and into the bathroom, where he put himself tenderly through the ordeals of a shower and a shave.

An illogical, unreasoning hope began to quicken his heart as he dressed. What if it hadn't been a dream? What if she really had come and sat there on the bed and spoken to him that way? And when he went into the kitchen it seemed that his hope was confirmed. It was astonishing.

The table was carefully set with two places for breakfast. The kitchen was filled with sunlight and with the aromas of coffee and bacon. April was at the stove, wearing a fresh maternity dress, and she looked up at him with a shy smile.

"Good morning," she said.

He wanted to go down on his knees and put his arms around her thighs; but he held back. Something told him—possibly the very shyness of her smile—that it would be better not to try anything like that; it would be better just to join her in the playing of this game, this strange, elaborate pretense that nothing had happened yesterday. "Good morning," he said, not quite meeting her eyes.

He sat down and unfolded his napkin. It was incredible. No morning after a fight had ever been as easy as this—but still, he thought as he unsteadily sipped at his orange juice, no fight had ever been as bad as that. Could it be that they'd fought themselves out at last? Maybe this was what happened when there was really and truly nothing more to say, either in acrimony or forgiveness. Life did, after all, have to go on.

"It certainly is a—nice morning out, isn't it?" he said.

"Yes; it is. Would you like scrambled eggs, or fried?"

"Oh, it doesn't really mat—well, yes; scrambled, I guess, if it's just as easy."

"Fine. I'll have scrambled too."

And soon they were sitting companionably across from each other at the bright table, whispering little courtesies over the passing of buttered toast. At first he was too bashful to eat. It was like the first time he'd ever taken a girl out to dinner, at seventeen, when the idea of actually loading food into his mouth and chewing it, right there in front of her, had seemed an unpardonably coarse thing to do; and what saved him now was the same thing that had saved him then: the surprising discovery that he was uncontrollably hungry.

Between swallows he said: "It's sort of nice, having breakfast without the kids for a change."

"Yes." She wasn't eating her eggs, and he saw that her fingers were shaking a little as she reached for her coffee cup; otherwise she looked completely self-possessed. "I thought you'd probably want a good breakfast today," she said. "I mean it's kind of an important day for you, isn't it? Isn't this the day you have your conference with Pollock?"

"That's right, yes." She had even remembered that! But he covered his delight with the deprecating, side-of-the-mouth smile he had used for years in telling her about Knox, and said: "Big deal."

"Well," she said, "I imagine it *is* a pretty big deal; for them, anyway. What exactly do you think you'll be doing? Until they start sending you out on the trips, I mean. You never have told me much about it."

Was she kidding, or what? "Haven't I?" he said. "Well, of course I don't really know much yet myself; that's the thing. I guess it'll mostly be just a matter of what Pollock calls 'blocking out objectives'—sitting around letting him talk, I guess. Acting like we know something about computers. And of course the main reason for this whole thing, at least I *think* it's the main reason, is that Knox may be getting ready to buy up one of these really big computers, bigger than the '500.' Did I tell you about that?"

"No, I don't believe you did." And the remarkable thing was that she looked as though she'd like to hear about it.

"Well, *you* know—one of these monstrous great things like the Univac; the kind of machine they use to forecast the weather and predict elections and all that. And I mean those jobs *sell* for a couple of million dollars apiece, you see; if Knox went into production on one they'd have to organize a whole new promotion program around it. I think that may be what's going on."

He had the odd sensation that his lungs were growing deeper, or that the air was growing richer in oxygen. His shoulders, which had been tight and high, came gradually to rest against the back of the chair. Was this the way other men felt, telling their wives about their work?

". . . Basically it's just a terrifically big, terrifically fast adding machine," he was saying, in reply to her sober wish to know how a computer really worked. "Only instead of mechanical parts, you see, it's got thousands of little individual vacuum tubes. . . ." And in a minute he was drawing for her, on a paper napkin, a diagram representing the passage of binary digit pulses through circuitry.

"Oh, *I* see," she said. "At least I think I see; yes. It's really sort of—interesting, isn't it?"

"Oh, well, I don't know, it's—yeah, I guess it *is* sort

of interesting, in a way. Of course I don't really know much about it, beyond the basic idea of the thing."

"You always say that. I bet you really know a lot more about it than you think. You certainly do explain it well, anyway."

"Oh?" He felt his smiling cheeks get warm as he lowered his eyes and put the pencil back inside his crisp gabardine suit. "Well, thanks." He finished the last of his second cup of coffee and stood up. "Guess I'd better be getting started."

She stood up too, smoothing her skirt.

"Listen, though, April; this was really nice." The walls of his throat closed up. He felt he was about to cry, but he managed to hold it back. "I mean it was a swell breakfast," he said, blinking. "Really; I don't know when I've ever had a—a nicer breakfast."

"Thank you," she said. "I'm glad; I enjoyed it too."

And could he just walk out now? Without saying anything? Looking at her as they moved toward the door, he wondered if he ought to say "I can't tell you how awful I feel about yesterday," or "I do love you," or something like that; or would it be better not to risk starting things up again? He hesitated, turning to face her, and felt his mouth go into an awkward shape.

"Then you don't really—" he began. "You don't really hate me, or anything?"

Her eyes looked deep and serious; she seemed to

be glad he had asked her that question, as if it were one of the few questions in the world she could answer with authority. She shook her head. "No; of course I don't." And she held the door open for him. "Have a good day."

"I will. You too." And then it was easy to decide what to do next: without touching her he began as slowly as any movie actor, to bend toward her lips.

Her face, as it came up close, betrayed an instant's surprise or hesitation, but then it softened; she half closed her eyes and made it clear that this, however brief, would be a mutually willing, mutually gentle kiss. Only after the kiss was completed did he touch her with his hand, on the arm. She was, after all, a damned good-looking girl.

"Okay, then," he said huskily. "So long."

SEVEN

APRIL JOHNSON WHEELER WATCHED her husband's face withdraw, she felt the light squeeze of his hand on her arm and heard his words, and smiled at him.

"So long," she answered.

She followed him outside to stand on the kitchen steps and watch, hugging her arms against the morning chill, while he started up the station car and brought it rumbling out into the sunshine. His flushed profile, thrust out and facing the rear as the car moved past, revealed nothing but the sobriety of a man with a pardonable pride in knowing how to back a car efficiently down a hill. She walked out to a sunny place in front of the carport to see him off, watching the crumpled shape of the old Ford get smaller and smaller. At the end of the driveway, as he backed it out and around into the road, a gleam of sun on the windshield eclipsed his face. She held up her hand and waved anyway, in case he was looking, and when he came into view again as the car straightened out it was clear that he'd seen her. He was bending and grinning up at her, neat and happy in his gabardine suit, his blazing white shirt and dark tie, answering her wave with a small, jaunty wave of his own; then he was gone.

Her smile continued until she was back in the kitchen, clearing away the breakfast dishes into a steaming sinkful of suds; she was still smiling, in fact, when she saw the paper napkin with the diagram of the computer on it, and even then her smile didn't fade: it simply spread and trembled and locked itself into a stiff grimace while the spasms worked at her aching throat, again and again, and the tears broke and ran down her cheeks as fast as she could wipe them away.

She got some music on the radio, to steady her nerves, and by the time she'd finished washing the dishes she was all right again. Her gums were sore from too many cigarettes during the night, her hands were inclined to shake and she was more aware of her heartbeats than usual; otherwise she felt fine. It was a shock, though, when the radio announcer said "Eight forty-five"; it seemed like noon, or early afternoon. She washed her face in cold water and took several deep breaths, trying to slow her heart down; then she lit a cigarette and composed herself at the telephone.

"Hello, Milly? . . . Hi. Everything all right? . . . My voice sounds what? . . . Oh. Well, no, actually, I'm *not* feeling any better; that's really why I called. . . . Are you sure you don't mind? I mean it may not be for the whole night again; maybe Frank'll want to come over and get them this evening, depending how things work out; but I guess we'd better leave it open, just in case. . . . Well, that's really wonderful of you, Milly, I do appreciate it. . . . Oh no, I'm sure it's nothing serious; it's just—you know, one of those things. . . . All right, then. Give them a kiss for me, and tell them one or the other of us'll be stopping by to pick them up, either tonight or tomorrow. . . . What? . . . Oh, well—no, not if they're outdoors playing. Don't call them in." The cigarette broke and shredded in her fingers; she let it drop into the ash tray and used both hands to grip the telephone. "Just give them—you know; give them each a kiss for me, and give them my love, and tell them—*you* know. . . . All right, Milly. Thanks."

And she barely managed to get the phone back in its cradle before she was crying again. To control herself she lit another cigarette, but it gagged her and she had to go to the bathroom and stand there for a long time, retching dryly even after she'd lost what little breakfast she'd managed to eat. Afterwards, she washed her face again and brushed her teeth, and then it was time to get busy.

"Have you thought it through, April?" Aunt Claire used to say, holding up one stout, arthritic forefinger. "Never undertake to do a thing until you've thought it through; then do the best you can."

The first thing to do was to straighten up the house, and in particular to straighten up the desk, where the hours and hours of her trying to think it through, last night, had left a mess of remnants. The heaped-up ash tray was there, and the opened bottle of ink surrounded by spilled ashes, and the coffee cup containing a dried brown ring. She had only to sit down at the desk and switch on its lamp to bring back the harsh, desolate flavor of the small hours.

In the wastebasket, lumped and crumpled, lay all the failures of the letter she had tried to write. She picked one of them out and opened it and spread it flat, but at first she couldn't read it: she could only marvel at how cramped and black and angry the hand-writing looked, like row on row of precisely swatted mosquitos. Then part of it, halfway down the page, came into focus:

> *. . . your cowardly self-delusions about "love" when*
> *you know as well as I do that there's never been any-*
> *thing between us but contempt and distrust and a*
> *terrible sickly dependence on each other's weakness—*
> *that's why. That's why I couldn't stop laughing today*
> *when you said that about the Inability to Love, and*
> *that's why I can't stand to let you touch me, and*
> *that's why I'll never again believe in anything you*
> *think, let alone in anything you say. . . .*

She didn't want to read the rest because she knew it wasn't worth reading. It was weak with hate, like all the other abortive letters on all the other crumpled papers; all of them would have to be burned.

It wasn't until five this morning—and could that really have been only four hours ago?—that she'd finally stopped trying to write the letter. She had forced herself up from the desk then, aching with tiredness, and gone in to take a deep, warm bath, lying very still under the still water for a long time, like a patient in therapy. Afterwards, feeling absent-minded and greatly calmed, she had gone into the bedroom to get dressed; and there he was, on his back.

The sight of him, in the early blue light, sprawled out and twisted in his wrinkled Sunday sports clothes, had been as much of a shock as if she'd found a stranger in the bed. When she sat down in the reek of whiskey to get a closer look at his flushed, sleeping face, she began to understand the real cause of her shock: it was much more than the knowledge that she didn't love him. It was that she didn't, she couldn't possibly hate him. How could anyone hate him? He was— well, he was *Frank*.

Then he'd made a little snoring moan and his lips had begun to work as he groped for her hand. "Oh, baby. Oh, my baby, don't go away. . . ."

"Sh-sh-sh. It's all right. It's all right, Frank. Go to sleep."

And that was when she'd thought it through.

So it hadn't been wrong or dishonest of her to say no this morning, when he asked if she hated him, any more than it had been wrong or dishonest to serve him the elaborate breakfast and to show the elaborate interest in his work, and to kiss him goodbye. The kiss, for that matter, had been exactly right—a perfectly fair, friendly kiss, a kiss for a boy you'd just met at a party, a boy who'd danced with you and made you laugh and walked you home afterwards, talking about himself all the way.

The only real mistake, the only wrong and dishonest thing, was ever to have seen him as anything more than that. Oh, for a month or two, just for fun, it might be all right to play a game like that with a boy; but all these years! And all because, in a sentimentally lonely time long ago, she had found it easy and agreeable to believe whatever this one particular boy felt like saying, and to repay him for that pleasure by telling easy, agreeable lies of her own, until each was saying what the other most wanted to hear—until he was saying "I love you" and she was saying "Really, I mean it; you're the most interesting person I've ever met."

What a subtle, treacherous thing it was to let yourself go that way! Because once you'd started it was terribly difficult to stop; soon you were saying "I'm sorry, of course you're right," and "Whatever you think is best," and "You're the most wonderful and valuable thing in the world," and the next thing you knew all honesty, all truth, was as far away and glimmering, as hopelessly unattainable as the world of the golden people. Then you discovered you were working at life the way the Laurel Players worked at *The Petrified Forest*, or the way Steve Kovick worked at his drums—earnest and sloppy and full of pretension and all wrong; you found you were saying yes when you meant no, and "We've got to be together in this thing" when you meant the very opposite; then you were breathing gasoline as if it were flowers and abandoning yourself to a delirium of love under the weight of a clumsy, grunting, red-faced man you didn't even like—Shep Campbell!—and then you were face to face, in total darkness, with the knowledge that you didn't know who you were.

And how could anyone else be blamed for that?

When she'd straightened up the desk and made Frank's bed, with fresh sheets, she carried the waste-basket outdoors and around to the back yard. It was an autumnal day, warm but with a light sharp breeze that scudded stray leaves over the grass and reminded her of all the brave beginnings of childhood, of the apples and pencils and new woolen clothes of the last few days before school.

She took the wastebasket out across the lawn to the incinerator drum, dumped the papers in it and set a match to them. Then she sat down on the edge of the sun-warmed stone wall to wait for their burning, watching the all but invisible flame crawl slowly and then more rapidly up and around them, sending out little waves of heat that shimmered the landscape. The sounds of bird song and rustling trees were faintly mingled with the faraway cries of children at play; she listened carefully but couldn't make out which were Jennifer's and Michael's voices and which were the Campbell boys'—or even, with certainty, whether the voices were coming from the Campbells' part of the Hill.

From a distance, all children's voices sound the same.

"And listen! Listen!—you know what else she brought me, Margie? *Listen!* I'm trying to *tell* you something."

"*Wha*-ut?"

Margie Rothenberg and her little brother George and Mary Jane Crawford and Edna Slater were there, fooling around at the place by the hedge where all the grass was worn away, the place with the little cave and the flat rock where they kept their collection of Dixie Cup lids.

"I said you know what else she brought me? My mother? She brought me this beautiful blue cashmere sweater, for school, and socks that match, and this beautiful little perfume atomizer? This little bottle with a thing that you squeeze? With real perfume in it? Oh, and we drove into White Plains with Mr. Minton, that's my mother's friend, and we went to the movies and had ice cream and everything, and I stayed up till ten minutes after eleven."

"How come she was only here two days?" Margie Rothenberg inquired. "You said she was staying a week. George, you *quit* that now!"

"I did not; I said she *might* stay a week. Next time she probably will, or maybe I'll go and stay a week with her, and if I do that—"

"George! The very next time you pick your nose and eat it I'm gonna tell! I mean it!"

"—and if I do that, you know what? If I do that I won't have to go to school or anything for a whole week; ha, ha. Hey Margie? You want to come home and see my sweater and stuff?"

"I can't. I have to get home in time for 'Don Winslow.'"

"We can hear 'Don Winslow' in my house. Come on."

"I can't. I have to get home. Come on, Georgie."

"Hey Edna? Hey Mary Jane? Know what my mother brought me? She brought me this beautiful— Hey, listen Edna. Listen. . . ." There was the sound of an upstairs window rattling open, and she knew that if she turned around she would see the dim shape of Aunt Claire peering out through the copper screen.

"*Aay*-prul!"

"She brought me this beautiful blue sweater, it's cashmere, and this beautiful—"

"*Aay*-prul!"

"What? I'm over here."

"Why didn't you *an*swer, then? I want you to come

in this instant and get washed and changed. Your father just called. He's driving out and he'll be here in fifteen minutes."

And she ran for the house so fast that her sneakers seemed hardly to touch the ground. Nothing like this had ever, ever happened before: two whole days with her mother, and then, now, the very next day . . .

She took the stairs two at a time and flew to her room and began to undress in such haste that she popped a button off her blouse, saying, "When did he call? What did he say? How long is he staying?"

"I don't know, dear; he said he's on his way up to Boston. You certainly don't need to tear your clothes. There's plenty of time."

Then she was out on the front porch in her party dress, watching down the street for the first glimpse of his long, high-wheeled, beautiful touring car. When it did come into sight, two blocks away, she forced herself not to start running down the path; she waited until it pulled up and stopped in front of the house, so she could watch him get out.

And oh, how tall, how wonderfully slender and straight he was! How golden the sunlight shone on his hair and his laughing face—"Daddy!"—and then she was running, and then she was in his arms.

"How's my sweetheart?" He smelled of linen and

whiskey and tobacco; the short hairs at the back of his neck were bristly to the touch and his jaw was like a warm pumice stone. But his voice was the best of all: as deep and thrilling as blowing across the mouth of an earthen jug. "Do you know you've grown about three feet? I don't know if I can *handle* a girl as big as you. Can't carry you, anyway; I know that much. Let's go on in and see your Aunt Claire. How's everything? How're all your boy friends?"

In the living room, talking with Aunt Claire, he was marvelous. His slim ankles, beneath trouser cuffs that had been raised to just the right height, were clad in taut socks of fluted black wool; his dark brown shoes were so shapely and so gracefully arranged on the carpet, one a little forward and one back, that she felt she ought to study them for a long time, to commit them to memory as the way a man's feet ought to look. But her gaze kept straying upward to his princely knees, to his close-fitting vest with its fine little drape of watch chain, to the way he held himself in his chair and to his white-cuffed wrists and hands, one holding a highball glass and the other making slow, easy gestures in the air, and to his brilliant face. There was too much of him for the eye to behold all at once.

He was finishing a joke: ". . . so Eleanor drew herself

up and said, 'Young man, you're drunk.' The fellow looked at her and he said, 'That's true, Mrs. Roosevelt, I am.' He said, 'But here's the difference, Mrs. Roosevelt: *I'll* be all *right* in the morning.'"

Aunt Claire's thick torso doubled over into her lap and April pretended to think it was unbearably funny too, though she hadn't heard the first part and wasn't sure if she would have understood it anyway. But the laughter had scarcely died in the room before he was getting up to leave.

"You mean you're—you mean you're not even staying for dinner, Daddy?"

"Sweetie, I'd love to, but I've got these people waiting in Boston and they're going to be very, very angry with your Daddy if he doesn't get up there in a hurry. How about a kiss?"

And then, hating herself for it, she began acting like a baby. "But you've only stayed about an *hour*. And you—you didn't even bring me a present or anything and you—"

"Oh, *Ape*-rull," Aunt Claire was saying. "Why do you want to go and spoil a nice visit?"

But at least he wasn't standing up any more: he had squatted nimbly beside her and put his arm around her. "Sweetie, I'm afraid you're right about the present, and I feel like a dog about it. Listen, though. Tell you what. Let's you and I go out to the car and rummage through my stuff, and maybe we can find something after all. Want to try?"

Darkness was falling as they left Aunt Claire and walked together down the path, and the silent interior of the car was filled with a thrilling sense of latent power and speed. When he turned on the dashboard lights it was like being in a trim, leathery home of their own. Everything they would ever need for living together was here: comfortable places to sit, a means of travel, a lighter for his cigarettes, a little shelf on which she could spread a napkin for the sandwiches and milk that would comprise their meals on the road; and the front and back seats were big enough for sleeping.

"Glove compartment?" he was saying. "Nope; nothing in here but a lot of old maps and things. Well, let's try the suitcase." He twisted around and reached into the back seat, where he unfastened the clasps of a big Gladstone. "Let's see, now. Socks; shirts; that's no good. Gee, this is quite a problem. You know something? A man ought never to travel without a fresh supply of bangles and spangles; can't ever tell when he might come across a pretty girl. Oh, look. Wait a second, here's something. Not *much*, of course, but something." He drew out a long brown bottle with the picture of a horse and the words "White Horse" on its label. Something very small was attached to its neck by a ribbon, but he concealed it from view until he opened his penknife and cut it free. Then, holding it by the ribbon, he laid it delicately in her hand—a tiny, perfect white horse.

"There you are, my darling," he said. "And you can keep it forever."

The fire was out. She prodded the blackened lumps of paper with a stick to make sure they had burned; there was nothing but ashes.

The children's voices faintly followed her as she carried the wastebasket back across the lawn; only by going inside and closing the door was she able to shut them out. She turned off the radio too, and the house became extraordinarily quiet.

She put the wastebasket back in its place and sat down at the desk again with a fresh sheet of paper. This time the letter took no time at all to write. There was only one big, important thing to say, and it was best said in a very few words—so few as to allow no possible elaborations or distortions of meaning.

> *Dear Frank,*
> *Whatever happens please don't blame yourself.*

From old, insidious habit she almost added the words *I love you*, but she caught herself in time and

made the signature plain: *April*. She put it in an enve-
lope, wrote *Frank* on the outside, and left it on the
exact center of the desk.

In the kitchen she took down her largest stewing
pot, filled it with water and set it on the stove to boil.
From storage cartons in the cellar she got out the
other necessary pieces of equipment: the tongs that
had once been used for sterilizing formula bottles, and
the blue drugstore box containing the two parts of the
syringe, rubber bulb and long plastic nozzle. She
dropped these things in the stewing pot, which was
just beginning to steam.

By the time she'd made the other preparations,
putting a supply of fresh towels in the bathroom, writing down the number of the hospital and propping it
by the telephone, the water was boiling nicely. It was
wobbling the lid of the pot and causing the syringe to
nudge and rumble against its sides.

It was nine-thirty. In another ten minutes she
would turn off the heat; then it would take a while for
the water to cool. In the meantime there was nothing
to do but wait.

"Have you thought it through, April? Never
undertake to do a thing until you've—"

But she needed no more advice and no more
instruction. She was calm and quiet now with knowing what she had always known, what neither her

parents nor Aunt Claire nor Frank nor anyone else had ever had to teach her: that if you wanted to do something absolutely honest, something true, it always turned out to be a thing that had to be done alone.

EIGHT

AT TWO O'CLOCK THAT AFTERNOON, Milly Campbell had just completed her housework. She was resting on the television hassock, addled with the smells of dust and floorwax and with the noise of the children outside (six kids were really too many for one person to handle, even for a couple of days) and she always said afterwards that she had "this very definite sense of foreboding" for at least a minute before hearing the sound that confirmed it.

It was a sound of emergency—of Fire, Murder, Police—the deep, shockingly loud purr that an automobile siren makes when the driver has just gotten started and has had to slow down for a turn before opening up to full speed. She got to the window in the nick of time to see it, down over the tops of the trees below the lawn: the long shape of an ambulance turning out of Revolutionary Road, catching the sun in a quick, brilliant reflection as it straightened out and pulled away down Route Twelve with its siren mounting higher and higher into a sustained, unbearable shriek that hung in the air long after the ambulance itself had vanished in the distance. It left her chewing her lips with worry.

"I mean I knew there were plenty of other people on that road," she said afterwards. "It could've been anybody, but I just had this feeling it was April. I started to call her but then I stopped because I knew it would sound silly, and I thought she might be sleeping."

So she sat uneasily at the telephone until it suddenly burst into ringing. It was Mrs. Givings, making the receiver vibrate painfully against Milly's ear.

"Do you know what's happened at the Wheelers'? Because I was just going past their place and there was an ambulance coming out of their drive, and I'm terribly alarmed. And now I've been trying to call them and there's no answer. . . ."

"I almost died," Milly explained later. "After she hung up I just sat there feeling sick, and then I did what I always do when something horrible happens. I called Shep."

. . .

Slowly rubbing the back of his neck as he stood looking out a window of the Allied Precision Laboratories,
Inc., Shep Campbell was lost in a muddled reverie. For
a week now, ever since the incredible night at the Log
Cabin, he hadn't been of much use to Allied Precision,
to Milly, or to himself. On the first day, like any
lovesick kid, he had called her up from a phone booth
and said, "April, when can I see you?" and she'd made
it clear, in so many words, that he couldn't see her at all
and that he should have known better than to ask. The
memory of this had rankled him all that night and the
next day—God, what a loutish, unsophisticated clown
she must have thought him—and caused him to spend
many hours in whispered rehearsal of the cool, mature,
understanding things he would say when he called her
again. But when he got into the phone booth again he
loused everything up. All the carefully practiced lines
came out wrong, his voice was shaking like a fool's and
he started saying he loved her again, and the whole
thing ended with her saying, kindly but firmly: "Look
Shep; I really don't want to hang up on you, but I'm
afraid I'll have to unless you hang up first."

He had seen her only once. Yesterday, when she
brought her kids over to the house, he had hidden

trembling in the bedroom and peeked down through the dimity curtains to watch her getting out of her car—a tired, pregnant woman—and he couldn't see her steadily for the beating of his heart.

"Phone, Mr. Campbell," one of the girls called, and as he moved to pick it up at his desk he wondered, against all reasonable logic, if it might be April. It wasn't.

"Hi, baby—what? Listen, now, calm down. *Who's* in the hospital? When? Oh Jesus."

But the remarkable thing was that for the first time all week he felt a sense of competence. His rump dropped lightly to the felt pad of his chair, his legs flexed under it in a kind of squat, and he nestled the phone at his cheek with one hand and held his mechanical pencil poised in the other—a tense, steady paratrooper, ready for action.

"Calm *down* a second," he told her. "Have you called the hospital yet? Honey, that's the *first* thing we ought to do, before we start calling Frank. . . . Okay, okay, I know you're all upset. I'll call them and find out, and then I'll call him. Now listen, you take it easy, hear me?" His pencil made a number of resolutely parallel lines on a scratch pad. "Okay," he said. "And for God's sake don't let on to the kids that anything's wrong—our kids *or* their kids. . . . Okay. . . . Okay, right. I'll call you."

Then he had the hospital on the phone and he was briskly cutting through all the confusion of the switchboard, dismissing the voices that couldn't help him and taking just the right tone of quick, commanding inquiry with those that could.

". . . undergoing emergency what? . . . Well, but I mean treatment for *what?* . . . Oh. You mean she had a miscarriage. Well, look: can you tell me how she is? . . . I see. And do you know how long that'll be? . . . Doctor what?" His pencil jumped and wiggled as he wrote down the name. "Okay. One more thing: has anyone notified her husband yet? . . . Okay. Thanks."

Hunching still lower over the phone, he put through a call to Knox Business Machines in New York.

"Mr. Frank Wheeler, please. . . . He's where? . . . Well, get him *out* of conference, then. This is an emergency." And only then, while he waited, did his guts begin to tighten with anxiety.

Then Frank was on the phone, saying "Oh my God" in a shocked, insubstantial voice.

"No, wait, listen, Frank: take it easy, boy. Far as I know she's all right. That's absolutely all they'd tell me. Now listen. Grab the first train you can to Stamford, I'll meet you there and we'll be at the hospital in five minutes. . . . Right. I'm checking out of here right now. Okay, Frank."

Out in the parking lot, running at full tilt for his car and pulling on his flapping jacket as he ran, Shep felt his exhilaration returning with the fresh air that whistled in his ears. It was the old combat feeling, the sense of doing exactly the right thing, quickly and well, when all the other elements of the situation were out of control.

At the station, waiting for the train, he used the time to call Milly again (she had calmed down) and to call the hospital (there was no news); then he walked up and down the platform in the afternoon sun, jingling coins in his pocket and saying, under his breath, "Come *on;* come *on.*" This incongruously peaceful lull was like the war too—hurry up and wait. But suddenly the train was on him, shuddering the platform, and Frank was a frantic figure clinging to its side, dropping off and nearly falling on his face and then sprinting toward Shep with wild eyes and a flying necktie.

"Okay, Frank—" They were running side by side to the parking lot even before the train had stopped. "Car's right here."

"Is she—are they still—?"

"Same as when I called you."

They didn't talk on the short, slow ride through traffic to the hospital, and Shep wasn't sure his voice would have worked if he'd tried to use it. The way

Frank's eyes looked, and the way he huddled and trembled in the seat beside him, had filled him with fear. He knew now that all his opportunities for action would soon be over; when he had steered up this final hill to this ugly brown building, he would pass into an area of total helplessness.

As they bolted through the whispering doors marked VISITORS' ENTRANCE, as they paused to husk and stutter at an information desk and then struck off down the corridor with the intense, swift heel-and-toe of competitors in a walking race, Shep's mind went mercifully out of focus in the way that it had always done, sooner or later, in combat: a dim, protective inner voice said, This isn't really happening; don't believe any of this.

"Mrs. who? Mrs. Wheeler?" said a plump freckled nurse near the end of the corridor, blinking over the rim of her sterile mask. "You mean the emergency? Well I don't *know*, offhand. I'm afraid I can't—" She glanced uneasily at a closed door over which a red light shone, and Frank made a lunge for it. She skittered in his path as if to stop him by force, if necessary, but Shep grabbed his arm and held him back.

"Can't he go in? He's her husband."

"No, he certainly can't," she said, her eyes growing wide with a sense of responsibility. But at last she agreed, reluctantly, to go inside herself and speak to the doctor. A minute later he came out, a slight, embarrassed-looking man in a wrinkled surgical gown.

"Which is Mr. Wheeler?" he asked, and then he took Frank by the arm and led him away for a private talk.

Shep, respectfully keeping his distance, allowed the inner voice to assure him that she couldn't possibly be dying. People didn't die this way, at the end of a drowsing corridor like this in the middle of the afternoon. Why, hell, if she was dying that janitor wouldn't be pushing his mop so peacefully across the linoleum, and he certainly wouldn't be humming, nor would they let the radio play so loud in the ward a few doors away. If April Wheeler was dying they certainly wouldn't have this bulletin board here on the wall, with its mimeographed announcement of a staff dance ("Fun! Refreshments!") and they wouldn't have these wicker chairs arranged this way, with this table and this neat display of magazines. What the hell did they expect you to do? Sit down and cross your legs and flip through a copy of *Life* while somebody died? Of course not. This was a place where babies were born or where simple, run-of-the-mill miscarriages were cleaned up in a jiffy; it was a place where you waited and worried until you'd made sure everything was all right, and then you walked out and had a drink and went home.

Experimentally, he sat down in one of the wicker chairs. One of the magazines was *U. S. Camera*, and he toyed with a temptation to pick it up and look through it for photographs of women in the nude; but instead he sprang to his feet again and walked a few steps one way and a few steps another. The trouble was that he had to go to the bathroom. The pain in his bladder was abrupt and keen, and he wondered how long it would take him to find his way to a toilet and back.

But the doctor had gone back inside now and Frank was standing there alone, rubbing his temple with the heel of his hand. "Jesus, Shep, I couldn't even *understand* half the things he told me. He said the fetus was out before they got her here. He said they had to operate to take out the whaddyacallit, the placenta, and they did, only now she's still bleeding. He said she lost a lot of blood even before the ambulance came, and now they're trying to stop it, and he said a whole lot of things I didn't get, about capillaries, and he said she's unconscious. Jesus."

"How about sitting down a minute, Frank?"

"That's what he said too. What the hell do I want to sit down for?"

So they continued to stand, listening to the janitor's low humming and to the rhythmic thud of his mop against the wall, and to the occasional rubber-heeled thump and rustle of a nurse walking by. Once Frank's eyes came into focus long enough for him to accept a cigarette, which Shep offered in a little excess of friendliness and courtesy—"Cigarette, fella? Atta boy. Here, I got the match"—and then, encouraged by the good cheer in his own voice, he said: "Tell you what, Frank. I'll go get us a cup of coffee."

"No."

"No, that's all right. I won't be a minute." And he escaped down the hall and around the corner and down another hall until he found the mens' room, where he stood trembling and very nearly whimpering as the pressure on his bladder was slowly relieved. Afterwards he went out in the hall again and asked directions until he found the canteen, which was hundreds of yards away at the other end of the building and was called the Hospitality Shop. He hurried through its toys and cupcakes and magazines to order two containers of coffee; then, holding the hot paper cups gingerly to keep from scalding his fingers, he started back to the emergency area. But he was lost. All the corridors looked alike, and he got all the way to the end of one of them before discovering he was going in the wrong direction. It took him a long time to find his way back, and he would always remember that this was what he was doing—mincing down hallways carrying two containers of coffee, wearing a silly, inquiring smile—this was what he was doing when April Wheeler died.

He knew it had happened as soon as he'd turned the last corner, into the long hall with the red-lighted door at the end. Frank had disappeared; that whole part of the hall was empty. He was still fifty yards away when he saw the door open and a number of nurses come spilling out and hurrying efficiently off in all directions; behind them, slowly, came not one but three or four doctors, two of them supporting Frank like polite, solicitous waiters helping a drunk out of a saloon.

Shep looked frantically around for a place to put the coffee down; squatting, he set both containers on the floor against the wall and then broke into a run, and then he was in the midst of the doctors, aware of them only as a mass of white clothing and bobbing pink faces and a discord of voices:

". . . terrible shock, of course . . ."

". . . hemorrhaging was much too severe to . . ."

". . . here, look, try to sit down and . . ."

". . . capillaries . . ."

". . . actually she held on for a remarkably . . ."

". . . no, look, sit down and . . ."

". . . these things happen, there's really . . ."

They were trying to make Frank sit down in one of the wicker chairs, which squeaked and skidded under their efforts, but he remained stubbornly on his feet, silent and expressionless, breathing rapidly, his head wobbling a little with each breath as he stared at nothing.

The sequence of events after that would remain forever uncertain in Shep's memory. Hours must have passed because it was night before they got home, and they must have covered many miles because he was driving the whole time, but he had no real idea of where they traveled. Once, in some town, he stopped at a package store and bought a pint of bourbon, which he tore open while the engine idled at the curb. He handed it to Frank—"Here, fella"—and watched him suck at its mouth with lips as loose as a baby's. Somewhere else—or was it the same place?—he went to a roadside phone booth and called Milly, and when she said "Oh God! No!" he told her to for Christ's sake shut up before the children heard her. He had to stay on the phone until she'd pulled herself together, keeping an eye on Frank's unmoving head in the car outside. "Now, listen," he told her. "I can't bring him home until the kids are asleep; what you've got to do is get them in bed as soon as you can, and for God's sake try to act natural. Then I'll bring him home to our place for the night. I mean we sure as hell can't let him go home to *his* house. . . ."

The rest of the time they were on the road, going nowhere. He remembered the trip only as a succession of traffic lights and electrical wires and trees, of houses and shopping centers and endless rolling hills under the pale sky, and of Frank either silent or making faint little moans or mumbling this phrase, over and over:

". . . and she was so damn nice this morning. Isn't that the damnedest thing? She was so damn *nice* this morning. . . ."

Once, and Shep could never remember whether it was early or late in the ride, he said, "She did it to herself, Shep. She killed herself."

And Shep's mind performed its trick of rolling with the punch: he would think about this one later. "Frank, take it easy," he said. "Don't talk crap. These things happen, that's all."

"Not this one. This one didn't happen. She wanted to do it last month and it would've been safe then. It would've been safe then and I talked her out of it. I talked her out of it and then we had a fight yesterday and now she—Oh Jesus. Oh Jesus. And she was so damn *nice* this morning."

Shep kept his eyes on the road, grateful that there was plenty to occupy the alert, front part of his mind. Because how would he ever know, now, how much or

little truth there was in this? And how would he ever
know how much or little it had to do with himself?

Alone in her darkened living room, much later, Milly
sat chewing her handkerchief and feeling like a terrible
coward. She'd done pretty well up to a point; she had
managed to do a good job of acting with the children
and to get them all in bed an hour early, well before
Shep's arrival; she had made some sandwiches and set
them out in the kitchen, in case anyone got hungry
later ("Life goes on," her mother had always said, making sandwiches on the day of a death); she had even
found time to call Mrs. Givings, whose reaction to the
news was to say "Oh, oh, oh," over and over again; and
she'd done her very best to be ready for the ordeal of
confronting Frank. She'd been ready to sit up all night
with him and—well, read to him from the Bible, or
something; ready to hold him and let him weep on her
breast; anything.

But nothing had prepared her for the awful blank-
ness of his eyes when Shep brought him up the kitchen
steps. "Oh Frank," she'd said, and started to cry, and run
for the living room with her handkerchief in her mouth,
and ever since then she'd been completely useless.

She'd done nothing but sit here and listen to the

dim sounds the two of them made in the kitchen (a scraping chair, a clink of bottle on glass, and Shep's voice: "Here, fella. Drink it up, now. . . ."), trying to work up the courage to go back. Once Shep had tip-toed in, smelling of whiskey, to consult with her.

"Oh, sweetie, I'm sorry," she had whispered against his shirt. "I know I'm not being any help, but I *can't*. I can't stand the way he *looks*."

"Okay. That's okay, honey. You take it easy; I'll look after him. He's sort of in a state of shock, is all. Jesus, what a thing." He sounded a little drunk. "Jesus, what an awful thing. You know what he told me in the car? He said she did it to herself. You believe that?"

"She *what*?"

"Gave herself an abortion; or tried to."

"Oh," she whispered, shuddering. "Oh, how awful. You think she did? But why would she do that?"

"How the hell do I know? Am I supposed to know everything? I'm just telling you what he *said*, for Christ's sake." He rubbed his head with both hands. "Hell, I'm sorry, honey."

"All right. You better get back. I'll come out and sit with him in a little while, and you can get some rest. We'll take turns."

"Okay."

But more than two hours had passed since then, and still she hadn't found the strength to carry out her promise. All she could do was to sit here and dread it. There had been no sounds in the kitchen for a long time now. What were they *doing* in there? Just sitting, or what?

And so in the end it was curiosity as much as courage that helped her to her feet and across the room and down the hall to the brilliant kitchen doorway. She hesitated, taking a deep breath, squinting her eyes in preparation for the glare of the lights, and then she went in.

Shep's head was in his arms on the kitchen table, an inch away from the untouched plate of sandwiches; he was sound asleep and faintly snoring. Frank wasn't there.

The Revolutionary Hill Estates had not been designed to accommodate a tragedy. Even at night, as if on purpose, the development held no looming shadows and no gaunt silhouettes. It was invincibly cheerful, a toyland of white and pastel houses whose bright, uncurtained windows winked blandly through a dappling of green and yellow leaves. Proud floodlights were trained on some of the lawns, on some of the neat front doors and on the hips of some of the berthed, ice-cream-colored automobiles.

A man running down these streets in desperate grief was indecently out of place. Except for the whisk of his shoes on the asphalt and the rush of his own breath, it was so quiet that he could hear the sounds of television in the dozing rooms behind the leaves—a blurred comedian's shout followed by dim, spastic waves of laughter and applause, and then the striking-up of a band. Even when he veered from the pavement, cut across someone's back yard and plunged into the down-sloping woods, intent on a madman's shortcut to Revolutionary Road, even then there was no escape: the house lights beamed and stumbled happily along with him among the twigs that whipped his face, and once when he lost his footing and fell scrabbling down a rocky ravine, he came up with a child's enameled tin beach bucket in his hand.

As he clambered out onto asphalt again at the base of the Hill he allowed his dizzy, jogging mind to indulge in a cruel delusion: it had all been a nightmare; he would round this next bend and see the lights blazing in his own house; he would run inside and find her at the ironing board, or curled up on the sofa with a magazine ("What's the *matter*, Frank? Your *pants* are all muddy! Of *course* I'm all right. . . .").

But then he saw the house—really saw it—long and milk-white in the moonlight, with black windows, the only darkened house on the road.

She had been very careful about the blood. Except for a tidy trail of drops leading out to the telephone and back, it had all been confined to the bathroom, and even there it had mostly been flushed away. Two heavy towels, soaked crimson, lay lumped in the tub, close to the drain. "I thought that would be the simplest way to handle it," he could hear her saying. "I thought you could just wrap the towels up in newspaper and put them in the garbage, and then give the tub a good rinsing out. Okay?" On the floor of the linen closet he found the syringe in its pot of cold water; she had probably put it there to hide it from the ambulance crew. "I mean I just thought it would be best to get it out of sight; I didn't want to have to answer a lot of dumb questions."

And his head continued to ring with the sound of her voice as he set to work. "There; now that's done," it said when he pressed the newspaper bundles deep into the garbage can outside the kitchen door, and when he returned to fall on his knees and scrub at the trail of drops it was still with him. "Try a damp sponge and a little dry detergent, darling—it's there in the cabinet under the sink. That ought to take it up.

There, you see? That's fine. I didn't get any on the rug, did I? Oh, good."

How could she be dead when the house was alive with the sound of her and the sense of her? Even when he had finished the cleaning, when there was nothing to do but walk around and turn on lights and turn them off again, even then her presence was everywhere, as real as the scent of her dresses in the bedroom closet. It was only after he'd spent a long time in the closet, embracing her clothes, that he went back to the living room and found the note she had left for him on the desk. And he barely had time to read it, and to turn the light off again, before he saw the Campbells' Pontiac slowing down for the turn into the driveway. He went quickly back to the bedroom and shut himself inside the closet, among the clothes. From there he heard the car rumble to a stop outside; then the kitchen door opened and there were several faltering footsteps.

"Frank?" Shep called hoarsely. "Frank? You here?"

He heard him walking through the rooms, stumbling and cursing as he felt along the walls for light switches; finally he heard him leave, and when the sound of the car had faded away he came out of hiding, carrying his note, and sat in the darkness by the picture window.

But after that interruption, April's voice no longer spoke to him. He tried for hours to recapture it, whispering words for it to say, going back to the closet time and again and into the drawers of her dressing table and into the kitchen, where he thought the pantry shelves and the racked plates and coffee cups would surely contain the ghost of her, but it was gone.

NINE

ACCORDING TO MILLY CAMPBELL, who told the story many, many times in the following months, everything worked out as well as could be expected. "I mean," she would always add, and here she would give a little shudder, "I mean, considering it was just about the most horrible thing we've ever been through in our lives. Wasn't it, sweetie?"

And Shep would agree that it certainly was. His role during these recitals was to sit and stare gravely at the carpet, occasionally shaking his head or flexing his bite, until she cued him to make certain small corroborations. He was glad enough to let her do most of the talking—or rather, he was glad of it in the beginning, throughout the fall and winter of the year. By spring, he had begun to wish she would find other things to talk about.

And his annoyance grew all but intolerable one Friday evening in May, when she was going over the whole business with some new acquaintances named Brace—the very couple who had recently moved into the Wheelers' house. The trouble was partly just that: it seemed a betrayal and a sacrilege, somehow, to be telling the story to people who would go home and talk it over in that particular house; and it was partly that the Braces made such a dull audience, nodding and shaking their polite, bridge-playing heads in remorse for people they had never known. But mostly it was that Milly's voice had taken on a little too much of a voluptuous narrative pleasure. She's *enjoying* this, he thought, watching her over the rim of his highball glass as she came to the part about how awful it had been the next day. By God, she's really getting a kick out of it.

". . . and I mean Shep and I were just about out of our minds by morning," she was saying. "We didn't have the faintest idea where Frank was; we kept calling the hospital to see if they'd heard from him; and then we had to go through this horrible thing with the kids of pretending everything was fine. They knew something was the matter, though; you know how kids are. They sensed it. When I was giving them breakfast Jennifer looked at me and said, 'Milly? Is Mommy going to come and pick us up today, or what?' And she was sort of smiling, you know? As if she knew it was a silly question but she'd promised her brother she'd ask it? I almost died. I said, 'Well, dear, I don't know what your mommy's plans are, exactly.' Wasn't that awful? But I didn't know what else to say.

"Then about two o'clock we called the hospital and they said Frank had just left: he'd gone in and signed all the papers, or whatever it is you have to do when somebody dies; and a little later he came driving up here. The minute he came in I said, 'Frank, is there anything we can do? Because,' I said, 'if there's anything at all we can do, just say so.'

"He said no, he thought he'd taken care of everything. He said he'd called his brother in Pittsfield— he's got this much older brother, you see; actually he's got two of them, but he never used to mention them; I'd forgotten he *had* any family—and he said the brother and his wife were coming down the next day, to help out with the kids and everything, and the funeral. So I said, 'All right, but please stay here with us tonight.' I said, 'You can't take the kids back to your house alone.' He said okay, he would; but he said first he wanted to take them out for a drive somewhere, and break the news to them. And that's what he did. He went out in the yard and they saw him and came running over, and he said 'Hi!' and picked them up and put them in the car and drove away. I really think it was the saddest thing I've ever seen in my life. And I'll never forget what Jennifer said when he brought them back that night. It was past their bedtime and they were both kind of sleepy, and I was helping Jennifer get ready for bed and she said, 'Milly? You know what?' She said, 'My mommy's in Heaven and we had dinner in a restaurant.'"

"God!" said Nancy Brace. "But I mean how did things work out finally?" She was a sharp-faced, bespectacled girl who had worked before her marriage as a buyer for one of the top New York specialty shops. She liked her stories neat, with points, and she clearly felt there were too many loose ends in this one. "Did his relatives stay on here awhile? And then what?"

"Oh, no," Milly explained. "Right after the funeral they took the kids back up to Pittsfield with them, and Frank went along for a few days, to help them make the adjustment; then he moved into the city and started going up there for weekends, and that's the way things are now. I guess it's more or less a permanent arrangement. They're very nice, the brother and his wife—wonderful people, really, and very good with the kids; of course they're, *you* know, a lot older and everything.

"And then I guess we didn't see anything more of Frank after that until March, or whenever it was, when he came out to see about closing the sale of the house. And of course that's when you folks met him. He spent a couple of days with us then, and we had a long talk. That was when he told us about finding the note she'd left him. That was when he said that if it hadn't been for that note he thought he would've killed himself that night."

Warren Brace cleared the phlegm from his throat and swallowed it. A slow-spoken, pipe-clenching man with thinning hair and incongruously soft, childish lips, he was employed in the city by a firm of management consultants, a kind of work he described as well suited to what he called his analytical turn of mind. "You know?" he said. "This is the kind of thing that really—" He paused, examining the wisp of smoke that curled from his wet pipestem. "Really makes you stop and think."

"Well, but how did he seem otherwise?" Nancy Brace inquired. "I mean did he seem to've made a— a fairly good adjustment?"

Milly sighed, tugging down her skirt and curling her feet up into the chair cushion in a single quick, awkward gesture. "Well, he'd lost a lot of weight," she said, "but I guess he looked well enough, except for that. He said being in analysis was helping him a lot; he talked a little about that. And he talked about his job—he's got this different kind of job now? I mean he's still sort of vaguely working for Knox, but it's under a new setup, or something? I didn't quite understand that part of it. What's the name of his new company, sweetie?"

"Bart Pollock Associates."

"*Oh* yes," said Warren Brace. "They're up at Fifty-ninth and Madison. Very interesting new firm, as a matter of fact. Sort of industrial public relations in the electronics field. They started out with the Knox account, and now I believe they've got a couple of others. They ought to be really going places in the next few years."

"Well," Milly went on, "anyway, he seemed to be keeping busy. And he seemed—oh, I guess 'cheerful' is the wrong word, but that's sort of what I mean. I really felt his attitude was—well, courageous. Very courageous."

On the mumbled pretext of refilling their glasses, Shep made his way out to the kitchen, where he banged and clattered a tray of ice cubes in the sink to drown out her voice. Why did she have to make such a God damn soap opera out of it? If she couldn't tell it the way it really was, to people who really wanted to

listen, why the hell tell it at all? Courageous! Of all the
asinine, meaningless . . .

And forgetting his guests, or rather coming to the
abrupt decision that they could damn well get their
own God damn drinks, he poured himself a stiff one
and took it out to the darkness of the back yard, letting
the door close behind him with a little slam.

Courageous! What kind of bullshit was that? How
could a man be courageous when he wasn't even alive?
Because that was the whole point; that was the way
he'd seemed when he came to call that March afternoon: a walking, talking, smiling, lifeless man.

At first sight, getting out of his car, he had looked
pretty much the same as ever except that his jacket
hung a little looser on him and he'd taken to wearing it
with the top button fastened as well as the middle one,
to gather up some of the slack. But after you'd heard
his voice—"Hi, Milly; good to see you, Shep"—and
felt the light, dry press of his handshake, you began to
see how the life had gone out of him.

He was so damned mild! He sat there arranging the
crease of his pants over his knees and brushing little
flecks of ash off his lap and holding his drink with his
pinkie hooked around underneath the glass, for safety.
And he had a new way of laughing: a soft, simpering giggle. You couldn't picture him really laughing, or really

crying, or really sweating or eating or getting drunk or getting excited—or even standing up for himself. For Christ's sake, he looked like somebody you could walk up to and take a swing at and knock down, and all he'd do would be to lie there and apologize for getting in your way. So that when he finally did come out with that business about finding the note—"I honestly think I'd have killed myself, if it hadn't been for that"—it was all you could do to keep from saying, Oh, bullshit! You're a lying bastard, Wheeler; you'd never have had the nerve.

And it was even worse than that: he was boring. He must have spent at least an hour talking about his half-assed job, and God only knew how many other hours on his other favorite subject: "my analyst this"; "my analyst that"—he had turned into one of these people that want to tell you about their God damned analyst all the time. "And I mean I think we're really getting down to some basic stuff; things I've never really faced before about my relationship with my father...." Christ! And that was what had become of Frank; that was what you'd have to know about, if you wanted to know how things had really worked out.

He took a gulp of whiskey, seeing a quick blur of stars and moon through the wet dome of his glass. Then he started back for the house, but he didn't make it; he had to turn around again and head out to the far border of the lawn and walk around out there in little circles; he was crying.

It was the smell of spring in the air that did it— earth and flowers—because it was almost exactly a year now since the time of the Laurel Players, and to remember the Laurel Players was to remember April Wheeler's way of walking across the stage, and her smile, and the sound of her voice (*"Wouldn't you like to be loved by me?"*), and in remembering all this there was nothing for Shep Campbell to do but walk around on the grass and cry, a big wretched baby with his fist in his mouth and the warm tears spilling down his knuckles.

He found it so easy and so pleasant to cry that he didn't try to stop for a while, until he realized he was forcing his sobs a little, exaggerating their depth with unnecessary shudders. Then, ashamed of himself, he bent over and carefully set his drink on the grass, got out his handkerchief and blew his nose.

The whole point of crying was to quit before you cornied it up. The whole point of grief itself was to cut it out while it was still honest, while it still meant something. Because the thing was so easily corrupted: let yourself go and you started embellishing your own sobs, or you started telling about the Wheelers with a sad, sentimental smile and saying Frank was courageous, and then what the hell did you have?

Milly was still talking, still embellishing, when he went back indoors to pass around the fresh highballs. She had reached her summing-up now, leaning earnestly forward with her elbows on her slightly spread, wrinkled knees.

"No, but I really do think it was an experience that's brought us closer together," she was saying. "Shep and me, I mean. Don't you, sweetie?"

And both the Braces turned to stare at him in mute reiteration of her question. Did he? Well, didn't he?

The only thing to say, of course, was "Yeah, that's so; it really has."

And the funny part, he suddenly realized, the funny part was that he meant it. Looking at her now in the lamplight, this small, rumpled, foolish woman, he knew he had told the truth. Because God damn it, she was alive, wasn't she? If he walked over to her chair right now and touched the back of her neck, she would close her eyes and smile, wouldn't she? Damn right, she would. And when the Braces went home—and with God's help they would soon be getting the hell on their way—when the Braces went home she would go in and bustle clumsily around the kitchen, washing the dishes and talking a mile a minute ("Oh I like them *so* much; don't you?"). Then she would go to bed, and in the morning she'd get up and come humping downstairs again in her torn dressing gown with its smell of sleep and orange juice and cough syrup and stale deodorants, and go on living.

For Mrs. Givings, too, the time after April's death followed a pattern of shock, pain, and slow recovery.

At first she could think of it only in terms of overwhelming personal guilt, and so was unable to discuss it at all, even with Howard. She knew that Howard or anyone else would only insist it had been an accident, that no one could be held responsible, and the last thing she wanted was to be comforted. The memory of that ambulance backing down out of the Wheelers' drive, at the very moment when she'd come bringing well-rehearsed apologies ("April, about yesterday; you've both been wonderful but I'll never ask you to go through that sort of thing again; Howard and I have agreed now that John's difficulties are quite beyond our . . ."), and then of little Mrs. Campbell's voice on the phone that same afternoon, telling her the news, had filled her with a self-reproach so deep and pure it was almost pleasurable. She was physically sick for a week.

This, then, was what came of good intentions. Try to love your child, and you helped to bring about another mother's death.

"And I know you'll say there was probably no connection," she explained to John's psychiatrist, "but frankly, Doctor, I'm not asking your opinion. I'm simply saying that it's quite out of the question for us ever to think in terms of bringing him into contact with outside people again. Quite out of the question."

"Mm," the doctor said. "Yes. Well, of course, matters of this sort are entirely up to you and Mr.—ah, Mr. Givings to decide."

"I know he's ill," she went on, and here she had to sniffle back an alarming threat of tears, "I know he's ill and he's much to be pitied, but he's also very destructive, Doctor. Impossibly destructive."

"Mm. Yes. . . ."

After that they confined their weekly visits to the inner waiting room of John's ward. He didn't seem to mind. He would ask about the Wheelers from time to time, but of course they told him nothing. By Christmas they had slipped into the habit of allowing two or three weeks to elapse between visits; then they tapered off to once a month.

Little things make a difference. One sleeting January day, at the shopping center, her eye was caught and held by a small, brown, mixed-breed spaniel puppy in the pet-shop window. Feeling absurd—she had never done anything quite so silly and impulsive in her life—

she went in and bought him on the spot and took him home.

And what a pleasure he was! Oh, he was troublesome too—paper-training and housebreaking and worms and so on; it takes a lot of plain, hard work to make a good pet—but he was worth it.

"*Roll* over!" she would say, sitting cross-legged on the carpet in her slipper-socks. "*Roll* over, boy!" Then she would knead his fuzzy little ribs and belly with her fingers while he squirmed on his spine, his four paws waving in the air and his black lips drawn back from his teeth in giggling ecstasy.

"*Oh*, you're such a good little dog! *Oh*, you're such a good little wet-nosed sweetie-pie—aren't you? Aren't you? Yes you *are*! Oh, yes you *are*!" It was the puppy, more than anything or anyone else, that made her winter endurable.

Business began to pick up with the coming of spring, which never failed to give her a sense of life beginning all over again; but one ordeal remained to be survived: the selling of the Wheelers' house. Her dread of the inevitable meeting with Frank in the lawyer's office, at the closing, was so intense that she hardly slept at all the night before. It turned out, though, to be much less awkward than she'd feared. He was cordial and dignified—"Good to see you,

Mrs. Givings"—they talked only of business matters, and he left as soon as the papers were signed. Afterwards, it was as if she'd closed a door forever on the whole experience.

The next two months kept her exhaustingly, deliriously busy: more of the sweet old houses coming on the market, more of the more presentable new ones being built, more and more of the right sort of people coming out from the city—people who wanted and deserved something really nice, and who didn't care about haggling for bargains. It soon developed into the best real estate spring of her career, and she took a craftsman's pride in it. The days were long and often very difficult, but that only made the shrunken evenings more exquisitely restful.

Between playing with the puppy and chatting with Howard, she found any number of simple, constructive little tasks to do around the house.

"Isn't this cozy?" she asked one fine May evening as she crouched on spread newspapers to varnish a chair. Howard, bored with the *World-Telegram*, was sitting with folded hands and looking out the window; the puppy was curled up asleep on his little rug nearby, sated with happiness. "It's wonderful just to let yourself unwind after a hard day," she said. "Would you like some more coffee, dear? Or some more cake?"

"No, thanks. I may have a glass of milk later on."

Turning the chair carefully on its spattered papers and seating herself on the floor to reach its underside, she went on talking as her brush trailed back and forth.

". . . I simply can't tell you how pleased I am about the little Revolutionary Road place, Howard. Remember how dreary it looked all winter? All cold and dark and—well, spooky. Creepy-crawly. And now whenever I drive past it gives me such a lift to see it all perked up and spanking clean again, with lights in the windows. Oh, and they're delightful young people, the Braces. She's very sweet and fun to talk to; he's rather reserved. I think he must do something very brilliant in town. He said to me, 'Mrs. Givings, I can't thank you enough. This is just the kind of home we've always wanted.' Wasn't that a sweet thing to say? And do you know, I was just thinking. I've loved that little house for years, and these are the first really suitable people I've ever found for it. Really nice, congenial people, I mean."

Her husband stirred and shifted the placement of his orthopedic shoes. "Well," he said, "except for the Wheelers, you mean."

"Well, but I mean *really* congenial people," she said. "*Our* kind of people. Oh, I was very fond of the Wheelers, but they always were a bit—a bit whimsical, for my taste. A bit neurotic. I may not have stressed it, but they were often very trying people to deal with, in many ways. Actually, the main reason the little house has been so hard to *sell* is that they let it depreciate so dreadfully. Warped window frames, wet cellar, crayon marks on the walls, filthy smudges around all the doorknobs and fixtures—really careless, destructive things. And that awful stone path going halfway down the front lawn and ending in a mud puddle—can you imagine anyone defacing a property like that? It's going to cost Mr. Brace a small fortune to get it cleared away and replanted. No, but it was more than that. The kind of thing I mean goes deeper than that."

She paused to press the excess varnish from her brush against the side of the can, frowning, working her lips in an effort to find words for the kind of thing she meant.

"It's just that they *were* a rather strange young couple. Irresponsible. The guarded way they'd look at you; the way they'd talk to you; unwholesome, sort of. Oh, and another thing. Do you know what I came across in the cellar? All dead and dried out? I came across an enormous box of sedum plantings that I must have spent an entire day collecting for them last spring. I remember very carefully selecting the best shoots and very tenderly packing them in just the right kind of soil—*that's* the kind of thing I mean, you see. Wouldn't you think that when someone goes to a certain amount of trouble to give you a perfectly good plant, a living, growing thing, wouldn't you think the very least you'd do would be to—"

But from there on Howard Givings heard only a welcome, thunderous sea of silence. He had turned off his hearing aid.

*"Soft-spoken in his prose and terrifyingly
accurate in his dialogue, Yates renders his
characters with such authenticity that you
hardly realize what he's done."*
—The Boston Globe

A SPECIAL PROVIDENCE
by Richard Yates

A Special Providence follows a young man,
Robert Prentice, and his mother Alice, a sculptor.
Robert has spent all his life attempting to escape
his mother's stifling presence; Alice, for her part,
struggles with her own demons as she attempts to
realize her dreams of prosperity. As Robert goes
off to fight in Europe, hoping to become his own
man, Yates portrays a soldier in the depths of war
striving to live up to his heroic ideals. With haunt-
ing clarity, Yates crafts an unforgettable portrait
of two people who cannot help but hope for more
even as life challenges them both.

Fiction/Literature/978-0-307-45595-6

YOUNG HEARTS CRYING
by Richard Yates

In *Young Hearts Crying*, Yates movingly portrays a man and a woman from their courtship and marriage in the 1950s to their divorce in the 70s, chronicling their heartbreaking attempts to reach their highest ambitions. Michael Davenport dreams of being a poet after returning home from World War II Europe, and at first he and his new wife, Lucy, enjoy their life together. But as the decades pass and the success of others creates an oppressive fear of failure in both Michael and Lucy, their once-bright future gives way to a life of adultery and isolation. With empathy and grace, Yates creates a poignant novel of the desires and disasters of a tragic, hopeful couple.

Fiction/Literature/978-0-307-45596-3